PRAISE FOR *FALCON IN THE DIVE*

"With as many twists and turns as an eighteenth-century Parisian alley, *Falcon in the Dive* draws readers into the dark, beating heart of the French Revolution. From the dank mines below Nord-Pas-de-Calais and cellar hideouts crowded with ordinary Parisians to the exquisite palaces of the nobility, Leah Angstman tells the story of one remarkable woman whose courage and complexity changes—and saves—lives. There is no one writing today who can approach Angstman's ability to blend profound erudition with a rollicking plot and indelible characters. A compelling page-turner, *Falcon in the Dive* will challenge everything you thought you knew about the French Revolution."

—Ashley Shelby, author of *Muri*, *South Pole Station*, and *Red River Rising*

"Entrenched in historical detail, Leah Angstman's *Falcon in the Dive* is the kind of book most authors wish they had the stomach for. No one is lucky in Angstman's Paris, and the realism with which she crafts her tale will have readers white-knuckling the book, cringing and cheering on the same page. *Falcon*'s daredevil protagonist, Ani, is no exception to the rules of the world, and her losses are as tragic as her victories triumphant. Ani's courage is without bounds, and in her, Angstman has realized a heroine as vital to today's reader as she is to *Falcon*'s gritty, riotous France."

—Eric Shonkwiler, author of *Above All Men*, *8th Street Power & Light*, and *Moon Up, Past Full*

Also by Leah Angstman:
Out Front the Following Sea
Shoot the Horses First

FALCON IN THE DIVE

A Novel of the French Revolution

Leah Angstman

Regal House Publishing

Published by
Regal House Publishing, LLC
Raleigh, NC 27605
All rights reserved

ISBN-13 (paperback): 9781646034338
ISBN-13 (epub): 9781646034345
Library of Congress Control Number: 2023934867

Cover images and design by © C. B. Royal

A timeline of the major events of the French Revolution, a Dutch-language glossary, a breakdown of the major political and miliary factions involved, a glossary of terms used in this book, a conversion of 1792 French currency to 2019 (pre-pandemic) U.S. currency, and an extensive glossary of the real-life named individuals mentioned in the novel can be found on the author's website at https://leahangstman.com.

There are many real-life historical figures named in this book. Although some of their dialogue comes from their own verbal and epistolary words, the characterizations are fictional.

Regal House Publishing, LLC
https://regalhousepublishing.com

Printed in the United States of America

For Lafayette, in sleep, and Mike, awake.

For Heidi, who never let the stairs slow her down.

If God did not exist,
we should have to invent Him.
—Maximilien Robespierre, after Voltaire

When the government violates the people's rights,
insurrection is, for the people
and for each portion of the people,
the most sacred of the rights
and the most indispensable of duties.

—Marquis de Lafayette

The time has come that was foretold,
when people would ask for bread
and be given corpses.

—Madame Roland

ENGLISH
CHANNEL

CELTIC
SEA

Brittany

NORTH
ATLANTIC
OCEAN

BAY OF
BISCAY

Pas-de-Calais
Nord-Pas-de-
Calais   Valenciennes
Denain
Cambrai
Saint-Quentin   Port-Gayant
Gauchy
RIVER SOMME

SEINE

Reims   Varennes
Valmy   Verdun   Metz
Lorraine

Paris
Gentilly
Versailles
Rambouillet
Chartres

Alsace

Le Mans   Orléans
Ronchamp

CHÊZINE   LOIRE   Beaugency
Angers
Luxon
Nantes   Maine-et-Loire
Cholet
Bocage Vendéen   Thouet
Marais   The Vendée
Deux Sèvres

Moulins

Lay

Lyon

Provence

Couserans
Foix

Marseille

MEDITERRANEAN
SEA

France
1792

Scale of 100 Miles
0   100

N

1 Grande Rue du Chaillot
2 Esplanade des Invalides
3 Place de la Révolution
4 Pont de la Révolution
5 Les Feuillants
6 Les Jacobins
7 Restaurants of Palais Royal, inc. Café de Foy
8 Grande Taverne de Londres
9 Boutique de l'aquatinte
10 Pont Royal
11 For-l'Evêque
12 Grand Châtelet
13 Carmelites
14 La Force
15 Hôtel de Ville
16 Pont au Change
17 Quai de l'Horloge
18 La Conciergerie
19 Pont Saint-Michel
20 Île du Palais Streets, inc. Rue de la Barillerie & Saint-Barthélemy
21 Notre-Dame
22 Théâtre de l'Odéon
23 l'Abbaye
24 Rue Sainte-Marguerite
25 Les Cordeliers
26 Jardin du Luxembourg
27 Lycée Louis-le-Grand
28 Sainte-Pélagie
29 Les Gobelins
30 Hôpital de la Salpêtrière
31 Église Saint-Médard

PARIS
1792

Scale of Half Mile
0   1/2

PART I

The Past Is
Fragments of

CHAPTER ONE

AN INTRODUCTION; OR, AN EXPOSITION

Your People, sir,
is nothing but a great beast.

—Alexander Hamilton

Now, Paris, mid-July 1792

The National Razor glittered above the roture like a jewel of monarchies past, a proud member of the Assembly, of the courtier, of Parlement, of the Bourbon. It was a veritable head of state, a baron, a marquis, a viscount, a bishop—as much an unelected supreme and autocratic ruler of divine right as any individual in the Versailles or Tuileries aristocratic noblesse, and well-oiled to lop any head into the arms of a regal Madame: the guillotine.

It was the year of Someone Else's Lord, Seventeen Ninety and Two. Six-hundred-thousand citizens from borel to baron crowded every livable corner of Paris in manufactured caste. Starving or highbrow, taillable or upper class, gabelled or bestowed with appointed seats. Those who held loftier societal positions would scarce confess it to a passing stranger wearing laces instead of buckles, pantlegs instead of culottes.

Ani could see the glistening metal of the blade from where she stood at the edge of the Seine. She'd once watched this very river freeze solid to the bottom. Three years prior, during the severest winter of the century, when epidemics of murrain ran rampant and deadly. When famine held true autocratic rule of the land. When financial heads collapsed banks in their wake as they were deposed one by one, and the country bankrupted itself. When nine-thousand famished citizens had rioted through the city, and guns came more abundant than bread. Between black and white were factions of gray in so many shades one daren't count them.

Devastation knew no class bias; rich and poor alike were swept into the anthem of those riots past, when mobs fled toward the fork that closed travel from the eastern mouth of Paris to the faubourg Saint-

Antoine, where had stood the medieval dungeon with a personality, a life, a birth and death all its own: the Bastille. A building steeped in legend, a symbol of oppression for the starving and overtaxed Third Estate—*the commoners*. Built as a fortress in the fourteenth century, it had since been used to imprison men arrested in accordance with the lettres de cachet, men who were not guilty of any offense that law could punish but who'd offended the king or his royal cabinet. The prison's destruction had meant the acquisition of countless barrels of gunpowder. The lower borel needed only munitions to propel its way upward; thus fell the Bastille and Hôtel national des Invalides, and thirty-thousand muskets therein were granted the common man through means of force. Paris now stood armed, but in the three years since, it had gained no bread.

Her father had been in that prison. That infamous Bastille. Her father—rotting away on a piss-covered mattress.

Thus, an aristocrat now swinging by his neck from a pont over the Seine shouldn't have given her pause. It was common enough these days. Yet, Ani found it hard to stomach sometimes—a man, a *life*, no matter what he'd done. But some things…some things that men did were unforgivable. She knew this too well.

Keener to the discomfort as she hurried, exposed and vulnerable, across the bridge, she lamented wearing a dress too elegant to be skirting the Palais Bourbon and the Jardin des Tuileries in this milieu. The color stood out, even under the dark cape that wrapped her. Her wooden shoes thumped each step mercilessly. She clutched her satchel, kept constant watch over both shoulders.

She wasn't used to a dress like this. Its cumbersome petticoats hindered her gait—a detriment if she had to run. Past the outer edges of faubourgs Saint-Germain and Saint-Honoré, a body might have to run. Footfalls behind her, crowds at the rear and off in some nearby courtyards. A cane clicked on the pont. Tallow lamps popped to life where a lamplighter lit the bridge's mouth from a torch. The sky lightened with the lamps. Too late in the morning for her to be out like this. Dressed like this. This silly pomp for a silverware accountant.

That's what she'd been hired as—a glorified butler, a counter of wall hangings, wine casks, and heirlooms. Well, some young *man* had been hired. She was simply going in the young man's place. *He's indisposed*, she was supposed to say, *quite likely the pox*.

Steps grew louder behind her, and she quickened her pace. Nearly off the bridge, nearly off the bridge, nearly…standing over the dead body swinging below it. Her gut tightened. The decaying flesh stung the back of her throat, a scent so potent she could taste it. But she couldn't show an inkling of repulsion—not here, so nicely dressed—or she'd stand out even more. She knew many people in the city, but she certainly didn't know everyone. Falling into the wrong hands might mean she would join the swinging man on the bridge, even if she wasn't one of them, one of the 'crats, one of the bourgeoisie, one of the gentry, one of the…

A woman in a cluster of women at the end of the bridge made eye contact with her, and Ani glanced down quickly, but it was too late. She heard the suspicions, saw stances shifting, foot to foot. She couldn't afford a confrontation. She wadded a piece of yellow paper she carried, a missive, and threw it into the Seine. The Tuileries palace loomed on the opposite bank, its hordes of red-clad Swiss Guard mercenaries like paintstrokes on the gray shore. Off to the north, throngs of mob and shopkeep and market women waited to pounce on anything that seemed out of place, and to the south, scouts and patrolmen, a herd of young men with dogs, walked across the bridge at her back. She squeezed by the women at the end of the pont, but the one who'd made eye contact knocked into Ani's shoulder. The woman opened her mouth to shout something, but Ani didn't wait around to hear it.

Ani bolted from the bridge toward Champs-Élysées, avoiding the puddles, her skirt hiked to her waist. Past the quay, she swore aloud at her wooden shoes and stopped to remove them and carry them beneath her arm. She'd always been better at running barefoot, or in shoes with soles so rotten that she might as well be barefoot. Crowds of people yelled, threw stones. Some pursued in chase. New menacing figures materialized from hedgerows and followed.

Ani kept running, her lungs heaving until they gave way to a wretched cough, and she tucked into an alleyway at Grande rue du Chaillot. Curse her weak lungs. She bent over, her hands on her knees, until the cough subsided. Catching her breath, she checked around the corner, but the mob had lost interest. They were fickle in chase and thankfully as fickle in giving up the chase.

She leaned her head against the wall. Lightheadedness momentarily overtook her, but she breathed, breathed. The danger of what she was doing came fully to her, but she pushed it away and stood upright, composed herself. Assessed. So she'd been mistaken for one of them, so be it. That had always been a gamble of the plan, and she knew the risks. But sweat now coated her hairline, and mud stained the bottom trim of the dress that Dr. Breauchard had paid someone to clean and flounce the hems. Perhaps no one would notice. Oh, whom was she kidding, she groaned—of course they'd all notice. She closed her eyes, and when she next opened them, she faced the Chaillot—a district that did not belong to her kind.

༄

Now, the Chaillot on the outskirts of Paris
Noon came and cast its heat onto Grande rue du Chaillot, running between the gardens of l'Étoile and the Champs-Élysées. Hunger tugged at Ani's insides, but she kept walking, her shoes rubbing painful blisters into her heels. The lightheadedness was gone, but the uncertainty remained. She took a deep breath and looked around her. Anchored her bearings. Counted the mansions. Saw the nameplates. Took a longer breath and steadied her racing nerves.

There were no alleyways now, no marketplace mobs. The upscale townhouses, chateaus, and small palaces were shelters of gentry. She was out from the center of the city toward the Chaillot, where the niceness of the properties ran contrary to the niceness of their proprietors. But one modest palace—if such a word could describe a palace—was the right one. *The right one.* A pit formed in her stomach. When she spotted guards lined inside the front gate, indicating the possibility of a fortified stone garrison, she hesitated, then walked toward them with all the confidence she could muster.

Palais d'honneur was pounded into an iron plate, capped with what she figured to be solid gold. Beneath it: *Beaumercy.* The words, the name, *that name*, sat like a cannonball in her stomach, but she moved forward through the weight. Of course his palace looked like this. Of course the plate was capped in solid gold. Bile rose in her throat. The neoclassical palace was marbled stone, smoothly faced in an enormous rectangle with four picture windows along the front ground level, five picture windows along the second story, and a third three-quarter-story along the roofline with four gabled windows protruding from it. A marbled Beaumercy coat of arms leaped from its own gabled centerpiece at the front roof. Orchards lined each side, ending at the street. Across the front, a stone-and-iron gate separated the property from the marshy, crowded lands of faubourg Saint-Honoré and northern Paris.

"Pardon me," Ani called, leaning against the wrought-iron gate.

"Please." She squeezed her hands through the bars and waved the guards down.

"Who enters here?" one of the red-coated soldiers said in a heavy Swiss accent. "Alert Mademoiselle Journeaux." The guard kept his musket drawn and moved toward Ani. "What business have you with the palace?"

Ani curtsied, but she was clumsy at it. "I am your clerk, your figurer for the palace accounts."

"Our clerk, scheiße." The man laughed. His eyes went to the mud on her dress hem. "The clerk is a boy."

"He's indisposed," she said as she'd rehearsed, "quite possibly the pox."

The soldier's face reflexively contorted, but he kept his musket on her.

"Please," she said, holding her satchel behind her back, "I have an appointment with his lordship the Marquis de Lourmarin, and as you can imagine, I've no desire to be late for my first day in his employ. I beg of you, kindly withdraw your weapon and grant me entrance."

"Lourmarin?"

"Yes, his lordship."

"The Lord Lourmarin's not—"

"Please, sir, I don't mean to be rude to such an honorable man as yourself," she stepped closer and whispered, "and might I add handsome," and she watched him fight a smile as he blushed to his collar, "but I cannot be late, please, sir."

He cocked his head at another guard, and two of the blue-and-white-coated soldiers ran through the front door. As the man unlocked the front gate, Ani counted the number of guards, the windows, gauged the distance between the fence and the front door, the outer walls and the inner, listened to how sound traveled the expanse.

ജ

Now

The soldiers' cries heralded down the interior hallway. "Marquis, my lord! There is a lady at your gate." The men yelled, tripped over one another to be the first to inform the nobleman.

"Ah, is there not always a lady at my gate?" the marquis said, walking down the hall toward the commotion. He hastened to the door to see his soldiers stepping cautiously toward the young woman with their bayonets drawn. "Has she a weapon?"

"None that I can see, my lord. She says she's your new clerk."

The marquis laughed heartily, then stopped when the soldier's face stayed blank. "Oh, you're serious." The marquis looked back at the woman. "My clerk is a gentleman, a scholar from Montreuil. Most certainly not a girl."

"She said he is indisposed with the pox," the second soldier said.

"The pox, huh. An unfortunate thing to be indisposed of." He studied her closer. Shapeless and petite, but shoulders straight, bearing solid. Her dress was fine enough, though clearly not even gentry, let alone noble, and the hem was splattered in mud, indicating that she didn't know how to walk with any grace. "Instruct them to lower their bayonets, Monsieur Porcher."

"Sir," Porcher said, "she might be—"

"—a lady," the marquis said. "She might be *a lady*."

"Sir—"

"Oh, come, a weak sneeze could bowl her over. Go into Paris, and fetch Monsieur d'Arcy, and he'll sort out this debacle of the clerk." The marquis fished in his pocket for his change purse, but when he held out a handful of coins, the soldier's face went pale.

"I'm not going into the city, sir. Have you seen the city?"

"You're not afraid of a few riots, are you?"

Porcher's eyebrows rose.

"Well, then, Monsieur Moulin," the marquis turned to the next soldier, "you go to the city, and tell Monsieur d'Ar—"

"General, no!" Moulin said and crossed himself.

"You'll do as you're told," the marquis said, but he couldn't keep a straight face. "I kid, I kid," he said, laughing. "Fine, fine, no one goes to the city. Such brave soldiers you are." He slapped their backs.

"Is it safe to bring her into the garrison?" Porcher asked.

"Heavens, no," the marquis said and crossed himself. "It's never safe to bring a woman inside anywhere. But I can't have her making a scene in my courtyard."

"We could deposit her in someone else's courtyard to make a scene," Moulin muttered.

"My friends, be kind!" the marquis said. "Imagine what the neighbors would think of all the mud on her skirt." He placed his hands on the shoulders of both guards. "Madame Balland would have the vapors for a week."

The two men exited, and the marquis watched as they ushered Ani toward the palace yard, stopping her before the front steps. He stood across the open doorway, one extended arm leaning into the jamb, thinking through what ruin this woman could harbor. Her eyes were bright, fiery—striking as if blue textile dye had washed into them. It was not just her best feature; it was her only feature. The rest of her face was pointed or rounded without consistent pattern. Her crooked canines looked like primitive carrot peelers, and her top lip slightly snaggletoothed on one. Her eyebrows were light, barely there. A clerk was one trouble all his own, but *a woman* changed things. She curtsied frightfully, and he made a half bow and a gesture of lifting a hat he wasn't wearing, then much to his surprise, she took the steps up to his same level.

"My lord," she said and curtsied again. "I have been sent to be your—"

"—new reckoner. So I heard. And the gentleman—"

"Indisposed, sir," she said. "Quite likely th—"

"—the pox, yes, yes. A poor way to go for Monsieur Joubert."

Ani's eyes flicked to his. She hadn't imagined Lourmarin to be clever. "It's *Au*bert, sir."

"Right, right, Aubert. Traveling from Montpellier."

She didn't flinch. "Mont*reuil*, sir."

"Ah, yes. The scholar."

"A graduate of Faculté de droit," Ani said, meeting his challenge before he could say it, but akilter at his adeptness when she'd always assumed him an oaf.

She had to get inside—she had to step one foot inside his palace. This man's palace. This man who had everything. Her lip snarled involuntarily at his ruffles and flairs, too disgusted to let it sink in that he was in a military uniform. His eyes remained on her, then he transferred his gaze downward to the rows of brass buttons on the front of his overcoat, with which his fingers incessantly fidgeted, and she ducked beneath his arm outstretched across the doorway and found herself suddenly in the inside foyer. The marquis gasped, and the guards mounted the steps, but Ani waved her hand toward the hallway.

"Oh my, what lovely—" She stepped farther in, then stared wide-eyed into the elaborate ballroom. "You have the sculpture of *Abel Dying*," she said, walking into the room and toward an outstretched bronze man. *There* was all the lost fine art she'd been mourning to Dr. Breauchard only days ago. How unfair that one man should have all this.

Even more unfair that *this family* should have it, that they should get to
have anything at all.

The bayonets of the armed guards were still trained toward her as
the men scaled the stairs. The marquis held up a hand for them to stop.
"Oh dear." He sighed. Should he send the men back to their places?
Had he ought to think of his own safety—or should he at least have a
bath drawn for her to clean the mud from her ankles, procure a dress
that wasn't so sodden. He thought for a minute. Would he trouble?
Did this warrant troubling? That wasn't too much to ask, was it? He
flicked his wrist. "All right, men. Smartly to your posts." There were still
two guards down the hall should he find necessity to shout for them.
The men hesitated, and he waited until they were out the door before
turning back to Ani, following her into the ballroom. "You can at least
conduct mathematics, yes?"

"I wouldn't be here if I couldn't count, sir." Her attention remained
fixed on the bronze statue.

"And how old are you, Mademoiselle—?"

"Ani," she said, and it wasn't a lie. "Seventeen." Not a lie.

"Have you a husband, any children?"

"No, my lord." Also not a lie.

"And credentials?" He held open his palm.

She drew forth some folded papers from her satchel. *Those* were a lie.
"Yes, Marquis de Lourmarin."

"Lourmarin?" he said, squinted his eyes and thought to correct her,
then closed his mouth and looked at the papers.

Out the corner of her eye, she watched him reading them, holding
them to the light from the window. He even smelled the paper. She
remained calm, kept her eyes on the artwork, on ledgers and stacks of
parchment on the table; she took note of escape routes through the
windows and alternative exits suggested by closed doors. Outside, past
thick panes, she could see faubourg Saint-Honoré in the distance. She
wouldn't be able to elbow her way through the window this time. Just as
well, she thought—her elbow and forearm still throbbed from the last
time she'd had to escape that way. When he looked back up at her, she
was staring at the statue.

"You are familiar with Stouf?" the marquis said, pleasantly surprised.

"I've seen the work in the Louvre hall, right next to—"

"—Le Brun," they both said in unison, and Ani turned to him, her
brows high, then creased with caution. He knew about art? She hadn't

imagined their conversation would go like this—art, the Louvre. She thought he'd be easier to despise immediately.

A lightness crept into him. "You have attended the Académie Royale?"

"Never attended, but I've—" she stopped abruptly before admitting she'd sneaked in through the sewage door, "—have, uh, looked through many a window."

"I see," he said. "What was your favorite piece?"

"*Leda and the Swan.*"

"O-oh. Ah." He misstepped and reddened, then cleared his throat. "Wertmüller?" he attempted respectably, but his voice was an octave higher as he forced away the image of Leda's naked legs wrapped around the feathered body of a swan.

"Yes, and his painting of Lady Imbert, though she looks like—"

"—she has a turkey on her head," he finished for her.

"Yes!" she said, and she smiled unexpectedly, though it vanished so soon.

That sudden crooked smile flustered him. He'd never been flustered by women; he'd been taught to handle them at court before he was even breeched. But who was this one? Surely not who she said she was—the papers were false. "I thought I was the only person who saw the turkey," he said. "I revealed that to my brother, and he said I'd maddened like our uncle Denis." The marquis made a throwaway gesture. "Though I'm not at all certain he knows the piece in question. Most likely seeks *any* excuse to think I'm maddened."

"Your brother?"

"Yes." He looked her in the eye. "Lourmarin."

"Uh," she stammered and glanced away. She had the wrong brother? But he was certainly a Beaumercy—he looked just like them, like their father, had the Beaumercy nose. She caught herself. He was still a Beaumercy, likely still a marquis of something. How much had she already blundered? "It's definitely a turkey." She hoped her airiness didn't sound false. "Bet he swiped one from market to use as a model."

The marquis laughed. "Men of means don't swipe things from market. He surely had one brought in from the fields to place upon her head."

"You gentry think *artists* are men of means?"

"I'm not gentry. I'm landed nobility."

Ani remembered anew her surroundings, why she was there, standing in a room of commissioned royal artwork that cost enough to feed everyone she'd ever known for a lifetime. She took a step back from him. Was this the right place? Was it even a garrison? Did the duke make his weekly visits here? "It doesn't matter now," she said quietly. "The artists are gone. They're relegated only to private salons these days."

"Yes, I heard. What…what is it now?"

"You don't go to the city?" she said, surprised.

"Oh, heavens no." He laughed and crossed himself. "I stayed far away from there even before they started hanging men I'd once dined with." His laugh petered out mirthlessly. "My concern is with the countryside, this unholy war with Austria." He crossed himself again.

War? Lourmarin wasn't an officer. She definitely had the wrong brother, but which one? There were seven of those blasted Beaumercy sons. She studied him closer. The very symbol of nobility, appropriately handsome, though with stubble around his mouth—what tedious business to be bothered with daily shaving. Dressed to the hilt in double-barreled pistols and a custom-made saber strapped across his waist. Ruffled and powdered with a willowy silk cravat tight about his neck and tucked into his double-breasted, gold-embroidered waistcoat and blue velvet cutaway coat with polished brass buttons down each breast. The outer pieces were tailored and laid perfectly over the top of a fitted linen stock shirt that was tucked with a buckle beneath white doeskin culottes attached at the knee with brooches to pristine white wool stockings, which were, themselves, stuffed into shiny-buckled, dark-brown, low-heeled leather shoes. He appeared the living embodiment of the Second Estate itself—and clearly a general. Why hadn't she noticed that at the entrance? Had she been so distracted?

She tamped down her confusion and focused on his question. "I believe they call it Musée Central des Arts now. Probably will add *Republic* at the end of it, like everything else."

"And they are filling it with…?"

"Art confiscated from the First Estate," she said, and the marquis nodded to the floor disappointedly. "The paintings that backed assignats."

He cocked his head. "You know about clergy bonds?"

"I'm here to do your figuring, am I not?"

"And you said *they*. You are a royalist, then?"

Ani's face blanked. "I—"

"I see," the marquis said. "Mine is not to judge," but he absently crossed himself again and looked down at the papers he was still hold-ing. "Baillairgé," he read from the top sheet. "I don't know that family name."

It wasn't hers. That was also a lie.

"Who is your father?"

Her face went pale. Her father? How could she explain to this man who her father was?

✑

Before, a month prior, Paris, June twentieth, 1792
Ani Pardieu's fists clenched around the bleeding hearts of two rotten tomatoes and one disintegrating fish carcass as she stood shoulder to elbow in the packed square. The stench of man rose from gutters near the Place de la Révolution, and flailing crowds knocked off Ani's hat and mashed her feet. Hands struck the back of her head, followed by knitting needles from the sewing women who'd come for entertain-ment, to sew and watch, watch and sew. But Ani was rugged and sturdy and not easily shoved. Mistaken for a boy more often than not, she'd come to dress the part in her father's old clothes, too plain to be no-ticed, easily thrust about in the folds, invisible, yet she didn't lose her footing, and she shoved back every elbow that smacked her.

A line of men formed at the neck of the Razor. Ani coughed a hard, painful heave that sat deep in her chest, and she fought her way toward the platform in the corner of the confiscated land of Comte de Crillon. Little more than political prisoners and pettifoggers, the disposal of these men was the attempt of the Second Estate—*the nobility*—to make an example of the rioting and pamphleteering kindlers of a revolution's budding fire. But the crowd didn't care about the why or whom; they'd come to watch men die, come to feel immortal in themselves—their own hands untied, their own heads unbowed.

Ani frowned, scanned the line of men, and her mind always went back to the same place: Flickers of a jewel in her mother's hair, fresh lilies on the table. A long room filled with highbacked chairs, lit by glass chandeliers. Ani'd had dolls once, handmirrors and paintbrushes and a wooden horse, books that she read to Dr. Breauchard—before some-thing had gone terribly wrong. She closed her eyes. The past was noth-ing more than disordered fragments. She'd had her mother and father, afternoons in parks and carriages, evenings in the marketplace watching puppets dance on sticks in children's theaters.

Then, there'd been famine. Volcanic ash had fallen from the sky and covered all of Europe. Mother, Father, the house, the toys—they left her one by one. But here she stood. She'd lived through it, all the failed crops and the depraved mounting violence. She'd been arrested for theft and vagrancy and repeatedly sent to forced labor in coalmines, and she'd lived through that, too—escaping time after time, lying her way out of most any situation in which she found herself. Hundreds lost their lives to riots and capital punishment for petty crimes. But still thousands upon thousands more stood to their feet, like Ani. They had witnessed the independence of the North American colonies across the ocean. Their millions of francs of levied taxes had gone to support the impossible achievement so that Louis XVI, like his infamous third-great grandfather before him, could see his longtime British enemies fall. The United States won France's bread, while Paris still hungered for it.

And now, *here* were the men who had been prisoners in the Bastille before its demise, joined by prisoners from the Temple, La Force and La Conciergerie, Grand Châtelet and Sainte-Pélagie. Paris had more prisons than food and more guns than bread. No onlooker knew the crimes these men had committed, but each was certain the deaths signified justice. One man's bloodshed was somehow synonymous with another man's liberty.

Unlike the women with their knitting needles, Ani didn't want to watch this. She recognized some of the chained men: a tax protestor, a bread thief. Men sent to the scaffold to clear out prison space. Her eyes fell on an older man half a dozen back in the processional, and her heart thumped at his appearance. Haggard. Steps sluggish, shoulders sloped. His weight shifted from foot to foot with the grace of a crippled leper. Five and a half years in the Bastille, followed by three in Grand Châtelet prison, had begotten white hair. A hollowness employed his eyes. His spirit was clearly broken, and she imagined he didn't even know who he was anymore.

Ani knew. When last she'd seen him, she was eight. She wondered if he'd respond if she called his name, or if prison had sequestered all memory from his memory, all life from his life. She pushed her way through the crowds nearer the scaffold, dipping beneath arms, ducking around blows and the city's garbage, both rotting and living, never taking her focus from the decrepit figure. She prayed she could reach the Razor before he did. Three men stood in line before him at the blade. Then two. Then one, faster than she'd imagined. A fragment, a blink.

"Papa! Papa!" She waved wildly toward the broken man at the block.

๛

Now, Palais d'honneur, the Chaillot

"We shall get you rinsed, Mademoiselle Baillairgé," the marquis said, "find you something suitable to wear."

"Trousers would be fine if I might borrow some."

"*Borrow?*" He wrinkled his nose, then straightened and crossed himself. "Trousers? 'A woman shall not wear men's clothing.'"

She faced away from him, rolled her eyes, and muttered to herself, "What use have I for your deuterocanon?"

"A good deal of use for it, seems."

She hadn't expected him to hear her. She pointed at a statue. "Even your revered Joan of Arc wore men's clothing."

"And she burned in pyre for it, you might recall."

"They're burning her again. Torching her relics and banner at the Carrousel."

"They are?" He sounded more sad than mortified.

"Men's pantaloons being comfortable was not one of the miracles she was blessed for." She pointed to his culottes. "But I could assume those halflings."

"These?" He tugged on the skintight cloth at his thighs. "*Halflings?* This is a uniform." Ani shrugged, but the marquis held up a finger and pointed to the mud she'd dragged beneath the hem that she didn't properly lift as she walked. "Let us get you rinsed and into a clean *dress* before you get that mud all over the Chevalier de Non's engraved marble."

"Better that than on his *Point de lendemain*," she said. "Certainly you have a copy?"

He flushed red. He certainly did have one, but he wasn't going to own to reading erotic novels. Well, not yet. Though he had a suspicion that it might be rather enjoyable discourse. He let the question hang unanswered and called down the hall, "Josette!"

Ani jumped at the suddenness of it.

He motioned his head for Ani to follow and extended a hand toward the hallway. When they'd neared the end of it, he yelled down an adjoining hall, "Josephine!" The echoes bounced down both halls and through each hollow room like the call of a loon across a still lake.

A slim woman came forward, exquisitely clad in a silk and velvet dress of layered pinks and dusty rose bunched beneath the deepest reds, petticoats aflutter, like that very loon taking off across the lake, wings flapping and water parting beneath her feet. Her hair sat in tall, twirled buns with carefully hanging curls. A clip the size of an apple adorned one side of her head. The woman wasn't plump enough to be the Marquise de Lourmarin—notoriously the butt of pamphlet jokes—so Ani figured the woman must be the marquise of whoever this marquis was and gave the lady a curtsy, while Josephine, a woman nearing twenty or just past, triumphed down the hallway as if trumpets should be exulting her entrance. She approached the pair and motioned for Ani to stop curtsying.

The marquis smirked with amusement. "I apologize for putting more work on you, Mademoiselle Journeaux, but there is this young woman," he motioned, "who shall be our reckoner for the fire insurance. She's sent from Compagnie d'assurance contre l'incendie directly and will be staying with us. She'll require—"

"I understand, my lord," Josephine said, her eyes already on the mud at Ani's hem, the splashes up the girl's ankles.

What Ani understood was that this beautiful woman was not the marquise, but such extravagance bestowed upon a servant?

Josephine ushered Ani through the hallway toward the washbasin in the nearest boudoir, and Ani emulated the woman's proud gait. When Ani glanced back down the hall to the spot where the cross hallway joined, there still stood the young marquis, watching intently with one hand cupping his chin, fingers splayed across his jawline in a pose befitting some ancient Greek scholar.

CHAPTER TWO

TWO LIES AND A TRUTH

*A little rebellion
now and then
is a good thing.*

—Thomas Jefferson

Now

In the bathing room, Josephine laid out a piece of linen along the wood floor at Ani's feet and positioned her before the washbasin. She instructed Ani to strip down and not to worry about getting mud on the linen. Josephine left the room to fetch hot water and returned a dozen times to fill the tub, each time finding Ani standing in the same position with clothes still donned.

"Girl, you'll have to follow instructions better than that. You're in a military garrison. Men bark orders around here like they're unleashed hound dogs, and you'll learn right quick which ones to throw a bone and which ones to let starve. The marquis gets the bones. Whatever I say comes from him, so best mind it. Now strip and get in that tub before the water cools. You are a filthy mess of a girl."

"Did that come from him?"

"Oh, sakes alive. You're a smart one, I see. It is twice my lucky day, then." Josephine stood with her hands on her hips.

Ani hadn't anticipated standing before a washbasin, but she was intrigued. This would give her time to think, to be alone. So it was the garrison. Right palace, wrong Beaumercy. But she'd never been wrong like this before. She wished someone would say his title or given name instead of *my lord this* and *the marquis that*. He was too clever to say his own name. He was a step ahead of her, and she wasn't used to being so precariously balanced. Josephine still stood behind her. Ani waited, then said, "Are…are you remaining here?"

"Remaining here?" Josephine grunted and reached for the laces on Ani's dress. "I'm going to bathe you, foolish girl."

Ani jerked away. "I prefer to bathe myself, if I may."

"You may certainly not. No woman of any worth bathes herself."

"But I—"

"Turn around. Stop being obstinate." Josephine took Ani's laces and untied the back of her dress. The servant inhaled audibly when she saw Ani's back and neck, the tops of the girl's arms; whip gashes traveled Ani's backside like a map of battlefield maneuvers. Josephine stayed silent and undressed Ani the rest of the way. "Do you have no under-garments?" she asked quietly. "Any corset or stockings?"

All Ani had was her dress, one thin layer of petticoats, wooden shoes over bare feet, and the trousers and men's blouses hidden at the bottom of her satchel. She shook her head and stepped into the brass basin. Dirt shed from her skin in gray rings and misted through the bath. She touched her finger to the top of the water and dragged tiny circles through the surface like bugs skittering along capillary ripples. The water warmed her skin. Moisture soaked into the tips of her fingers, slowly pruning the pads. She smiled. It was certainly better than lakewater. Flickers of a different time returned: A copper basin with ivory handles, her mother's long fingers around a wooden comb dragged through Ani's wet hair, often Dr. Breauchard's lye cloth on her tiny back, long before the skin was mapped in scars. A balsa swan that floated on the water's surface.

Josephine leaned Ani forward in the tub and held her breath. Her cloth barely grazed the whip gashes along Ani's torso, arms, and shoulders, as if the old scars would rip open again on contact. But Josephine didn't miss a beat when she unmangled a heavily soiled linen from Ani's forearm and pressed the cleansing cloth into a deep glass cut. "What do you call yourself?" Josephine asked.

"Ani."

"Well, Ani. This is grotesque." She looked at it closer. "It's infected, and looks like...like glass shards in your skin?" Josephine touched it lightly, and Ani drew breath. "You have another on the back of your elbow, here, split up bad. We'll require a doctor if this is to heal properly. Else you'll end up losing the hand or the skin if it gets rotted." She sighed. "What house do you belong to, Ani? I'm not permitted to address a guest by first name."

"Just Ani will do. I'm not really a guest."

"An intruder, then."

Ani glanced at her, then examined the cut herself. No matter how bad it looked, she'd survived worse. But the thought of it rotting gave her pause. Her motion stirred steam that tickled her lungs into a cough. She gripped onto the side of the basin to brace herself and coughed forward into the water. Dirty bathwater splashed onto Josephine, crouched at the side of the tub.

The servant pinched her face together. "All right, Just Ani. I'm inclined to call it a day and let it rot—"

"A doctor once had to cut two fingers from Gret's hand that rotted."

"Did you ever talk to this Gret's doctor?"

Ani bit down on her tongue. Why had she mentioned Grietje? She'd have to be more careful. Couldn't name any names. "No. I don't know any doctors." She tapped against the tub anxiously.

ဆ

Before, the Bastille, faubourg Saint-Antoine, almost nine years prior
"Dr. Breauchard?"

The doctor reached toward the tiny voice and took the hand connected to it. "Stay close to me, Allyriane." He didn't really have to tell her—she was already standing on his heels.

The stench of the building was nauseating. Prisoners with boils over their lips, styes on their eyelids, sitting in their own vomit, feces. Rotten apple cores covered in insects and mice. Blood pooled beneath bodies of men sprawled on the floor in their own tubercular, consumptive messes.

"Where's Papa?" the little girl said, holding her nose.

"We'll find him," Dr. Breauchard said, but he didn't want to lie. He didn't know if they'd find him, but how could he say that to a child of eight? A child he'd known since before her birth, as a friend of her father's and closer friend of her mother's, before the woman had died years before. He'd tended to the young girl's infant care when she'd suffered first from jaundice, then breastmilk contamination, then colic, and throughout her childhood of lead poisoning, famine, dehydration, heatstroke, the loss of both parents, and already the undeniable symptoms of blacklung.

And when finally he did see Simon—eyes barely hanging in his head, one showing inflamed sockets through an abscess in his temple, his fingers scratched to bloody nubs from clawing crazedly at the wall—Breauchard turned the girl toward his own knee and walked her back, back, away.

"He's not here," Dr. Breauchard said. "Must not be here. We'll look somewhere else."

But Ani had seen her father's vacant face, smelled his overflowed chamber pot. *Her father.* A republican-minded pamphleteer, he was one of the heavily taxed men who stood up against the monarchy. He'd thought it intolerable for merchants to pay forty separate tolls for one single box of wine making its way from Provence to Paris, despite his appointed position to enforce it. His rebellion posed a threat to the monarchy, clutching desperately at its royal reins—the new Constitution merely a flimsy parchment at the time. Now, true rebellion was here, and her father, who had called for it to come, was jailed because of it. She turned away, but for a second a string had connected them, and she'd known the hollowness creeping through her insides like a hunger.

"Allyriane, why don't you recite for me a verse," Dr. Breauchard said. "Something cheery?"

Ani stayed silent for a moment, but then recited, "*The curfew tolls the knell of parting day, The lowing herd wind slowly o'er the lea, The plowman homeward plods his weary way, And leaves the world...to darkness...and to me.*" She turned her head and looked back at her father, but he was a ghost. She willed him to recognize her, to *see*, but an infection had taken his mind.

"I said 'something cheery,' child," the doctor said. "Is that all I've taught you? Darkness and weary ways?"

Ani stopped walking and pulled her hand from Breauchard's. "Are you going to leave me, too?" A tear ran down her cheek.

Breauchard knelt and pulled her forehead to his lips. "No. No, not ever." He closed his eyes and held her to his neck. He knew he couldn't promise that, but what could he say to a child of eight?

Now

Josephine rubbed the lye cloth over the fresh cuts, and Ani winced. "I'll talk to the marquis about a doctor," Josephine said.

"Oh no," Ani said, "please don't."

"That won't heal on its own."

"I don't want to trouble the Lord Lourmar—" She stopped herself. He wasn't Lourmarin; that much she'd figured out. "—to trouble *him* wi—"

"Eh, he's a troubler." Josephine waved her hand as if swatting a fly. "He'll trouble himself if you don't trouble him first. Might as well get it out of the way. And we'll have to get you a new dress. You're smaller than me, but nothing a little altering won't fix. I'll fetch you something to wear that should fit fine enough."

Josephine stood and went to the door, then saw the satchel. She looked at Ani, whose head now rested on the lip of the basin, her eyes closed. Josephine snatched the satchel and ducked out the door, closing it quickly behind her. She leaned against the wall and clutched the bag to her chest, her heart pounding. She opened it and looked inside. The stench of unwashed garments hit her first, and she closed the bag abruptly to keep from gagging, then opened it again. Men's clothing, tucked and pinned for a smaller fit. Shoes with soles so thin she could put her fingers through them. Some small brown pouch that looked empty. A vial of something powdery. A ball of twine. Then she gasped and closed the bag and whirled herself around the corner to find the marquis standing where she'd left him, one hand glued to his chin, the other twisting his buttons. The smell of rye malts haloed him.

"Are you drunk?" she asked. "I'll have to pick your wits up off the floor and give them a good dusting."

"I may have had a dram of whisky, yes, Mademoiselle Journeaux. Your concern has been noted." He peered around her toward the bathing room. "Brief me."

She sighed and whispered, "I'm frightfully concerned that she is not what she seems. She's lower class, quite obviously. Her body is a battlefield of scars. She's got an unpleasant cough—heaven help us if it's the typhoid. Her mouth is smart. She has men's clothing!" Josephine held up the clothes. "And she has cuts all over her arms that are infected with what look like glass shards in them." She lowered her voice even further. "I believe she's escaped from somewhere."

"Well now, see. This is why a man takes a drink."

"She needs a doctor, but she won't go to one. I doubt she can afford it, I'd say."

"Put her in a sleeveless frock, so I can administer to her arms. That should give me something to do with these fidgeting fingers. You know what I say about idle hands."

"Yes, sir, 'they make for excellent drunkards.'" She said it as if a practiced proverb. "And I believe she thinks you are the Lord Lourmarin."

"Yes, I've surmised that. Yet, I am the one who requested a new clerk. Right palace, wrong Beaumercy."

"And, my lord, when I looked through her satchel—"

"You looked through her satchel?"

"Of course! And I found this!" She raised the glass vial of a pow-dered mixture.

The marquis took the vial and examined it closely, rolling it around in his fingers. "Huh," he grunted. "What do you suppose it is? An inhal-ant or a dissolvent?" He popped the lid, stuck the tip of his finger into the powder, and dabbed it on his tongue.

Josephine gasped. "Or a poison!"

He smirked. "Could have been a poison, I suppose."

"Do not you toy with my nerves, sir!"

"Hallucinogenic anesthetic. She knows an apothecary somewhere."

"Then she is also a liar."

"Oh?" He grinned and smacked his lips together. "Pain deadeners to mask…something else quite indistinct. Huh. Perhaps our new friend is an addict. And a liar. Naturally."

"And a murderer!" Josephine hissed. "I found these!" She held up two sheathed knives that she'd pulled from the bottom of Ani's bag. "She might have slit your throat!"

"Well, is she going to poison me or slit my throat, which is it?" He handed the vial back to Josephine.

"And I found this!" She held up the ball of twine. "She means to bind you with it!"

"My! Is that before or after she poisons me and slits my throat?"

"I am not in jest!"

"I believe you are not." He smiled sadly. "But did you consider that perhaps she just desperately needs the job? You of all people ought to have a little compassion for that, Josette, no? We weren't all born into this. She's scrambling for that wealth as you once did. Let's not judge our new friend too quickly. Everyone's got some kind of knife and poison these days, bah, and I could break that twine with my teeth. Besides…I do believe this dreary place could use another touch of gentler fingers."

"You don't mean to let her stay?"

He shrugged. "I let you stay, didn't I. You came to me under much darker circumstances, yet you're the one thing in this palace that I can-not do without." He turned toward the front parlor, but then turned back. "But, Josette…hide the knives."

"I was already going to, sir."

Josephine watched him walk away at his thinking pace, then contin-ued down the hallway to exchange Ani's soiled clothes for a sleeveless dress and undergarments. She returned to the bathing room to find

Ani still soaking in the tub with her head thrown back, eyes closed, murmuring the chorus of "Ça Ira."

"Don't sing that here, Just Ani," Josephine said, startling her. "This is not the National Guard and certainly not the Commune. You're among the king's men now. Come, up, up, up." Josephine unfolded a dress, stockings, undergarments, corset, and shoes at the dressing table. "Call for me when you get to the corset. Then right back down the same hallway you entered, and go into the last door on your left before the front door," the servant added on her way out the bathing room. "Understood? Last door on the left before the front door. That's the front parlor. Hurry along, and don't make him wait. Not because he won't wait, but because he'll wait forever without complaint. I, however, will not."

❧

Now

Ani, dressed in elegant new clothes, walked down the hallway toward the front parlor, moving from plaque to plaque under the portraits, searching for a clue to his identity. The large wall-sized portrait at the head of the hallway was of Josephine, the oddity of it all, for that was the position reserved for the master of the house. What nobleman didn't fill his own hallways with portrait after portrait of himself?

A servant stepped into the hall and cleared his throat, not at all subtly. He held a letter too dearly to be for anyone but the marquis. Ani seized her opportunity.

"Is that for me?" she said and stepped forward with her hand outstretched.

Before he could reply, she had hold of one edge and tugged. His grip too fervent, all she managed to do was rip a corner, but it was enough to see the title. The servant pipped, his mouth wide open, but Ani quickly read the name. *Collioure*. She felt as if she'd been stabbed. This name of all the Beaumercy names. He had the duke's title—was the son to inherit the duke's lands in Collioure. She collected herself.

"My thousand pardons, monsieur." She curtsied clumsily, but the servant's jaw hadn't closed. She frantically tried to remember everything she knew about the Marquis de Collioure. How could they have told her the wrong Beaumercy? Did they know?

She brushed by the servant before he could admonish her, entered the front parlor, and stood in front of the marquis as he sat reading *Modern Chivalry: Containing the Adventures of Captain John Farrago and*

Teague O'Regan, His Servant. His eyes were alight, scanning the page, and she wondered if he'd noticed her enter. Perhaps she could back out quietly and poke around in the next room without detection? But she thought better of it—the Marquis de Collioure wasn't as distracted and blockheaded as his brother was purported to be.

She approached his desk, neat piles of parchments pressed flat with fancy stone paperweights. There, on the top, a law case with his name typed in roman plate lettering. If only she'd been patient, she wouldn't have had to put herself at risk and rip a corner of his letter, but patience wasn't her strong suit, nor was it usually required of her. Aubrey-Catherine Martin Gilbert Montchamb Beaumercy. Twenty-two years of age and already an established marquis-general in the field. The only Beaumercy whose name never made the papers. She knew far too little about him.

Josephine called this room the front parlor, although it appeared to be everything but, including a library, a study, an office, a meeting room—and oh yes, there in the far corner at the farthest window were two fabric chairs with tall backs squeezed in around a dainty table harboring two upside-down teacups on saucers and a fine china teapot that Ani supposed could be misconstrued as an area resembling a parlor.

She stepped forward, glanced over his book, but he still didn't look up. He was waiting for her to strike first. "I see Captain Farrago has newly stumbled on a horse race where the crowd is engaged in bitter arguments over the race results, and Farrago maintains the voice of reason," Ani said, then listened to her own words echoing back to her around the high ceilings.

"You're quite right," the marquis said, his attention still on the book. "It is humorously written, though not of much substance, and—" He looked up at her. "Holy God, strike my faith, rap my knuckles, and call me a scoundrel." He crossed himself, but she was clean and in a court dress that made her look like a queen. Her startling blue eyes matched the fabric of her dress. He caught himself. "Well. Mademoiselle." A smile kept the words light, but there was an air of caution in his tone.

He clunked his boots against the floor, stood from his chair, and walked toward her. He carved a slow circle, taking in all angles of her, settling on the cut along her right forearm before steering her to a chair. She sat nervously, her skin crawling with the idea of him standing behind her. After she'd been seated, the marquis walked around his desk to seat himself again behind it. It was a grand display.

"So, you can read full passages. That is," he paused, "unexpected."

"I, uh—someone read it to me."

"I see." He was disappointed but decided not to question it. Josephine had warned him the girl was a liar, after all.

But Ani winced and relented. "No, my lord, I can read full passages, full books. Much more than the usual." She'd have to be more careful with her lies here. This was one he'd surely notice when she hoarded every book from his library as soon as she found it.

"Quite remarkable for a woman on its own. But you can also do numbers—that is extraordinary. Who taught you?"

Dr. Breauchard, she almost said, but settled on: "An educated friend."

"I see." He looked disappointed again. "It seems you don't know who I am—"

"General Aubrey-Catherine Beaumercy, the Marquis de Collioure." She brought her eyes to his. "Intelligence officer of the field, military strategist, and three-star general. And a cousin of the king."

He raised a finger. "Very distant."

"Distant cousin of the king."

"How pedantic of you." This caught him off guard. He'd expected his brother's name or something equally as offensive to his sensibilities. "Should I recognize you from somewhere? Did my carriage run over your kitten, or some sundry, to mark me listed?"

"No, Marquis, sir, you don't know me. Everyone knows who you are."

"Mmm," he grunted. "But the real question is, mademoiselle, who are you?"

"What do you mean, sir? I'm—"

"Not the lie. Who are you, really? And what are you doing in the Chaillot?"

"I'm—"

Aubrey shook his head. "Not the lie. Please. You have a hundred tells: your lips pucker, your cheek twitches, your fingers tap, your brows crease. Please. Give me the truth."

The truth? She almost laughed out loud. What if she really told him the truth, this curious man who waited for her response as if it would be poetry? She reminded herself he was a Beaumercy, that he didn't deserve the truth, but what would be his reaction if she told him? Why she was here, who he was to her? She shrugged, made an effort to appear calm, but she had to tell him something. Those eyes so brown they appeared diabolical. His face angled. Eyebrows arched as if an architect had formed them just for practice. Cheekbones prominently set. Ears too small, and the tight curls above them pulled back on his temples, fetching his hair into a queue down his back, past the shoulders. She couldn't tell what color it actually was, but it seemed dark under the remnants of lazy powdering. All of him dark. Ani looked away. She felt the fire in her lungs rising again and wished she could reach her inhaler.

"Let's start with why you're here. It will take two days for my message to Compagnie d'assurance contre l'incendie to come back to me, and what will it tell me?"

Ani blinked rapidly and looked away.

"It will tell me that they didn't send you."

"Sir—"

"Please, call me Aubrey. Not marquis, not my lord, not sir."

"Aubrey." The name turned to lead on her tongue. And what now? Could she draw out sentiment or pity or guilt? Could she tell *some* of the truth? What was the easiest? "Please don't send me away. I need this job, and I can do it well. All right, so I'm not gentry, but I can work—anything—washing and mending, polishing and…" She petered out. To beg a Beaumercy was more sour metal in her mouth.

He splayed his fingers on his desk but said nothing.

Good lord, was she going to have to cry? She breathed in deep through her nose to bring water to her eyes, quivered her lip as her lower lid filled with tears. "I need a chance."

"Aaaah," he sighed long as if it were painful. "Right arm out. Put it here." He tapped one finger to the top of his desk and retrieved a pair of magnifier lenses from his drawer. He pulled closer his medical chest, the oil lamp. "Might I ask how you acquired this cut, and might you tell me the truth about that?" He slid the spectacles over his ears, took hold of her hand, and tugged her arm closer.

Ani's skin burned as if she'd thrust her hand in flame. It took every effort not to yank it from his grasp. All right, the truth. She could burn him right back. "Guardsmen and one of your deputies broke a riot and corralled me through a window."

Aubrey pulled a pair of tweezers from his medical chest. His hand cupped Ani's small forearm. He picked a shard of glass out of her skin, heard her subdued whimper, and clinked the piece into a porcelain dish. "He wasn't my deputy. I have no more deputies. The Civil Guard has control of that department now. Blame the insurrection." He flicked his gaze at her, gauged her pokerfaced response. "Once I get this glass out, I'm going to swab a sublimate in it, and that's going to send you howling. So much so, that you'll want to reach for the pistol in my top drawer, but I do kindly ask that you refrain from such an impulse." *There.* The gun. If she had it, what would she do with it? Should he test her so? The rush of adrenaline to find out was nearly palpable. Amid wars and generals and stone walls, it was so much more exciting to dig glass and truth from a woman who was clearly hiding something.

She watched the side of his face as he worked close to her arm, and there were long stretches of silence and her whimpering in between his breaths that he held in at-length, then released in a rush when a new piece of glass clinked in the dish. She asked, "Are you going to turn me out?"

He slid his magnifiers off his nose and looked at her. "Not until you're healed. Do you think I would be unkind to you? I'm a man of chivalry."

Oh! what she could say to that! She could spit a thousand venomous unchivalries committed in his family's name. She bit her tongue. Her arm jerked.

He bent his head over her wrist with a final look through his magnifiers, his eyes owling. "You are mistaking me for my father," he glanced up, paused, "or brother," but she didn't react, "my misfortune of being a Beaumercy, as you clearly know the family name. My stature is a title bestowed upon me in a feudal history of lunacy that means little more than dressing in frills and wooing unmarried women into believing my title means something more than being my father's son, in hopes one will bear a son, in turn, to continue the line of lunacy with a new title. But I'm the disappointing son. The son that the duke sends off to wars he cannot win, in hopes I won't return from them."

A sober moment passed. "But you're still a Beaumercy," she said.

"That I am." He cocked his head. "May I ask you—did you get to choose who your father was?"

She felt like she'd been kicked the thought struck her so hard.

୭

Before, the execution of her father the previous month, Paris, June twentieth
"Papa! Papa!" Ani yelled toward the scaffold processional as the line of men moved forward.

Life flooded the old man's face. He called, "Ani? Be that my Allyriane?

Turn from here, and do not watch!" He faced the executioner and begged, "Please, monsieur, don't let my daughter watch this. You've already took her mother. I'm all she has left."

The headsman didn't reply. He shoved Ani's father toward the block and the imminent blade above it. The prisoner rose to see his daughter's face, but the guard struck him in the knee with the musket. Ani cursed and flung her fistfuls of tomatoes and fish at the executioner, pelting him, crests of black mold splotching his tunic, though he took no notice. He dragged the prisoner up and positioned the man's head against the nook of the block, then fitted the neck clamp in place with a grotesque dull thud.

"Papa, no!" Ani shouted, tears stinging her eyes. She occupied a bubble of retarded time, her arms outstretched, reaching no target. "Please, let him go! He's done nothing!"

"Be strong, my girl," her father called. "Vive la Révolution!"

The words hardly passed his lips when the blade flashed the sun's reflection across the crowd. Deliverance fell swift. His head rolled from the platform and landed at the gutter's edge alongside others. Ani turned her face, but too late. The image brushed her eyelids like a paintstroke. The twitch to the eyes after the severance, a sign still of life, of knowing. Her knees buckled, and she tottered at the kicking feet of passersby. Darkness folded around her, dizziness overcoming, a blue-black hole canyoned into her face, through to the back of her skull. For eight and a half years, she'd held out hope that her father would be released and returned to her—if even half the man he'd once been, that ghost she'd seen so briefly—that the day would come when he would exit the garrison walls and remember her, embrace her. She'd hardly known him—he'd been distant and cold and unapproachable for all her life—but he was hers. As long as he lived, there had been some sort of hope. Reconciliation, the chance to know and understand each other at long last. But now her hope lay dispatched in the gutters of the Place de la Révolution without even the dignity of a burial bag.

Chapter Three

In the lion's parlor

*If we could read the past
histories of all our enemies,
we would disregard
all hostility for them.*

—Napoleon Bonaparte

Now

That image of her father, how he'd stood in line, called out to her blind-ly, the tufts of grass at the esplanade that held what was left of him. "No, my lord, no one ever asked me what I wanted my papa to be. But if they asked me now, I'd say…alive. I'd like my papa to be alive."

He missed a beat, then pressed a cleansing cloth to her forearm, and she seethed and held her breath. "Sorry," he said. He wasn't sure which terrible thing he was apologizing for. Maybe a little of all of it. He finished disinfecting her wrist and reached for a threaded needle to make his first stitch. "Painful so far?"

"Only a little. But I'm," she shifted uncomfortably, "stuffed in a suf-focating corset."

Too quickly he said, "You're wearing a corset?" He trailed his glance up and down her, still looking through his magnifiers. "Hm." It gave her no shape. "It shapes you exquisitely," he said, but he had a hundred tells, too.

An unexpected laugh escaped Ani. "At least my parts aren't stuffed."

"Oh, come. Every member of the Second Estate stuffs. Button, cuff, powder, stuff. Button, cuff, powder, stuff. It even has a rhyming order." He sang it, "Button, cuff, powder, stuff." He chuckled, but good sense told him to lower his lens. He completed his sutures with meticulous precision and a theatrical pull of every stitch. His gaze wandered her when she wasn't looking. Wrapped around the curve of her shoulders were jagged, raised scars from whip lacerations that he imagined had left quite a map across her skin. *What had she done?* His gut tightened. "Is it all right with you if I take a drink?" He hated the apology that seeped into his voice.

"I never trust a man who doesn't drink."

"You'll never trust me anyway," he said lightly. "I'm a Beaumercy." He walked his fingers across the desk toward an uncrizzled flintglass whisky decanter, making a show of it. He upturned two matching, short-footed, lead-crystal glasses that looked to be something between a cordial glass and a snifter. A victim of practice, he filled each to the same volume, sliding one across the desk with signature epicurean precision in front of Ani. "I always say idle hands make for excellent drunkards." He winked, lifted his own glass in tilted salute.

"I'm not sure that makes sense. It's not your hands drinking."

"Well. A drunkard should only be quoted when you're also drunk."

She smirked, took the elegant stemware, watched him take a drink first, then downed the liquid before raising her arm to point out the cut on the underside, spreading across her elbow.

He whistled low and sat on the edge of the desk in front of her, lifted her arm over her head, and adjusted his magnifying lenses toward the glass shards embedded at the back of her elbow. A warming swell draughted him to touch her skin again. But for Ani, only coldness shot through her. There was a sharp intake of breath as the ends of his tweezers dug around beneath her skin, but neither was sure which one of them had breathed.

Ani trembled violently beneath his touch, a repulsion inside her that wanted to shed the skin right from under his fingers and slither away like an asp. She felt so small. He reigned over her with such privilege, towering like a giant. She hated that he was a tall and strong man, limber but fit, active, quick. Why couldn't he be puny and shrunken-in like his brother or fat and slow like his father? She cringed to think of his father—*the duke*—then sucked in through her teeth at a sharp poke.

"If you'd let me get you a doctor, this would be easier," Aubrey said.

"No, please. No doctors."

"You've surely surmised that I would pay for it."

"No." She swallowed the lump in her throat. "No…thank you."

Aubrey stood and walked around to his medical chest, opened the top tier, and rummaged through it for two small vials. He read the labels of each; all the contents of his chest consisted of identical vials in matching sets. He came before her, served her more whisky, then untwisted the tops of the vials and poured a drip of each into her glass, giving the liquid a swirl. The light filtered through the glass as he held it up to his lenses then placed it down in front of her. If she'd sucked on a lemon, her lips could not have sealed together any tighter.

"You do not trust me, I know," he said. "But killing you just means I have one more body to bury in the cellar." He sighed theatrically. "So much shoveling. I'd really rather not."

She gasped and laughed in one sound. He tapped the glass, and she took it but didn't drink it.

"If you can trust me, we'll get through this all much faster."

Ani pushed the fear from her eyes. She had to show him she trusted him, damnit, she had to. She threw the tincture back in one throw. Inside of a minute, her head swirled as it had on Dr. Breauchard's inhaler powder. Aubrey dug around within her wound to find the deepest shards, and she hardly felt a thing.

When his work was finished and he'd stitched her up, she looked at him through a haze. "What did you give me?"

"Opium and ether with snake venom. It'll shake off in a couple hours."

"What?"

"It worked, didn't it." He lifted another upside-down glass from beside the decanter and poured her a fresh snifter of whisky, setting it down on the arm of the chair. In her haze, she'd loosened, and he wanted to get her talking, wanted her to slip up and say the wrong thing, so he could know everything inside of a careless syllable. "So, Ani, where would you be if you were not here?"

"Saint-Marcel."

"Saint-Marcel," he repeated, thoughtstruck. "Filthy, overcrowded Saint-Marcel." He sipped. "I assume, then, that your family was inflicted by my father's impositions, moreover those of his deputies, and that is how you know who I am."

She wanted to scream it, but she kept calm. "That is a fair assumption, sir—Aubrey."

"And would you tell me if you were a revolutionary?"

She didn't respond.

"Don't want to be politick?" More silence, and he sighed. "Do you think I'll try to change your mind?"

"No," she conceded. For some reason, that felt like the truth.

"I beg of no one to change ideals if he should enjoy them." A horse whinnied outside the window, and he turned his head toward it. "So. You wish your father alive, then I surmise that he is dead."

Her heart dropped. "Yes."

"And your mother?"

She tensed, then said too sharply, "They both died."

❧

Before, following her father's execution, an insurrection at the Tuileries, Paris, June twentieth

His head rolled on the ground. She thought she heard its thud above the mob, so obsessed she was with it. Thunderous feet smacked the cobbles down the alley behind her. Ani drifted toward the sound, absently, another angry march of protestors, this time to the palace of the Tuileries. The headsman didn't collect the heads or bodies of the slain men, just rolled the last one aside and ducked for cover from the approaching mob. The crowds shouted for regicide of the king and queen, unless the royals ceded to demands for more bread. Someone drove a cart through the crowd, and it ran over a boy who writhed on the ground in its wake, screaming, clutching a leg of execrable bent. A cask of ale rolled from a flatbed and burst onto the soil with a crack. Protestors squatted above it and licked the ale from the mud, from the broken cask cradle. Shouts fell in line with footfalls: "Liberté! Égalité! Fraternité!" The fractious National Guard general Antoine Santerre swore drunkenly at children as he led the rioters past the scaffold.

Girondins, the newly defeated political faction, marched their sore egos against the slow moderation of the Feuillants, the ruling faction that implemented the Constitution and upheld the monarchy above it. Extremist Girondin ministers had been replaced by these Feuillants under the command of the Marquis de Lafayette and Antoine Barnave, and the king had been granted the power of constitutional veto, which outraged the barrage of market women, machinists, starving furniture builders, and armed guardsmen marching from the working-class faubourgs of Saint-Antoine and Saint-Marcel. General Santerre flooded the street beneath the scaffold with his processional masses and streams of muskets and symbolic burning lily bouquets. Petitions waving, declaring the king to be treasonous. Liberté. Égalité. Fraternité. *Or death.*

Ani huddled near the scaffold as the mob roiled toward the Tuileries in a dark wave, their red liberty caps like bobbing buoys above a tidal swell. She curled herself into a culverted dugout, scrunched in the makeshift drain barrel below the platform. Rainwater, human waste,

and blood lapped over her ankles. Insects swarmed, and dead ones
sloshed against her clothes and stuck there. She made a conscious effort
to breathe through her mouth, but breathing at all felt like a length of
rope dragged up from her bowels, dredging behind it a barbed anchor.
From where she hid, she could see the heads of the prisoners in the
slanted gutter. They were kicked by the hooves of the stampede like
so many scraps of trash in the street. Her eyes settled on her father's
severed head, and she dry-heaved in the back of her throat—her belly
empty, but her gut too tight to keep still.

Flashes of blue uniforms, men atop horses. Red and blue so distinct,
steadily rippling, consistent. When the mob moved on, pushed forward
and out, Ani hauled herself, damp and filthy, from the culvert and stood
on shaky legs. Her head reeled with dizziness. Stars dotted her eyes like
lightning bugs, and she almost sat back down in the filth. The shouts
began in her head and filtered out through her ears as if screens covered
them, then joined the outside shouts, until she realized it was the other
way around. What was in filtered out, out slithered in. She crept toward
her father's severed head, not knowing what she would do with it when
she got there but knowing she couldn't just leave it in the street. She
approached and lifted it from the ground and cradled it in her arms like
an infant. She wiped the mud away from his starkly open eyes, brown
so unlike hers, and her body convulsed in retches. Heaves, dry and consuming. A deep throb that knocked her lungs around like a paddle. Snot
bubbles popped and drained from her nose down to her lips. His head
was still warm.

She carried it in her arms through the slums, away from the gilded
statues of the Place de la Révolution and the stretching gardens of the
Tuileries, moving in the opposite direction of the mob of extremists,
back along the Seine toward the far bank. Dirty walls and low archways
and the thud of wooden wheels on cobblestones and halved logs. A
pounding that might have been the drumroll of the city guard. With
half a million people crammed into every corner of the city, it was
difficult to find green land untouched by machinery, industry, factories,
textile mills. Taverns, mud. She thought she carried a cannonball for all
his head weighed, the flesh of it stiffening beneath her fingers as she
shifted it from arm to arm, her balance swaying left and right with it.
Her feet led her past Cours-de-la-Reine, to the edge of the Seine, and
out onto Pont de la Révolution, parts of the masonry made with the old

dimension stones of the Bastille, sections of the bridge still unfinished, moldering into the rushing water.

After walking until her arms weakened, propping herself repeatedly against the limestone of the Palais Bourbon garden wall, Ani sought a patch of grass near the edge of the Esplanade des Invalides, and she dropped to her knees in the miniscule tuft, setting her father down gently and digging with her hands into the ground like a disinterested dog. He was a soldier after all, she wanted to think, a soldier asleep in the esplanade of soldiers. The soil was warm from the June heat and overdry from half a decade of drought and rain coming in the wrong seasons. It crumbled beneath her fingernails and slid back down into the spaces she'd carved it from, until she dug into it again, again, again, the repetition a thing of numbing mercy. She placed her father's remains into the shallow grave, closed his eyelids with her muddy hands, and carefully packed the dirt in around his face. She looked across the Seine toward the Tuileries and felt its expanse. Men's voices carried for miles and miles across the open river, yet all around Ani there were serene patches of green grass and forced quiet.

She rolled the largest stone she could find over the burial spot and pulled her weary body upright, intending to go back toward the center of the city. Instead, her legs gave out, and she fell back to the ground without strength to attempt it again. She curled her knees to her chest, cradled her father's makeshift gravestone, and pulled into a tight ball, stiff and exhausted, famished of stomach and heart, the shadow of the approaching patrolman stretching across her body like a dense cloud.

༉

Now

"How old were you when they died?" Aubrey asked.

"Very young when my mother passed. I hardly remember her, but Papa said I look just like her, except my eyes." She pinned him in place with them to be sure he'd remember the discomfort of his question. "Papa…" she trailed, "his death was…more recent. But he was already dead to me long before then."

"I'm sorry, Ani. It isn't cordial of me to pry." He lifted his glass and slid from his seated position, walked to the closest window that overlooked the horse posts then on to Paris in the near distance. Taking a sip of his aged whisky, he wrestled the guilt. That was always one of his flaws, according to his father, *everything always according to his father.*

Aubrey looked back at her from the window where he raised his tipped glass. He felt drunk, actually felt drunk. That was rare. The sunlight filtered in over his dark eyes, illuminating them. "So," he said, "you have no family to support, and no more family to support you, correct? Seems to me that you don't need the job so much as you need the room and board, yes? Food and—"

"Food," Ani repeated, her stomach growling.

Aubrey spun, spilling a dribble of whisky down the front of his embroidered lapel. "You need food right now?"

She looked back at him as if he might be joking.

"Oh, galleypock, of course you do. Why didn't you say so?" He crossed himself, then dabbed at his lapel with his cuff. "When was the last time you ate?"

She squeezed her bottom lip between her teeth. "I borrowed an apple this morning from a just-price cart, but—"

"Borrowed? You were going to give it back?"

Ani sighed. "*Stole*." She winced. "And I shared half of it with Isab—a girl."

"An apple? You are living on one half of an apple?" He shook his head, set down his whisky hard on his desk, and put both hands first upon his hips, then across his chest. "Arnaud! Valéry!" He shouted toward the hall, walking brusquely to the parlor entryway to meet two men hurrying to heed the marquis' call. "Messieurs Thénault and Fergniaud, please let me introduce Mademoiselle Baillairgé."

Ani blushed. That wasn't her name, and she couldn't get used to hearing it. The blush deepened when she realized the servant he'd called Arnaud was the one she'd encountered in the hallway with the letter. Arnaud scowled at her before he hid the gesture from the marquis.

Aubrey waved a hand toward her in the chair and motioned for her to stay seated when she attempted to rise. "Ani: Monsieur Arnaud Thénault and Monsieur Valéry-Marie Fergniaud, at your service eternally for whatever you require of them from the kitch or pantry at any time, day or night." Aubrey turned back to the men. "Messieurs, this young lady requires sustenance. She is famished quite literally." To Ani, he added, "What do you like?"

"Any scraps you can part with."

He grimaced, as did the men. She was far worse off than he'd first surmised. "Get our guest the remaining supper portions. Something hearty." He ushered the two men toward the kitchen and turned back

to Ani. "Really. One half of an apple? All right, food is handled." He
looked her up and down. "You've got some nice dresses of Josephine's
now."

"Is she your wife?"

"My wife?" he choked around a gulp of whisky. "Heavens, no. I'm
unmarried, another constant boon to my father's disappointment." He
crossed himself. "She's my sempstress. And she's the only female in
Palais d'honneur, so don't make an enemy of her."

Arnaud and Valéry entered the room with two large trays of food.
The smell of freshly prepared dinner wafted over her, and she thought
of how much the girls back in the Saint-Marcel cellar would appreciate
a catered meal. Dr. Breauchard would feed them—the girls wouldn't
starve. But a catered meal was beyond anything they'd had in a long
time, if ever. The marquis seemed proud of himself, his absurd kindness, but Ani's mind was only on the prospect of food.

≈

Before, a faubourg Saint-Marcel cellar, earlier in the month, July
Grietje was first to arrive, soon pacing the floor of the cramped cellar
space, plotting a way to find food. Grietje usually protested every presented idea, but today she was too hungry, and instead she worked her
bottom lip with her teeth, nibbling nervously.

She was an orphan dropped over the Alsace border by her Dutch
father who could no longer afford to keep her during the disastrous
winter of 1788. The number of orphans had quadrupled then, and
Grietje Hindricks was one of them. Now nearing fifteen, she'd given
up hope that her father would return to find her. She resigned herself
to the black existence of the black coalmine that all the girls had been
in and out of their whole lives. She'd lost two of the fingers on her
left hand and the hearing in one ear to an explosive cave collapse, and
no longer noticed that her blond hair was now pitched in coal. Grietje
dressed in boys' clothes like Ani, with items pilfered from the body of a
dead boy who drowned in the belly of one of the mines when the rain
flooded the tunnels and pinned the lower miners inside the main pit.
The pumping-out took days, and by the time the galleries were flushed
of their excess water, twenty miners had drowned, and another dozen
deaths followed in the subsequent mudslides that diminished the foun-
dation of the props and collapsed new portions of the tunnel. While
the floods were devastating to the mine, they were a jackpot to the

pickpocketing Grietje, who scavenged every stiff and helped herself to coins, pocketwatches, precious metals, and clothing, without so much as a wince.

Eleven-year-old Isabeau Léandre arrived next, strong-willed and even stronger-spirited, and they all waited for Béatrice. Ani snapped shut the book she'd been reading that she'd stolen from a rich man's library, and she tucked her shirt into her pants and tugged the high waist into place. They were her father's pants, one of several articles that had been returned to Dr. Breauchard after Simon's body had been dumped, beheaded and naked, into the catacombs that ran beneath the city outskirts. Ani twisted her hair around her fingers, shoved it under her cap, and gave the girls a cursory glance before checking the street. By the time Béatrice made it to the safety of their musty cellar, the rain let up, but the humidity stuck to the girls like a constricting net, and Béatrice, too, was acutely aware of her hunger.

"I'm going to find us something to eat," Ani said through the opening beneath the stairs once the girls were settled.

In the street, she studied starving peasants and mismanaged capital, the bustling of market stands, too costly and mostly empty. She filled her pockets with pamphlets. Women took off their skirts and petticoats and wrung the rainwater out of them in the open. A cough forced its way out of Ani's lungs, and she reached into the pocket of her father's pants for the inhaler and powdered mixture that Dr. Breauchard had concocted for her. Pinching a tiny bit of the powder, she held the wooden funnel up to her lips, flicked the mixture out of her fingers, and inhaled sharply, holding her breath to the slow count of five. But by the time she got to three, she gagged on the mixture and doubled-over, grasping hold of her throat and coughing fiercely. The powder was potent, and the nightshade hit her quickly, its anesthetic properties not outweighing the burst of toxin it shot through her body. Hallucination was an understatement. Her vision blurred and tripled. The marketplace zipped by in illuminated streaks of color and warped-moving slugs of people cast against a cloudy villagescape that melted in on itself, sinking into the cobblestone. She held her hand out in front of her and counted her fingers again and again to keep her focus from floating. *Food.* She was after some food. A gray haze covered the street that rolled like floodwaters around her legs. *Food.* Gray haze and food.

She got to her feet, stuffed the inhaler into her britches, and lifted her head to float erect over the shifting marketplace. She coughed the

mixture loose from her throat and swallowed hard. Food. Through
her hallucinations, she walked down the street until she came to a row
of just-price carts, where empowered women stole items from merchants in order to sell the goods at what the women considered *just
prices*, only to turn around and give the just-priced earnings back to the
merchants. It was a display of feminist intolerance toward inflation that
Ani couldn't understand. The women spent all day doing the labor, and
the merchants still came out ahead. But the goods weren't the women's
belongings to sell in the first place, so Ani felt more justified in stealing
them.

She walked along the rows of carts with her hands low, pulling red-
currants, dates, greengages, apples, sacks of lentils, a small loaf of stale
bread, and even a head of cabbage out from under the women's noses.
They bickered about women's rights in the workplace, inequality in marriage, and low wages for working women, while food disappeared from
their carts into Ani's pockets. With her spoils in hand, she made her way
back to the cellar to dole out her plunderings to the hungry girls. But
Breauchard hadn't spoken lightly about not using the inhaler when in
need of alertness. The streets still rose to meet her, all the way back to
the cellar.

Béatrice took an apple from Ani's bounty upon return. "I landed in
calaboose when I stealed one fig. And you!—you could walk an entire
cart from under the woman leanin' on it, and she'd just be leanin' on air,
none the wiser."

Ani smiled. "It's all in the timing. You've got to read people, know
when they're turning their backs on you." She glanced quickly at Grietje,
noted her scowl.

❧

Now

Aubrey motioned for the trays of food to be set in front of Ani. Without hesitation she dived into more food than she'd tasted in years:
rice soup, rump of beef with cabbage, loin of veal on the spit, grilled
mutton cutlets, sweetbreads en papillot, casserole with rice, artichokes
a la galigoure, cauliflower with parmesan, eggs with partridge gravy,
chocolate profiteroles, raspberry tarts.

"What, no Grace?" Aubrey asked.

"I don't thank any gods," Ani said. Few of the city dwellers did anymore.

"I'll pretend I didn't hear that."

"'Belief in a cruel god makes a cruel man.'"

He grunted. "Thomas Paine is an indecent role model."

She stopped chewing.

"Yes, I've read Thomas Paine. The man is an idealist."

"An atheist."

"A deist," he compromised. He bowed his head and put his glass of whisky to his face, clasped between both folded hands. "Bless her, O Lord, and these Thy gifts, which she is about to receive—well, is already receiving, forgive her—from Thy bounty, through Christ my Lord if not hers, Amen. There, I felt guilty enough for the both of us, so that should do." He looked up from his hands, and she had her mouth filled like a chipmunk, food stuffed in each cheek and pressed against the roof of her mouth to the point she could hardly close her lips. "My, you'd think it's a Solemnity. Slow down. No mutt is going to tear it from your claws, I assure you."

But she didn't slow down, digging into both trays at once, eating from every plate in a round, one right after the other. She barely chewed, completely forwent utensils. It was an awful and messy sight, but Aubrey was contented to witness the entertainment.

"As I was saying," he continued, motioning toward the food, "you need room and board, and I have fourteen empty rooms. I certainly don't mind company."

"Fourteen empty rooms?" she echoed, spitting food from her mouth. "What on earth for?"

"It's a palace. Empty rooms are all that palaces are for. The noblesse collect empty rooms like you collect apples from a cart. And this isn't even a particularly large palace. The disappointing son gets relegated to the small one. If you'd wanted a larger one, then you really should have ended up on my brother's doorstep. Alexandre—Lourmarin, as you call him—is our father's favorite." He was quick to add, "Though he doesn't have a marquisate paired to our father's duchy in Collioure as I have, of course."

"Of course," she said, colder than she'd meant to. The mention of his father ran through her veins like ice to the bottom of the Seine.

"I would be honored if you'd take a room. I should never allow such a one who has already endured the misfortune of being my medical patient to be venturing about the marshlands unattended whilst recuperating." He gestured toward her arm. "Shoes, dresses, trinkets, baubles, whatever you need."

"No one *needs* baubles."

"All right, you don't need baubles like I don't need whisky, but some things improve the quality of life, no?" He grinned. "I can supply you with quality of life at no particular loss to myself, and perhaps someday you can supply me with a son."

She choked on a cutlet. "Excuse me?"

"Just a jest," he said. "The Second Estate collects sons like empty rooms."

His gaze sparked, and she felt it sear through her before he broke it by nodding at her food. But she couldn't take another bite. What repugnance—a son, a Beaumercy. Her head still swam as she focused on loin of veal, and she thought it changed colors. She leaned back in her chair to give her belly room to expand. She hadn't felt this full in quite some time. As a child she'd eaten food like this, endless portions. But most nutritious food was so scarce now that Dr. Breauchard would make her ration it when they did manage to acquire it.

"You could get used to that, no?" Aubrey said.

"Not in a corset."

He smiled and laid both of his hands across the back of his chair and leaned in. "She gives Thee thanks, Almighty God, for all Thy benefits consumed here. She simply doesn't know it yet. Pray show her Thy patience as she learns. World without end, Amen."

Ani kept quiet amid his platitudes to his Catholic god, but she found herself silently thanking the marquis, even as that thought repulsed her. His generosity was not a god's; it was his own. He simply didn't know it yet. But she wouldn't be the one to tell him. Let his Catholic god sort them all out in the execution line.

"Fourteen empty rooms," he lured again.

How could she say no to that, after sleeping in leaking cellars or on Dr. Breauchard's hospital cots? As long as she didn't have to share a room with the marquis, she could bear it—she'd have to bear it. This was exactly where she needed to be. Though she'd never imagined that she wouldn't have to continue the lie to get here.

Chapter Four

One of fourteen

Every man is guilty
of all the good he didn't do.

—Voltaire

Before, the aristocratic quarter of Le Marais, Paris, seven years prior
Dr. Breauchard made an incision down the dead man's chest. A ten-year-old Ani heard the skin pop from where she sat, writing the doctor's notes into his files.

"Write this down," he said, careful not to get blood on his pristine whites, his cravat pressed neatly against his neck, never falling out of place. "Thermal injuries in the upper airway, reminiscent of smoke inhalation. Spell that for me."

"I-n-h-a-l-a-t-i-o-n," Ani spelled.

"Excellent. No burns. No outer damage. Throat and esophagus chemically peeled. Repeat that for me."

"Throat and e-s-o-p-h-a-g-u-s chemically peeled."

"Excellent."

Ani slid from her chair and brought the notebook toward the body. "What does that mean? He choked on something?"

"Breathed something in."

The man's wig flopped off his dead head and brushed Ani's hand. "Can I wear his wig?" Ani asked, pulling it from the table.

Breauchard laughed, despite himself. "Just don't mangle it. I must return it to the family."

Ani plopped the wig on her head and affected an air of elitism.

"See here," Breauchard pointed to the man's shriveled black lungs. "These lungs have been irrevocably burned."

"But not by fire?"

He looked up at her, and it was hard to take her seriously with the wig on her head. He laughed and said, "No—gas. Write this down. F-l-u-o-r-o-s-p-a-r, fluorospar. Heated manganese dioxide, you can sound that one out. Dephlogisticated muriatic acid, you've heard that one before. You can spell it?"

"Yes." She wrote it down.

"He breathed in contamination."

"He worked in a coalmine?" Ani wrinkled her nose.

The dead man was obviously an aristocrat, his cheeks rouged to ridiculousness, his lips outlined in a pink pencil and filled in with pink facepaint. An artificial mole was dotted in black char above his lip. She straightened his wig that she still wore on her head.

"Clearly not," Breauchard said. "Just look at those clean fingernails. But I'd say he lived next to a factory."

"Factory smoke killed him?"

"If you breathe in enough of anything, it'll kill you." He put aside his prodding tools. "Let's stitch him back up."

Ani held the dead man's skin together while Dr. Breauchard stitched the incision. "I'm going over to Bibliothèque Mazarin," she said. "There's supposed to be new broadsides in."

"Do you want to see your father?" Breauchard asked.

The question was unexpected. Ani froze with her hands on the dead man's skin. She remembered the Bastille, her father's sagging face in that dark prison—his ghost, how far gone he already was, as far gone as this dead body. She knew Dr. Breauchard could never witness Simon like that again. "No," Ani said quietly.

Breauchard nodded. What else could he say to a child of ten? "Stay away from the marketplace at Richelieu. They're snatching you kids left and right to make up for the labor shortage. You get hauled off somewhere, and it'll be hell to find you."

"I'm good at escaping." Ani smiled to ease the tension and wiped her hands down the front of her apron, then walked toward the door.

"I mean it!" Breauchard called after her.

"I know!"

"Ani," he said, as her hand hit the door latch. "The wig."

She pulled it off her head and tossed it on the table, its tail dangling over the edge like a dead animal.

❧

Before, Paris, late in the previous month, after her father's execution, June 1792
Ani jolted awake, wheezing through the fine dust that coated her lungs, until green-black mucous landed on the pillow. As her eyes adjusted,

they settled on the flicker of a candle, and her nostrils filled with the acrid smell of blood. Medical tools lay on the tray beside her cot. A pitcher of clean water sat next to a bowl of dark red water. Her stomach felt full, its endless growling having been answered by food from somewhere. She reached for the tools and noticed that her fingernails had been scrubbed clean, no longer coated in coal dirt. Lye wafted from her skin.

"Naht-aht, no touching," a voice spoke from across the room. "Those tools are worth more than your life."

"Jacques." Ani smiled, and it made her ears ring. "I thought I was at Hôpital de la Salpêtrière."

"You were. I paid a great deal to sneak you from the Salpêtrière in a cadaver box. You'd get no good care there unless some bloodstock is paying. That blacklung, Allyriane." He shook his head seriously and clucked his tongue. "It's gotten so bad. You'll die of pneumoconiosis before you're twenty."

Dr. Jacques-Marie Breauchard now neared forty yet still looked half that. He'd once been upper class, servicing the medical demands of aristocrats and royalty, but these days, in light of the devastating income disparity throughout most of Paris, he applied his practice to those who couldn't afford it rather than to those who could. His wire-rimmed spectacles slipped off his nose constantly, alternately revealing and magnifying a pair of clear-blue eyes. A full head of brown hair hung about his neck and cheekbones in clean strands, circling in loops around a smirk that creased into dimples. He pressed an ear trumpet against her chest and his flat palm into her back, lifting her to a half-seated position and breathing deeply as a prompt for her to follow.

"I'm not sure what—"

"Your lungs gave out, and you collapsed. Stop talking and breathe." Breauchard looked away and rubbed at his eye with his forearm. He pushed his hand deeper into her back and lifted her to him. "Is that the deepest breath you can take? How long have you been breathing this bad?"

"Months."

"Has it got worse since your father died?"

She shrugged and hung her face away from him, exhaled another deep cough, and scooted to the edge of the cot. "I hadn't thought of it much."

He lifted her chin. "Think of it, yeah? I promised him I'd keep you alive, and so far, you're only that way by sheer luck. Don't make me waste a perfectly good promise."

"Ah, I waste those all the time."

He glared at her. "You didn't always. You used to be a girl I didn't have to worry so much about. Now those revolutionaries got you all muddled up. Pray, keep more of your mother and less of your father in you." He took a deep breath and tapped her knee. "Ani," he paused, then asked quietly, "why did you never ask to see him?"

I wouldn't have done that to you, Jacques, she wanted to say. Instead, she said, "I hardly knew him at Le Marais, when he was still my father and not just a ghost of one. He wouldn't have even recognized me at the Châtelet." She remembered the Bastille—he'd looked right through her then, invisible. But she also remembered the execution block, how he'd recognized her voice calling above the crowds, how he'd known her despite the years. She wiped it from her mind. What was done couldn't be undone. "Have you got any new books?"

He thumbed at a stack over his shoulder. "Probably a few to like in there."

"Any new pamphlets?"

"Lord, no. Stop reading those. But I do have an invitation for a salon at Lachapelle's if you want to clean yourself up to go with me. Members of the Académie will be there."

"Will they have their paintings on display or just be talking about themselves?"

Breauchard laughed. "Mostly talking about themselves, I'll wager, but it's an opening for Houdon's new marble figure, and it's a woman this time. So that will be there."

"Have you already seen it?"

"I have."

"Any good?"

"Quite."

"Well…maybe I'll clean myself up." She wrinkled her nose.

"Don't put yourself out any," Breauchard grunted. "Wouldn't want you to have to wear a dress and be a lady. Gasp, what horrors."

She smiled, but she knew that all the times she'd been kidnapped on the street and forced into labor at the coalmines weighed even heavier on Breauchard than they did on her. The Industrial Revolution had shaped her into something he'd never meant for her to be. "Well, you should have raised me proper."

He laughed. "Neither of us would have turned out all right if I'd tried. But I *could* have gotten you into one of those salons—your paintings were always as good as theirs. Could have at least made a nurse out of you."

She wrinkled her nose further. That had only been his dream, never hers. "I'm good at what I do." And she was. Sneaky, good with throwing knives, documents, floor plans. Good at escaping. A child born into a shifting Paris that ate up those who couldn't adapt fast enough. She'd learned to adapt.

He looked at her sadly and handed her a crude dry-powder inhaler funnel carved of teak, followed by a glass jar of a loose Epsom clay, magnesium sulfate, and henbane powder mixture. "A pinch, small as a dust mite. Place the funnel to the back of your throat, dump the powder quick, and inhale it at once, then hold your breath for five seconds. It will sponge some of that coal dust. With some divine interference, it'll keep you breathing for a few more years."

She studied the inhaler, poking her finger into the hole.

"That powder contains nightshade. Easy does it and not when you need to be alert, or you'll hallucinate. And, Ani…" He took hold of her shoulders and squared her to him. He wanted to say more, but what could he say to a woman of seventeen? She'd do what she wanted, no matter what he said—she always had. She was still too much like Simon, all the more for having lost him to debt and prisons and revolution and the bloody Razor. Breauchard kissed her forehead and brought her face against his chest and listened to her poor breaths. Loath to release her, he fished in his pocket, pulled out a coin, and placed it in her palm. "Go down to Café de Foy and get a coffee, and give Henri the denier this time."

"He won't take it," she laughed.

"Not too much coffee, now. All that hot air at Desmoulins' table, and you'll be breathing far blacker stuff than coal." He gloared at her preemptively. "Don't cause me stress, girl. Stay far from the Cordeliers. The men don't like it."

She smiled, stuffed her hair under her cap, and slid off the cot, wincing at her stiffness. Camille Desmoulins was an impassioned orator, if plagued by a painful stammer, and if he were standing on a table in the Café de Foy or the garden of the Palais-Royal, his hat garnished in foliage, giving one of his revolutionary speeches calling citizens to arms, then Ani would be there, listening with rapt attention, and both the

doctor and she knew it. Though the heralding of the militant behavior
that Desmoulins and the other Cordeliers proposed frightened her and
went against the Fayettists—the constitutional faction she followed—
she thought it exciting, and unlikely to gain much momentum beyond
bragging rights. Most men of Paris delighted in bragging rights. The
mob insurrection at the Tuileries had shaken them both, however, and
the Constitution was still so fragile. He dug into his pocket and pulled
out another coin.

"If I give you two deniers, are you going to buy food or a pamphlet?"

"Food."

He cocked his head. "Food for stomach or food for thought?"

Ani took the denier from his outstretched fingers. "Paper is digest-
ible, yes?" She gave him a nod and headed for the door of the small
room and out into the unstable streets of Paris.

✌

Now

Aubrey led Ani down the hall. He extended his hand to hers, but she
pretended she didn't notice, so he withdrew it. She felt as if he were
leading her in a waltz, keeping her in that state, like a flake of snow
shaken inside a snowglobe, floating within a protective dome, unheed-
ing a world beyond the glass barrier, beyond his own stone walls. She
curled her fingers into fists. Let him drop the enchanting snow—she'd
never forget what was outside these stone walls. He led her into a room
at the end of the long back hallway, located adjacent to his, outfitted for
guests of the highest distinction.

The ceilings vaulted into a main cathedral arch up the center. Multiple small cathedrals circled around the edge of the first, swooping
birdlike, and adjoined with high walls masked in light-red velvet with
ornate gilded gold trim, reflective mirrors, and carved Roman Catholic
idol balustrade. The velvet met the marbled tile floor at perfect angles
and complemented the swirling bronze-and-white design of the tiles,
the swirls leading luridly toward the bedroom's attached boudoir. Inside
the boudoir were matching upholstered velvet chairs, dark-brown wood
vanities, and wardrobe closets to match the bronze tiles. At the far wall
of the room, two large windows looked out across a courtyard garden.
Evening sunset cast over the plump covered bed at the room's center, highlighting bed hangings of matching light-red gossamer dimity
queued in bunches with gold-laced ribbon. Ani realized the evening had
escaped her and that the hour was late. She had to send a message to Dr.

Breauchard that could get to him by morning. But she did like the view of far-off Paris and the orchard overlook this room afforded. She liked how easily she could jump from the window.

Aubrey watched her face as she took in every strip of cloth, every piece of furniture, every crevice of the high vaults and gables and flying buttresses. She faced the mirror at the dresser and stared at her own reflection. She hadn't really seen herself like this for years, not this clearly, not in a court dress since she was a child. Ani ran her hands down the smooth fabric. *She was wearing a court dress.* Aubrey walked toward her. His reflection matched his portrait behind him, the first oil she'd seen of his own likeness in the palace so far, near the mantel—though in it he looked displeased, his right hand tucked into his waistcoat at his belly, the sign of good breeding. She wished his demeanor had been more like that, as she'd expected a Beaumercy to be—powerful, full of self-righteousness and entitlement. Displeased with trivialities. But his reflection didn't look displeased now. He looked thrilled, energized with the breath of something new to him. Ani took a step away.

"Is that your mother?" She nodded above the dresser toward the portrait of a beautiful noblewoman who shared his face, finely painted in oils that outlined a fur collar silhouetted against a backlit fireplace of gold gating.

"It's my sister."

"You have a sister?" she asked. She knew he had six, but she'd let him tell it.

"I have six," Aubrey said. "And six brothers. Their separate portraits are in each room along this hallway. I could not put them all in the same room, or there would be no space left around their grandiosity for the guests to sleep."

She gazed back to the portrait, then at his reflection in the mirror, standing far too near to her, behind her shoulder, much taller than she, with his eyes fixated coldly on his sister. The nose bore the most prominent resemblance, the nose of their father, the duke. That icy cold Seine shot through her veins again.

In an unexpected gesture, he lifted the portrait from the wall. "You shouldn't have to look at this impious woman with four—yes, four!—illegitimate children." He turned the frame in his hand, pulled out the securing nails, and punched the oil canvas through the back and out of the frame. "I know you have no pity for my station, but I'm at war, surrounded by men I can't trust, and I have everything of high cost and nothing of value." He shrugged. "All the money in the world doesn't buy my way out of the annoying infliction of feeling…detached from it all." He raised the empty frame in front of Ani's face, capturing her head and shoulders inside the four corners, and outlining her in the lavish gold-scrolled wooden border. His gaze softened. "There, much better. Maybe I'll have you painted."

"Waste of paint." The idea that her portrait would hang in this room made her want to climb the wall it would hang on.

"On the contrary," he said. "Even bad portraits go to good use. They make savory fire starters. As flammable as Joan of Arc."

Just then, Ani's eyes darted to a chain and pendant lying on the dresser, and she let out a careless gasp. A plate of antiqued silver with a raised ivory cameo of court lilies circled about a cross was strung through a long, cheap metal chain. Something sparked in her memory. The women who used to wear France's lilies, the marketplace of her youth. With desirous fingers, she lifted the chain and held the pendant in the palm of her hand, awed by its simple beauty, the remembrance of so long ago. Dust drifted into her hand and left a ring on the dresser where the pendant had sat unmolested for some time. It reminded her of something she couldn't name. A symbol she'd seen once. Something stuck in the rear of her mind that wouldn't step forward, refused to step forward. Yet refused to step back.

"Where did you get this?" she whispered.

"It's my mother's."

"That's not what I asked."

"She would never know if you took it. It might do you some good to wear a cross."

"Where did she get it?"

"You don't really want to know, Ani."

"I do. I must know. Tell me."

❧

Before, the aristocratic quarter of Le Marais, Paris, fifteen years prior
A fist flew into Dr. Breauchard's nose, then a stick came down across his back. He yelled and struck out, but gendarmes overpowered him. The scream of a woman clattered around high ceilings. The gendarmes tore her away and out the door. Another officer kicked Breauchard in the stomach, and the doctor rolled over onto broken glass from smashed lamps and thrown porcelain plates. He seethed through clenched teeth

and got to his feet, his pain ripping through him like electricity, but when he reached the door, the men had gone. Marie was gone.

"Bro-sha?"

As always, the tiny voice, tiny hand Jacques Breauchard knew well. Fingers slid into the doctor's palm, and he looked over absently, panting, his face dripping with sweat and blood. Tears streamed down the child's cheeks.

"It will be all right, Allyriane," he said. "I promise."

He couldn't really promise. It wasn't all right. But what could he say to a child of two? He rubbed his fingers over her hair and turned her from the door, back into the parlor of what had been an impressive upper-class home before being ransacked and raided by gendarmes. The home wasn't his, but that didn't matter now. The girl clutched a wrinkled sketchpad in her hand, still opened to a scribbled drawing of her mother's apron, adorned in misshaped lilies. Breauchard stared at the wall, wiped the blood from his lip with the back of his hand.

"You stay?" the small voice said.

He couldn't promise that, either, but he bent to hug her as her father came through the door. The two men straightened and stared at each other. Breauchard put his hands over the girl's ears. "Your wife's gone, Simon," he said. "They took her. I tried…"

Simon's jaw fell open, and he looked like he'd been gut-punched. He took two steps toward the child, his fists tight, but Breauchard came between them.

"I'm taking Ani," Breauchard said. "She's going with me, Simon, for a while—"

"Like hell—"

"She'll get tutored. She can learn a trade. She won't be at risk from all your—"

"Get out."

"Just until you're better, Si, until you—"

"I said get out."

"What kind of life will you give her?"

Simon turned away, but Breauchard still saw the tears. The doctor lifted Ani into his arms. She dropped the sketchbook and closed her eyes against his neck, converted to memory the color of her mother's apron, the lilies. She already knew she'd never see it again.

‌ ‌

Now

"Please, I must know where this pendant came from," Ani said, squeezing it.

Aubrey went quiet, his rhythmic breathing interrupted by unease. "My…" he started and stopped. "My father…collected trinkets from the prisoners he locked in the prisons his deputies ran. They were… trophies to him." He made a disgusted face that she saw in the mirror. "He gave this one to my mother. She left it here years ago." He dragged his finger through a spot of dust on the dresser. "Étienne should have cleaned this. I'll see to it."

Ani cupped the pendant tight in her palm, and tears welled in her eyes. She wanted to smack him, but it would be misdirected. Or would at least not get her any closer to the answers she sought.

His voice cracked. "I told you that you didn't want to know."

"Where did your father get this one?"

"Maybe Sainte-Pélagie?"

"No. It came from For-l'Évêque, before the prison was emptied."

"Yes, that sounds correct." His eyes narrowed. "How did you know that?"

She swallowed. "The lilies. Sainte-Pélagie has no females, and its walls are not old enough for this," she scowled, "this *trinket*. Judging by the dust." She wiped the surface of it and rubbed her fingertips together.

She couldn't take her eyes from it. Aubrey took hold of it and lifted the chain at the clasp and secured the necklace around Ani's neck. She gasped audibly at the touch and shrank from it, but his hand remained, his fingers following along the length of the chain to smooth the links. She held her breath and tensed. The touch was of someone who was not a laborer. Soft, rich.

"Give it a better future than its past," he whispered. He pulled his hand back when it grazed a line of raised whip scars. "Your skin is cold. These old stone walls can keep a chill. Let me make you a fire."

She ran her hands over the pendant. That symbol of France so lost now.

Within moments, he had a fire crackling, and he leaned against the fireplace poking the flames with an iron rod, contemplating her shifts in mood, trying to understand where she'd come from, where she'd been, endeavoring to be patient. He lifted the portrait of his sister, and he carried it to the fireplace and threw it on top of the fire. *Just be patient.* The oil made the flames burst forth. "See. There you have it. The Beau-mercys can also burn."

"Like Joan of Arc," she said quietly, stroking the pendant.

CHAPTER FIVE

MASSES OF DESPERATION

*The secret of freedom
lies in educating people,
whereas the secret of tyranny
is in keeping them ignorant.*

—Maximilien Robespierre

Before, Paris, earlier in the month, July
The city brimmed with distrust, a fount of woes and mourning for
bygones, a caricature of its former self. This was where Ani knew best
now, the faubourg of Saint-Marcel, a poor, industrial side of the city,
dirty of face and brittle of being, slow to rise in defense of a stranger, more so should he be powdered. She pulled up her collar, but the
streets still felt like home. The curves of rococo homefronts swooped
into delicate ornaments at the arches, pastel horses running along the
banisters, and oval chambers protruding from the roofs of once-great
halls. Scrolling asymmetrical rocaille shells and vines stillframed in sea-
green plaster and outlined in gold that peeled and flaked into piles in the
streets. Devilish putti played in swirling frescoed laurels along the front
of a loom parlor where the sounds of flying shuttles thudded in unison,
and Ani jerked out of the way of a man stepping from a marquetry
shop carrying a tabletop of inlaid ivory too tall for him to see around.
Another man spit at the tabletop and rasped, "Vive la Révolution," just
above his breath, then tripped over a mound of lime plaster that had
crumbled off the corner of a commonhouse.

An hour out from the Palais-Royal, where the cobbles narrowed into
residential alleyways, a mob gathered around two aristocrats, dragging
the overdressed men through the street by the tails of their coats. A
woman yelled, "À la lanterne!" and the crowd hauled the screaming
men toward a lamppost stretching from a cement arch. Ani's eyes went
wide, and she saw their fear, the men clawing to free themselves. For a
moment the fear registered as something human, and then her breaths

went ragged, and she clenched her fists. *The hood fell again over her father's eyes, his face in black cloth.* Men in dress like this—tight tan breeches, unwrinkled jackets—had put her father away when she was eight. There'd been fear on his face, too, when they arrested him, dragged him, and she remembered it with the memory of a child, how tall the men had seemed, how she'd faced thighs and crotches, and they'd passed through her as if she were invisible, so easily brushing her aside.

The mob draped ropes around the necks of the pleading men. A deputy was part of the swarm, and Ani watched him with unease, though in this crowd, she wouldn't be singled out in any way, she knew. Safety in the tide, a ripple in an ocean. One of the flailing men knocked over a cart of mushy strawberries. Men down the alley tore paving stones out of the road and piled them into a hasty barricade. "Vive la Nation!" someone shouted too close to her ear. Her heart pounded in the back of her teeth, and she listened through it. Why could she hear the gasps of these aristocrats so plainly? She shook it away, looked for something to pick up. A standing shelf of milk bottles clattered to the street, and children in the crowd broke from their mothers' skirts to lap it up, heedless of the cracked glass, slipping on the mess. Next, a broken piece of glass in her hand. Her heart rose into her neck, and the rope looped the streetlamp, tautening. She could cut it down. A window broke in a neighboring building. Someone screamed. More glass. She could cut the men down.

The second rope, and the crowd chanted in unison. A yank and a following one, and the bodies fell suddenly, snapped against the ropes, kicked and struggled, *and the hood came over Ani's father's eyes.* Swaths of the crowd peeled away, not even caring to see the culmination of their doing, on to the next. One of the men stilled and swung lifelessly, urine running down his leg. Ani held the glass, then dropped it, hearing it singularly shatter on the ground, a sound impossibly apart from all else. The second man went limp, though he still audibly choked, and Ani focused on his tan culottes, the boots that scrambling men were pulling from his feet. Then, hooves pounded in the alley, and the horde of blue was coming.

The crowd dispersed on quick cue, but Ani stayed, staring at the men, one still choking. She bent again for another piece of glass, but the National Guard came around the corner, and she left the glass and the space and ducked for the window that had been smashed out of the office building next to her. The windows sat too low to the ground, too easy to climb through, and the place looked nearly abandoned inside. Out the window, she watched the guardsmen cut the ropes, the men falling hard to the street. One jerked and coughed and rolled around. One didn't.

⤎

Now

Josephine entered the room, knocking at the open doorframe without pausing long enough for the knock to be registered. "Out with you, my lord," she said, "so that I may get her into her gown and proceed with my evening peace." The servant ushered Aubrey toward the door, and he let her push him out without any argument. Josephine went to Ani, throwing a clean nightgown at the younger woman.

Ani dodged and caught the flying gown.

"Put that on, and take this." Josephine extended her hand with a tincture glass filled with cranberry-red liquid. "This will help with any pain from that arm."

Ani frowned at the liquid but didn't take it.

Josephine spilled a little and bent to the floor to swipe the spot with the hem of her skirt. "Don't be obstinate about it. It's only cramp bark."

Ani took it, examined it, and set it on the nightstand.

Josephine grunted. "Suit yourself."

Outside the door, Aubrey stood watching the swiftly moving figures of two men approaching. "Barons d'Egrenant and Bellon, I presume by the clicking of the boots," Aubrey called down the hallway. "Clop-clop, like lazy horses. It's past your bedtime, messieurs, so do tell what I may do for you."

"You didn't tuck us in yet, Mother," d'Egrenant replied, coming closer into the dim light at the end of the hall. "We've been summoned by an alarming admission from the ears of your palace."

"I do not doubt it," Aubrey said. "It's news worth investigation, I'm sure."

"And thus we've been sent to investigate, General," Baron Bellon said, coming to soldierly attention before the marquis. "You understand."

Baron René-Gervais d'Egrenant was a military man sworn to protect and uphold feudal property recently stripped of him by the new Constitution, leaving him a man unemployed. This led to his appointment to follow the marquis into the inevitable war with only minor complaint. He was the secretive sort, but the marquis had never minded that trait in a man, even before it became a necessity for survival in this paranoid country.

Baron Pierrick-Anne Bellon was a Breton hailing from Western Brittany, with a heavy accent resembling Cornish, a head full of staunch Catholicism and wiry hair, and the gesticulations of a puppet whose strings were always held completely taut. His movements, jerky and cumbersome, looked as though his skeleton were too heavy for his skin. His face had a regally handsome set to it, but his mouth eternally cocked higher on one side into a snarl. He would follow the levelheaded marquis into any battle in any place at any time for any cause, just sound the horn.

"Did my father send you?" Aubrey asked.

Baron Bellon said, "Fast rumor tells that she is seventeen and unmarried and may be occupying a room in this garrison. As a fellow Confessionist, I caution that having an unwed woman in your home, not employed for services, will undermine members of the First Estate who have supplied us for quite some time. Your father may turn you out without an inheritance."

"Your concern is noted. The lady is, however, employed for services. As it is your duty, you can report to my father that there is nothing to report." Aubrey's smile could have melted butter.

"But is she landed nobility?" d'Egrenant asked.

It seemed to Aubrey like he already knew the answer. "No," Aubrey said. "She's fascinating is what she is, entertaining as a puzzle jug filled with wine at a wedding, but no, not nobility."

The two men looked long and hard at him. The young marquis was reckless where his family name was concerned, and the men had to respond to the duke—Aubrey's disenchanted father. Only Josephine storming out of Ani's bedroom broke the tension.

"That insolent girl fears my tincture. She thinks it's poison!" Josephine pushed past Aubrey, slamming the door behind her and nodding toward the two barons in brief acknowledgment. "Barons d'Egrenant and Bellon, good evening, my lords." She curtsied. "I do hope you are here to loose that child back out where she belongs. She's got the talons of a bird of prey, so you ought release her in the field like one." Josephine walked off in a huff.

The men watched after her and listened to the clunking of angered brocade heels pounding down the hall until the echoes were gone.

"Looks to me like the bird caught a little mouse," Aubrey laughed.

∾

Now

When the sounds of the palace hushed to nothing, Ani sat up in bed. Her heart pounded deep into her throat. Her arm throbbed. She clutched the letter she'd written for Dr. Breauchard. *Arrival was amiable, though not flawless.* She slid out of bed, her feet still hurting from running in wooden shoes. *An egregious error—he's m. de C, not m. de L, and he's not as witless as his brother or father.* The floor was cold; the palace held no warmth in its walls. Which brother it was didn't really matter, as long as the palace was the hidden garrison, but now there were a few hitches. For one, the duke didn't visit the disappointing son as often as he visited the favorite son. That was a setback. *Furthermore, he's unwed, so I cannot befriend the chatty wife as planned. Did É know? Did you?* She turned the iron crank on the French casement windows. *It is indeed a garrison, though I've not found where munitions are located.* She pulled the two meeting casement leaves inward. *I have mapped the front rooms.* After rifling through the satchel that Josephine had unceremoniously plopped on the floor in the corner, Ani retrieved the ball of twine, wrapped it around the letter and some documents. *The orchard lacks guards, as we supposed it did.* She lit a tallow lamp and placed it in the window, the light flickering across the expanse of the massive yard, the fields beyond. *I am otherwise safe, I believe.* She didn't tell Dr. Breauchard about her cut arm—he'd be at the door to retrieve her at once, no matter what the cost of such a hasty move. *I am endeared to you always.*

When shadows moved below toward the lighted lamp, she lowered the documents on the twine and blew out the flame. She held her breath. Watched the twine jiggle. Barely heard quiet footsteps. She pulled the empty twine back into the window, closed the casement, put the ball into her satchel, then cursed. Her knives, damnit. Someone had removed them from her bag. She scrounged for her inhaler—it was thankfully still there.

The latch on the door was louder than she wanted it to be, but she exited the bedroom and went barefoot down the hallway, her back to one wall. She'd start in the parlor. She traveled along each wall, each crevice. Ran her fingers along dusty top shelves. Got down on her knees to look between furniture for hidden doors or traps in the floor that could lift to reveal passages and lockboxes. Felt along the seams of statues and behind the frames of artwork.

She made her way along cases and bureaus, and finally around to his day desk, lifting papers. A lawbook lay cracked to a page on religious divorce proceedings, outdated lines struck through, and a ledger was pressed open beside it with paperweights. Scrawled in what she now recognized as Aubrey's hand were the notes: *a divorce may now occur through the mutual consent of the spouses* and below it, *the abandonment of the wife by the husband, or of the husband by the wife, for at least two years*. She imagined that must have pained him to write, though she somehow didn't doubt he'd still defend it to the letter, this thing that went against his nature. She studied his perfect cursive. Beside his notes, the manual *English Composition for French Scholars*. A scholar. In her mind, the aristocrat swung from a lamppost, and she recalled how she could have cut him down. She'd since learned he was a mathematician. The world needed learnèd men—surveyors of fine art, lawyers, statesmen, and mathematicians. Perhaps what the world needed were sons that weren't their fathers.

She opened his desk drawers and rifled through each, then slid open his top middle drawer. Her eyes rested on the pistol. She grasped it, and her finger eased over the trigger.

୬

Before, after the hanging of the aristocrats, Paris, earlier in July
Uncomfortable quiet surrounded Ani inside the building, where she'd fled from the National Guard after the lynching. She didn't know whose office she occupied, but it didn't look freshly vacated; she figured it was empty of anything viable, but she'd still search through the paper stacks for whatever someone might buy from her. Revolutionaries would pay handsomely for certain types of information, and even less-valuable ledgers or confessionary letters could still buy her a soup from Procope, a pot-au-feu from ol' Henri, or one of his cods stuffed with garlic and truffles. She didn't dare light the oil lamp next to the broken window. Her muted steps landed on the bare pads poking through her soles. Her hand felt sticky, and she knew it was blood from the glass, though she couldn't feel clearly where the cut was.

On the bookshelf, she saw a long, narrow ledger sandwiched between other books. She slid it off the shelf, then ran her hand along behind where it had been. Another book fell to the side, revealing a second ledger. She whistled low at her quick luck but imagined that if it were that easy, then the ledger didn't contain much. She tucked the first beneath her arm and opened the second to the pages where the binding cracked. Her eyes fell to choice lines: livres paid outgoing to men of stature, some to the First Estate—*the clergy*—corrupt names she'd memorized from pamphlets. Some, names with deputy rankings before them. The logs were in cipher, mostly coded shorthand, but they appeared to mark payments exchanged for delivering children to detention halls, notably the Bicêtre in Gentilly: equal parts juvenile detention center, orphanage, prison, hospital, and lunatic asylum. The lines read like nothing new, the same old corrupt system. Incoming funds from industries—one marked *Purchased four, strong, male*—appeared to be purchasing detained orphans for industrial labor. Bassin Minier du Nord-Pas-de-Calais was listed, as figured, and she knew well the name that followed—*that name*. A payment to the city's mayor was marked *Bypass*. What had been bypassed? Ani considered. Was the mayor being paid to look the other way? The orphan trade was as much a smooth-running machine as any metal press or textile weaver or irrigation system of the Industrial Revolution—and as had always been the case throughout history, the rich man got richer while the poor man was only promised Marie Antoinette's cake in passing jest. Ani snapped the ledger shut. It might be worth something.

She stuffed both books beneath her shirt, grabbed another choice selection from the reading shelf, and walked toward the open window. The guardsmen were still outside, a doctor among them, bent over the writhing man, inspecting the windpipe Ani imagined was likely crushed. She walked down the long room to another window at the far end, over-looking a gravel carriageway. A door latch clanked in a far hallway, and Ani shielded herself with her neckerchief, picked up a heavy counting frame, and threw it against the lower pane. She slammed her elbow into the hanging pieces of glass and shimmied her way through the opening, cursing as the shards cut at her skin, then she dropped feetfirst to the ground outside and vacated the site.

Blood seeped from her arms and stained her father's shirt. The back of her wrist and elbow got it the worst. She stopped periodically and picked out slivers embedded in her forearm and wiped the cuts against her pants, wincing. Alleys afforded her discreet cover, and she kept her back toward the buildings. In her bloody state, she might seem suspicious. She went cautiously through an empty expanse of countryside, ventured onto rue Mouffetard near the border of faubourg Saint-Marcel with the Hôpital de la Salpêtrière and the Marché aux Chevaux horse market in far view, and beyond that, the slight green of the Jardin du

Roi. The air smelled of fermented indigo, ammonia, and sulfur from the textile dyeing at Les Gobelins, and the spillover from the manufactory waste dyed the cobbles and grasses an uneven brown with spots of vibrant purple. She blended in amongst the women of the brothels and the drunk gamblers that pervaded the city streets, and here, even blood didn't get noticed on clothing. The stench of manure overtook the dye, and then the sour smell of unclean women.

A stone house sat snug against the street, so snug against its neighboring rowhouses that a body couldn't fit between them, and she made her way to it. She checked over her shoulder for onlookers one last time, then dropped the accounting books through a wide, handcarved slot beneath a plated-glass window. After a minute, slim fingers wedged a slip of browned cardstock through the slot for her, the front side decorated with an image of a bundle of rods surrounding a two-headed ax—the fasces—on a billet de confiance to collect one sou from an account at a dying bank, if the bank still backed it or gave even a percentage of face value. She sighed. It was effectively worthless.

For a moment, she collected her thoughts. Considered her bleeding forearm before continuing to the busy rue Saint-Victor. She'd find the girls in one of the cafés if they hadn't been rounded up by patrolmen, and her destination was any nearby one—with Café de Foy now too far of a journey to begin anew. Two deniers weighted her pocket, but when she thought of coffee, she still saw the dead man swinging at the end of the rope, and she lost interest in buying a cup.

When dusk fell, the summer rain started, and she moved on. Finding habitable spaces in the city was a challenge. A swarm of homeless stood outside newly vacant rooms, waiting to claim occupancy. Despite this, Ani had discovered a crawlspace under some stairs that led to a boarded cellar about the size of a kitchen pantry, clearly not in use for some time. The occupants above didn't notice that she'd burrowed into it, and she crawled in now and curled into a ball, cracking open the book she'd taken from the office shelf—some sea adventure about the coast of New England—and listening to the quiet hymns from the neighboring Église Saint-Médard before someone heckled and hushed them. She slept out the rest of the rain that poured outside, muddied the streets, and flooded under the dilapidated doorframe in a small pool. She drifted off thinking about marble statues in an Académie salon she was missing—the head of her father cast in marble, what that would look like. Just the head.

The air was sticky and humid when Ani woke. She stretched and realized afresh the severity of the glass cuts on her forearm. She tore off a band of fabric ringing the bottom of her shirt—a surprisingly difficult endeavor considering the fabric's thinness, the holes clear through it—and laid it out on the ground and rested her arm on it. Carriage dust had clotted to the drying blood. She worked spittle into her mouth and drooled it out onto her arm, rubbing the spit around the cuts before wiping her arm across her pants and leaving a streak of rusty brown down her thigh. That would have to do for cleanliness. She wrapped the linen around her forearm and wrist and around her thumb and knuckles. Dr. Breauchard was too far away for now, and the other girls would gather soon.

⌘

Now

"Yes, the gun is there. I wasn't lying," Aubrey spoke across the silent room.

Ani jumped and instinctively pointed the pistol at the marquis, who'd materialized from thin air in the darkness.

"It's loaded. All you have to do is cock and pull." He walked toward her as she held the gun on him. "There are also a hundred other weapons within these walls if it's your desire to use them on me, so don't settle for that one simply because it's there. You might be more interested in our shiny, new iron maiden device. A simple lead ball is so archaic. But the iron maiden, ah! Stick a few spikes in her, and I'm sure I'd confess every tax I ever raised, every mouth I ever starved, every peasant I ever cheated." A tense silence blinked between them. He stood in place before her outstretched pistol, testing her resolve. He drew a quiet breath and gave her more than a clear shot if she should want to take it, then closed his eyes, muttered something to God.

Ani thumped the gun down on the desk and pulled her fingers away from it swiftly. A backbone of iron ramrod couldn't have erected her straighter. Aubrey crossed himself and cleared his throat.

"If you were going to kill me, that was your chance," he said, "and you probably should have taken it."

Yes, she wanted to scream. *Yes*, but that wasn't part of the plan. That would ruin all other plans to come. She shirked away from him and looked anywhere about the room but at his face. "No, sir. I just found the gun. You…you scared me…in this dark. It was…impulsive." Ani was used to impulsive, but she couldn't be so injudicious here. "Some-one…someone stole something from my satchel, sir, and I—"

"You don't feel safe here without a pistol?"

Safe? She almost laughed out loud. "Out there, though, sir." She gestured toward the door. "It's a violent world out there, you know." She suffused her tone with forced lightness, and a hint of an embarrassed smile played across her mouth. "You might have heard there's a war."

"Is there? I hadn't been informed. Do you know how to fire this?"

"Yes."

The answer didn't surprise him. "I wish I could be foolish enough to put a gun in your hand." He opened his palm and stared at it, gripped the barrel. "But you aimed it at me, Ani. None of us is safe if you shoot me. I'd be dead, and guards would shoot you dead in the same instant."

"But I didn't shoot you, sir," she said to the floor.

He breathed deep. "Don't call me sir. Not marquis, not sir, not sire, not my lord. Please. Just Aubrey." He managed a smile.

Josephine appeared at the entryway, and loudly whispered, "My goodness! What is the matter, my lord?"

Aubrey hid the gun in his palm and turned to her. "Ani lost her way back to her room is all. I'm escorting her, and there is no matter. Please, my dearest Josette, don't trouble yourself."

Josephine blew a breath like a horse out her nose, then turned and walked off.

Aubrey went around the desk and laid his gun in the open drawer and stared down at it. He couldn't contain this woman. He had let her in, carelessly, and now he could either cage her or set her free, dictate or trust. It was a moment he abhorred, choosing what kind of man he wanted to be, how to see himself. Nothing organic in it, the repulsion of blind faith, the urge to be collected but swept up, never made a fool but open to the rules of engagement. What kind of man was he if he didn't engage? He glanced at her quickly, left the gun loaded, and left the drawer unlocked. "It is my flawed nature to consign, and I want to trust you." He walked around to her. "Can I do that?"

Her nod was slow, but he looked grateful when she did it. "May I escort you?" he said, holding out his hand.

"No, I—"

"—can find your way back to your room and are not lost at all, I know." He withdrew his hand. "I pray you'll have pleasant sleep,

Mademoiselle Baillairgé." He walked away slowly, trusting her to the room, the gun.

She realized she was shaking. She hadn't truly meant to hold a gun on him, had she? Could she be trusted with her own willpower? A door latched somewhere, the hiss of a lantern coming to life, while her inner light seemed snuffed. The room he'd vacated was shrouded in darkness.

She'd be more careful with him, she promised to the dark parlor. She'd go slower, ease in. *This had to go slower,* or she'd spin out of control. His walls were safety, and the gun really was too impulsive, though her fingers had known it wasn't an accident—she'd felt so bereft without her knives. She lifted his paperknife from his desk, the sharp steel point twisting into the globus cruciger orb of royalty, and she threw it at the marble statue of a crowned woman holding her midsection. To her surprise, the statue was not marble at all, but a plastered papier-mâché, and the knife stuck right into the crowned woman's cheek. Ani stifled her unexpected laugh and fled the parlor before anyone else came to see what was the matter.

༈

Before, the faubourg Saint-Marcel cellar, earlier in July
Béatrice took a lentil sack to soak in a miniature cauldron she'd "borrowed" from Dr. Breauchard, and she begged Ani to make a fire in the brickpit, despite the room's lack of ventilation. They collected rainwater, and the cellar grayed with smoke, and Béatrice complained of it the whole time she soaked her sack, in between smothering her laughter at Isabeau's constant gagging.

Béatrice Meschinot was a younger girl, fourteen years old, scrawnier than Ani, abandoned by the side of a road as an infant at the height of famine. A deputy found her and turned her over to the First Estate, who housed her until she was old enough to work off the debt accrued for eating under their roof. This debt sent Béatrice working in the collieries as a galibot, first at Ronchamp and finally at Nord-Pas-de-Calais, by the age of five. The rewards of her forced labor now lined the silk pockets of the clergy, six renowned marquises, and one arrogant duke. The dress she wore was the only dress she had. Blue with fragile, torn lace, and she was fast outgrowing it. The long sleeves now reached the middle of her forearms, and the once floor-length skirt exposed the better part of her calves. The only thing that hadn't changed on the waif was her waist size. The roomy fabric bunched about the middle was enough to make half of another dress. Had she the luxury of needle and thread, she might have done just that. Ani would have to tell Dr. Breauchard to buy Béatrice a new dress.

"Hey," Béatrice said quietly to Ani, but Ani's mind was elsewhere. "Psst, hey." She threw a wet lentil at Ani.

"Fine fiddles, what! I'm right here," Ani said, picking the lentil out of her hair and eating it.

"Did you hear about the 'crat what hanged off the merchant bridge?"

"The one choking, or the one died?"

"Aw, not the one choked," Béatrice said. "That'n only got his neck broke. Bit off his tongue and can't walk or some such as don't matter."

Ani winced.

"That other one, though, the one died, he was a mathician."

"A magician?"

"No, math," Béatrice enunciated. "Math. Like numbers."

"He was?" Ani remembered anew how she could have cut him down.

Béatrice giggled. "Guess he didn't *count* on that mob, eh?"

"Bet."

"Aw, come now, I been waiting all day to say that." She scooped a handful of hot lentils into her hand, blowing on them and shifting them from palm to palm until they cooled. "Wait, I got more," she said around full cheeks.

"No."

"Wait, wait. I'll bet his *abacus* sure broke in that fall." Béatrice threw herself backward to the floor and rolled from side to side, gasping through laughter, wiping her lentil-covered hands down her dress.

Ani looked at the fire, coughed in the smoke, and blinked her drying eyes rapidly. "We don't want mathematicians dead, Bet," she said. "The world needs them."

"But wait, wait, wait. I wonder if he could sense his days was *numbered*." She laughed so hard, holding her abdomen, that she hardly got the words out. She choked on a lentil and kept laughing.

Ani pictured the man swinging, the moment the life had left him. His tan breeches. She respected mathematicians. Breauchard could nearly have been one, so good he was at arithmetic. And the swinging man had been so afraid. He'd begged for his life, as any scared man would. He had pissed himself. The final throes of Béatrice's laughter faded, and Ani stared blankly into the fire. There didn't seem to be any warmth from it. She wondered if the man had had a daughter.

Chapter Six

Iron maiden

If to be feelingly alive to the
sufferings of my fellow creatures
is to be a fanatic,
I am one of the most incurable fanatics
ever permitted to be at large.

—William Wilberforce

Now

"Come now, up with you," Josephine called over Ani's bed like a tocsin beckoning all of Paris to arms. "The marquis expects you presentable by the hour succeeding his dawn drills. Don't make me speak it twice."

Ani stirred in bed, too comfortable to pull herself from the covers, twisting in the silk bedclothes. Rays of morning sun streaked across her eyes. She thought of Béatrice sleeping on the hard floor, Grietje curled on some old linen she'd found, Isabeau maybe on one of Dr. Breauchard's vacant cots. Ani blinked her eyes hard a couple times, wishing it were not too dangerous to bring the girls here. But it was not a place for her, let alone for all of them. She thought of the fourteen rooms and balled her fist into the pillow, murmured, rolled away from Josephine's dissuasions.

"I writ your schedule, and I'm leaving it on this desk for you," Josephine said, doing as she stated. "It lists your appointments. There are expectations. You should be in the social hall—the second room on the left, adjacent to the front parlor—for morning tea by ten when he finishes his drills, and he will escort you to dine. You do not enter the dining area without him, ahead of him, behind him, or late at any time. In the meantime, you may keep yourself preoccupied in the library on the second floor—last room on the right, overlooking the orchard and the olive grove—until he requires you. He will then meet you for afternoon tea in the front parlor, until he wishes to retire to law work or a briefing with his men, at which time you will leave him to his studies and find yourself preoccupied elsewhere until he requests you for supper. I hope you got all of that because your closed eyes are not giving me the concordance I would like to see."

"I stopped listening at 'there are expectations.'" But Ani registered the library and the olive grove, too. Those would prove interesting. "I'm up, I'm up."

Josephine stomped to Ani and ripped the covers from atop the resting girl's head, then skulked out the door. Ani lay there, listening once again to Josephine's displeased clomping moving farther down the hall and the sounds of men shouting off in the fields where the officers were running drills. Ani got up, wrapped herself in a bayan, and watched the soldiers out the window. Aubrey rode down the line on horseback, an elegant, easy rider, using his sword for emphasis of verbal direction. He looked powerful among the smallness of the men, so far in the fields. She shivered and waited for Josephine to return to apply clothing and false eyelashes, hair clips and powdered rouge. Ani couldn't get used to someone else dressing her.

The hallway was dim when she finally stepped into it an hour later, the light newly filtering in from the cathedral window at the end of the corridor. She was so taken that she nearly stepped into Aubrey, silhouetted in it. She hadn't heard him enter from the fields. He nodded and held up a finger and briskly marched through the hall at the side of another man. This man was of equal age and breeding to his noble counterpart, although admittedly not as handsome as the marquis—Ani decided no one should ever be as handsome as the marquis; it was unfair. The less-handsome man was leaving, too quickly for introductions, and Aubrey parted with him hastily.

"Farewell, Émilien, our little mother," the marquis said, kissing the man's cheeks. "Give my love to Lorraine and the little ones, and I'll see you at Vigil on Saturday. Tell Grégoire he still owes me a battledore rematch." Aubrey waved off Émilien, then turned to Ani and simply stared. "Well, well, don't you look like royalty."

"Like a marquise." She curtsied, though it was clumsy.

The corners of his mouth dropped. New worry cloaked his face.

She grinned. "Just a jest. We ladies collect noblemen like you collect empty rooms."

His eyebrows rose. "Well," he said after a moment of speechlessness. "I think that rather made my heart seize a bit."

"I'm sure you've a remedy for a weak heart in that medicine chest of yours. Perhaps something with snake venom?"

He leaned in close, and all her feigned confidence left her. His eyes flashed so dark, even in the light. "Are you sparring with me?" he said, a wry smile on his lips. "Or do you really seek to be the marquise?"

She gasped. What a dreadful thought. "You can take a spar, can't you?" She hoped her composure remained outwardly stable.

He smiled. "Indeed, I can. I'll take two spars if you are also apt at counting my silverware." He put out his arm.

This time she took his elbow. The repulsion momentary, she was getting used to overcoming it. His uniform jacket, which he still wore from his morning drills, was so surprisingly soft and pressed, didn't smell like horses and sweat as she imagined it would. She allowed her hand to close around his arm, telling herself it was only fabric, only fabric. Ignoring the skin it covered.

He led her to the social hall, across from the front parlor, and gave her a polite half bow. "Make yourself comfortable. I shall return with valuations." A sense of foreboding overcame him when he left the room. He walked across the hall and stopped before the parlor, glanced quickly over his shoulder, then went to his desk. It was how he'd left it last night. He took a breath and opened the drawer. His pistol lay there, untouched, and he slowly crossed himself and held a thumb to his lips, then raised his eyes to the knife protruding from the statue's cheek, and crossed himself again. "I'm sorry for that, Isabelle," he whispered to the statue, then retrieved his valuations log and followed the sound of light coughing back to Ani in the social hall, sitting under a cast of Our Lady of the Assumption, with her index finger tracing the outline of ghouls on a page of woodcuts in Aubrey's hand-transcribed *Ars Moriendi.* "That copy dates to the fifteen hundreds," he said over her shoulder.

"What language is it?"

"German."

"And you can read it?" She swiveled to look at him.

"Yes."

"How hard would it be to teach me to read it?"

"Harder than it would be to simply read it to you." He clucked his tongue. "Did you throw a book-knife into the face of Saint Isabelle?"

"Is that who that was?" Ani didn't look up from the book but heard his passive sigh. "I didn't know it was soft plaster," she said more apologetically. "I thought it marble the knife would bounce off—that worse for worse, there might be a chip you'd never see for all the bilious décor in this place." She heard another sigh, but it hid a short laugh. "And who is this one holding his own head in his hands?" She indicated the idol above her and shuddered.

"Saint Denis. Reminding me I could lose my head," he said, and watched Ani's expression pale suddenly. "Besides being the patron saint of France, the monarchy, and all of Paris, he's also the patron saint of madness, so that's fitting."

"And who is the patron saint of," she looked away from him, addled, refusing the headless image, "...falsely accused prisoners?"

"Saint Roch," he said with a curious uplilt, almost a question for her.

She recovered herself. "And the patron saint of..." she looked out the window, "of horses?"

"Saint Vincent de Paul."

"Ohh, you are sick, you poor fool."

"Saint Quentin and Saint Michael can heal me of that." He opened the ledger of valuations and laid it out before her. "This is for the art pieces."

Her mouth fell open at the astounding figures. Her gaze flitted between the numbers, the books on the table, the window. A gentle rain fell outside.

"Many of the pieces will have no doubt increased in value, and I trust you will look into that."

She nodded, then pointed to a glass of clear liquid on the table. "I poured you an eau-de-vie instead of tea."

He lifted the clear fruit brandy to his lips, sipped eagerly, then made a sound in his throat. "This is water."

"You locked me out of the liquor cabinet." She turned the page and held in a gasp at the prices.

"I locked myself out, you mean. It is for everyone's good that Josephine holds the key." He grimaced at the water. "I hope you at least boiled it."

"I got it out of that bucket by the horses in front." She held in her pleasure when he visibly gagged. "You mean that wasn't boiled?"

He groaned. "I shall remind myself to get you a key to every lock."

A key to every lock. Her pulse quickened. "Including the iron maiden?" she pressed.

"Are you going to ask me to demonstrate how it works?" He smiled.

"Yes, the garrison shall be the hardest room to keep count of, but come, I'll show you." He held his hand down to her.

"You're not going to reprimand me for last night?"

"No," he said. "You reprimanded yourself already." He was not any good at reprimanding. He preferred to let grudges and mishaps go the way of all things. And how could he explain to her that she'd terrified him but also thrilled him? That this morning, he'd awakened feeling more alive than he'd ever been?

The sun filtered unevenly through some clouds and into the two windows of the social hall. Ani watched the stretching variegated lines dance across the floor as the dust kicked into each beam, and then the gray overtook it again, and the rain fell harder. She took his hand, touched the noble skin, stood, felt the distance between them escape her, her footing give way at the edge of a great canyon.

Aubrey pulled an oil lamp from a wall sconce and led her from the social hall through the corridor toward the boardroom. As they walked, he shifted closer to her. She knew she must be shaking, but he didn't address it. "Ani?" he asked softly.

Heat crept up her neck. What would be required of her?

"I know you have steered from the politick, but I sense that it hasn't entirely abandoned your sensibilities. You are not a Catholic, plainly, and I can...possibly guess that you are not a monarchist at all."

Ani made to speak, but he held up a hand.

"That is fine," he said. "Our beliefs in no way make us decent." He drew closer. "But if you'd heard anything near the Louvre clubs about columns against the Sacred Heart in the Vendée, would you tell me?"

"Maybe," she said, flustered. "Perhaps, yes. I don't know." She tapped her fingers on her thigh. "It depends, I suppose."

"Supremely decisive. Ani—"

"Please stop saying my name like that." The pleading softness was getting to her conscience.

"Mademoiselle Baillairgé—"

God, that was worse, and it wasn't even her name.

"There are women and children in the Vendée being beaten in the streets on their way to Mass." He felt her quick exhale, her grip droop at his elbow before she could reclaim it. "Women and children, Ani. Beaten for their beliefs."

The deep rivulets of agony that a whip could cause—Ani knew the pain. But what could she tell him? Something new, something personal.

Something he hadn't yet found out but would find out anyway. Something that cost her nothing. "I know who's leading men to Cholet," she said.

His eyes widened. "You do?"

She nodded. "Comte de Marcé."

"Marcé? With reinforcements?"

She shook her head. "He doesn't have any."

Aubrey caught himself before he dropped her arm and paced the hallway as he'd usually do with his men. "We can beat Marcé with our eyes closed. He keeps marching insurgents through the streets of Paris for mere riots. The saps are bedraggled and haggard as dishrags. That column is weak."

"He'll be followed by the Duke de Biron."

His sudden enthusiasm broke. "Well, that will be harder." He murmured to himself, "How am I supposed to fight Biron? We used to fight on the same side."

"But you aren't going to the Vendée, are you?"

"Not if I can help it. Dear graciousness, the eastern countryside is turmoil enough." He crossed himself. "If I go to the western countryside, I come home in a box."

Beyond the last door at the end of the corridor, a cathedral window offered a gray view of a rainy orchard. Aubrey whisked her around a façade to a staircase she hadn't previously noticed. The steep stone steps led to the second story, then around another façade to the third half-story, where he presented her at the mouth of the grandest library she'd ever seen.

The books went clear up to the ceiling, all the way into the gabled roof, in perfect columns and rows, so high that a lofted walkway circumvented the room to access the upper echelon of the collection. Protruding from both the lower and upper levels were two sliding ladders that moved on a track around the oval layout of the room. The wood was the rich dark brown that matched her bedroom furniture, and every shelf was carved with a decorative arch at the top of each section, resembling the trimming of an ancient gothic castle.

In Ani's excitement, she read titles aloud, following along the spines with her finger: *Rheims-Douay Latin Vulgate Translation, Uniformity with God's Will, Confessions of St. Augustine, The Plays and Poems of William Shakespeare, Travels to Discover the Source of the Nile, Philosophical and Political History of the Settlements and Trade of the Europeans in the East and*

West Indies, Reflections on the Revolution in France (preemptive, that one), *L'Homme de Désir.*

Aubrey raised a brow. "If you can read all of those, it makes it considerably easier to learn German, should you wish for a tutor to do so."

"You'd get me a tutor?" The only other man she'd known who thought women should be tutored was Dr. Breauchard. He'd insisted that Ani learn everything he could get his hands on.

"Certainly," Aubrey said. "All women should be educated in any subject they desire."

Ani exhaled in audible admiration and faced away. A tutor? How much could she take from this man?

"What is your favorite book?"

"You'll be afraid you asked."

"Try me," he said. "I'm fairly well-minded. And even more well-read."

"Voltaire's *Candide.*"

He let out a chaff chuckle and walked toward a row of books. "Anything less...intractable?"

"I also enjoyed *Common Sense* by Thomas Paine."

"No, no. No one 'enjoys' *Common Sense*. I may forgive you for being more Lumière than Romantic, but no. Too seditious."

"How about *The Decline and Fall of the Roman Empire?*"

He glared at her.

"*A Vindication of the Rights of Men? Declaration of the Rights of Woman and the Female Citizen?* Anything by the Marquis de Sade?"

He grunted defeatedly. "All right, all right. *Candide* it is." He slid his hands along the far top shelf and retrieved a tiny pair of spectacles. "The only good thing to come out of the Colonial War of Independence was bifocal lenses." He perched the glasses on his nose and searched along the rows of books until he found his copy and pulled it off the shelf. Carrying the book over to a spot on the opposite wall next to Ani's head, he exchanged it with a different volume that had been in that slot. "There, now you can remember that it's *Candide*, and I doubt I'll ever forget that, either." He returned his bifocals to the nearest shelf, then tilted the copy of *Candide* and reached his hand beneath it. He stopped. His heart pounded with the anticipation and furtiveness of the act to follow, butterflies releasing in his chest. He turned to her. "What I am about to show you must never leave this room, must never be uttered to anyone outside of this palace except the certified insurer. Tell me you understand."

She nodded.

"Say it."

"I understand."

Hesitation wefted into his fingers. A scar from a whip gash creviced the back of her neck, another along the side, and his own neck tightened with imagined pain. What had she done? The latch beneath the book jiggled, and the bookcase made a muffled popping sound. The corner of the case came forward nearly imperceptibly. Aubrey took hold of the edge of it and pulled it toward him, revealing a stone passageway that wound back behind the wall and down into the floor, beneath the palace into a cellar. He led her by the arm within the passageway, then reached behind him to pull the bookcase shut. He lifted the oil lamp to illuminate the cramped space.

The passage was no wider than a prison escape tunnel, stone-lined, dirty, and unfinished. It was so dark that Ani couldn't make out anything past the first few feet. She thought about the coalmines. The stones looked more secure than the prop-plank tunnels she'd walked through a hundred times. But the darkness—the darkness was always the same.

♨

Before, Bassin Minier du Nord-Pas-de-Calais, northern France mining basin, several years prior

Damp tunnels wound beneath the surface of Nord-Pas-de-Calais in lightless, snaking trails that shrank into the mine. Rusted nails protruded from oak prop-planks supporting the walls and ceilings, and they nipped at Ani as she walked, snaring hair, nicking cuts into her temples. Notches scarred her ears. Along the narrow path, she felt her way through blackness and carried a wooden bucket of coal weighing half her own weight.

Not yet a teenager, her hair hung in scraggly brown curls about her face, escaping from beneath the peddler's cap that kept dust from her eyes. Despite the cap and a neckerchief over her nose, she swallowed the dust; it churned in her stomach with remnants of rotted food. Her shoes were worn through, and the balls of her feet scraped rocks where she tripped along the mine on her father's pantlegs left too long. Her father's shirtsleeves flopped down her forearms. The cuffs draped bony fingers that had memorized their way toward the lighted end of the tunnel.

The ten-hour mark in an unbroken twelve-hour day approached. The few scraps of egg and bread crust she'd stolen from a man's breakfast hadn't lasted her past dawn. Her arms quaked as if plagued by tremors, but she durst not set the bucket down, lest she never lift it again.

"Passing the line," a voice spoke, nearly on top of her.

She exhaled and reached out. "In line," she replied, and oriented herself to step out of the way.

"Ani?"

She couldn't place the man's voice. "Yes?"

"They pick you up again?"

"Is there a girl here of her own will?"

There was a rustle of fabric like he shook his head. Coarse wool brushed her arm and hot breath floated above her and he was gone up the line. She still hadn't recognized him, but her mind whirred.

She'd been caught on the street again. Scouts roamed the city in search of orphans and scrappers, avoiding the law, snapping them up to work the coalmines and mills. Derelict children made cheap labor in a time of bankruptcy. This corrupt industrial machine, fed off the burgeoning era of fossil fuel, supplied the energy-hungry country's needs.

Ani was no stranger to the mine; she'd labored now and again in the dank tunnels until she learned the ways to escape them. Yet here she was again. She treaded miles upon miles back and forth, thirsting, carrying hundreds of pounds of coal each day, and stumbling over passed-out, drunk miners. Carrying the buckets and the oil lamps was the easy part. Standing erect with a lamp lifted over a miner's head for twelve hours was not. The days she lugged buckets to the surface, she was thankful to be permitted some movement.

As Ani felt her way around the next corner, a faint glow silhouetted a miner leaning over his lighted lamp, but she hadn't spotted him soon enough to avoid his cloud of coal dust. The stabbing, low cough of blacklung came from deep within her, and she staggered with the force of it. She secured the neckerchief tighter around her mouth, clenching it between her lips. His light gored her eyes.

"Passing the line," she managed, and squeezed by the miner without further conversation. She watched her footing on the path for as long as his lamplight allowed. By the markers it lit, she figured she must have walked half a mile from the end of the tunnel with the forty-pound bucket and that the next spot of light she'd see should be the other end of the mine. As she neared another corner into darkness, she felt a shoulder brush past her. Ani startled.

"Pardon me," a small voice said.

"You got to call out. In line."

"Pardon. Passing the line."

Ani paused. "Béatrice?" She set down the bucket of coal before she could remind herself not to, and reached for the elbow that touched her. "You going back down now?"

"Allyriane?"

"Yeah, it's me. How far to the surface?"

"You's at the last turn, there." Béatrice pointed a finger that neither could see.

Ani lifted the bucket, cursing herself for having put it down. A cramp shot through her shoulder, and she flexed it away. "Wait for me, Bet."

"Hurry. I inn't being whipped for being slow again. Last time—"

"Yeah, yeah, last time."

Ani trudged the rest of the tunnel toward the light that seeped into the darkness at the final corner, then she squinted like a surfacing mole at the garish brightness that pinned her eyes. Warm summer air whooshed into the cave and threw her into a daze, her mind drifting back to the outside world. She squeezed her eyes closed, then open, closed, and grew faint. Vertigo enveloped her. Her footing broke loose, and she slid downward. She dropped the bucket of coal when she landed, first against the walls of the cave, then hard onto the path, and tears stung her eyes.

"Stupid galibot," a surface miner yelled down. "Get your ass off the ground, and pick up that coal."

The man slid his legs into the mine's mouth, and Ani knew she had to be on her feet with the coal collected before he reached her, or he'd plant a whip across her back. She scrambled for the coal and reclaimed her lost ground, handing the man the unwieldy bucket. He snatched it and knocked her down again, where her exhaustion kept her crumpled.

"Get up. Here, kid." He tossed an empty bucket into her gut and hauled her to her feet. "Back down there. Keep moving." He pushed her toward the tunnel, then turned for the surface.

Ani's hip ached from the fall, but she inched back into the mine with one outstretched hand. As the darkness overtook the light, it choked her with claustrophobia. The walls bent inward to touch her, to scrape her face like claws, and she arched into each curve, but it was like being folded into a box, regardless of joints or bones.

"Is that you, Ani?" The damp air swallowed Béatrice's voice.

Ani kicked up stones near the bend, and the two girls joined their hands together to carry the empty buckets back down into the mine's center.

"I heard you fall. Did you get dizzy again?"

"I've got that bad cough."

Béatrice squeezed Ani's hand.

Another voice called in the darkness, "Ani, is that you?"—a much louder one with the squeaky keening of a hawk and the careless echo of a girl who'd forgotten she was in a collapsible tunnel. "I'd recognize that awful cough anywhere," the heavy Dutch accent said, and Ani knew the voice of Grietje.

"Yes, Gret, it's me," Ani said. "You going back down with empties?"

"Ja. Lille is on lamp down there. It's my turn to relieve her."

"Lucky, lucky. Have you seen daylight?"

"Not since dawn," Grietje said. "And it's hotter than a dutch oven down there today. They's digging deeper."

The three girls approached a glow near the end of the corridor, and Ani knuckled the bill of her hat to the lamp-carrier boy who was casting the light for the trapper, releasing his trap flue door to ventilate the methane buildup throughout the tunnels.

"You're doing a fine job, Pere." Ani nodded.

The boy with the lamp had the hardest job in the tunnel; one errant puff of air or one tiny break of the seal on the lamp, and the firedamp would become explosive in the presence of a flame. But Pere Dinault-briand, day in, day out, held this lamp. When their eyes met, he smiled at her and nudged the trapper to let the girls through.

Ani lifted her neckerchief over her nose and held her breath. Going through the trap meant crawling into some of the highest concentrations of methane in the mine, a rotten sulfur smell that made her eyes water. Lifting her knees, she pulled herself into the shallow crawlspace and dragged her empty bucket through behind her, then reached back for Grietje. Ani didn't want to turn around; the mine pinholed as it wound down, like a tornado funnel, and the weight of it was crushing, oppressively damp and heavy. Pere pushed Grietje and Béatrice from behind while Ani pulled from the front, and she counted heads to make sure they were extracted safely from the trap. The younger girls soon followed her along the path away from the light.

ॐ

Now

Aubrey's grip tightened, and he pulled Ani to him. She went rigid and resisted every urge to fight him. As her eyes adjusted, she looked to the left and saw why he held her so securely. The tunnel dropped straight into a steep flight of stairs that, had Aubrey not known it there, would have sent her plummeting down a twisted stone dropoff, just as the architect had intended. In the dark, she could smell his lye soap, the mint sprigs he'd used to cover it. Her mouth was so close to his chest she could feel her own breath coming back to her. She willed herself to relax. When she was steady, he took her arm, keeping her tight behind him as they descended. Her dress tripped her first step, and she lifted it higher.

"There are over a hundred steps here," he said after the first several. "Tell me if you get dizzy, and we'll rest."

The stairs went on eternally. Lightheadedness caught her as the steps twisted around and around. She kept her eyes on the back of his head, his small ears, what she could scant see of him, to keep the walls from closing in around her, the claustrophobic memories coming back to her in nauseating waves. The stairs leveled off, and then, to her surprise, started upward again. She'd been descending, and now she was climbing. She could not place where she was along the inner walls. Her legs grew tired, but she kept quiet. The stairs evened again, and a faint glow came from ahead of them.

When Ani's focus returned, she saw, there, before her, what must have been the most heavily stocked military garrison in the city. Row upon row, crate upon crate, rack upon rack of gunpowder, saltpeter, muskets, swords, and various torture devices. She inhaled sharply. There were enough munitions here to wipe out half of Paris. And they were in the hands of royalists.

"I told you," Aubrey said, holding the lamp to his face so she could see his proud smile. "We run alongside the first floor of the palace now, to the westward side and back, behind the false windows. The front parlor is about there." He pointed. "Your room would be over there. And by the time you get to the bottom of that incline at the front, you are below the first floor, and it continues into a cold cellar for storing the powder. The iron maiden is straight to the back, there."

Ani followed the direction of his finger and walked along the huge room that went forward the length of the palace, then dropped steeply. Thick, reinforced walls lined the inside—walls that could absorb the brunt of battle damage. Muskets, both primitive and new, were heaped in crates, and laid out in rows beside them were bayonets arranged by varying length. Trébuchets towered over her, and hand cannon were butted in rows against the innermost wall.

"How did you get this in here? Is there another entrance?"

"The stairs are the only entrance, treacherous by design, but what you see before you over here is a false wall, a very thin façade, easy to knock in or out for accessibility to the munitions without any demise of the old palace stone."

"So, you built the wall around all this, already inside?"

He held the lantern to his face and nodded.

"Remarkable," she muttered, and walked between tidy rows of munitions, marked and crated, that she was to inventory and value. A room of munitions in the hands of the royalists—and now she knew the entrance. Along the wall, she saw the freestanding iron figure of the mythical maiden. It was larger than a person, with inlets and traps for knives and spikes. Multiple folding compartments corresponded to the locations of the various body parts to receive the spike. She slid her finger along the curved metal of the morbid invention.

"I have heard of her," she said, "but seeing her in person is horrifying."

"Me, personally—I don't like the thing. She is one of only three in existence. Her torture is medieval in nature, but she is flawlessly new."

Ani stood before the propped-open iron cabinet and squeezed through the crack to stand inside it, seeing the spikes aimed at her and the open slots for more torture knives to be driven in and out. This nobleman could close it on her now—he could end her, right here. But he just smiled giddily.

As she started back through the open crack, the dust and moldy, damp air tickled her lungs. A deep, asthmatic cough came from low inside her, and she snagged her elegant dress on the spikes. She twisted to free herself, but the cough deepened. Ani fell to her knees, unable to stop the cough, and clutched her neck. A spot of red blood shot out her mouth as a tear ripped in her throat.

Aubrey sprang forward as if he'd been kicked. "My God, Ani." He crossed himself and dropped beside her. "What is happening?"

His words were lost. The pain of the sudden attack coursed through her, and she fell limp, lightheaded, then regained herself, though her breathing was harsh and strained. She patted herself, but she'd forgotten her inhaler.

ॐ

Before, the mine

The girls neared the center pit where miners extended the tunnel along a coal seam. The ground and walls lit with the lanterns of other children. On one side of the cave, Isabeau Léandre stood with her lamp lifted between miners extracting coal with peaks and shovels; and on the other side, Lille Vigny struggled to hold her lamp for too many miners to share one light. Lille was fragile, too much a part of the dust to keep from being stepped on. Yet, she stood for hours without complaint, her feet bare and arms shaking to hold her lantern high, and she tolerated drunk and abusive miners like a barmaid.

"Where's your shoes, Lille?" Ani asked as she ducked her head below the overhang of the extended gallery.

Lille looked embarrassed. "I think they been took. When I woke, they was gone." Her quavering voice leaked out among the steady smell and taste of methane released by the miners' tools, a garlicky egg flavor always on the air.

"I'll find you another pair." Ani set her empty bucket near the miner with the fullest exchangeable one. The cramp shot through her shoulder again, then farther down her arm. This time, she couldn't flex it away. "Gret is here to relieve you. Take Monsieur Montien's pail before it gets too full, and get some surface air. You look like death. I'll be right behind you to help you through the traps."

Lille lowered her arm, but as she took a step, her bare foot caught a chunk of rock. She rolled her ankle and fell toward the ground before anyone knew what was happening. Flitters of light swung across the cave like flying bats, and the miners watched in horrified anticipation as Lille toppled, her lamp smashing open across sharp bedrock. In a split second, Ani screamed and shoved Grietje and Béatrice back into the mineshaft and down to the ground as the firedamp gas struck the lamp's flame and sent an explosion, fingers of sparks, across the gallery and through the tunnels, catching new pockets of leaking methane. Ani reached for Isabeau and dragged her to the ground, pushed her along on her belly as the flames shot overhead and sucked the breathable air from the tunnels.

Ani pressed her neckerchief tight over her nose and looked back to Lille across the noxious plumes. A leg and hand draped over the bedrock, unattached from a body. The rest of the arm stuck to the propboard wall, blown onto the protruding nails that held it there. Lille's torso rocked in flames, yet the screaming girl was alive and holding on to what was left of the lamp with the only limb still attached. Ani gasped, then coughed, her mind refusing the image she saw, and she yelled toward Lille. *That couldn't be Lille—she wasn't put together.* Miners on fire fell to the ground of the gallery, rolling. Indistinguishable body parts burned in small clusters throughout the pit.

"Allyriane!" Isabeau called from the ground in front of Ani. "You can't save her. She's gone. Come, or you'll burn with her."

"Go!" Ani yelled back, coughing hard into her neckerchief. She took shallow breaths, then held each one as long as she could. "Get the girls to the trap, and get it closed behind you."

"You can't go back!"

"Go. Get out of here."

Ani crawled in the direction of Lille, but the sudden stillness of the girl stopped Ani in her tracks, and against her very nature, she turned instead to the trapped miners. Then a hand grabbed hold of her wrist and pulled her toward the tunnel. The hand was not a girl's, and through the smoke, she made out the lamp-carrying galibot who helped them through the ventilation trap.

"Let go of me, Pere! They're still alive." She kicked at him.

"You can't save them, girl. Come on with me." He crawled closer.

Flames lapped at the gallery ceiling above them. Ani stuck out her hand and kept her head low to the ground. Her lungs deflated into empty sacks. The flames grew hotter, wilder, hitting methane pockets farther down the tunnels behind her, collapsing walls beyond the gallery. Lille. *Lille, Lille.* There was no movement from that side of the cave. Flames chewed the right lining of the pit.

"Lille?" Ani offered, halfheartedly. "Lille, can you hear me?" Only the crackle of fire. "Lille?" Ani choked, and Pere clutched her again, directed her to the path. She coughed hard and gagged on the smoke, then reached for Pere's body to orient herself in the lifeless gray. "Lille!" she screamed hoarsely, and a bolt of heat burst toward Ani's face until she had to retreat from it.

Pere dragged her up the tunnel backward until he had her close to the first trapdoor. He released her, then jerked up on her britches and collar and righted her against his chest. Her head lolled, then snapped-to. He pounded his fist against the trapdoor over his head, muttering, praying for a response—praying they hadn't been abandoned.

"Get ready to be quick," he rasped, his vocal cords fried.

The trapdoor opened, and buckets of water poured over the two exhausted galibots. The water held off the flames that lurched toward a fresh opening while their bodies were pulled through the crawlspace by miners on the other side. With the latching of the door, the inferno was closed off behind them.

The air in the second corridor was much more breathable, but smoke stuck in Ani's insides such that she couldn't stop coughing long enough to catch a breath. The coal dust was fine, and as it stirred through the air, it clung to the walls of her lungs, and she collapsed unnoticed half-way through the corridor, the rest of the miners fighting their way to the surface. As more clean air poured in and the ventilation increased, the methane lessened, and the fire dwindled under the buckets of water being poured down the hole. Ani felt the rushes of water washing over her, seconds before blackness fell.

⁊

Now

Aubrey looped his arm through the lantern bail, helped Ani to her feet, and held her steady against him, whispering soothing words to calm her. He could not get her back up the steep, winding stairs. Carrying her was out of the question, and if they fell, it could end them both in one instant, and no one would know they were there. He envisioned someone knocking out the wall and finding corpses in the midst of war and didn't feel like dying that way today.

Though he was sworn to secrecy about the two other garrison entrances he'd said didn't exist, he had to take one, the closest and easiest that led past the decline and back up to open behind the boterie off the kitchen. The powder casks turned into wine casks at the boterie entrance, and none but a discerning eye could tell the difference. But there were thankfully no stairs, only a series of depressions and inclines, so he directed her that way. She clung to him with one hand, his fabric bunched in her fist, the other hand pressed firmly to her chest, and Aubrey repeated brief mantras to keep her focused on her steps: *You're all right. We'll get a doctor. You're safe. Rest on my arm.* Her cough still hung onto her lungs in small breaths, and once outside the boterie, she collapsed against a cask.

"Ani?" he said, tapping her cheek, propping an elbow against rows of port wine. "Are you all right? Talk to me?" He pulled the lantern up to her face.

She squinted and pushed the light away. "Yes," she managed, but she coughed again, groping for the inhaler that wasn't there.

He thought about calling out. Arnaud might hear. Étienne might be dusting the hallway. "Ani." He shook her. "What is it? Do you have consumption?"

"No. No, it's…" She pushed away from his embrace, becoming too familiar, becoming too known. She was certain he knew what it was. After she caught her breath, she lifted the hem of her skirt and leaned away from him as they weaved through the last kegs and out the boterie door. She took note of the entrance, the powder kegs that turned to wine kegs. She even thought she saw one more entrance that she'd have to come back and map out.

Two guards standing inside the front foyer, avoiding the rain outside, glanced briefly at Aubrey, and then away, their faces registering only flickeringly the sacred protocol he'd broken.

৯৮

Before, the mine

The miners pushed their way through two more ventilation traps and, at the surface, were marked off on a roll call, counted as alive. Some badly burned, but alive. Isabeau, Grietje, and Béatrice made it to the surface, and they stood heaving deep breaths, waiting for Ani to emerge. When the last of the miners had been extracted, Pere looked at the girls, and they were looking back at Pere, wanting to know where was Ani. He glanced down the hole, cursed, then slid his legs through the opening with a bout of claustrophobia like none he'd ever known. Making his way against the smoky darkness, Pere climbed through two trapdoors and crawled along the path, feeling for signs of life.

Halfway between the second and third traps, his hands struck a linen shirt attached to an arm attached to very small female fingers. He gained Ani's positioning, then lifted her to him. "Ani." He shook her.

"Pere," she said, opening her eyes and coughing. "Pere, did they bring the wagons?"

"There's some up there, aye."

"And you can drive a carriage?"

"You bet I can," he said.

He helped her along the tunnel, through the trapdoors, and hoisted her past the opening at the mouth of the mine. The girls' eager hands pulled her up, onto the clean soil. Green grass and stems of angel's tears haloed her head like an Enlightenment painting with its subject out of place. Pere emerged from the hole and lay on the ground next to her, his chest heaving.

"Bring more carriages around for these men," a velvet-vested mine warden said. His cheeks were swollen and dark, blotched with the red-marked symptoms of smallpox. "Get the burned miners down to Paris. Not the street urchins." He waved his hand at the girls and Pere. "The roture do not undergo care at the mine's expense. Only the wage workers." The warden turned to the smoke billowing out of the hole and counted how many other men were still trapped inside, and the group of miners hefted ropes, buckets, and pulleys to get anyone out who might still be alive.

With the miners occupied, Ani, Pere, Grietje, Isabeau, and Béatrice stood and meandered slowly toward the closest carriage, avoiding attention. The traces were set and ready to go. When the girls were in the backend, Pere came around the frontside to the driver, yanked the man out and climbed inside in one motion, and the conveyance was galloping off toward Paris before the warden knew what all the commotion was.

♀

Now
Aubrey and Ani were back in the first-floor corridor, then inside her bedroom, where Aubrey eased her onto the soft blankets of her bed and felt her forehead, but she wasn't running warm. He sat on the edge and pulled the covers over her, noticing a speckle of blood on his vest.

"Josephine! I need water and clean cloths," he yelled toward the hallway, but Ani pushed on his arm and pointed to the satchel in the corner.

The powder that Josephine had shown him, of course. He knew at once what it was. He retrieved the powder and the inhaler and cupped them into her open hands, helping her upright to inhale the mixture. Within minutes, her cough subsided, her pain leveled, and her head fell back on the pillow in a hallucinogenic haze. Josephine rushed in with clean rags and a ewer of water for the porcelain basin.

"Goodness, what happened?" she asked, wringing out a cloth and placing it against Ani's head.

"Miner's lung, isn't it," Aubrey said. "And here I thought you were an addict."

"I'm not rich enough to be an addict," Ani said with effort. "Nord-

Pas-de-Calais. I'll carry this cough till it takes me under." There was no humor in her words.

"I am from Pas-de-Calais," Josephine refuted. "My great grandpapa's cough was like yours, and he made it to his late eighties, so hush."

Aubrey said, "Nord-Pas-de-Calais. You were a galibot in the collieries?" Perhaps she wasn't even bourgeoisie, he wondered. Was she so lowborn as to be a coal worker? "Do you know who owns that mine?"

Ani shook her head and let the daze take her, pulled her hand from Aubrey's. "I could use some coffee."

"Coffee?" he said. "Why would you want that foul substance? Only revolutionaries drink coffee."

"Well, you said yourself I'm not Catholic and possibly not monarchist at all." She chuckled and closed her eyes.

Josephine and Aubrey exchanged a glance. "I'll see if the scullery knows how to make it," he said. "Don't bate your breath."

"Fret not. I can't."

CHAPTER SEVEN

A TREASONOUS COMBINATION

A revolution is an idea
that has found its bayonets.

—Napoleon Bonaparte

Now

"Shhh. Come this way," Ani whispered to Béatrice as Ani led her to the back of the palace through the orchard.

The southeastern side was not walled, and the orchard served as its only barricade. The summer trees stretched for a thousand rods southward, grouped into apples, cherries, pears, and a tiny orange fruit Ani had never seen. She stopped abruptly, and Béatrice ran into her as Ani pulled one from its branch, cupping it. It was softly fuzzy with a point of slight pink blush.

"Hm," Ani murmured.

"Them's rich-people fruits," Béatrice said.

Ani nodded and took in the deep scent of the orchard, its fermented sweetness, a wooded graininess behind the fresh redolence, before putting a finger to her lips and quietly pulling open the back palace door. She ushered in her friend and pointed to the meetingroom where she heard Aubrey's voice, muffled and too gentle, placating some man or other who had ideas of his own that didn't match Aubrey's. Ani felt his voice comb over her, crawling fingers of quickened blood, and she grabbed Béatrice's wrist and yanked her down the hall, ducking behind the podiums and waist-high bureaus that dotted the way. At the doorway to the kitchen, she paused, listened for voices, popped the fruit into the air, caught it in her hand, and took Béatrice around the corner into the dark pantry. A tall flame blazed hot on firedogs with swirling tracery, spitrests, and iron baking drawers filled with warming potatoes.

"I can't tell you what half of it is," Ani said, "but fetch it up."

When her eyes adjusted to the darkness of the room, Ani dug through a wicker hamper for some soiled cheesecloths and linens, and she laid them out on the counter in large rectangles. Béatrice squealed.

"Hush," Ani said.

"I don't think anyone's here to hear me." Béatrice giggled, too loud.

"They are. The ears of this place are everywhere. You've got to hush, or I'll tell Jacques you stole his cauldron."

"You wouldn't!"

"I would."

"I haven't stole it. I only…borrowed it…forever."

Béatrice started with the tarts and sweetbreads, filling the cloths with whatever her fingers were touching that was closest. Large blocks of cheese hardened with wax, salt-cured bacon slabs preserved in slackwax and pitch. Ani tied the bundles together as they were filled and slid them onto the end of a cauldron paddle. She winced. No one would notice a few missing tarts or linens, but Arnaud would miss that paddle.

"Bring a basket next time," Ani said. As she said it, a lamp came around the corner from the kitchen into the pantry.

"Who's in here?" asked a voice connected bodilessly to the lamp, and the women froze. He lifted the light to his face. It was Valéry-Marie Fergniaud, Aubrey's sculleryman, one hand on the lamp and the other on the handle of a cast-iron flatpan, raised as if to strike.

"It's me," Ani said quickly, pushing Béatrice out of the way of the light and shoving the bundles of food at her. "I was hungry."

"Hungry enough to eat this whole shelf?" He swung the lamp to the two shelves that the young women had picked stock clean.

It was then Ani could see how ragged he was, dressed in full trousers, his hair loose. She wondered why Aubrey let him get away with the slouchiness—but then, Aubrey wasn't a man to beat vices out of other men, it seemed. Valéry ran a hand through his dark hair and lowered the lamp, and Ani could see he was smiling to himself, amused.

He sighed heavily and slid the flatpan onto a shelf. "Don't let the guards shoot your friend on the way out. There's pickets at the back of the orchard."

Ani already knew this. She'd skirted them easily, and her messengers skirted them without incident every night. On occasion, she'd even found them sleeping at their posts in broad daylight. "Thank you," she said.

Valéry waved Béatrice out from behind the tall end shelf. "You can come on out. You're not invisible; I saw you. No harm in it." He urged her forward with an extended hand.

"Bet," Béatrice said and kissed his hand awkwardly, kneeling as if knighted. "I won't stay any. I got a room at Dr. Breau—"

Ani stepped on her foot.

"Ow, you frogbottom!" Béatrice cried but threw her hands over her mouth, dropping the bundle paddle, then swooping to pick it up. "Oh, look at me. I'm befuddled up."

Ani lifted the tiny orange fruit to Valéry. "What is this?"

"What do you mean, what is that?" he huffed. "It's fruit."

"Well, yes, fruit, but what is it?"

"It's a plain ol' apricot is what it is. You've never seen an apricot?"

Ani shook her head.

"Well, did you try one? Go on, try it."

She looked at it, wanting to bite into it, but she polished it against her dress and slipped it into the apron pocket. It was too beautiful to puncture, a symbol of a life that wasn't really hers.

"Well," he said, "when you do try it, you'll be back to pick those trees clean." He folded closed the last unfinished bundle and tied the knot, handing it to Béatrice. "Don't make a habit of depleting the master's pork, but I'll tell you, no one eyes the orchard trees, and a body can last for quite some time on apples and pears." He threw a thumb over his shoulder, and Béatrice looked once at Ani, then slinked out of the pantry.

Ani studied the floor. "You won't tell him?"

"I have to tell him."

She nodded, not looking up.

"But he won't say a word." He leaned forward conspiratorially. "It's Arnaud we can't tell. Especially not once he finds his paddle missing. I'll have to feign some mighty termite infestation." He winked.

Ani smiled hesitantly and walked out after Béatrice, glancing behind her once or twice to see if he'd change his mind.

"Imagine if I really was invisible, though!" Béatrice said, giggling.

The two women sidled down the hall, but nearer the orchard exit, the meetingroom door came open, and the sounds of men's voices spilled into the expanse. Ani tugged Béatrice inside the doorway of the closest room, and they watched the men pass, Béatrice nearly tripping over herself to get a look at the marquis. When the officers had taken the bend in the hallway, Ani shoved Béatrice forward and toward the door, then out of it, into the orchard.

"My, but he is a beauty!" Béatrice almost shouted. "I didn't know he was such a beauty. How can a man so awful be such a beauty?"

Ani swatted her, but then pulled her into an embrace and held it there until the cauldron paddle left an indent in her thigh, and Béatrice wriggled free and turned away without a word, swiping at her eye. Ani watched her go, inching through the orchard, tree to tree, then Ani stepped back into the hallway. At the other end of it, Aubrey walked toward her, his sides oddly bereft of men. A rare second of quiet, solitude. When he saw her, he stood straighter and brightened and touched an open palm to a hat he wasn't wearing. *He won't say a word*, she heard Valéry-Marie say in her mind, and she watched how the marquis moved, sturdy, certain, fluid. Yes, he was a beauty. A peerless remnant from an ancient time, a consummate mold that had been broken by careless creators. And he wasn't even that awful, she found herself thinking before blotting the thought.

∾

Now

The weeks passed, and the battles in the countryside grew closer. Ani's arm healed well enough. Aubrey commissioned doctor ministrations when he was home, though he was rarely home these days. She'd long since stopped pretending that she was counting or inventorying anything, and everyone else either forgot it, as well, or chose to ignore it. She could have left Palais d'honneur, but she didn't, and no one seemed to expect her to. In the evenings, she even had a tutor, schooling her in architecture, German, and natural philosophies. Every few days, Ani found a basket of salted meats and goat cheeses propping open the orchard door, left there by Valéry-Marie. If Aubrey knew about it, as prophesied, he'd never said a word. She thrilled at the rare days that Béatrice sneaked through the orchard to meet her. Everything else would have to wait until the riots lessened in the streets. Soon, she kept thinking. *It must be soon.* The people couldn't really go on like this indefinitely, could they? *Could they?*

Aubrey briefed her daily, sometimes hourly when he was present, about war goings-on, where the fronts moved, and how many men each maneuver took. She was curious and helpful, and he put her in charge of paperwork, recording numbers, at which she excelled. She could read and write better than some of the barons, saving Aubrey the expense of other tutors, harder to come by as the strains of war encroached on an increasingly anxious and penurious city. She had her own stake in it, as did he—to know what would happen to the peasants. He reminded himself constantly that it was her Paris, too.

But outside the palace walls, ill-conceived violence escalated. A fledgling revolution had intensified among struggling would-be leaders throughout the poorer faubourgs and down the center of the city, branching outward. Generals, republicans, monarchists, atheists, anarchists. The scales of power shook unstably and could tip in anyone's favor. Paris' time had come. The people waited, waited, waited for something to break. Ani inwardly rejoiced in having stone walls around her and not being left standing in the thick of the rioting city—even if the stone walls were his.

But the unrest ate at Aubrey. He grew sullen as he came and went on various appointments. He managed some small victories, but also some crippling failures with the young, inexperienced mercenaries who'd been assigned to him. His troops were often outnumbered, and his conflicted men—fighting against their own people—switched sides in alarming numbers, minute nuances of their opposing stances upended in the mire. They'd soon lose the garrison as a place to regroup, unable to risk bringing attention to the hidden arsenal. If he didn't die in battle, he would eventually not be allowed to return to Paris. Insurgents would know he fought for the monarchy against the uprising, and as those insurgents took over cabinet seats, they would displace the men who fought against them, first in the government and then in society. When that day finally came, he would either have to flee or be imprisoned.

He paced the floor of his boardroom, outwardly calm despite his unrest, staring at the manifesto issued forth from the Duke of Brunswick. What fresh hell was this? "When Brunswick's proclamation hits this city, there will be massive conflict. Have you seen this?" Aubrey said to his strategists, waving a copy of the Brunswick Manifesto and reading directly from it: "*The members of the National Guard who shall fight against the troops of the two allied courts, and who shall be taken with arms in their hands, shall be treated as enemies and punished as rebels to their king and as disturbers of the public peace. The inhabitants of the towns and villages who may dare to defend themselves against the troops of their Imperial and Royal Majesties and fire on them, either in the open country or through windows, doors, and openings in their houses, shall be punished immediately according to the most stringent laws of war, and their houses shall be burned or destroyed.*" Aubrey paused and took a sharp breath. "This will bring the destruction of Paris. The insurgents will never comply with this. What is Brunswick thinking? If we bring

more foreign powers into this, we'll be viewed as treasonous enemies."
He wadded the manifesto and threw it on the table, crossing his arms.
"And this from a man who sympathizes with the Constitution."

"As do you, General," Baron d'Egrenant reprimanded, "but we don't
question your resolve, now do we?"

"Noted," Aubrey said. "But the insurrectionists will take this manifesto as proof that our king has been corresponding with foreign governments. He'll be held unjustly treasonous of the very laws he vetoed."

Baron Bellon stepped forward and picked up the crumpled manifesto from the table, peeling open its edges to read it. "I disagree entirely,
General. It will threaten the insubordinates of Paris into submission.
They fear losing their homes and being imprisoned, so they will be
willing to keep their homes and arms in exchange for not harming the
king—something I don't think anyone is willing to do, anyhow."

"They fear nothing but being afraid," Aubrey said. "The poor have
no homes to protect, and any danger of losing anything more than they
do have will make them even more fiercely protective of it. They are
starved animals."

"But these insurgents will be nothing against the armed forces," a
third baron, Loïc Corbière, argued.

"That's what I once thought, too," Aubrey said. "Yet, look how often
they have defeated us."

"Brunswick has Emperor Leopold's soldiers and the king of Prussia's combined armies beneath his single command. And we have kingsmen north of Lorraine and in Alsace. The Republic will not get across
the borders, nor will they be able to push us back." Baron Loïc Corbière
was another West Brittany Breton, short and older, with only one remaining eye, bearing a patch like a badge of honor for the sovereign
enterprise.

"It is not wise to brush off these insurgents," Aubrey said, his finger
raised toward Corbière. "We lost a hundred of our own men at the
Bastille under a white flag against eight thousand insurgents more than
capable of carrying out a massacre. They don't follow the rules of civi-
lized warfare. Those very fédérés acquired forty thousand muskets in a
matter of days, set half of Paris ablaze, and are getting stronger every
minute. They're not to be underestimated."

"But, General," Corbière said, "they've had those muskets now for
years and have done little more than threaten. I don't think they have
the courage to follow through with deposing the king."

"We have a larger problem that should be addressed," a fourth voice arose in the room. "Captain Bonaparte. The man is unstoppable." The voice belonged to General Édouard-Valentin Aimé de Béquignol, a general without noble title whose authority challenged Aubrey's at every turn. While the two men led matched divisions of soldiers, they seldom agreed on how it should be done. The fact of the matter was de Béquignol was a better general, not for any good reason save that he was utterly ruthless. "Bonaparte has won every skirmish what's been throwed at him. Should he set his hat to Brunswick, then France has a new leader."

"Bah," Aubrey dismissed, and he glanced at the man to his right, Baronet Chicoine, who nodded too eagerly.

Baronet Chicoine, unaesthetic and unathletic, rarely said a word. He donned the full red uniform of the Swiss Guard by choice, in solidarity with his fellow Swiss guardsmen, even though he was French. He, in turn, set his nod to the final man in the room: the complicated Yves Lenoir, Aubrey's trusted military advisor, who sat almost always as silent as Chicoine, observing the opposition until came his need to speak. Lenoir's eyes were dark as any Beaumercy's, his convictions constant. He looked a man so squarely in the eye when he spoke that one felt intimidated even when complimented.

"Yes, Bonaparte seems effective," Lenoir spoke up, "but he's in Corsica. He don't look to be moving any time soon. If he marches toward Paris or the borders, we'll know about it long before he can approach them. There be pressing problems closer to home." He counted them on his fingers. "The Vendée. Nantes. The fortress belt along the countryside. Areas closer to Paris that have men faithful to the First Estate, to the divine monarchy, alongside us. Those men will rally to protect the king in full force and bring the war right into our city walls."

General de Béquignol broke in over Lenoir's advice, "Marquis, the most extreme left of the Assembly has been informed by some rat of the Marquis de la Rouerie's royalist plot in the Vendée. Rumor has it them so-called Girondins of the Assembly," he snarled as he said it, "may be preparing to send troops against the Vendéens."

"I know," Aubrey said.

"If this happens—"

"—I know what happens, General," Aubrey said.

Before, the faubourg Saint-Marcel cellar, mid-July, two days before arrival at the palace in the Chaillot

When night fell again over the cramped cellar, the girls huddled together and found sleep. All except Ani. Her mind drifted back to her father, the scaffold. His eyes remained, hovering, the flame of enmity threatening to explode like a firedamp. As she played this image over, a soft tap came at the door, and she bristled. The knock wasn't enough to wake the sleeping girls, and Ani didn't rouse them. A shadow moved beneath the crack. She stilled and held her breath. When the shadow moved on, she shuffled to the door and lifted the latch enough to allow a strand of lamplight to streak across her eyes. No one was there. Whoever it was had slinked away into the faubourg. Dr. Breauchard? No, he would have stayed. He would have hugged her, asked when she'd last eaten, brought her a stack of books or a new treatise on something medical. She stood there and waited, scanned, but only an eagle-owl woohooed somewhere far off.

As Ani slipped back into the cellar, she stepped on a letter in the threshold. She lifted the folded piece of yellow paper into the lamplight. Her real last name was written on the front. She looked once more up and down the alley before she broke the wax seal and read the curly, well-practiced hand. *Not yet*—she wasn't ready yet. Not with her father's death still so fresh. She stared at it for a minute longer—the name she knew so well, *that abhorred name, her next assignment*, to find a marquis' hidden garrison, raid a hated duke's war plans—then folded it, tucked it into her britches, and closed the door to her cellar. She pondered it, then replaced the thought with that last image of her father, and she shivered and bit down into her lower lip until she tasted blood. *Not yet.* She squeezed her eyes tight. She needed time to gain her composure, to ease her vulnerability. She hadn't fully hardened back to her old self.

"What's that?" Béatrice whispered, startling Ani.

"You know what it is." She led Béatrice to the wooden boards on the floor, and the two girls sat quietly. She put her arm around her younger friend and held her as she drifted, a slow tear running down her cheek and into Béatrice's hair, damp as it already was, and Ani could smell the mustiness of it as she pressed her lips to her friend's forehead.

This was it. This was it, and the weight was crushing.

Béatrice sniffled. "I'll miss you. I wish you didn't have to go there."

"I'll return," Ani whispered. "I swear it."

ഇ

Now

"I said I know what happens, General. I set Bonchamps to handle it." Aubrey paced about the meetingroom in agitation. "Messieurs, I think it's time we consider evacuating our families and munitions out of Paris. The garrison is safe for now, but our families are not. You should begin fearing for the safety of them. Pending Brunswick's actions, God help us," he crossed himself, "appointments will be handed thusly. If he submits this manifesto as he's threatening to do, we can only presume there will be a greater war to follow."

A sound came from outside the door, and de Béquignol's head turned to it, then back to Aubrey.

"Bellon," Aubrey continued, "you have only daughters. You're pardoned from participation in order to conceive a son to carry on your family name. The rest of you have sons and are expected at your appointments. Your youngest or healthiest son is not permitted to fight, even should he be of age. There will come a levée for the single men, I fear."

"General, sir, I thank you for the pardon," Baron Bellon said, "but I will be at my appointment. I can bear the end of my family name, but I cannot bear the end of France. I am besides blessed with nephews."

De Béquignol suddenly burst out of the door and into the hallway. Ani pipped at the unexpected charge that displaced her from where she'd been standing behind the door. De Béquignol grasped her arm tightly and spun her around to face the men who had followed him out of the room, all talking at once.

"This wench was spying!" de Béquignol shouted.

"Let go of me!" Ani said, squirming, clutching to her chest the library book she held. "Call me a wench! I was getting a book from the library!" She flung herself free of his grasp and landed against Aubrey, who instinctively closed his arms around her, then moved her behind him to come between Ani and an enraged de Béquignol. "I wasn't spying! Honest. I was only procuring a book. I…didn't even know you were in there…didn't hear a word." She constricted her throat and nose to force tears, and some of the men softened when her eyes welled. "Please, Aubrey," she said.

De Béquignol snarled, "You'll address him as *my lord general.*"

Ani gasped and looked at Aubrey, but he didn't dispute it. "My lord general," she whispered, her blood rising.

"You are all dismissed," Aubrey said, but the men didn't move. "Go!"

he said, and they stepped backward, then slowly walked down the hall.

Yves Lenoir made unnerving eye contact with Ani before he turned to leave. Ani prepared to follow but was stopped by Aubrey's arm extended in front of her.

"Not you," Aubrey said. "You are not dismissed." De Béquignol opened his mouth to speak, but Aubrey raised a hand, then rubbed at his own temples. "Just go, General. I'll attend to this." Aubrey pressed a hand into de Béquignol's back and urged him down the hall, then followed the men as they walked toward the front exit, turning back to Ani with: "You. Stay."

When he was around the corner, Ani exhaled hard. *You. Stay.* Like she were some kind of dog. She forced more tears into her eyes, though she knew they wouldn't work on him, and thought of what she'd say when he returned.

Aubrey led the men to the door, ushered them out quickly, then went to the front parlor. He walked to his desk in the center of the room, murmured a prayer, and opened the top drawer. The pistol was still there. He crossed himself, let his breath out slowly, and walked back to Ani. When he returned to her, tears streamed down both of her cheeks. He sighed. "I'm not looking forward to that conversation with my father."

Her eyes went wide. "Duke de Collioure? You'll have to face him because of this? All because that vile man," she gestured to the spot where de Béquignol disappeared, "claimed I was spying?"

"And were you spying?"

Ani gasped. "You don't believe me? I got a book from th—"

"—the library, yes, yes. But were you listening in on the conversation?"

His eyes were so pleading. She knew what he wanted to hear. "No," she lied, "…my lord general."

"Only when the officers are around. Forgive me that I didn't clarify that distinction. I would never make you address me—"

"The duke is really coming here?" Ani said, anxiety and hot blood and eagerness all colliding into her at once.

"Good mercy, not if we're lucky." He crossed himself. "Follow me."

He led her back into the boardroom. The Brunswick Manifesto was in a ball on the table, and as Aubrey walked past it, Ani snatched the wad and slid it into her pocket, flattening it against her hip.

"Most of France's class differences are not so great as they are here," he said, half to himself, half to her. "The nobility outside these walls isn't unpopular with the local peasants they benefactor. I don't know how six-hundred thousand peasants in this city—nay, the twenty-five million people of France, in her entirety—will agree on anything without a figurehead."

"The monarchy is destroyed?"

Aubrey lowered his head. "Welcome to the New Republic of France," he mocked, "a 'government of the people.'" He laughed without mirth. "They think they can achieve a new national order overnight. They want to start a civil war when we are eight-hundred million francs in debt and can barely sustain ourselves when united." He lifted his palms outward. "But this is what happens when a man who cannot read or write or pay taxes gets the same say as the man who," and for this, he puffed out his chest and struck a thumb to it, "graduated Lycée Louis-le-Grand, then with flying colors from École d'application de l'artillerie and practiced law by twenty. They are right to be outraged, but you cannot overturn these things with outrage alone. A change must be gradual, sensible. Rage is blind. It turns in on itself. It eats its own kind."

"What have they done with the Constitution?"

"You care more about the Constitution than the king?"

"I just mean…" she stammered, then said sheepishly, "the king has never done anything for me, for women."

Aubrey nodded, exhaled through his nose. "Neither has the Constitution."

Ani couldn't argue with that. Few of the new rights pertained to her.

"When I do not return—"

"Not return?" Ani said. "Where are they sending you?"

"There is something I need to show you," he whispered, at once keenly aware of the openness of the room. He led her to an oil painting of the Crucifixion and lifted the painting from the wall. Behind it, he revealed the metal square of a lockbox bolted inside the wall, secured with an elaborate wrought-iron-and-steel alphabetical combination lock of seven rotating cams. "I've changed the combination," he still whispered. "No one knows it but me. And you. Watch carefully."

He moved each letter slowly, beginning with a C, then twisting to an A, then N, and Ani chuckled as he finished the rest of it: C-A-N-D-I-D-E. She gasped when he opened the door of the safe. Inside were bundles of money, bank notes, jewels, gold bricks, Louis d'ors, marks, and fine coins, far more than she had ever seen in all her life. The vault seemed to go back into the wall for a yard.

"If word should come to you that I've been defeated," he said, "get to this and take it and run from here as far as it will take you. I have other material wealth—investments, accounts, property—but they'll require my insignia." He raised the stamper ring on his finger. "No doubt they will be inaccessible or tracked at some point, taken as the Church's property has been taken." He turned back to the safe, closed the door, and erased the combination from the lock, holding it for a few extra seconds.

"Why would you give this to me?" she asked.

"I..." he said. A moment of silence passed between them. His body slouched, his fingers softening around the lock. "Just stay safe." He stepped away but couldn't look at Ani. "There will be more guards stationed around the palace, until they can no longer do so, and men will come at some point to move the garrison munitions—"

"Move the garrison?" she said.

"Yes. I fear it isn't so safe or secret anymore. Josephine will look after all your other cares as long as she can."

Ani snorted. "She'll care to poison me first."

"Try kindness on her," he dismissed. "You remind her of where she came from, and it's not a memory she relishes."

As if on cue, a knock sounded at the door, and Josephine's voice squeezed its way through the crack. "Sir, pardon, there's a receiver at the door who says you sent for him."

"Thank you, Mademoiselle Journeaux." He hung the picture back in place, adjusted it, stepped back, adjusted it again. Then he gathered some papers from the table, carried them to the desk in the corner, madly shook a jar of ink, and scrawled a message across a piece of parchment with a fountain pen.

Ani fixated on the process. "What's that letter?" she inquired when the marquis ran an ink blotter over the script and rolled several pages together into a tight square, slit an edge, and looped a piece of parchment through the slit—a security lock. His restlessness unsettled her.

"It's for the Duke of Brunswick, the king of Prussia, and the Austrian emperor. A warning not to release that manifesto." More to himself, he added, "And an outline of where our men are stationed so foreign forces don't just march right into us, God help them." He crossed himself.

She watched intently as he melted a stick of deep-brown mahogany wax over the curled edge of the letter and onto the security loop. With a balled fist, he pressed the raised insignia of the pewter ring on his right middle finger into the wax, flattening the center section against the desk. From his jacket pocket, he retrieved a shiny écu and extended both the letter and the coin to Ani.

"Would you kindly hand this to the messenger at the door?" he asked, rubbing the bridge of his nose to relieve tension. "Make no mention of its contents and be sure he gets the coin. Then go and get pretty because there is a surprise in the parlor upon your return."

"What surprise?"

"It wouldn't be a surprise if I told you, now, would it." He whisked his hands at her. "Go. Letter. Pretty. Parlor. In that order."

Ani opened the door to find Josephine still standing in the hall outside the boardroom. She gave the servant a polite curtsy, then hurried down the hallway toward the messenger at the front door, one thumb sliding back and forth over the wax seal of the letter, and the other hand gripping tightly about the shiny silver écu. As she neared the door, her fingers squeezed around the guts of the letter, ashamed to be holding it. The Girondins, now in power—the faction that Dr. Breauchard now followed—had passed laws that anyone corresponding with, joining with, or showing sympathies for foreign powers or the advancing foreign armies was to be tried for treason, a crime punishable by death. She breathed in. That was Aubrey. Treasonous Aubrey. Treasonous, *merciful* Aubrey—how did he keep forgiving her, trusting her, and looking the other way? He'd be put to death if anyone got hold of this. And why should she care about that? She sucked in air and stopped before the door and looked over her shoulder. The hall was empty. Impulsively, she tucked the letter down the front of her dress and opened the door to the messenger.

"Good day," she said, shakily at first, calming herself. "The letter. Has been ruined. Spilled upon by, uh…coffee."

"Coffee?" the boy replied slowly.

"Yes. Coffee," she also repeated slowly. "*Coffee*," and nodded until he nodded in return. "Here is a silver écu for your troubles." Her manner became controlled so as not to alarm any guards at the gates.

The boy lifted his hat from his head and bowed to her. "I'll return a hundred times to be sent away empty for a whole écu, mademoiselle."

"Tell no one you were sent away empty."

The boy nodded. He understood. "Coffee," he whispered.

Ani nodded and stood between the front steps and the foyer watching the boy leave, his clothes looking as hers once had. He glanced back, and she nodded again. Guilt struck her that she floated through this pretty palace, this false and falling world. She shook it out of her mind. It certainly couldn't be much longer—this war, this post. This couldn't go on forever, this suspension, this upheaval. As she was about to close the door to the world beyond her snowglobe, her eye caught a singular thing: a stem of angel's tears pushing its way through a patch of green near her feet. The flower had littered the rocky landscapes near Nord-Pas-de-Calais where she'd seen the creamy white and yellow fields many days, so briefly, outside the coalmine, but the *Narcissus triandus* didn't come this far south of the rocks. The memories brought on by that little yellow bud penetrated the glass shield and made her stop floating. She bent and picked the flower, staring into its droopy pools of yellow in a trance.

Then she remembered her surroundings, the guards at the gates, the second and third parts of her instructions, all the collapsible things that hindered on her ability to keep herself together. Her safety. She stood to her feet, raced up the steps, and closed the door abruptly, leaning her back against it and taking deep breaths. Uncomfortable breaths. Second-guessing breaths.

"Pretty. Parlor. In that order," she repeated, then went down the hall to her bedroom before there could be questions. Back in her room, she shoved the documents into her satchel, focused on the pretty, and within minutes, Josephine was at the door to help her achieve it. "Please come in," Ani said.

"Please?" Josephine opened the door slowly, suspicious. "Since when do I warrant a please?"

"Mademoiselle Journeaux, if I may—"

"Oh no, don't you start calling me that just because he does. He's touched with the idiocy of a male and can't help it." Josephine wagged a finger. "You have no excuse. You're bright as a lamplight and know how to start a good fire with it—could light the entire theater sector with one thought."

"The theater sector?"

"Don't you know that street?" Josephine said. "All those hundreds of lamps lighting the carriageways?" She waved her hand. "No matter—his lord the Duke de Collioure takes his mistress there every night, so it's fresh on my mind. Likes to tout that he doesn't fear this city."

"The duke?" Ani brightened like a lamplight. "Every night?"

Josephine nodded.

Ani softened and extended the plucked stem of angel's tears toward the servant. "You said you were from Pas-de-Calais. I remember seeing these all over the countryside there. This one was all alone in the front court, as if saying hello, and I thought, well…it is not so terrible to be reminded of where we come from." She broke off the stem of the narcissus just below the flower, leaving enough to tuck the sprig of two ivory cupped bells into Josephine's updo. Ani stepped back, smiled, and curtsied.

Josephine reached a hand up to pat the flower, and Ani walked out the door for the front parlor, as instructed. It was to be a full five minutes before Josephine followed.

Chapter Eight

A portrait of revolution

Every man has a right
to risk his own life
for the preservation of it.

—Jean-Jacques Rousseau

Now

Ani entered the front parlor. A large, blank canvas sat on an upright easel with an array of paints to one side of it and a round man to the other. Round was polite; he was set as only a nobleman could afford to be. His height mercifully balanced him out, but his birdlike face featured high, curved eyebrows, thin lips, and flared nostrils saddling an aquiline point. Ani gave him a pleasant nod. Aubrey stood dressed with his usual flair, in fine Parisian fashion, ruffled at the neck with a fully fastened high collar, and clean-shaven. His eyes sparkled like new coins.

"Allow me to introduce to you Monsieur Lethière, Paris' finest work of art himself," he said, taking Ani by the wrist and leading her toward the back of the parlor where he paraded her before the painter.

Her eyes widened. She bent into the practiced curtsy she'd learned at the palace. "How do you do, Monsieur Lethière? Please allow my admiration for your *Horace and Camille*."

The painter beamed and bowed.

The table by the window had been arranged with an upended teacup and saucer set before a chair, intended for her. Aubrey situated her in the seat, spread her dress in a peacock-tail about her ankles, fixed her hands around the cup and saucer, and positioned her face as if looking out the window beyond her shoulder. When his fingers left her cheek, she was acutely aware of the space, the abrupt absence of his skin—but for the first time, the touch didn't repulse her. She found herself closing her eyes and pretending he wasn't a nobleman.

"Open," he said.

And when she did, he bid her raise the teacup and hold it suspended in mid-drink. Arnaud brought in a steaming kettle, and Aubrey had him fill the teacup with a black tea. When Aubrey looked up, Ani was displayed in the parlor chair like a museum exhibit. His breath caught.

"I really have to hold actual tea?" she refuted.

"Yes. It's not merely art; it is for you to drink. I think the fine Monsieur Lethière can imagine it being there or not being there and will not be interrupted if you actually consume the tea."

The painter cleared his throat.

"It's imported black leaves from the Russian caravans," Aubrey said. "Dark and smoky. Expensive, so you should appreciate it accordingly."

"Mademoiselle," Lethière said, looking over his canvas, "you must sit more still than that."

"My apologies, sir," she said with a false smile, though inside she was thrilled at the prospect of a portrait. She'd once been painted as a child, but gendarmes had burned it in a pyre with her father's belongings when they'd confiscated his house in Le Marais. To be seated here—like this. Her heart fluttered. A portrait meant a person might be remembered.

"Nonsense. You shall do as you please," Aubrey said, despite the painter's grunt. "She'll do as she pleases, Lethière. Is she not a fantastic specimen? Be sure to catch that light across her hair."

The painter grunted again. "Yes, Marquis."

"And those eyes must be that truest blue of lightning," he nearly whispered it. "That's what will make the portrait."

"Of course, my lord."

"If I'm such a fantastic *specimen*," Ani said, "then why do you never take me out of these walls?"

Aubrey tilted his head. "You do know that would light some controversy, yay? High society won't know what to make of you if I were to escort you. They'd call you *my mistress*, a bevy of colorful misdirections. And more importantly for your reputation…they'd know that I no longer employ you for services, that you are simply…staying…with me. It might hurt you."

Ani's face reddened, but she remained unmoved.

A breath of air puffed out his cheeks. "Then where do you want to go?"

"The theater."

Aubrey groaned.

The painter let out a loud ahem and barked, "Mademoiselle, please! You must sit still."

"What captures your fancy at the theater?" Aubrey asked.

She figured *your father* would not be an answer that went over well. "*Figaro,*" she said instead.

"Beaumarchais? A bit subversive, no?"

Lethière shouted again, "Please, subject, I need you to remain still. Very, very still." He slammed his brush too hard into the paint, and the bristles bent. Splashes of blue landed on the floor.

"You've too easily won me," Aubrey said, pouring some whisky into his own tea. "*Figaro,* it is." As she repositioned, he strode toward Lethière's canvas. "I hope you are painting something equally as subversive for this unconventional woman." Aubrey peered over Lethière's shoulder.

"Sir!" the painter ejaculated.

"Paint the Bastille." Aubrey laughed.

"My lord!"

Aubrey glanced to the harrowed look that filled Ani's face at the mention of the Bastille. Her eyes emptied, and she blinked it away. Her father. In her childhood, when she'd seen him there. Slumped against the wall of the Bastille, dozens of other prisoners sharing his jammed cell, pushing in against him. Open sores on his mouth. Eyes vacant, gone. Blisters on his hands, clutching a tin cup. The buckets of feces at the bars adding to the nauseating stench of rot and decay.

"Relax, Lethière. I jest." The marquis waved his hand, unsettled by Ani's new, painful expression. "Just paint the window and the light and the…blasted teacup."

"I can't paint a damned thing if she can't sit still!" Lethière shouted, throwing his paintbrush down onto the palette.

The outburst broke the spell over Ani, and she pulled herself back, attempted a smile.

"Make it a little blurry," Aubrey said. "She'll learn it for the next portrait."

The painter turned to him. "It will not be I who paint the next portrait."

Before Lethière could be castigated, the marquis' military advisor, Yves Lenoir, appeared at the doorway of the front parlor, accompanied by the scowling General de Béquignol. Aubrey went rigid, the humor gone from him. Lenoir motioned to him and nodded, and the two unwelcome visitors headed down the hallway toward the boardroom.

Aubrey draped his arm around Lethière. "Would you rather I get my next portrait from Monsieur David, that old swollen-cheeked tumor face?" The two men exchanged glances. "Portraits are on their way out. Paint them while society can still afford them." Two pats on the older man's chest, and Aubrey left the room, leaving Ani to continue posing.

He walked toward his own funeral. He held his head high, but he knew what news the men brought. As he entered the boardroom, de Béquignol and Lenoir stared back at him with the hollow look of war, and the marquis closed the door behind him, waiting to hear the message they bore from the duke.

The strategists spent a half hour in the room with their discussions before the painter dismissed a stir-crazy Ani from her seat. Alarmed by the expressions of the men who'd fetched the marquis, she flexed her sore muscles and tiptoed down the hall to stand outside the boardroom. Placing her ear against the door, she listened for any key words that might stick out. The men's voices were muffled, but she gathered phrases and heightened undertones. At once, the door opened, and she lurched to the side, behind the bureau, not to be caught snooping again by de Béquignol. The men came into the hallway, headed toward the front doors of the palace.

"The area would be south of the Loire to the Lay," Lenoir said, "covering Marais, Bocage Vendéen, Collines Vendéennes, part of Maine-et-Loire west of the Layon, and a portion of Deux Sèvres west of the Thouet."

"That's a big area," Aubrey said.

The Vendée. Ani waited until they got past the podium that held the bronze statue of Saint Gertrude the Great, the patron saint of the West Indies—where, Ani imagined, the Beaumercys had slave plantations of sugarcane for this saint to watch over—and she darted behind the podium. The Vendée was at war. *Real war.* The men who went there did not return.

"Yes," Lenoir agreed. "You'll assist the Comte de la Rochejaquelein as he gathers some support to protect Cholet, Nantes, to march inward into our city for protection of the monarchy."

"It's treason according to the New Republic," de Béquignol said. "Should you find yourself outmanned, retreat rather than surrender. If they catch you…"

The marquis looked to Lenoir. "When does my father request I depart?"

"Tonight. After dark. Very quietlike."

Ani bumped into Saint Gertrude, and it teetered. The men looked back, but Ani tucked in her knees behind the podium, and the statue rocked in its place until it stilled. The men continued.

"What about that mistress you have here?" de Béquignol asked.

Aubrey stopped and snapped, "She is not a mistress."

"Well, you can nay marry her."

"I know," Aubrey said, then continued walking. "I know. Obviously."

Ani waited for the footsteps to fade away, then stood and stepped from behind the podium. She looked to Saint Gertrude and frowned at the statue, then simply stood there, immobile. Josephine came down the hallway toward her. One cursory look at Ani, and the servant pushed her through her bedroom door and situated her on the bed.

"What is it?" she asked. "You look dumb as an infant in a room of strangers. Did one of those generals say something to you? If he did… Oooh, that de Béquignol. You don't mind him. He's the dog to let starve on the chain." She crossed herself and cupped Ani's face. The flower still bobbed in Josephine's hair. "What did you hear?"

Ani shook her head and picked at old scars on her wrists and hands.

Josephine released her cheeks. "You are a stubborn thing." She sat onto the bed next to Ani. "Slide." She wiggled against her. "Slide, slide."

Ani laughed grudgingly. "I'm sliding." She made room for Josephine next to her.

"When I was young," Josephine said, folding her hands in her lap, "we discovered my papa had a second family in Valenciennes. I was an only child, and I didn't understand it, found it wonderful that I'd now have brothers and sisters." Josephine rubbed her hand across the quilt. "Mother packed the two of us into a carriage, and I thought, 'This is it! She's going to murder Papa!' but we pulled up to his manor, and she told me to get out. I was standing alone on the steps when her carriage drove away, and my astonished papa opened the front door." She brushed a strand of Ani's hair behind her ear. "That is where I come from. It seems like only a breath later I was brought here and received another new family." She scooched off the bed and cupped Ani's cheeks again. "I live for this household and all who are in it, and you are in it." She kissed Ani's forehead. "So, as long as I live in it, I'll not let de Béquignol harm you." She ran the back of her hand down Ani's cheek and turned toward the door.

"But don't you ever wonder," Ani said, "what would've happened if you'd stayed in that carriage?"

Josephine paused with her hand on the latch, turned slowly, looking at the floor. "Yes," she said. "But we can only face one direction at a time. I choose forward." She walked out but was careful not to slam the door behind her this time.

Ani's chest seized, and she grabbed hold of it, bunched the cloth of her dress, tugged at the lace. There had never been another way. But. *The Vendée.* She slid off the bed and paced from wall to wall, a sour sensation beneath her tongue as if she might vomit. It was treason to support the divine right. Tithes were made illegal; prayer in public was punishable; clergy were arrested. To support the monarchy publicly now, with the Girondins in control, was—suicide. Death. The Vendée would bring that death to Paris. Right here. The thing her own father had once fought for was coming right to Paris' door, and Aubrey would die to stop it. This clash of two worlds met right across her breastbone. Her knees weakened, and she fell back down on the bed. She wasn't supposed to care if he died. He was one of them, and she wasn't supposed to care. Was she? Did she?

She fretted for hours into the night, skipping dinner, remaining alone in her room that closed in around her like a storm. When the darkness came, she lit no candles. Not tonight. Tonight she'd send no missives to Dr. Breauchard, no messages to the orphans and men who awaited her replies. Aubrey wouldn't be able to return to Paris if they caught him. She sat quiet on the edge of her bed nearly half the night, until she heard his footsteps lightly graze the hallway. She slid from her bed and flung open the door.

"You're going now," she spoke in the hallway behind him, louder than she'd intended.

He turned. "I didn't mean to wake you." His blue-and-white uniform shown in the dim light of the hall, exquisite gold embroidery down the lapel and sitting high on his shoulders. A tricorne sat properly upon his forehead, and over one breast was the patch of the Sacred Heart. A decorated baldric crossed his chest and held his saber. Two pistols hugged his waist, tucked into a white sash knotted to one side with a red cord. Riding boots touched above his kneecaps. He was dressed to kill and dressed to die. "I must go quickly." He managed a pained smile.

"You were not even going to tell me?"

He didn't reply but gazed at her steadily.

"And if you don't return?"

He stepped toward her, setting each boot heel down with purpose.

When finally he stood before her, he leaned in close and whispered, "*Candide.*" As he righted himself, he took one deep look at her, into her eyes. Then he walked away, to the Vendée, to the father of all wars.

PART II

Now and

CHAPTER NINE

PHILIPPE ET GEORGETTE

If this be treason,
make the most of it.

—Patrick Henry

The first day of the stagnant palace, the rains came. It pounded so heavy against the orchard trees that Ani heard the hundreds of premature fruits dropping to the ground. There was no other sound but the endless thudding, all remaining bodies of the household avoiding collision with another, a funereal pall unspoken but walking among them as if it had been invited to stay. The second day, Ani sat in a washbasin until the water turned so cold she could finally feel something worse than anomalous silence, and by the end of the third day, she knew for certain he was in the Vendée, knew the horses would have made it, the marching columns behind, pacing into the fourth day, the fifth. She visualized his defeat, recovering some bridge, taking a high ground, imagined the files footslogging toward him.

When the summer heat returned, she woke next to Josephine pulling the covers over the edge of the bed, and the eighth day, Ani absorbed the unsympathetic energy of rue Neuve des Petits Champs—Béatrice in one of Josephine's hand-me-down dresses, and Ani in her father's old clothes, her fingers twirling the necklace cord of that brown pouch Dr. Breauchard had given her. Some parts of the city had emptied out; in others, riots reigned, and authority changed hands by the hour.

But that night, Ani was back in the safety of his walls, where her mission kept her until the second half of the task was completed, behind gates locked by guards, her eyes wide to the sounds of a horseshoe bat somewhere in the boudoir, the scratching of tree branches against stone walls. On the tenth day, she entered his room and drank his expensive barrel-aged whisky and sat on his bed with his tin of tobacco snuff and counted the golden points on his ceiling and rifled through his drawers, though there was little heart in it. He smelled like this from

time to time, this mustiness, the sweaty pores of alcohol and the lush
winter mint of cologne to cover it up.

Caddy corner at rue Sainte-Anne, a man was being beaten for his
shoe buckles, and around the curve of rue Neuve Saint-Augustin, the
wig of an aristocrat swung from a rope, only a disembodied tuft of
horsehair. Ani backed from it slowly, her gut tight, then she turned again
toward Palais d'honneur. At the gates stood new guards who didn't know
her and refused to admit her until Josephine instructed them to do so.
That was the twelfth day, and Ani could no longer come and go for the
constancy of new guards. She had to stay. Or go. The emptiness of both
worlds filled her with guttering absence, and she lost count of the days.
She'd fulfilled the mission of locating the garrison, though now she felt
compelled to know when someone came for it, so she could make sure
it ended up in the right hands. Was someone really coming to move the
munitions, and if so, to whence? But above all, *where was the goddamn duke?*
He should have made an appearance by now, and she wouldn't leave until
she'd seen him. What would she do when the duke came here? When
she had to face him alone? The next day the rains came again, and the
next day they stopped, and the day after that, the carriageway rattled to
life, gravel spinning against gravel with the purpose of speed. Ani's pulse
skipped. Was it finally the duke? Would she face him at last?

In unison, Ani and Josephine and Arnaud, Valéry-Marie and Étienne, and even Aimé, the wheezing cheesemaker only there for monthly
inventory, rushed to the foyer for the returning officers. Aimé removed
his hat. Josephine took hold of her dress, in preparation for a curtsy.
But the door opened slowly and without ceremony, and Barons Bellon and Corbière stepped silently inside, leaving the door cracked wide
enough to see four crude coffins stacked on the top of the carriage. A
sling held one of Bellon's arms in place. Josephine gasped and dropped
her skirt midcurtsy. Hairs rose on Ani's neck, and she shivered. As the
door closed on the view of the coffins, the barons removed their hats
and looked at the sudden solemn faces.

"We don't know," Corbière said preemptively and shrugged. "Everyone in the Bocage is either dead or captured, and more are coming from
the city. He had to ford the Loire, and his boys were cowards."

"Rot-belly cowards," Bellon seconded, and crossed himself.

"There were many retreats, many washed downstream." Corbière
shrugged again sadly and steadied his one working eye on them. "We
do not know."

Ani stepped backward, and Josephine moved to catch her, but Ani pushed her hand away, shook her head, grasped her chest that seemed to stop midbreath.

"But he's not in those coffins?" Valéry said, hopeful, pointing toward the door.

Bellon said no, and Ani put her hand to the wall to steady herself and backed down the hallway, her heart beating so fast her fingers tingled, her lungs seizing. It was better this way, she repeated, better if he didn't come home, better if she didn't think of this as home, better if she remembered who she was. Better if she *knew* who she was, *why* she was still here. *Better if.* Would it have been better if he'd just been in a coffin, a body to witness, cloth to touch? Something to mourn or hate or destroy or curse or burn or know too intimately? Something to make this suspension easier. *Better if.*

She turned for her bedroom and ran to it, then stopped, and went to the boardroom. She drew back the velvet curtain and stared at the Crucifixion, but she couldn't touch it, couldn't move it. Let them use the gold for his burial. What would come of it for her? She'd be beaten for her shoe buckles, swung from a rope by a wig. But nor could she look away from it. *Washed downstream*, she thought, a horse taken from under him, broken legs beneath the fallen beast and dragged to a ditch to die with his own kind, patches of the Sacred Heart ripped from royal jackets for rebel souvenirs. She held her breath. But that was what was supposed to happen, how the revolution was supposed to go. The insurrection was supposed to win. Now, *now*, she would come face to face with the duke. He'd have to come. To deal with the munitions, to oversee a movement of men and armory. Maybe to deal with her. To silence what she knew, to humiliate her for the rumors of a wayward son in the circles of society that still somehow swirled among all this chaos. Men still dined in parlors. Women still danced in heady gowns at lavish balls that seemed destined from another time. The world did not know itself, what spun around it, each in feeble snowglobes, paltry remnants of fading divides, worlds among worlds, and she a part of none of them, floating somewhere in between.

Each new day, she stood at the window that overlooked Paris. Fires burned. Smoke billowed from old buildings. She endured the solitude to ensure baskets of fresh cheese and figs made their way to Saint-Marcel, to have food, shelter, to watch the movement of the munitions, to get missives to Dr. Breauchard—waiting for word of what to do, waiting for the word from him that would expel her from this endless partner-less dance, send her back where she belonged. But there kept being tomorrow and tomorrow and another tomorrow. One foot in front of the other, choosing forward. By the end of another week, when the heat of a new August made the window a disagreeable perch, the elaborate carriage bearing the Beaumercy crest rolled up the carriageway, and she knew the duke had come.

The horse harnesses jingled. Men spoke boisterously. The front door burst open, and Ani heard it crash into the wall, and then Josephine squealed into peals of laughter. Ani left the room and walked cautiously down the hallway, and there was a sound her body knew before her mind did. Heat and ice shot through her, each sensation fighting to claim her. It wasn't the duke. Aubrey stood in the hallway, laughing, bedraggled and otherworldly, as if he'd been washed *up*stream instead of down. He sported an unkempt full beard, shaggy hair. His half-un-buttoned collar had no cravat or ruffle.

"So much for 'button, cuff, ruffle, stuff,' huh," Ani said, the sound of her voice so suddenly alien to her. She took a painful deep breath to calm her fidgeting.

"I clean up well." The smile on his face looked like it was stuck there. He smelled like horse lather and gunpowder, and was wearing the same clothes he'd been in for weeks. He stripped off his jacket in the middle of the hallway and discarded it in a pile on the floor, disregarding Jose-phine's audible shock as she swooped it up and disappeared around the corner, her arms full of items he'd dumped into them. Stopping inches from Ani, Aubrey sniffed himself and crinkled his nose, then retrieved from the pocket of his stock shirt two printed paper stubs and raised them in the air. "I believe we have an assignation."

"Tonight?" she said.

"Tomorrow." He stripped off his filthy cravat and flung it. "Tonight, I pass out." He smiled, looked at her longingly, water to a thirsting man, and walked past her toward his room as if his bones were too heavy for this world.

ꜱ

The next day, after an afternoon in the library, she turned the latch to her room, and the scent of flowers overcame her. A vase of creamy narcissus sat on the bedstand. Two candles lit either side of the bed. An elegant square-scooped dress in royal blue lay atop the bedspread with a pairing of a black art-glass chandelier neckpiece and a matching ti-ara-style, beaded-glass hair pick that would sit perched upon one's head like a layered cake. Laid at the very tip of the dress' Camelot sleeve—as if the phantom body inside the dress were holding it extended in out-stretched phantom hand—was a book: *The Decline and Fall of the Roman Empire*. Ani smiled. His olive branch.

"That certainly wasn't my idea," Josephine said behind Ani and crossed herself, holding her thumb to her lips.

Ani reached for the dress and the jewels sprawled out before her. What did anything else matter? Aubrey was alive, and Ani was going to the theater. She would come face to face with Aubrey's father. Anger burned inside her, but so did a thrill—what would she do when she finally met the duke?

After her bath, she sat at the boudoir's ornate dressing table, feeling like she were tucked in a hidden cave. Her corset pulled tight around her middle and gave her statuesque posture that she studied in the mirror until the faintest rap came at the boudoir entryway. Ani looked at the reflection over her shoulder and smiled.

"I've missed you like this," Josephine whispered. "Misery is never a good look for anyone." She fastened the buttons at the base of Ani's neck, then kissed the top of her head and lifted the black chandelier necklace to Ani's throat, clasping it and arranging its beads evenly down the front. "You know this hair won't do."

Josephine removed the single clip to unravel Ani's tight, simple bun. She opened the drawer of the dressing table to several dozen hair combs. Beginning at Ani's forehead, Josephine lifted sections of hair and ratted them into strands that stood on their own, then folded the ratted poof under and up, securing it with a comb into a large beehive bouffant on the front of Ani's head. Taking the next portion of hair, the servant did the same in an even higher bouffant, then higher and higher with the combs to follow, until Ani resembled Marie Antoinette herself. Josephine pulled a couple strands out of the sides of the bouf-fant and a long tailpiece down the back, offcentered to fall over Ani's shoulder. The servant licked her fingertips and ran her wetted fingers down each fiber, then wound each of the errant strands around tiny pins so tight that Ani winced.

"Beauty comes with a pinch of suffering," Josephine said. She placed the decorative comb of jewels and feathers to the left of center in Ani's bouffant. "There. Though you'll need more than this to contend with the noblesse. When they speak, their own voice is the only music they hear, even at an opera." She leaned in. "So, you must sing louder." With this, she pulled the pins out of Ani's tight curls, and the spirals bounced at her ears and neckline. Josephine kissed her head one last time. "Sing," she whispered before quitting the room.

Ani looked at herself in the mirror, then walked down the hallway toward the door, to find Aubrey awaiting her on the front steps of the palace. He had shaved and had buttoned his collar, and now rearranged a ruffle on a double-breasted waistcoat that matched the hue of her dress. His hair was washed and curled at the temples, and she smelled him and the smell was now familiar and bridled and kicked into her ribs.

Before she stepped to his side, she stopped to consider what tonight meant, the weight of it—that she was stepping out in the midst of chaos on the arm of a nobleman she tried violently to abhor. She'd be called his mistress. He might think she was positioning *to be* his mistress, and what would come after that? But if she could get up close to the duke, she wouldn't have to worry about what came after—there'd be no after.

A horsedrawn Berlin carriage waited in the roundabout, attended by a footman and a chauffeur. Decorative drapery swathed it, and it was equipped with illuminating oil lamps. The Swiss Guard surrounding the wrought-iron gates stood erect as pillars and applauded as she descended the stairs. She couldn't extinguish her blush as she curtsied to them. Aubrey led her to the carriage, lending a hand to lift her up, and she finally breathed when they were well out of the carriageway and down a quiet street.

Aubrey lifted his pocketwatch, read it.

"Won't we be late?" Ani asked.

"One never arrives early for an opera," he said. "I thought you'd read Chevalier de Non?"

"But will the play be already started?"

"Perhaps," he said indifferently. "Does it matter?"

"Yes! I want to see it."

"Then, my dear, you have entirely missed the point of an opera." He smiled.

The carriage finally turned onto the rue du Théâtre-Français, and Ani could see the expansive green of the Jardin du Luxembourg across the way, smell a patch of clean air from the rows of fruits and flowers as she arrived in a slow line of emptying coaches outside the Théâtre de l'Odéon. There shone all the hundreds of lamplights that Josephine had mentioned, lighting the streets, the carriageways, the entries to each theater as if from a separate ethereal world. Ani had never set foot on this upscale street before, its elegance stunning her quiet. Aubrey righted her, sturdy as a baluster, when she stepped from the carriage. He lifted his chin, tucked one arm across his lower back, and transformed. No matter how much he pretended otherwise, this was his world—and he, the center of it.

When they entered the theater's foyer with its high ceilings and oval curvature, Ani's attention went to the flying buttresses, the cathedral arches, that absolute romanesque quality of every pillar and stair and face staring back at her. The onlookers hushed, then hummed. The room ceased its dazzling spin, and whispers buzzed around it in currents.

"Pay them no mind," he said out the corner of his mouth like a ventriloquist, maintaining a stiff smile. "They will make a feast out of you, the vultures."

But she didn't care what they thought—she was looking for someone. "They all know you." She watched their stony, bored faces animate as Aubrey entered.

"Of course. Half of them are indebted to my father; a third of the other half manage my countships; and of the remaining two thirds, a third of them are kingsmen or royalist National Guard, a third of them just want to be important, and a third of them actually are."

"I don't mean to question that rithmetic, but there were a lot of thirds."

"I thought I'd hired you as my figurer." He grinned, and several well-dressed men approached Ani and him in a whirlwind of bows and curtsies and cheek kissing. The first to chat was tall and slender and analyzed Ani openly as if she were a specimen under glass.

"Monsieur Turcotte," Aubrey addressed with false politeness. "May I introduce to you—"

"Antonine Berthiaume, Comtesse de Foix," Ani spoke for herself, extending her hand and curtsying perfectly. "Pleasure to meet you, monsieur."

"Foix!" Turcotte gushed with infatuation. "Mademoiselle, the pleasure is entirely mine own. Your castle is the grandest ever was."

"Oh yes, isn't it exquisite, if I'm allowed to gloat?" Ani tried to pull her fingers away. "Am I allowed to gloat?" she said playfully to Aubrey, whose face had gone pale. If the name got around to the Duke de

Collioure, then Ani wouldn't have to go to him—he'd find her. She didn't know what the duke looked like outside of illustrations and portraits, but she had a feeling she'd know him when she saw him, that she'd recognize the hatred heating through her all the way to her toes.

Aubrey intervened, prying Ani's hand from the enamored Turcotte's, and turning her from the man. "Would you excuse us for a moment?" The marquis faced Ani. "Comtesse de Foix? Really? How can I compete with that castle?"

She smirked. "Is the worth of a man judged by the size of his… castle?"

"That's not too far from the mark. That man is a—"

Monsieur Turcotte tapped Ani on the shoulder and gestured to two female guests who accompanied him. Upscale tramps, emblazoned in jewels and caked makeup and too heavily powdered. Each woman took an exceedingly long curtsy when addressed.

While the ladies curtsied, Turcotte's unoccupied hand pulled the marquis from the circle of women. Turcotte whispered slyly, "While the ladies are talking, I'll inquire about her availability as a houseguest?" Turcotte winked as he said the word. "I pay handsomely and would make it worth your while. I never return a woman bruised, and you're of course welcome to watch or participate. I have new paddles."

Aubrey resisted the urge to grab Turcotte by the collar and throw him bodily against the closest pillar. "Perhaps I'll be your guest instead, Bastien," he said calmly, looking the libertine in the eye and leaning in. "I have new bayonets." Stepping away from a vexed Turcotte, Aubrey took hold of Ani's arm and pinched it, whisking her from the circle of libertines. "Don't bat those false lashes at sadists."

"Sadists!" Ani laughed in dismissal. "You should have warned me how much fun this would be. They all think they know me by name."

"Yes. They'll say anything to impress. Better hope you don't come across anyone who knows the real Comtesse de Foix, or your jig is up, as they say."

It was surprisingly fun, but Ani was also irritated at how hard it was to walk through the throngs of the noblesse, how hard to see over their heads as they just stood there like grazing sheep, blocking her view.

A nobleman hailed the marquis from across the room and moved through the herd of sheep like a hungry wolf. "Collioure," the handsome nobleman spoke excitedly, ignoring the nondescript, upright woman dragged in his wake. "How dare you not introduce me to this ravishing woman."

"This is Antonine Berthiaume, Comtesse de Foix," Aubrey said, pressing Ani's outstretched hand to her side before the nobleman could kiss it.

Ani said, "I hear this opera is so wickedly subversive that it's almost fashionable."

The plain woman inhaled sharply, but the nobleman shot a you-dog look at Aubrey and wetted his lips with his tongue. The woman sank into a shell and placed a hand over her heart.

Aubrey bowed politely. "Monsieur d'Evreux did not warn you of that, madame?" Aubrey looked at the nobleman. "Shame on him." He skirted Ani around them and spoke to her out the side of his mouth. "You're lighting gunpowder in a room of terrified Papists who have no idea that operas have meanings at all, let alone hidden ones." He crossed himself.

She scanned the room for the duke but saw no one who resembled Aubrey in the slightest. No one with that prominent, pointed Beaumercy nose. "I hear... Is... They say your father comes to the theater every night."

"Oh, do *they* say that...or does Josephine say that?" He smiled, but he clearly didn't want to talk about his father any more than he wanted to talk about the horrors he must have witnessed in the Vendée—he hadn't said a word on the subject all evening.

"Is your father here tonight?"

"Here?" Aubrey laughed. "Certainly not. He's no doubt at a bawdy hurly-burly down the road with his mistress."

Ani hid the disappointment. "And you're here with your mistress."

Aubrey's face blanked.

"Like father, like son," she said, though she managed to keep it light.

He recovered himself from her slight. "You may recall who asked to come here. I didn't realize it was in hopes of a family reunion."

She looked across the room toward a bar covered with velvet drapery and sporting a tender dressed as finely as the noblesse he served. "Are they serving wine over there?"

"Yes, they are." He led her to the bar and reached into his pocket for his folded notes. "I don't suppose you know what you want, mistress of mine," he teased and stepped to the bar to order for her.

She cocked a brow and answered, "Château Lafite."

Both the bartender and Aubrey snapped their heads to her. "Sir," the bartender cautioned, afraid there might be some chance the marquis didn't know what he was getting himself into. "That is the most expensive bottle we carry. Perhaps the most expensive anyone carries."

"I'm quite aware." Aubrey pulled more notes out of his pocket and laid them down. "Rouge. Not younger than ten, not older than twenty. Two glasses." The marquis held up two fingers.

Ani said, "Might I pop the cork?"

The bartender took offense. "Certainly not, m'lady. This is Château Lafite 1776."

"My, 1776!" Ani said. "It's wine of the Colonial Revolution!"

The bartender was offended again, and Aubrey made a quieting motion toward Ani. "Have you ever removed a cork?" the marquis asked.

"No. That's why I'd like to do it."

"May she pop the cork, monsieur?" Aubrey laid another note on the bar. The bartender growled and slid the whalebone corkscrew and the wine across the bar toward Ani.

She held the neck of the bottle, and Aubrey assisted as she twisted the helix and pulled against the cork. As it popped, she said, "Liberty or death!"

Aubrey put his hand to his forehead and laughed into the crook of his elbow against the bar. His face had turned the color of the wine.

Ani slid the bottle back to the bartender. "Thank you, monsieur. That was enjoyable." She shrugged to the crowd of astonished onlookers. "Not too many Patrick Henry followers in the room, eh?"

Aubrey passed her wine glass down the bar and raised his filled stemware to hers in a salute. He whispered, "Let them have death, then," tinking the lip of her bowl with a clink, then they both took small sips.

A voice came from behind them, and Aubrey straightened. "Well, well, Marquis de Collioure." He didn't turn to face the graceful, lavishly dressed woman who called his name. "Is *this* why you've not returned my correspondence?" the woman said, looking Ani up and down with feigned interest. She flicked her hand at Ani.

"Baroness Annette Butte," Aubrey acknowledged in introduction to Ani. "This is—"

"Comtesse de Foix," Ani said but didn't curtsy. "Pleased to make your acquaintance."

"I'm sure it is your pleasure," the baroness said solecistically. A smile oozed from her mouth. "I'm sure he's told you that he and I are—"

"Would you look at that," Ani said. "What lovely flowers." She walked away from the bar and Baroness Butte, wine glass in hand, to feign looking at flower arrangements propped upon an arched altar near the entrance doors of the theater, but really to regroup, to think through a new plan now that this one had folded. She might as well simply enjoy a night at the theater if the duke wasn't here.

"Marquis, come now. The Comtesse de Foix?" the baroness said. "Foix has had no provencial-states for over two years and has joined with Couserans."

"I know this," Aubrey said, "but most of the people here do not. She's playing, so I'll let her play." He watched Ani as she touched gold trim on the decorations and listened to the conversations of important noblemen.

"Is she a patrician?"

"No. Not even close."

"Has she proper lineage?"

"I'm still figuring that out."

Baroness Butte waved dismissively in the direction of Ani's amorous affections with neoclassical decorations. "Does she support the decisions of the king?"

"Oh, come, we all know that the king doesn't actually make any decisions. He's a handful of oiled ivory marbles that we're trying to hold in one hand, while packing our bags with the other."

"This may all amuse you, but you are a man spoken for. The wealth and property, the prosperity that would come from the blessed union of our two houses. Your father—"

"Do not mention my father when talking about 'blessed union,' Anne. Makes me limp as a fish."

Baroness Butte recoiled, and Ani made her way back across the room toward the two conversers, perturbed that the baroness was still there.

"Comtesse," the baroness addressed Ani as she approached, "I was inquiring with the marquis as to when you were going to inform us of the prospect of your becoming the next marquise?" The baroness beamed with a self-satisfied gaucherie.

Aubrey whipped toward her and opened his mouth to rebuke, but Ani reached out her hand to him. "My lord general," she said, and he took her hand without hesitation. "They're playing the clavichord in the ballroom. Would you care to waltz?"

"My pleasure, m'lady." He tucked Ani's hand around his elbow and led her through the partition between the social hall and the enormous ballroom where guests gathered before the opera began, the social aspect of which was enjoyed more than the actual performance.

"It is a clavichord, right?" Ani asked discreetly.

"It is." He spared only one glance back toward the pouting baroness, and the glance was one of victory.

A staunch, erect man with an expressionless face stopped the couple at the threshold to the ballroom. "How may I announce you, your grace?"

"No announcement. Thank you, monsieur." Aubrey didn't wait in the entranceway for the man's astonished eyebrows to curtail themselves back to expressionless.

"I'm delighted you know how to waltz," Ani said, when Aubrey escorted her onto the floor, "because I haven't the faintest."

"Oh, dear God," he cursed through tight lips, then crossed himself. "Can you at least follow my lead?"

"Most likely no."

He sighed through his nose. "I'll instruct as we go," he said, smiling that smile he always smiled when he wanted the world to believe all was as it should be. He executed the movements as he instructed. "I bow; you curtsy. Give me your right hand; hold it high. Don't look at me; look over my shoulder." He took her right hand in his left, then reversed his direction, looking over her shoulder. "Your left hand on my epaulet, left elbow on mine; keep it high. Don't look at me." He stuck his right foot between her legs unexpectedly, and she chirruped as he wiggled her thighs apart with his kneecap. "Keep your legs shoulder-width apart. Don't look at your feet. I step in between your legs. Keep a count of three, two, three, one, two, three. Move in a box, but move with the box as the box moves. I step to you, two, three. To my right, your left, three."

His body pressing into her made her tense, taut as a bow string, but with her face that close to his neck, she could smell him again, and she hated how she knew his scent. French shave soap and chalky powder and skin oil made with clovers. Gone were the odors of the Vendée and the death that seemed so far away, where they moved in this box. She lost count. She looked down at her faint reflection in his shiny leather shoes and let him whisk her back to position.

"Loosen up," he whispered. "Step toward me. Don't look at your feet. Over my shoulder. Step, then my left, your right, two, three. Then we move toward you, two, three. Don't look at your feet; just feel my thigh leading you. Don't look at my thigh. Don't look at me. Over my shoulder. Stay with me, right against me." He pulled her into him so close that she couldn't breathe without heaving her chest into his. "Good enough, two, three. If you can breathe, you're not doing it right. Press against me like I don't have the plague."

"I'm not convinced that you don't," she said breathlessly.

"Two, three; don't lose count. Don't count aloud; it makes you speed up. Don't look at your feet." He tilted her chin with an imperceptible lift of his shoulder and corrected her posture with a tight grip on her shoulder blade.

"Baroness Butte," Ani said, eying her at the edge of the ballroom. "She's trying to dance with you."

"She's trying to marry me," he said. "I can still see your lips counting; don't count aloud. My father and her father have it all arranged for me. Look over my shoulder, not at me."

He lowered his hand from her shoulder blade to the small of her back and pressed her torso into him. She felt that any minute the iron-maiden cabinet would completely close around her, and he'd stick torture spikes into her.

"We are on three," she said, looking at her feet. "I think you lost count that time."

"I most certainly did not. I could do this in my sleep. Don't look in my eyes. Over my shoulder."

"You were looking in my eyes."

"Certainly not," he said. "Ready for your next test? Song and composer."

He spun her, and her eyes landed again and again on Baroness Butte who had moved farther into the ballroom to watch them with contempt.

"Do you realize the baroness has been watching us this while?" Ani asked.

"Yes. She wants to see you fall." He twirled her in the opposite direction, so she didn't have to face the woman. "Better? This is a medley from last year's opera, *Philippe et Georgette*, by Nicolas d'Alayrac. All beautiful love songs by a noble Frenchman."

"The baroness has wealth, beauty, breeding. I'm sure she knows this song's composer. So why don't you marry her?"

He allowed a pause. "I believe that I would like to marry you instead."

Ani breathed in sharply, and he gripped her tighter so she couldn't pull away. The sudden rush of air and anxiety stopped her midbreath, and she choked and coughed from the bottom of her lungs. The two came to a standstill in the middle of the dance floor as swiftly as those around them. She clutched her throat, her chest, and heaved such guttural coughs that she thought she might spit up more blood. The dancers stared in fascination. Even the violinist ceased his bowing to gawk at her. The ballroom echoed with whispers and the fit of coughs.

Aubrey waited patiently until she righted herself, and he extended his arm to her. When she'd caught some breath, she took his arm, and they walked from the dance floor as if it had never happened. They rounded the corner of the social hall and entered a private hallway where several noblemen were wistfully cooing to would-be noblewomen in the dim lighting. Pulling from his inside pocket her inhaler and powder, he held it to her mouth and inserted a pinch of her medication, ignoring her expression of surprise. He took calming, deep breaths in hopes of her emulation and shielded her from the prying eyes of the curious onlookers.

By the time the indecent noblemen had cleared the hallway, Ani had regained her breath, though she'd lost her false composure in the ballroom. "I'm sorry about that," she muttered.

"Yes," he sighed. "It was not quite the reaction I had envisioned."

"I'm going to pretend you didn't say it."

"Are you?" He groaned. "Well." He looked down at his hands, absently holding the inhaler he'd remembered that she'd forgotten. "Think on it. We could both do worse than one another."

A muted clarion trumpeted throughout the theater, indicating that the opera was beginning. Baroness Butte appeared at the end of the narrow hallway, clutching the arm of a nobleman from the ballroom. She glowered at Ani. Ani stiffened and righted herself, stepped away from the wall, and set an arm on Aubrey's.

"I simply love d'Alayrac's *Philippe et Georgette*, my lord general, don't you?" Ani laughed loud enough to be heard, while quietly clearing a residual cough. "It steals the very breath from me."

Aubrey looked to the baroness at the end of the hallway and back to Ani. "It happens to be my favorite," he said, entwining his arm with hers and strutting past the baroness and toward the auditorium doors.

Ani raised an arm theatrically, her head still whirling. "Beautiful love songs by a noble Frenchman, don't you think, my dearest lord general?"

CHAPTER TEN

REVOLUTIONARY COFFEE

*Why has government
been instituted at all?
Because the passions of men
will not conform to the
dictates of reason and justice,
without constraint.*

—Alexander Hamilton

Aubrey woke suddenly in the false dawn, but he wasn't sure if it were from a sound or a premonition. His nightshirt was sweat-through, but from the wine or sweltering heat or some kind of nightmare, he didn't know. Quiet rustling came from the hall, he heard it now, and he drew the pistol from beneath his pillow, stood in his bare feet, and went to the door. He opened the latch quietly, stepped into the black hall.

Light came from beneath Ani's bedroom door, and along the edge where it was cracked and stuffed with something soft. Some fabric. Aubrey walked closer to it, his gun drawn. It was a man's shirt, and even in the dimness, he could see that the collar of it was coated in dried blood. He put a hand to her door and pressed it enough to see the flickering lamp on the sill, the windows drawn inward, twine rolled out the casement. Through slivers of the boudoir, he saw Ani, putting items into her satchel. She wore loose men's trousers and an overly long men's shirt. On her feet she still wore her floral silk brocade shoes, but she left her pantlegs long enough to cover them. She secured the court lilies and cross pendant beneath the top buttons of her shirt and twisted her hair around her fingers into a knot that she covered with a dirty peddler's cap.

Aubrey watched for a moment, then closed the door on the muffling shirt and went down the hall, around the corner toward the servants' rooms. He couldn't risk the sound of knocking, so he softly entered Arnaud's and Valéry-Marie's quarters and lit a lamp.

Valéry woke instantly, and his eyes darted to Aubrey's gun. "Sir, what is it?"

Aubrey shushed him and whispered, "I need your clothes."

"My clothes, sir?" Valéry said sleepily. "You want clothes at gunpoint?"

Aubrey set the pistol on the dresser.

Arnaud stirred and woke. "My lord?"

"Clothing," Aubrey said. "I need you to dress me pedestrian."

"Sir," Arnaud said, "you could never look pedestrian. Even your nightgown has gold leafing on it."

"It's not the time for flattery," Aubrey said. "Just make it work."

Valéry stood and rifled through his clothespress for an old blouse. He sniffed it and gurned.

Aubrey saw his disgust and said, "That one's perfect." Valéry protested, but Aubrey put it on, left it partially untucked, and was fastening the clasps of the cuffs.

"Oh no, my lord, you must not clap fetters."

"Fetters?"

"Cuffs," Valéry corrected. "Working men leave them loose."

Arnaud grunted, slipped by the men, and walked into the hallway.

"And you can't wear your halflings, so try these on." Valéry handed him a pair of full-legged fallfronts.

"*Halflings?*" Aubrey said. "Why does everyone say that? It is a uniform. Is that what you think of my uniform?" He put on the fallfronts.

"Your worst waistcoat, at most. The one you're embarrassed you own."

"I don't own one of those."

Valéry yawned and pulled yesterday's waistcoat out of the laundry basket, checked that it only had one row of buttons down the front, and handed it to the marquis, along with some dirty stockings. "No heavy or formal overcoat, certainly nothing military. Don't shave off that morning face. Don't curl your hair or pull it back." He tousled Aubrey's shoulder-length hair. "Leave it down and absolutely no powder. Don't rouge your cheeks. No moles, no lips, no brows. No white cockade. Don't polish your shoes."

Aubrey crossed himself and looked down the front of him. "Shall I stuff?"

The servant stifled his laugh. "I would advise against it, my lord."

Aubrey's legs felt loose with nothing holding up the stockings. "So…
I'm done, then? There are no ruffles?"

Valéry shook his head, and Arnaud came back around the corner
with a tray brimming with creamy pudding, jars of preserves, and ham
omelettes slathered in pheasant gravy. "Your breakfast, my lord."

"Oh, Arnaud, you're too good to me," Aubrey said, "but I haven't
time for that. Enjoy it yourselves, gents."

"You'll at least need this," Arnaud said, holding out Aubrey's flask.

"Now *that*, I'll make time for." Aubrey uncapped the flask and took a
swig, then slid it into his pocket along with the pistol, kissed them both
on the cheeks, and slipped back down the hall in his baggy stockings.
He sneaked a quick polish of his simplest shoe buckles, filled his pock
ets with coins, then couldn't stop fussing with his loose hair or fiddling
with his unfastened buttons. He craved a cravat. He cursed the nearly
tropical heat that encircled him, his body already sweating, and when
he crept back to Ani's room, the lamp was out. The door was closed
and locked from the inside, the male shirt gone. He listened, but he
knew she wasn't in there. The French panes squeaked quietly in their
casement, an indication that the sashes weren't locked—she'd gone out
the window.

Aubrey ran down the hallway to the front door and barreled out
of it. The guards swung their guns toward him, then lowered them
immediately.

"Where is she?" Aubrey said. "The girl, where'd she go?"

The guards murmured that they hadn't seen anything.

Aubrey crossed himself, and whispered, "The orchard." He turned
for the orchard, listening for sounds unmeshing with the night, seek-
ing shadows or lamps where they shouldn't be. Above his own ragged
breaths, he heard her coughing. He held onto the sound until he saw
Ani walking beneath a lantern down the Chaillot, toward Paris proper,
and he followed.

ॐ

Ani had the distinct sense someone was following her by the time the
sun rose and she'd made it into faubourg Saint-Honoré. She wanted to
stop at Dr. Breauchard's, to relay information and embrace him, but
she couldn't chance revealing any hidden locations if she was being
followed. Instead, she led the culprit around the city for hours until she
was sure he was exhausted, but he didn't seem to leave her tail.

She arrived at the Palais-Royal, lined down the middle by magnificent gardens and enclosed on three sides by stone buildings, courtyards, shops, tiny restaurants, and cafés. Among the latter, the revolution's finest: Café de Procope, Café de la Régence, Café de Foy, Méot's, La Véry, Beauvilliers', Massé's, Café Chartres, Trois Frères Provençaux, Café du Grand Commun. Arched galleries and awnings covered them, etched still with outlined remnants of the removed Fleur-de-lys of the Duke d'Orléans' coat of arms, just one of hundreds of symbols of the monarchy that had been torn down throughout the city. When she got within the courtyard, she took a quick turn at the corner of a stone wall and stopped, leaned against the wall, waited. Her fingers squeezed around the handle of a knife from the palace kitchen. She closed her eyes and steeled herself, waited.

When the man came around the corner, she grabbed him by the shirt, backed him to the wall, and stuck her knife to his throat. "Why are you following me?" she hissed, before recognition set in. "My lord general!" She withdrew the knife and stepped back, only then realizing that he had his pistol drawn and could've sent a bullet into her gut in a fraction of an instant. "What are you doing here?"

"Following you," he said, regaining his composure and lowering the gun. He recognized the knife from his own kitchen. "What are *you* doing here?"

"I'm…" *Think fast.* "Visiting a friend…in a café…"

"Dressed like this?" he asked.

"How can I be dressed any other way out here?" *Think fast.* "Remember Joan of Arc—men's clothing, full armor. It's too dangerous to—"

"Tell me the truth, Ani," he said. "Even Joan had to face a judge."

She paused, considered. The truth? "There's…there's a plot against you, and I…I think…I think I might be trying to stop it."

Aubrey sighed. "I said *the truth*, Ani. Please."

She looked at him, dumbfounded. What could be more the truth than that? It was the first time she'd even said it out loud, admitted how conflicted she'd become since she met him. "The truth," she said, "is that I'm getting coffee." *Think fast.* She couldn't lead Aubrey to Dr. Breauchard, but Henri was mostly harmless. "You might as well come with me since you're here. Keep your head down." That answer seemed to be truth enough for Aubrey, much easier to digest. "I can't say that you'll like what you see. You'll rather wish you'd stayed in bed."

Ani led Aubrey into her favorite, Café de Foy. Elegant tables and chairs lined the outside walkway for the distinguished guests, while the cramped interior reeked of a changing revolution, with crowded seating packed tight together, loud talkers playing draughts and chess, a bar for wine and coffee. Outside, the porters would serve customers on saucers of silver; inside, a body bellied up to the bar and took his chances. This particular establishment, haunted by its reputation as the starting place of the revolution's mob violence, had become less elegant than some of the other cafés in the Palais-Royal. The faint of heart even deemed it bad luck. Three years prior, lawyer and politician Camille Desmoulins had stood on this very café's tables and called men to arms to storm the Bastille.

"Ani, Ani, Ani," Aubrey muttered to himself as he entered and took a good look at the place. "Where have you brought me?"

The room was narrow with a standing-only area to one corner, a bar at the back, and tables with too many chairs shoved in every other corner. Tall ceilings featured candle chandeliers that dripped wax onto the tiled floor. Decorative bottles lined the shelves next to Enlightenment books and stacks of inked pamphlets. The stuffy heat was suffocating.

"Don't worry," Ani whispered. "Desmoulins doesn't come here anymore. He's mostly at Café de Procope with Danton, Robespierre, Bonaparte, and Hébert; but you're welcome to head over there if that's more your cup."

"What excellent company."

"You'll find the remaining royalists at Méot's or Massé's, but the Constitutional patrons here are mostly indifferent to nobility now, provided you don't make a show of it." She raised her brows.

"God help me, I'm among Constitutionalists," he cursed beneath his breath and crossed himself.

"Don't do that here."

Aubrey's gaze fell to a man in the far corner as they made their way to the counter. The marquis took a deep breath. The man had a high, slanting forehead that completed its flat plane down a long, slender nose. His receding red hair was whisked back in a queue, highlighting bulbous brow bumps that joined in a center crevice like the cheeks of an ass. His chin was reddened with rosacea.

Aubrey took hold of Ani's arm. "That's the Marquis de Lafayette."

"He's the closest friend you'll find here, so don't make enemies with him." She saddled up to the bar and slammed both fists down onto the countertop repeatedly. "Heya, tender," she intoned in an ungodly accent. "What's a boy gotta do t'get some service 'round 'ere?"

"Little boys gotta suck m'cock, that's what," the bartender said, much to Aubrey's shock. "Then ya gotta bend over and take it up the ramparts like a good little Cath'lic without cryin' to mumsy, 'cause fuck if she ain't gettin' it up the parts next."

Aubrey was too dumbstruck to say a thing.

"Well, whip it out then, big talker," Ani said, as the burly bartender made his way toward her. She puffed out her chest like she were ready to fight. "Your coffee could use a squirt of cream, fat man."

The heavyset bartender reached the spot where Ani was sitting and threw his hand across the bar, grabbed her by the collar, and dragged her chest over the counter toward him. Aubrey leaped from the barstool and lunged toward them, then stopped.

"My god, Allyriane, ya loveliest li'l dove that e'er was. 'ow the 'ell are ya?" the tender cooed as he kissed her on the lips and placed her back onto the barstool, smoothing down her collar and patting her on the cap like a master would to his loyal pup. "This place 'asn't been the same since ya stopped comin' 'round. Yer fatter. Got some meat on them bones. Ya got someone feedin' ya table scraps on the sly. But bless it if'n yer chamber mouth inn't filthy as ever."

"Sure, Henri," she laughed, "but only after you kissed it."

Henri Sault was a squat, common man, of the variety one didn't take home to mother, but he regularly fed the local orphans and scrappers of rue de Saint-Honoré. Sweat beads adorned his overworked face. His skin was blotchy and red, and he scratched it incessantly. A slightly hunched back accompanied by a slightly crooked smile was what the Constitutionalists remembered of this bulbous beast when they left the café.

The marquis caught Henri's eye, and the tender snarled protectively. "What alley did ya drag this chump outta?" Henri directed a thumb toward Aubrey. "And may yer god take ya, ya bastard, if'n yer the one keepin' this pretty li'l boy from comin' 'round 'ere to suck m'cock." Henri guffawed and smacked Aubrey hard across the shoulder, taking joy in his pale face. "Aww, come now, chap, loosen up. It's 'ow we do 'round 'ere." Henri abruptly shouted across the café at the crowd in the far corner, "'ey! Tell that blasted marquis o'er 'ere to keep 'is voice down. If Allyriane's back, then we got a set'a bigger balls than yours in the room, Fayette." The comment was handed with an exaggerated wink and returned with a mildly annoyed one.

Joining in, Ani climbed up on the barstool and shamelessly grabbed hold of her crotch in her father's pants and rallied, "You want to see grand balls? How about declaration of the rights of woman?" With that, she lifted her hat and waved it in the air like a flag, shaking her hair out of its loose knot. "Anniversary at Champ de Mars! Who's with me?"

Lighthearted boos and chuckles both reluctant and genuine rolled from full bellies. Even Lafayette laughed at the chiding, though his reputation had not recovered from the incident of the fusillade de Champ de Mars, where his contingent of National Guard fired on a group of retaliating insurgent republicans rallying for the removal of the king.

Ani sat back down on the barstool and spun around to Henri, who was laughing, and to Aubrey, who just stared, completely shocked. "Right, right, Henri," she said, nodding to her guest and slipping into and out of a gutter accent that was clearly affected, "the chump is Aubrey. We wants two of your worst coffees, and I'm nay paying you a liard for neither one."

"Since when's you e'er paid a liard for nothing?" Henri turned his back to fetch two coffees.

"*Allyriane.*" Aubrey looked more relaxed, even if he didn't feel it. "You never told me your name was Allyriane."

"My name is Allyriane," she said.

"How on earth did you ever get Lafayette to laugh about Champ de Mars? That massacre was the end of him. And he laughed at it. Astonishing. I didn't know that man had a sense of humor."

"It wasn't a massacre." Ani smacked the bar. "That man's got more character in his pinky than you'll have in all your life."

"Please," he brushed off, "he's just a marquis-general, same as I. I, in fact, outrank him."

"Would you like to wave your crotch at him from atop a table next?" She squeezed his leg hard under the bar and whispered, "Keep that rank to yourself."

Henri set before them two porcelain cups enameled with gold-leafed rims—far, far too sophisticated for this café—sloshing watery, lukebrown liquid over the gilt edges and onto the matching saucers beneath. "A'ight, two coffees, on the 'ouse like always." Henri beamed, leaning over the counter on his elbows. He scratched at his face, and white flakes of dead skin fell to the bar. One landed in Aubrey's cup. "'ave ya checked in with Jacques lately? Devil's been losin' hair over you."

Ani glanced at Aubrey, but he was picking out the flake in his cup. "Not lately," she said. "If you see him, tell him I was by." She regretted that her communication had been lax of late. She'd become more careful with what she said, what she confided.

"I get worried if'n ya don't come 'round, then show up with men like this." He shot a sly grin at Aubrey, then went on to Ani: "Not t'mention—well, a'ight, I'll mention it—when yer away, everyone's away. And them pretty girls've stayed right gone since ya split, too. Bet, Isi, Gret. You took all m'customers with ya, you filthy wretch. But you jus' be sure ya check in with the ol' bastard. Stopped in when 'e hadn't seen ya, askin' if'n I getted two deniers off'a ya for coffee. Even went lookin' at the bloody mine for ya."

"Eh, the mine," she said. "You know you aren't going to find any two deniers there. Never saw even a piece of a liard."

Aggrievance contorted Aubrey's face as that sank in. "You never received compensation for your work in the mine?"

She laughed humorlessly. "Don't look so shocked. Rights are expensive, and women don't get lawyers."

"Nah, shut yer chamber mouth, girl," Henri said. "Ya don't owe me nothin'. Yer deniers, if'n ya had 'em, would be no good 'ere. Ya might as well have assignats instead." He leaned over the counter and whispered, "Believe it 'r not, I still take Fayette's assignats off'a 'im. I plumb feel bad fer th' guy. They inn't even worth th' paper they's printed on."

"Right kind of you," Ani said.

"Right foolish, monsieur," said Aubrey.

A spray of coffee from Henri's mouth flew through the air across the bar and landed in an array of watery brown across the counter and Aubrey's shirt. "Did you just call me monsieur? Monsieur!" Henri laughed in hisses, and little veins popped along his hairline, streaked down his temples like map trails. "Monsieur! Ha! Ha! Best thing I's 'eard all week, lad." He set down his cup, wiped his sweaty hand on his apron, and extended the fat, shaky thing across the bar to Aubrey. "Henri, lad. Henri, Henri. I ain't 'er bloody father—rest him. Yer not askin' for my blessin', an' I sure-as-the-Church-can-cluck-me wouldn't give it to ya, chump, so it's just plain ol' Henri. Or hey you. Or keep, tender, horse's ass: I respond to any'a those'ns. Now drink yer coffee; it be fresh from the bottom'a the kettle."

Aubrey looked into the watery ooze with a faintness of the heart. Holding his nose was not on the menu of etiquette options, and Ani had nearly drained her whole cup before his was even halfway to his mouth. A bitter, expired smell overwhelmed his senses. With a deep breath, he took a mouthful and attempted to swallow, but the concoction was worse than he'd imagined. His body instinctively rejected the substance, and he spit it out, all over the floor, whereafter he commenced with violent gagging and combing his tongue with his fingers to strip the buds of any remaining trace of the stuff.

Henri doubled-over with laughter that made his eyes water. He called across the room, "Hey, Fayette, we's got another spitter!"

"Oh, Holy God, that is awful," Aubrey said, tonguing areas of his mouth that had been violated by this poison. He raised his hand to cross himself, and Ani stilled the motion.

"Nothin' 'oly 'bout it, boy," Henri replied. "It ain't *var. bourbon.* It's goddamn tar."

"With respect, I think tar might taste better," the marquis said, turning to face Ani with his lingering wince. "You drink this stuff regularly? It could kill you faster than arsenic."

"Or it might grow 'er a bigger set'a balls and give 'er some'a them shaman powers." Henri walked away, twiddling his fingers in the air down the bar.

Aubrey stared into his coffee and lifted his eyes to glimpse her madly consuming her third cup as if it held a tincture of immortality, and when they were finally left alone, he said, "So," and gestured, "this is definitely a revolutionary café. Worse, it is a propaganda shop with the recent spate of leaflets strewn from end to end filled with false and exaggerated maxims. All that's missing is a man standing on the table telling his public to come to arms." He glanced about the room as if expecting such a demonstration to begin.

"Lafayette may do that if you stick around long enough."

"Ani—" He was again startled by the fondness in her voice when she spoke the name of the other marquis, a nobleman, an upholder of the monarchy. Aubrey had long ago guessed that Ani was on the side of the Constitution, but he hadn't dared press her for her allegiances to the monarchy. "Allyriane, pardon—are you a Feuillant? A Constitutional *monarchist?* Do you believe in the king heading your Constitution, and not just the people?" He waited for her to speak, but she just looked back to the far corner of the room. "Look at your puppy eyes for that ogre. How long have you been in love with Lafayette?"

"Since 1777."

"Oh, you fell in love with him as an infant, did you? A hero in America is a hero here, is he?" Aubrey raised a finger. "He holds the same position as I, is even richer than I. This whole Constitutional insurrection was started by the nobility itself, not the least of which included that ego-headed reptile across the room. Things that begin on tennis courts and end up setting fire to half of Paris often have a way of burning their very own meager constitutions and Rights of Man to the ground. As a general, I empathize with the Fayettists for having to loose bullets on the monster of their own creation at Champ de Mars when those Cordeliers went rabid. To a point. But the monster will rise again, mark me. I was called to the Tuileries a month ago to quell that very same type of storm before it got out of hand. It will happen again. And again. And again. It will only end when there is nothing left to burn."

Ani hung her head. "I saw the Tuileries that night, too," she said. "It was the very night my papa died. Perhaps you rode your horse right past me as I sat in a gutter." She sneered, paused, the unwelcome flash returning to her. She sat up straighter. "So, all right, I'm not exactly what you thought. I believe in the monarchy, yes—and in the people. But something must happen. People will not starve anymore. You don't know what that is like, Aubrey, to starve—that rage and desperation. A man cannot always turn a cheek. Cannot spot prey and simply soar over it. He must take his chance at that prey or starve. Not as a pretty finch with some meager crusts of bread—but like a falcon in the dive." She stared hard at him, his hand cupped around his coffee.

"And you think Lafayette will save us all, that smug nobleman with his proud ideas of what's right for everyone because it happened to be right for the States?"

"You're jealous."

"Of him? Please. You know what he fails to see? Allyriane, look at me." He waited until she did. "He wants us to be America so bad that he can't see that we are not. The colonists of the New World are self-sustaining and resource-rich. They had industry and exports, food and livestock, were creating laws for themselves. It was working. They were self-governed. They were but a small step away from independence before the fighting even began. I'm not completely sure how I feel about it, but my monarchy supported it and paid for it and sent our best generals to ensure victory in it, so for the most part, I'm all for it. Huzzah, victory!" He wiggled his fingers in the air facetiously. "But we are not America, Ani. Our system is not working. We are not fighting a common enemy; we are fighting ourselves. Unmentionable depravity makes beasts of decent men. The government is not thousands of miles across a dividing sea; it is right next door to this very café." He pointed toward the Tuileries. "If it is overturned, the result will not be freedom. There is no question of 'liberty or death.' There is only death. The insurrectionists are no longer interested in higher constitutions, as you are. They've never read a book. They are not smart. They want goddamn bloodshed." He crossed himself before she could stop him.

Ani lifted her cup to her face, but she was listening, contemplating. Reeling hard from the strength of it. He wasn't right, she told herself—but nor was he wrong.

"I'll quote one of your Feuillants." Aubrey stood and went to the stacks and stacks of pamphlets and broadsides, looking for one he'd read earlier in the week. The newsletters and handpressed fliers littered one whole side of the room, scattered about onto the floor, and were used as wads to sop spills and dripping wax. He found the one he sought, scanned the page, and carried it back to Ani. "'*The moderate party, which, both in numbers and composition, should be regarded as the nation itself, has scarcely any influence; it throws itself as a make weight on the side which seeks to moderate the Revolution, but it scarcely dares to give public utterance to its wishes. This party has, always, coward-like, abandoned its leaders, while the aristocratic and popular party have always supported theirs.*'"

"Antoine Barnave."

"Your own Feuillant leaders doubt the ability of the moderate party to succeed."

"They're not all cowards," Ani said.

"Barnave is no coward," he agreed. "He may have been put off his stroke, yes. But his longwinded orations won't save him. Or us."

Henri sneaked up, surprising them. "What fancy romantic conversation're you two lovebirds spattin' 'bout down 'ere? A'ight, monsieur," he said the word with such contempt, "ya 'asn't drunk up yer coffee, an' yer fine lady friend is already on 'er third cup, an' I'm near on m'tenth. Ya tryin' to insult me?"

"You know," Aubrey said, smiling, dabbing sweat from his forehead, "the problem with coffee is that this hand has no task." He twiddled the fingers on his left hand as he propped himself on the bar with his right elbow, two fingers of his right hand secured around the handle of his cup. "You've got this dainty, effeminate cup, Henri, and I'm supposed to hold it ever so delicately with this one hand, see—not even the full hand, mind you, just these two silly fingers—and then what does this hand do?" Aubrey wiggled his left fingers again. "Nothing. It taps. It

waits for the other hand to hurry along and consume the wretched concoction. And you know, Henri," he reached his wiggling left fingers into
his mismatched waistcoat pocket, "I have this little saying, and you can
quote me on it." From his pocket, he pulled a too-expensive glass hip
flask encased in mulled leather, unscrewed the metal top, and poured a
wealthy amount of its liquid contents into his coffee cup, then swished
the mixture around with both hands. "I always say," he said, "that idle
hands make for excellent drunkards." He cocked his brow and poured
the whisky into Ani's cup, then into Henri's.

"Sounds right genius t' me," Henri said.

"Would you like to propose a toast, Monsieur Sault?" Aubrey smiled,
raising his coffee cup and sliding the flask back into his waistcoat pocket. When the flap lifted, it exposed the king's white lilies over a bayonet
and the three stars of a lieutenant general for the King's Guard. It was
the very cockade Valéry-Marie had instructed him not to wear, and Aubrey had fastened it inside his pocket flap.

Henri's expression changed at the sight of it, and he looked at Ani.
She didn't know exactly what had transpired, but she could hazard a
guess. She shook her head at Henri and lifted the pendant of court lilies
subtly up her neckline, into his view. Henri suddenly looked sad, took
a deep breath, and turned back to Aubrey, whose cup was still raised,
smile unceasing.

"I do want t'make a toast, come t'think on it," Henri said, raising his
own cup to meet Aubrey's and Ani's in two clinks. His eyes locked with
the marquis'. "Vive la Révolution."

"Vive la Révolution," Ani echoed without hesitation. It was not a
toast on which a tongue could hesitate.

Aubrey sensed the change in Henri. The marquis sat mute, leaning over the counter with his drink suspended before him. The words
wouldn't leave him. In this moment, he apperceived, the words meant
something very dark, and they sat like bricks in his mouth until Ani
cleared her throat, prompting him. "Aw, the hell with it," he mumbled.
"What do I really care? Vive la fucking Révolution." He clinked his glass
with Henri's, checked it on the bar, and downed the ghastly cocktail in
one swig, slamming the cup down on the counter and shaking off the
burn. The other two followed suit, and Aubrey crossed himself quickly
before they looked up.

Ani saw him mouth *Forgive me* to the air before the two of them stood from their barstools simultaneously. There hung a suspended note in the atmosphere that it was time to go, and its tocsin rang for everyone. Whether by coincidence or the jolt of whisky, the smell of revolution really was in the air.

Ani tipped her hat to Henri and kissed the big man goodbye across the bar. Aubrey fished around in his pocket, turned back to Henri, and set a handful of écu silver coins on the counter, more than enough to cover Ani's entire history of unpaid tabs in that café. Henri waved his palm in dismissal of the money, but Aubrey nodded politely and walked to Ani. As they approached the door, Ani tensed and dragged her feet.

"I forgot something for Henri," she said.

Leaving Aubrey by the exit, she weaved her way back to the bar where Henri stood. Shielding her hands from Aubrey's view, she removed a rolled stack of papers from the front of her pants. Henri held out his hands to receive them, and Ani felt guilty, small. She looked at the wax seal, thought of what Aubrey said, of Antoine Barnave's words, and she held fast to the edges of the letters. Henri gently but insistently pried them from her grasp, and she let them go.

"For Jacques," she said. "For safe-keeping. Tell him I'll stop by soon." Her voice shook.

"'ave you got to that cockfaced duke?" Henri said.

"Not yet," Ani said.

As she turned, a man appeared before her in a brown dresscoat that came to his thighs, revealing hose beneath. He stood too close, his mouth suddenly at her ear. "There is no sunshine in Austria," he whispered rigidly, "and the queen won't bring it back without a parasol." He pressed into her hand a note, sidestepped her, and muddied into the crowd.

She didn't turn, didn't look after him, just clutched the paper, then stuck it deep into her pocket without opening it. *Not yet, please*, she begged of the room, the enveloping heat. She heard the crinkle in her pocket and pushed the fear away, and when she rejoined Aubrey, he was approaching Lafayette's table.

Aubrey nodded coldly. "Marquis."

"Marquis." Lafayette nodded back, then sniggered. "Don't you know we can't say that anymore?" He laughed coolly. "You look a mess, Collioure."

"I didn't want you to be the only ugly one." Aubrey smirked, ushering Ani out the door before the café erupted into a battle of cockades and cockfights.

"You know him personally?" she asked, once they'd stepped onto rue du faubourg de Saint-Honoré.

"I fought with him before I fought against him. We were all kingsmen once. Best general I've ever seen. That man's got enough gall to be divided into three parts." As they made their way onto rue de Richelieu, Aubrey's voice lost its pleasant lilt. "You should not have taken me there."

"I know. I regret it."

"I could've been arrested."

Guilt constricted her chest, but she ignored it for her preoccupation with the eerie quiet of the empty street before them. They'd spent longer in the café than she'd planned, and the sun sank low in the west. The quietude nagged at her.

"Was that a game to you?" he asked. "To make me feel humiliated?"

"You're the one who followed me." Ani looked both ways down the empty street. There were no just-price carts lining the walk. Where were the minstrels with their hurdy-gurdies? The comédie en vaudeville actors playing Barbary organs and donning masks for livres? The pamphleteers?

Aubrey tossed up his hands. "Gah, a Feuillant! God, how could I not have seen that?" He crossed himself. "We are factioned by one Constitution, and that is it. A piece of paper. That is all that separates us. One piece of paper that I do not even disagree with in its entirety—just don't tell anyone I said that."

"A piece of paper and a god," Ani corrected.

He looked at Ani, but she had stopped and was no longer listening. At least, not to him. Then he stopped, and everything stopped. The change in the air had followed them from the café into the streets. It felt to him suspiciously not unlike the stillness that precedes battle. The prelude to war.

Chapter Eleven

Aux armes, citoyens

Give all the power to the many,
they will oppress the few.
Give all the power to the few,
they will oppress the many.

—Alexander Hamilton

The night crackled. Boarded shutters and drawn curtains closed shop entries like crossed arms. The baker down the street extinguished his lamplights. In front of one home, a flipped cart pushed against windows served as a barricade. Streets away, whooping, roaring, marching thumped through the veins of the city, a rhythm that shook cobblestones at their feet.

A stirring chorus filled the air, and Ani knew the words by heart: *aux armes, citoyens, formez vos bataillons, marchons, marchons!* The marquis rooted himself and stared in the direction of the noise, grasping absently for weapons he wasn't carrying. Ani took big steps backward, her heart pounding in her throat until it hurt. Aubrey would stand his ground against these men, she knew, and she'd watch him get slaughtered in the street. She forced the image from her mind, but it was replaced with a guillotine blade that fell from the sky, out of pure blue, merciless across her father's neck. But the face in the severed head was not her father's; she saw Aubrey's neck bleed, and she screamed for him to move.

He turned to face her, and, behind him, the armed band of rebellious insurgents flooded around the corner, their lips black from biting cartridges, feet donning clunky wooden sabots. Their fingers clenched around all manner of sharp iron objects attached to an assortment of bludgeons and clubs. His eyes scanned from her to them, then for somewhere to hide. He spied a saddled horse roped in front of a row of darkened shops and ran to it, loosed the highwayman's knot, stepped into the stirrup, and pulled Ani up behind him.

"You can't steal a man's horse," she said.

"I can't, or I shouldn't?" he replied, much too calm. "Those are very different things. One is untrue, and the other is not a current concern."

"You shouldn't."

"You shouldn't steal apples from carts."

He steered the horse out of the line of advancing men and away from the direction of the Tuileries, where he was certain the rebellious guardsmen were headed to mount a standoff, demanding the deposition of the king. When the two of them had ridden far enough from immediate danger that the shouting faded to mere echoes, he slowed the horse and searched for shelter. The shops were still boarded, but Aubrey spotted sanctuary in a dim, unbarred tavern. He lined the horse with the outside post and slid down the side of the saddle, straightening himself out and reaching to catch Ani.

"It's all right," he assured her. "We're safe. See now? I only borrowed the horse. Her owner will find her." He stepped away and roped the mare to the post and directed Ani before him through the door of a half-built restaurant, more assommoir than luxury, exposed wooden planks still showing, and a cloth sign handpainted to designate the moved location of the Grande Taverne de Londres.

A scurrying stump of a man, short and old, with pockmarks on his cheeks and missing teeth, piddled to and fro about the room in a quandary, extinguishing the flames of his lamplights and boarding his windows. Aside from the proprietor, they found not a soul in the tavern, but this room was no less sweltering than the last. The man ushered them in without any word but barred the door behind them.

"They'll thieve all my liquor dry," the man said.

"They've got plenty of their own," Aubrey said, checking the back exits to the bar that were boarded but easy enough to break through if he had to get out of there. He peered through the shutters at the deserted streets before him. "They aren't coming this way." But far down the road, he could still see the Marseillaise swarming the city center, met with heroes' welcomes by the Girondins, but visibly more rebellious and undisciplined than any city guard had intended them to be. The men were sheer animals lacking any military direction, though they still feigned a marching order. Aubrey cursed in his head and crossed himself for it, then crossed himself again for the death of moderation. The middle of the road was gone. He couldn't take his eyes from the end of it. Ani stood back from the shutters, huddled near the bar and a lone light, until Aubrey pulled himself away from the window. He knew he should be going. That was his call outside the doors, and he knew it. But it disgusted him. He wouldn't leave Ani locked inside some random tavern. And his files of mercenaries were still marching back to their camp from the last battle—they weren't even near the city if he'd wanted to call them to order.

"Monsieur, you do not want to go out there," the scurrying man said, pulling on the marquis' sleeve. "Have you saw the manifesto? Them wilt kill us in our homes!"

"The manifesto?" Aubrey questioned.

"From the Duke of Brunswick."

"He released that blasted manifesto? But I—" He stopped himself short, then shook his head. "These men aren't Brunswick's foreign troops. These are no one's troops at all. These are men of the gutters." His utterance was thick with disdain.

Ani flinched at its sharpness. Men of the gutters were still men.

The bartender tugged Aubrey to the bar and seated him next to Ani. An unmarked bottle of brown liquid hit the counter inside the tender's fist, and he snatched up two footed glasses. "Please, monsieur and mademoiselle: on the house," he said, patting the bottle and sliding it toward them. "Take it; take the whole bottle. Take whatsoever you like."

"Monsieur, I can pay," Aubrey said.

"Oh no, no," the distraught man said. "We wonnot be alive morrow to count deficits. Just drink down. Enjoy one last night."

"Thank you. Santé." Aubrey sniffed the top of the bottle, decided it brandy, and turned to Ani. "It's been a long time since someone called me monsieur, and today I've got it twice." He poured two glasses and set one in front of her, raising his in faint salute. "No amount of brandy can relieve me of the realization that I should be at the Tuileries, countering this uprising right now."

"You should go if you must," Ani said.

"With what army? You think those National Guardsmen will heed me? I doubt they'll even heed Lafayette anymore. People are going to die—there's no good I can bring it."

Ani gripped the countertop. "Your father will be angry."

"Furious." The marquis laughed humorlessly. "But you sure won't find him anywhere near there."

Her hand touched the foot of the glass, and it slid across the smooth countertop.

He lifted his glass to his lips and stuck the tip of his tongue in it like a frog, testing the unmarked drink's quality. "Have you considered further…what I said at the theater?"

"Are you still asking me?" Mirroring, she dipped her tongue through the surface of the brown liquid in her glass, wondering what he was sampling. "I put it from my mind."

"We're all going to die at some point, Ani." He clinked his glass to hers and took a sip. "But we don't have to do it as bachelors."

Her glass was emptied before his, and he kept it filled to filter from her mind the new trouble that sat on the edge of it. She motioned toward the windows, then her glass was empty again. Then refilled. Her head spun, and Aubrey hadn't even touched half his first glass, his snobbery toward cheap liquor relegating him to the tiniest of sips.

"That has nothing to do with me." He pointed to the windows, then sipped. "Do I just stay in bed with the covers over my head, then, because the world could collapse around me at any minute? Should I not try to make life pleasurable?"

Her eyes, glassy with drink, her face so close to his that he thought she might give in to the closeness, touch him, brush him. A bout of musketfire rattled off outside the windows like firecrackers, and she jumped and pulled away. He remained unmoved, well-accustomed to explosions.

"That sounded close." She swigged her drink in one gulp.

He cringed. Pushing the bottle of cheap cognac back toward the bartender, he waved the man over. "Please allow me your bottle of Rémy Martin, monsieur." When the tender set the new bottle down, the marquis sniffed its crown. "Much better." The aroma was smoother and nuttier, the color brighter filling Ani's glass. "We are safe in here. You do know I'm armed, don't you?"

"Armed?"

"Always." He unbuttoned two buttons of his waistcoat to reveal, protruding from the inside pocket, the handle of the compact custom bronze revolver prototype that had been in the top drawer of his parlor desk. "Look familiar?" The lightweight metal from which it was constructed reduced its effective range, but it would suffice in close quarters. He winked, buttoning his vest closed and patting the bulge of the revolver that matched the outline of a flask on the other side.

"You're a walking curio cabinet with all those pockets."

He smiled. "Do you know who those men are?"

She shrugged. "Radical fédérés, most likely from Marseilles."

"Or Finistère." He watched her drain another round. "Taking their charming little oaths." He raised his glass to the bartender and said, "Eh, you may as well bring the Martell, too. We may be here awhile." When the bartender brought the second bottle, Aubrey uncapped it and added, "And another stem, please, monsieur." Pouring more of the Rémy Martin into her empty glass and an equal amount of Martell into the new glass, he set them side by side in front of Ani. "Slow down, and tell me the difference in these two cognacs. Anything that comes to you. There's no wrong answer. Quality cognacs are not intended for a single throw." He picked up the bottle of Martin and ogled the stamped centaur.

"This one is coppery, like rust."

"There goes your Constitution."

"This one is fruitier, like a...wooden orange."

"Your Fayettist Feuillants must be terrified."

"No, wait, this one is woodier. And stings more."

"You think so?" He poured the Martell into his own glass and tongued the liquid against his lips, then said to himself, "Where is Lafayette now—fighting or running?"

She swallowed uneasily at the name. For once, she hoped Lafayette was running. "I like the second one better."

"Well, there's no accounting for taste," he said. "Just know that if anyone comes barging through that door to treat you in some manner that Saint Agnes would not approve, I'll be at the ready."

Ani put her hand to the bottom of the snifter at his lips and tilted it upward, causing him to swallow the drink in one shot. He almost spit it out.

"Or," he choked, "give me enough of this stuff, and I may be no use at all."

વ્જી

Hours passed, and the light in the tavern clung only to one dying wick. The bartender had fallen asleep at the other end of the bar, and Ani could hardly keep her eyes open, her drunkenness orbing inside her eyelids. When she opened her eyes, the marquis was there, considerably more sober; when she closed them, he was still there, adhered to what remained of her consciousness. The muskets had stopped, but neither Ani nor Aubrey knew the result of the reports across the Seine, nor did they want to know until morning would force them to.

Night shrouded Paris by the time all had quieted. Aubrey lifted the door bar to darkness, an eerie vacancy to the streets. The horse was gone. The only lights flickered far off, over the river. Ani weaved as she followed him out the door, stepping on his heels, propping herself on walls of shuttered buildings they passed. The air flourished with spinning dots and stale smoke. Leaves had already fallen so early in the season, and they crunched underfoot.

The two had stumbled most of the way home when Ani said, "Why couldn't you at least have followed me in your carriage?" She tripped and weaved, and Aubrey laughed. "Is there another course—horse!—horse to steal?"

"I can be your horse," he said, kneeling, tapping his back over his shoulder. "Come on," he laughed, trying to lighten the heaviness all around them, to push it from her eyes, but more so wanting to make sure she ended up in a safe bed and not passed out under some bridge.

"No, that's absurd!" She shoved away from him, but then came back.

"Steal me!" He kicked at the ground as if he had hooves.

"Wait, will you run with me on?" She climbed on his back and laughed too loud in his ear, and he jogged for a few steps before they nearly toppled. "I'm not getting down," she slurred. "I like the view from here."

Their drunken laughter rose and fell in swells through the Chaillot, knocking at the doors of the noblesse without humility, juxtaposing the horrific slaughter at the Tuileries they'd left over their shoulders.

Aubrey slowed and said, "I have a feeling the whole world changed tonight."

"The world is always changing."

"No, I had that gut feeling, that intuition. It's here, Ani, so close."

"You could just *not show up*," she said, slumping over his shoulder and crossing her arms around his neck, a warmth that no longer made her shiver. "Let's go to England."

"England? Dreadful. Why stop there?" He laughed. "Why not *New England*?"

"Would you take me so far as the Americas? Sail me on a ship—I've never been, you know—all the way across?"

"Sure."

"Have you been on a ship?"

"I have."

"Do you get seasick?"

"Only the first week."

"I'll get seasick and complain of it endlessly."

"Just don't get seasick here. I'm not the side of a ship."

"No, you're my horse!" she said. "You'll have to swear every day for two months not to throw me overboard. Then we'll go to Canada."

"Brrrr."

"I imagine those cold winters, though. You'll have to build me a fire each morning."

"I believe I could manage that."

From next to his face, she could see the lines of his smile, the creases around one eye and the tug at his jawline in the night. "You won't stay sore at me for long, will you?"

"No, no." He sighed. "I won't ask again."

"What will you do?"

"Most likely marry Baroness Butte and pray the war takes mercy on me and kills me right quick."

Her head lolled against his shoulder, and her tone grew graver. "Or you could go."

"Paris is my home."

"Please. Let's go, Aubrey. Promise we will. Promise me that when I wake, we will be in the Dutch Republic where no one will harm you."

"How did we go from French Canada to the Dutch Republic? One minute I'm building you a fire every morning, and the next I'm exiled?" He laughed, but the lightness was gone from it. "Come, now. No more fear. Talk about running off to Canada again—that was the good part."

He arrived at the front gate of Palais d'honneur and dropped Ani down behind him. He made a shushing sound to the guards as they let him through the gate, and he shuffled up the walk, Ani on his heels. As his hand hit the door latch, it opened from inside, and Josephine met him through the crack with a finger to her lips. She nodded toward his father's disgruntled generals gathered in the front parlor. He nodded back and slipped through the door with Ani while Josephine created a diversion for the officers with a tray of warm rum. He kept Ani steady against him and crept past the front parlor, then down the hall to her room.

She was instantly asleep sitting upright on the edge of the bed, holding loosely onto him. He pushed her gently, and she lowered to the bed, murmuring, not letting go of his shirt. When she touched down, she opened her eyes, and whispered, "Please forgive me."

"For what?"

The drift of cognac exhaled, inhaled in the tight space. Her cheeks blushed with alcohol. Her body collapsed into the bed, and he knew he wouldn't get an answer. He unclasped her fingers and released her unemployed head to the pillow. A distorted reality impregnated the room and lulled her into a cloudy sleep and him into reverie. He laid her hands across her chest and flattened the chain of the pendant against her neck. Finally, he released the breath he'd been holding. The drawer of her nightstand slid quietly, and he removed from his pocket the inhaler and vial of medicine he'd carried and the loaded gun, and laid the items next to a dog-eared *Decline and Fall of the Roman Empire*. A brown drawstring pouch lined the very back corner, and he reached to see what it was, then withdrew his hand. He thought better of it and slid the drawer closed.

Stepping away from the bed and into the hallway, he latched the door behind him and fell in line next to Josephine. He leaned his head against the wall with a thud and closed his eyes and still smelled Ani's cognac breath. "Forgive me, Father, for I have sinned." He sighed. "It has been twenty-two years since my last confession." He absently crossed himself.

"If it had been twenty-two minutes, I was going to come in there after you."

"A man can accomplish a lot in twenty-two minutes."

She glared at him fiercely. "You did not."

"I did not." He smiled. "Aww, Josette, Josette, come now. I am capable of occasionally being a gentleman." He struck a finger to the air as if he had something wise he could add to that, instead reclining his head against the wall with another thump.

"What will you do with her?" Josephine picked at the hem of her sleeve.

"What will she do with herself, you mean." He shrugged. "She won't have me. I can send her off to a shelter in the Provence, when such is to be had, but I doubt she'll go." His chest deflated. "Perhaps I *should* just wake her in the morning in a different country, let her work off her bottle-flu over the railing of a ship bound for America with the rest of the exiled Feuillants." That thought made him laugh softly.

"Excuse me, sir?"

He waved it off and looked toward his bedroom door. "I'm off to evade some very unhappy generals with very happy sleep instead." The last of his smiles left him. The starkness of the hallway, of the fleeting moment sobered him. "My dear Josette, how good you've been to me. Much more than I deserved." He tried for a smile, but it failed him. "Take care of the household. Word will come when we have safe places for all of you. Until then, stay low and vigilant. Tell her gently when she wakes. She'll have a thunderhead, poor thing. I'll be lucky if she remembers which cognac she liked best." He instinctively fastened his two top buttons and his cuffs and turned down the hallway toward his room.

CHAPTER TWELVE

THE DEPARTURE

*Trust dies
but mistrust blossoms.*

—Sophocles

Aubrey left in the dark that night, still considerably drunk, and didn't
come home in the week and a half following the slaughter at the Tuileries. When he returned to Paris now, he'd find himself an outlaw, for
within one week, the city had turned inside out. New councils formed
proclaiming new laws. The mass of Parisian men and women calling
themselves the Commune, on the heels of the marching Marseillaise,
had claimed a victory in the storming of the Tuileries that could only
be called savagery. The massacre left thousands of the King's Guard,
Swiss mercenaries, and monarchist volunteer soldiers—Aubrey's side—
cut down in bloody masses throughout the halls and gardens of the
Tuileries to bleed out where they lay. The gutters of Paris ran red with
blood that trickled into the Seine and misted the waters pink.

Ani woke one morning on the library chaise longue to the jingling
of a horse's harness outside the gate, followed by the clank of iron and
scurrying of boisterous persons in and out of the house, and she knew
the sounds so well by now. She flung her legs over the side of the chaise
and landed barefooted onto the marble floor, wiping the sleep from
her eyes in the dawn's light that swelled in and out through the clouds.
She handled the door quietly, crept down the stairs, down again, then
through the hallway in her nightgown, toward the commotion near the
front parlor. She stopped when she saw Aubrey standing ceremoniously
in the front foyer between the parlor and the dining hall. He seemed
to be picking up officers like fleas. They flocked from whence they'd
been gathered in the front parlor to meet him at the door, doffing their
hats and saluting. They collected there and were moving out, on, to
someplace else, dirty and uniformed for battle, and Aubrey appeared
agitated. Ani hid around the corner of the cross hallway and watched

him at the other end, dressed head to toe in blue and white with high leather boots, his cockade splayed on both chest and tricorne, fiddling with the gold edges of his elaborate cuffs. There was an unnatural coldness about him that kept her rooted.

Arnaud, the finickiest of the male servants, stepped from the dining hall to wipe some lint specks from the back of the marquis-general's draping blue coat, fixing an edge that had turned under. The generals and barons of the front parlor stepped back, sensing the tension that curved Aubrey's brow downward.

Arnaud adjusted Aubrey's gold shoulder stripes, black neck collar, and the two decorative medals that clipped over the marquis' heart adjacent to the cockade of lilies. "How was London, my lord?"

"Gloomy this time of year."

"Is it not always gloomy?"

"It is, indeed. But you should have seen how hard it was to get here. A carriage with silver lamps is not exactly covert."

"I'll have the lamps removed, sir."

Aubrey retrieved the gun at his right hip and loaded it with a paper cartridge from his formal white pouch, then shook his head.

"Are you not returning again, then, sir?"

"We will have you all safe in England soon."

"Sir." Arnaud made a face.

"How has gone the household?"

"Morbid, as expected. Shall I rouse the others?"

"No. But…is she…"

"She's here. Shall I—"

"No." The marquis studied the loaded gun in his hand, and he visibly winced at his own cowardice. He could look no one in the eye today. He stepped back and straightened his uniform, smoothing the breast and twisting a button nervously. The loaded gun remained at his side. "How do I look?"

Arnaud smiled, eyed the marquis from top to bottom. "Like the good son."

Aubrey smirked, stepped to the side to face into the front parlor, and without any warning, drew his pistol swiftly upward toward one of the men—the ever-quiet Baronet Chicoine, dressed proudly in his Swiss coat, head to toe in deep red like a shooting target. A collective inhale filled the room. Chicoine froze, his face etched in fear.

"Did you really think I would not find out?" Aubrey said to the baronet, gun aimed between the man's eyes. "Were it not August 1792 of a New Republic, I would arrest you. You'd get a trial. But with prisons at capacity holding the maids and chauffeurs and young children of innocent noblemen, there is no room left for the insurrectionists who locked them away. So, I guess the rules of war change today." Aubrey never took his eye from the nervous baronet. "Draw your weapon. You get one chance. We can duel outside, or we can duel right here."

Chicoine remained in place, but started trembling, his fingers twitching at his side.

"Draw your weapon," Aubrey said louder, and Chicoine drew the pistol from its strap and aimed it back at the marquis. "Cock it."

Chicoine didn't cock his pistol, just gloared back at Aubrey.

"Cock it." Aubrey's voice quavered more than he wanted it to. "I know the names of all your sons. Say something, anything, to prove me wrong. Give me a doubt, and make me stall. Make me rethink this."

Instead of an answer, Chicoine cocked his gun.

Aubrey exhaled sharply and pulled back his hammer. "Count off."

When no one else started counting, General de Béquignol began a count to ten aloud, but at three, Chicoine's finger twitched on the trigger. Aubrey squeezed his trigger faster and released his bullet into Chicoine's forehead. In a spray of red that landed across the tea table and the matching porcelain cup and saucer sets, the baronet propelled backward to the floor. Men leaped out of the way, then swarmed over him and stared at the body as it lay bleeding onto seafoam marble. Ani couldn't see the body from her hiding spot, but she knew what had happened. Her hand hovered over her open mouth, and she blinked hard.

Aubrey slid his pistol back in his sash and crossed himself, three fingers from left to right, meticulously, unhurried. His eyes burned. He muttered to himself, "God and Saint Adrian forgive me." He breathed out and turned to the other men. "Not a word of this. General: Place someone in charge of returning his body to his wife. Tell her he died in battle as a brave man serving his king." Aubrey removed a medal from over his own heart and hooked the clasp upon the chest of the baronet as the men lifted the body. "Let her know that his proper burial will be afforded by the court, as will the needs of his sons, and do not breathe a word of his betrayal outside this circle."

General de Béquignol scoffed. "A spy does not deserve—"

"It is one horrible thing to take a man's life; it is another entirely to feel I get to judge him in death, as well. This war is forcing my hand in

ways I never imagined myself capable. Only God can forgive him his
trespasses now, and the rest of his family doesn't need to know that
he could be bought so easily. His children are innocent of his crimes,
and they should remain proud of their father." The marquis turned to
Arnaud and to Valéry-Marie, who had entered the room at the sound of
the shot. "Please. Don't think less of me for what you have witnessed."

"My lord," Arnaud said, "what if he'd been faster?"

"Then he would have spared my conscience." He looked over his
shoulder at the parlor floor. "I know it is unpleasant to ask of you to—"

"Consider it cleaned, sir."

"Before—"

"Before she wakes, sir."

Aubrey nodded. "And make her some coffee. Tell her I...tell her I
wish her well. Flowers for Josette from the orchard, if you think about
it. Keep sending fruit to Saint-Marcel as long as you can. Good luck,
Arnaud, Valéry-Marie." He kissed both men's cheeks in turn. "You've
been the best men I could hope to depend on. Word will come when I
have a safe place for your evacuation. Should it be too slow..."

"Don't worry for us," Valéry replied. "Godspeed you, sir. May the
Lord grant you mercy."

"It is His time that I need most. Pray He grants us time."

Valéry nodded and transferred the bayoneted musket from the hanging wall mount into Aubrey's hands. "Vive la France."

"Vive la France."

A few things were clear to Ani: Aubrey had just gotten there and was
already leaving. The barons were traveling with him. He'd killed one of
his own men. He was armed and uniformed for war. He wasn't coming
back. He was leaving her there.

In her bare feet and nightgown, she turned down the hall and sprint-
ed to the end of it, passing the valet sleeping on a truckle bed outside
Aubrey's chambers, then dashing into her bedroom for provisions—
brocade shoes, a simple daydress that slid over her head effortlessly,
a droopy net fichu for the neckline. From the back of her nightstand
drawer, she pulled the brown drawstring pouch and draped the long
cord around her neck, tamping it flat beneath her dress, then secured
the lily pendant inside her net fichu. Tying the dress ribbon about her
waist as she ran into the hallway, she stopped before the cathedral window to unlatch the door to the orchard and to slip out unnoticed.

Along the side of the palace, she ran atop the gravel of the orchard, the scent of apricots like a mocking idyll, then she squeezed through the opening at the front entrance and slinked against the front corner of the building toward the carriage. She came up on the rear of the conveyance, away from the driver and the onlooking guards. When the path was clear, she pulled open the trundle compartment just enough to stuff her slender body in it, providing—and for this she crossed her fingers—that the passengers had no other luggage. There had been none in the hallway, and by the looks of their uniforms, there was nothing clean to change into. Scooting as far in behind the seat as possible to remove her weight from the trundle-pull, she rocked and flung the pull upward, and it caught. She heard the unscrewing of the carriage lamps to make the carriage look more pedestrian, and then she heard men approaching the front of the carriage and felt more than heard the officers climb into the side, close the doors behind them, and lean into the seat that pressed against her. Aubrey was unusually quiet, but she recognized the voices of Barons Corbière and Bellon, the Bretons. She wasn't sure how many men were in the carriage, but she could hear them through the thin lining of the sliding trunk behind the fabric encasement of the benchseat.

"Delegates from the departments met at Hôtel de Ville at one in the morning on the dawn of the attack," Corbière said. "They have assumed control of the city."

"We can only assume, in turn, they are responsible for the Tuileries massacre," Bellon said. "Messieurs Danton, Marat, Hébert—they urged violence at the Tuileries and are keeping down the National Guard in favor of the more radical fédérés. The National Guard has become nothing. All General Lafayette's hard work at that command—Holy God, the man looks a saint by comparison. All that work, gone. For a rabble of murdering radicals overnight."

"Twenty-five hundred soldiers slaughtered by the Commune," Corbière added. "Mayor Pétion captured. The royal family now prisoners of the Assembly supposedly protecting them. Marquis de Mandat executed on the stairs of the Hôtel de Ville by the mob, with no one able to command his troops in his absence. The scene was horrifying, General. The bodies are still there. They just left the bodies right there."

"They are calling it l'Hôtel de la Fidélité now," Bellon sneered.

"It will always be de Ville to me," Aubrey said softly.

The men talked for a quarter of an hour about the violence of the insurgents, how the National Guard—once in the reasonable hands of

Lafayette—had turned from city protectors into city rioters at the new command of the reckless fédérés who'd marched in from Marseilles. The men were still briefing Aubrey when the carriage arrived at the driveway of an enormous palace. As the conveyance rounded the carriageway and came to a standstill, a rolling thud was heard from behind the bench, and something bumped the back of the cushion. The men looked at one another and listened for a moment but heard nothing further. One of them cocked a gun. Taking hold of his bayonet and slowly unlatching the door of the carriage, Aubrey climbed out and moved toward the trunk, listening closely. With one quick motion, he jerked open the trundle drawer, and as it rolled out, he extended his bayonet before him. Ani came tumbling forward over the edge of the trundle and onto the ground, landing inches away from the tip of Aubrey's bayonet.

He withdrew it quickly. "Allyriane?" He helped her from the ground. "What are you doing here?"

"That depends on where I am."

"At my father's palace," he growled.

The barons and—to Ani's surprise, since she hadn't heard him in the carriage—that bastard General de Béquignol stepped from the coach and watched the scene with sour faces. Aubrey put up a hand and waved them off.

"That was foolish," he said. "What do I do with you now? Stuff you back in the trunk?" He drew back, took her by the forearm, and dragged her to the side door of the carriage, depositing her on the bench. "Stay here. You cannot come inside."

"Who was that man you killed?" she asked.

He stopped midmotion. "You saw that?" He patted her knee and faced away from her. "He was a spy."

"You went to London? Why didn't you tell me?"

"I couldn't."

"What did you do there?"

"I can't tell you that, either."

A moment of silence, then: "You were going to leave forever and not tell me?"

"Yes."

The clipped reply stung. "Why?"

"It's very complicated." He paused. "I will send for you when I have a safe place outside of Paris."

"There is no life for me outside of Paris."

"So be it." He nodded solemnly. "It seems there is no more life for me inside of Paris. Twenty-five hundred men died at the Tuileries."

"Your father will be angry that you were not one of them."

"Yes."

"You're afraid of him."

"Yes."

"I'm not afraid of him." She stuck her chin in the air. Her pulse quickened.

"You've never met him."

"I have thick skin."

He harrumphed. "You need a suit of fucking armor." He crossed himself.

She looked out the carriage window at the home of the Duke de Collioure. *There it was.* It could be mistaken for nothing but a palace. Everything Aubrey's was, this was ten times over, yet it wasn't even a garrison. Walls so tall no human could scale them. Stone so smooth Ani could wipe her cheek against it with nary a scrape. Windows so large she could see the whole of Paris' southern skyline reflected in them.

Aubrey nodded to the other men and walked toward them, and Ani realized it was a nod of farewell and that the men were not staying at the palace. They might have been headed to the countryside or fleeing France altogether. She craned her head around the side of the carriage to see another conveyance waiting in front to take the other officers to their destination. Aubrey spoke to that conductor for a few minutes, then the coach pulled away with the rest of the officers, and Aubrey stood there, lost. Ani's confidence sank at the sight of him so bewildered.

He walked to her, slumped, and said, "The coach will return to take you back to Chaillot." Then he drew himself upright, twisted a button, breathed hard through an O on his lips, and started toward the palace.

As he came upon the steps, the hefty door creaked open. Armed men filled their decorated blue-and-white uniforms with grandeur, and he wondered how they could muster it. They marched out to line the steps for him. At the top of the stairs, his father approached, smelling of woods and dirty linen, the strong odor forcing Aubrey back a step.

"I see you've brought the little whore with you." Duke de Collioure watched his son deflate, and the man puffed out his chest. "You, girl." The duke pointed to Ani through the carriage window. "Come here."

"Father, don't."

Ani exited the coach and made her way toward the steps, climbed, and stopped level with the marquis. Hot blood flooded her veins—*this man, this monster.* She balled her fists.

"You don't stand equal to a marquis unless you share his rank," the duke said to her.

"Father."

The duke ignored his son. "Stand down a step."

Ani bit at her lower lip and stepped down one step below Aubrey and studied the duke's cold stare. There was little of Aubrey reflected in his father's face, and likewise, Aubrey was only his father's son in nose, name, and uniform.

The duke seethed and rolled his tongue through his mouth and across his teeth. "No doubt this is the occupation entertaining you while Marseillaise marched streets of Paris, and fédérés destroyed Swiss Guard at the Tuileries. How loud she must be to drown out their Republican choruses. I hope your whore's wet thighs were worth the men we lost."

Aubrey's voice sharpened. "Our men would have died whether I'd been there or not. I would've merely died alongside them. Most fathers would be delighted their sons survived."

The duke stared his son down until the young man crossed himself reflexively. "You are growing bolder. Your defeats on the battlefield have built bones, son."

"My boldness I inherited from my mother."

"You've also grown a good deal less respectful."

"Now that trait I got from you."

"You knew you would be called to respond—"

"Rioting Parisians are commonplace as day."

The duke barked, "Whores are commonplace as day."

Ani squeezed her fists. "I'm standing right in front of you."

"Women do not speak." The duke took a step toward her and loomed where she stood two steps down. "I'll discuss you right in front of you, and you'll say nothing of it." He looked to Aubrey. "Where did you get this whore, the gutter?"

"Father," Aubrey said. "Call her whore one more time," and the guards sniggered. His eyes cut to them, and they instantly ceased.

"You and your weaknesses." The duke waved in dismissal and bent toward Ani. "Not a whore? Fine, a cunt. You failed your post for a cunt."

Ani took two stairs deftly and slapped the duke across the cheek.

Recoiling, he threw a backhand that might have toppled her, but Aubrey caught his father's arm and pulled him off-balance. The guards hefted their muskets forward in unison, and Aubrey let go of his father's fist, pulled Ani down behind him, and drew his saber.

"My God, Father, you'll have an army kill me on your doorstep?" Aubrey spat. "Is this the noble battle you'd have me fight—your pride over who can shout loudest?" He pointed his saber in an arc in front of the guards. "Back at attention! Don't you aim at me, you blackguards! Use your goddamn sense."

Their muskets dropped back to their sides like lead weights, and their chests thrust forward. The duke hissed but stepped back, his mouth half-cocked in a tight smirk.

"Would you like to invite me in civilly?" Aubrey said through gritted teeth. "Or shall we dance in the courtyard?"

The two men glared at each other until the duke looked at Aubrey's extended saber and snorted like a dissatisfied beast, then turned inward for the dining hall, motioning for his caravan to follow. The uniformed guards marched inside, leaving Aubrey and Ani to linger on the front steps.

Aubrey let out a long breath, sheathed his sword, and rubbed his fingers into his temples. "You just slapped a duke. God Almighty." He crossed himself, and again for good measure. "A duke. I know he deserved it, but. If I were not his son, he could've..." He shook his head. "Wait in the carriage. A driver will come soon. Don't slap him, too."

Ani raised her nose. "I'll not go back," she said too hastily before seeing that his hands were shaking. "I choose forward."

He sighed and met her eyes and held them in his. "Then go forward," he muttered as he ushered her into the palace.

If Ani thought she'd ever before seen anything elegant in her life, she'd been mistaken. The walls dripped with damask curtains. A tapestry hung down a joined hallway depicting French Indies slaves in sugarcane fields. The dining table ran the entire length of one room that stretched nearly half the first floor of the palace. Except for the duke, who was already seated with knife and fork in hand, the room was empty of people and echoic.

"Where is your mother?" Ani asked, too late to realize how far her voice carried through the high ceilings.

"They cannot tolerate each other," Aubrey whispered. "They live entirely in separate rooms."

He pulled out her chair at one end of the long table where she was forced to face the duke at the opposite head of the table. Aubrey removed his hat and seated himself on the wing next to her. The table felt strangely off-balanced.

"Continuing," the duke said. "Marquis de Mandat is dead. The Assembly just butchered him. His fifteen hundred soldiers combined with the thousand Swiss infantry of the king's household troops couldn't hold back the insurgents. Hundreds of thousands of them. De Mandat's incompetent replacement couldn't command the respect of the National Guard or any of the volunteers for the king. Half of them broke ranks and changed sides, God help us. We needed a good general. That should have been you, son."

The sound of the resonating voice took a full three seconds to get to the other end of the table, to stop overlapping itself in echoes, and to register fully what was spoken. Aubrey, used to the delay, replied, "Sir, you sent me to London to gather British allies to assist in the safe deportation of noble families. It was dangerous-enough work, rest assured. I cannot be two places at once, despite how that would please you."

The sound floated back like ghosts haunting the room and was finally returned seconds later. "The King's Guard were cut down in the gardens and corridors. Do you hear what I'm saying? Not just killed, but their bodies mutilated, heads mounted on pikes, butchered in the technical sense. The king was forced to flee, and the royal family is being held hostage by the Assembly at de Ville."

"Yes, sir, I have learned all this. What would you like me to do about it?"

First course came around on the forearms of miserable servants and competed for the echoes of the room when the china plates landed before each diner. Croutons with cabbage soup, Spanish pâtes, rabbits on the skewer, fowl wings à la maréchale, larded breasts of mutton with chicory, green beans and cucumbers with beef consommé, and capers.

"You are a superior general and statesman," the duke said.

"Is that so."

"You will negotiate and aid in the safe return of the king and queen back to the Tuileries, replace the King's Guard with more Swiss mercenaries, gather any of the royalists left in the National Guard willing to protect the monarchy, and take over de Mandat's post. The mercenaries are already on their way."

"Sir!" Ani blurted.

"Aht," the duke replied. "Quiet."

"That is suicide," she went on. "Do you want your son to die in a fight he can't win?"

"Aht, girl, I said quiet."

"You have uprisings sprouting all over the countryside like weeds. Forget the Tuileries. The Tuileries is already lost to you."

The duke pounded his fist on the table. "You will not speak!"

Ani jumped but continued, "The Assembly's not going to hand over the king and queen as if this never happened. They will summon your son to Ville and butcher him on the stairs just like Mandat. He'll end up like Launay and Foullon with his head on a pike and a mouth full of nettles and peppered vinegar. Do you want your son to die?"

"Women do not speak at the table!"

"If you're truly concerned for the monarchy," Ani said, her voice shaking slightly, "then send him to the northeast. Have him take those royalist guards and join with Brunswick's troops or the Swiss mercenaries in Lorraine and the frontier fortress belt to push on Paris from outside. He can do more good there. If you send him back to the Tuileries, he will die. So, you want your son to die?"

The duke threw his knife and fork across the room, and they smashed against the iron of the fireplace with echoing cacophony. "You will not speak at this table! Men discuss; women stay silent."

"Father, don't be a child," Aubrey intervened. "Women don't stay silent when they've something to say. Surely you've been married long enough to know this." He turned to Ani and motioned for her to remain calm. "She knows what she's saying, and there's truth in it. I would be of better use in the northeast. They'll soon be inside of Valmy, Reims, Metz. I could form and march troops from the outside in, rather than the inside out. Paris is the largest pocket of violence; we've had to evacuate our homes, for godsake." He crossed himself.

The duke brushed him off. "I will not listen to anything that girl says. Rumor has it she's low class—some peasant. Has she even bled?"

Aubrey choked on his chicoried mutton, spitting out both the meat and his words. "Father, for godsake."

"Yes," Ani answered and stiffened, lifting her chin. Her heart thumped hard, and her hands were slimy with sweat. "I have bled. I can bear your son a son. That's what you want to know, isn't it? I can bear your son an army of sons. But why would I? The tainted blood of a Beaumercy?"

Aubrey looked at her sharply.

"Enough!" the duke said, spraying chunks of food into the air and back onto his plate. "You'd be lucky to birth his blood from your peasant cunt."

Ani slammed her hands down on the table, threw back her chair, and rose to her feet. She thrust her finger at him. "Duke de Collioure, I have slaved in your miserable coalmine for half my life, receiving none of the pay I earned lawfully, to keep you on your lofty throne. You better be respectful to those *peasant cunts* who put you there, or the angry masses that butchered your kingsmen will pull your comfy cushion right out from under your fat ass."

Aubrey's eyebrows rose like strings pulled them. "You told me you didn't know who owned that mine."

"I lied," she spit back. "But no more a lie than your silence in not telling me it was your father when you thought I didn't know."

She threw her fork down onto her plate, cracking the china, and stormed out faster than Aubrey could catch her. He stood, folded his napkin respectfully, laying it next to his plate, and pushed in his chair.

The duke's voice stopped Aubrey from proceeding. "Please tell me, son, that a borel coal slave is not the one you've chosen for your marquise." His rude laughter echoed about the room.

"You'll be happy to know she refused the offer."

"Refused?" He wasn't laughing now. He snapped upright. "She *refused* your name?"

"She's not terribly fond of the name."

"A peasant whore refused your name?"

Aubrey breathed out slowly, his body tensing behind the chair. "If I give in to your provoking, then I'm no better than you."

"Just stuff a son in her before you crawl off to die somewhere."

The marquis grunted. "We are done here. I'll be at the Tuileries. Up on a pike, as you'd have it."

His father stood in a huff of self-righteousness, throwing the napkin from his lap onto the floor, but Aubrey had already quit the room.

✀

Ani made her way through the hallways of the palace, easily three times the size of Aubrey's, carefully tiptoeing by guards and maids and men too busy with war preparations to mind her. She peered in each room and ducked inside what appeared to be a den. A desk served as the centerpiece of the room, and she approached it. She pulled open the drawers and retrieved whatever sketches, letters, documents, maps she found inside, without discrimination, and rolled them into a tight curl. She pushed aside her drawstring necklace and slid the roll in the slim space of her breast fabric. She slid her hands along shelves and bookcases but found nothing of further interest there. When she turned for the exit, she jumped and inhaled audibly. It was blocked. Not by guards or Aubrey—but by the Duke de Collioure.

"Tsk, tsk, tsk," the duke said coldly as he advanced toward her, covering the door and forcing her back toward the desk. "Where is your knight in armor now?"

He grabbed hold of her dress, and she pushed against him, fingering for the pouch at her neck. He pulled the cord taut against her throat, and she choked and broke it loose, dumping the pouch into her palm. His hand went to her mouth and her own hand followed, digging into his fingers with her nails until he broke away. He pushed her against the desk, yanking her hand away and twisting both of her arms behind her. Her pouch fell to the floor.

"Don't scream," he hissed and unfastened the buttons of his fall-front culottes with one clumsy hand, pressing his groin hard against her to keep her pinned. "Refuse my son, did you? His name's tainted, is it?" He leaned in and licked her ear. "His name's going to sound like a holy prayer when I'm through with you." He raised his knuckles to her cheek, then a backhand across her mouth, then another in succession, bringing blood to the corner of her lip. It took him only seconds to push aside her skirts, and his hand clenched against her bare thigh. "Keep quiet," he growled, groping with his fingers between her thighs and fumbling to pull his cock from his culottes.

To silence her upon his entry, the duke pressed his mouth down over hers and made a show of tasting the blood from her lip. She didn't fight the kiss, and he tightened, then relaxed, surprised to find her opening her lips to receive his mouth willingly. He parted his in return, wide enough for her to slide her tongue inside. The motion startled him into releasing her hands as she slid something along her tongue and onto his back molars. He started to spit, but she brought her hand hard against the bottom of his jaw, pushing up and forcing his teeth to close over the capsule. She heard the crunch, and she pushed his jaw up to make him swallow. Within seconds, his mouth foamed, and his body shook where it stood, the smell of bitter almonds wafting from his breath.

He gripped his throat. His face flushed red, and he grabbed at her but couldn't make purchase.

She put her mouth to his ear and said, "You will not hurt me like you hurt my mother."

She watched until he slumped to the floor, his culottes still unfastened with his stubby, ugly cock hanging out, red with infection and puckered with sores. His foaming mouth mixed rosy with the blood he'd stolen from her lip. She retrieved the knife scabbard from his belt and tucked it up under her skirt and through the side lacing of the nightgown she still wore beneath. It wasn't worth the effort to move his excessive body, so she went to the door, opened it gingerly, and stepped out. The door closed too loudly behind her, and a servant looked at her with narrowed eyes, but Ani jerked her gaze away and walked calmly down the hallway. She rounded the bend, maintaining steadiness, but halfway down the adjoining hall, she heard the loud click again and knew the den had been entered. She picked up her pace. Voices built behind her as she rounded the main hallway toward the foyer.

"Stop her!" a man called out behind, and Ani ran at a sprint toward the front door.

Before she could reach it, she was twisted sideways, and Aubrey caught her in his arms as her hands hit the latch. He whirled her to him and lifted her face, and her lip pressed against his chest, spreading a trail of crimson across the clean white.

"What happened? Why are you bleeding?"

Someone screamed behind them. "Marquis! My lord!" a shout came from the other end of the hallway. "Come smart! Your father!"

The marquis looked back to Ani with new concern. "What did you do? God, what did *he* do?"

She spat with a bubble of red blood, "He won't touch a woman again," and she twisted from Aubrey's grasp and out the door, taking the front steps in two bounds, her skirts no hindrance to her flight.

"Marquis! Your father!" The voices of the panicked men rang out again, giving Aubrey a moment's pause before he darted through the door after Ani instead.

She had a considerable lead. She neared the two guards stationed at the front gate and drew from beneath her skirt the knife she'd lifted from the duke's belt. The first advancing guard swung his bayonet in confusion, and she dodged it, and came up beneath him to drive the tip of her knife under his ribcage, felling him to the dirt. She pulled the blade out and dragged it across the second guard's throat, spilling his neck open. He dropped like a sack of sand.

Aubrey stopped stock-still at the swiftness of her actions, how she'd scaled half the locked gate before he could get halfway down the steps. By the time he approached it, she was over the other side, running down the street. The guards lined along the gates, and Aubrey heard the clicking of guns. He shoved the barrel of a guard's musket into the air, sending a shot ringing across the skies.

"Don't shoot! For fucksake, do not shoot her." He threw his hands against the iron gate like a caged prisoner, not bothering to cross himself. "Open this fucking gate!"

Then he was through the gate with his adrenaline pumping and more surefooted in his uniform than she in a dress, but she'd already made it to a market street, and his uniform was dangerous there. He caught up to her and grabbed her around the waist, then spun her and trapped her against a wall with a tight grip around her collar.

"Don't you run from me," he spat out. "What did you do to my father?"

"Let me go," she shouted, writhing wildly in his grasp. Her nails sank into his arms.

He sucked air through clenched teeth. "I won't hurt you. Don't fight me." He shook her a couple times, then clutched her to him, but she pushed away. "God, Allyriane, hold still." He tried for eye contact, but she refused to look at him. "Did my father touch you?"

She brought her knee up to his groin.

He deflected it and took hold of her arms again. "You gutted my guardsmen like roe deer!"

She finally stilled herself, the struggle fruitless.

"Tell me what's going on."

As Ani turned her head from him, she saw a man crossing the street toward them. His hair was pulled back in a tail beneath a hat long out of fashion that he didn't raise in greeting. The tail was powdered, though great efforts had been taken to make it appear not so. His eyes were dried fruit pits, and his mouth bunched into a tight knot beneath a nose the size of three, and he fixated specifically on Aubrey's uniform. The man's hand reached to his breast pocket. The marquis' glance followed Ani's, and all else waited, hinged on this. Ani pushed against Aubrey's chest and yanked him aside.

A shot pealed from a Nock pepperbox, and Ani's expression blanked.

The marquis reached for his gun to fire in return, but the man was swallowed in the haze of gunsmoke. Aubrey heard the clink of a rotating gunbarrel and many feet in all directions, but the man was impossible to see through everyone running. Aubrey looked at Ani. She stood still in front of him for a breath, an instant, then collapsed into his chest. His arms circled her impulsively.

"Oh my God," he whispered.

She folded against him, her head lolling limp on her neck. Tears came to her eyes but didn't fall. His hands lowered to the small of her back, and he felt the sticky warmth. When he drew his hand back, red washed over his knuckles, his palm, over the gold cuff of his jacket, in between his fingers.

"Oh no," he said, lowering her to the ground and rolling her to her side. "No, no, no. Please, no. God in Heaven, not this, I beg you." He untied the scarf from his neck and pressed it into the wound at her back.

Her breaths shallowed. She whispered, "You must leave me here. Go before he returns for you."

"I will not leave you like this. You can't ask that of me." He took off his jacket and wrapped it around her to hold the cloth in place. Though blood had never made him squeamish before, hers did. The lightheadedness coated him like a sickness. He felt that he moved in a fever dream when he scooped her limp body into his arms and turned back toward his father's palace.

"No." She gripped him. "You can't take me back there. I." She stopped.

"What have you done?" he said. "Damnit, Ani, I don't care what you've done. I need help with this. This is beyond my capabilities. You need a doctor. I must get you to a carriage." He kept moving toward the palace.

"Please." She lowered her eyes to her chest and slid her fingers along the inside seam and pulled from her dress the faded piece of yellow paper that she'd received at Café de Foy. "There is…note…" She unfolded it enough for him to read Dr. Breauchard's directions.

"Rue Saint-Honoré? That's over the Seine! Three and some kilometers from here. You don't have time."

"Please," she whispered, a tear streaming down her cheek until it joined with the blood at her lip. "There is a doctor."

"We'll be arrested if I go into the proper dressed like this. I'll be shot and quartered. What then? We need a provencial doctor."

"Then leave me here."

He glanced down at her. Eyes that he once believed held affection for him now seemed impassive. The seconds slipping away. Against his better judgment, he turned and trotted as fast as he could manage toward rue de Saint-Honoré. Her consciousness drifted in and out.

"Aubrey." Her lips quaked. "I can't feel my legs."

He held her tighter. He wanted to cross himself for the curses passing through his muttering mouth. The limpness in her body had already told him the worst of it, but now he knew she knew, too.

"I can't feel my legs," she repeated. "I can't feel my legs."

"I know," he replied with calmness that he didn't feel. His eyes scanned constantly for guns, for rocks in fists, or batons that would strike him down. A few blocks east onto rue du Bac, and he choked back his fear and hailed a passing hack.

"No," Ani pleaded.

"Shhh. I can't go fast enough, and I can't carry you that far. I'll take the chance."

A passerby saw the blue of the uniform wrapped around Ani, the queue of Aubrey's hair, and shouted, "À la lanterne!" He pointed to the marquis, and two others joined in: "À la lanterne! Hang the 'crat!"

"Long live the nation!" another shouted.

And another, "War on castles! Peace for cottages!"

"Jesus," Aubrey whispered, and he stepped quickly to the slowing hack. He looked down at his feet, away from the driver's eyes, when it halted. "Rue de Saint-Honoré, please, monsieur."

"Inn't no Saints now," the driver grumbled and pointed at some sign pounded into the masonry that had been chipped away. "What's matter 'at one? Blood on her?"

"Monsieur, I pay in livres."

The driver spit on the ground at Aubrey's feet, eyed the oncoming mob with disinterest, and jerked the reins on his stepping horses. "Get in." He cracked his whip toward the mob, and they stepped back, scattered. Once on their way, the man slid open the carriage-slide and sized up Aubrey out of the corner of his eye. "Where to on rue de Honoré?"

"I don't know. Just." He looked down at Ani, and she'd drifted out of consciousness again. "Just go there. Anywhere."

Aubrey closed his eyes and murmured to nothing as the coach flew across Pont Royal, and the smell of the rotting Seine gripped him low in the belly. It took ten minutes to arrive at rue de Saint-Honoré, and the site Ani pointed out when consciousness returned was a nondescript printshop, a hole-in-the-wall single-story building, architecturally unsound, that had been constructed in the alleyway of two already existing buildings. A washed-out sign hung from it, faintly reading: *Boutique de l'aquatinte*. And above it, a different sign pounded into the building, sure enough, with the Saint chipped out of rue de Saint-Honoré until it was just a hole in the masonry, inscrutable. He knocked against the carriage-slide, and the slider slid open.

"Ninety livres," the driver said.

"Ninety?" Aubrey echoed.

The driver looked at the blue-and-white jacket wrapped around Ani, the gold cuffs, the powdered hair. His eyes slit at the marquis. "Ninety."

"That's a fair price, monsieur." Aubrey smiled tightly and fished through his waistcoat pocket for his change purse, then pawed through the coins. Three Louis d'ors and some sols. King Louis XVI's head floated on the obverse, ominously prophetic. *Roi des françois*. The reverse: The standing Genius writing the Constitution. *Règne de la loi, l'an 4 de la liberté*. Aubrey sneered at the dark irony on the coin. The Rule of Law, Year 4 of Freedom. He handed the coins to the gouger and stepped out, holding Ani. "Are you with me?" He tapped her on the face, and she groaned.

The driver shook his reins at his horses and spoke low to them, then snarled, "Vive la Révolution," as he drove off.

Aubrey cursed below his breath and turned where her finger pointed. "Ani, this is a printshop. I thought you said there was a doctor here."

"There is. Please. Leave me at the door and run away."

"Absolutely not."

"You must." Her tears started again. "You must."

He allowed the instincts to surface that he'd been struggling for so long to suppress. "Is something going to happen? Is someone going to arrest me? Merde," he'd entirely lost control of his mouth, "if someone's going to arrest me, then so be it." He butted the door open and carried her into the center of the tiny, obsessively clean shop where another young girl of maybe ten or eleven looked back at them with panic.

Ani called out to the younger girl, "'Pick pink posies by palace steps,' says Simon's sister Simone."

The girl gasped and yelled, "Dr. Breauchard! Come quick!" She ran to the back wall and pounded on a case of drawers containing cut, flattened, and sized pieces of zinc and copper for aquatint matrix printing plates.

Ani had not let go of Aubrey's neck while he carried her inside. She watched his expressions grow more and more concerned with each passing second of realization. "Go, Aubrey. Go now," she said. "There is a doctor here. Go. Do not even look back. Flee Paris. Flee France. Go quick."

He moved his eyes from the case of aquatint plates down to Ani's face so deliberately slowly that she could feel the strength drain from him, inch upon inch.

"I trusted you." His voice cracked. "I wanted so much to trust you." His grip grew tighter on her body. His stomach cramped, and he thought he might get sick.

"Go now, before someone sees you," she pleaded again.

"Let someone see me," he said fiercely. "Let someone know I trusted you. What the hell difference can it make now?" He yelled toward the wall on which the young girl still pounded: "This woman is shot! She is bleeding! Please. Someone. A doctor. Please. Where is the doctor? She cannot feel her legs."

Lowering Ani's broken body to the floor, he held up her head and placed it on his knees, cradling her in the crook of his elbow and splaying his crimson hands out in front of him so as not to wipe them on her face. There was hardly an inch of the front of him that wasn't coated with her blood. Before him, the frantic shopgirl jumped out of the way as the case of drawers shifted to reveal that it wasn't a case of drawers at all, but a painted mural disguising a hidden door that had only a tiny slit for a finger to pull in or push out. Dr. Breauchard stepped through the door and into the shoproom, then stopped. He dropped the cloth he'd been holding. The marquis looked up with temporary relief to stare into a doctor's eyes as crisply blue as Ani's.

"Allyriane! Oh, God." Breauchard pulled a gun from his coat pocket and aimed it at Aubrey.

The marquis didn't move. Didn't wince, didn't put up a fight, didn't let go of her. He just stared at the gun as if he didn't recognize it as a dangerous object.

"Jacques, no." Ani held her hands in front of Aubrey's chest. "Please, do not hurt him. Not him."

"Oh, Allyriane." The doctor lowered his gun hesitantly and fell to his knees beside her, prying her gently from Aubrey's grasp and looking her over.

"The back," Aubrey said. "She's shot in the back."

"God." Breauchard looked at Aubrey, and tears were clinging to the tips of the young man's eyelashes. "God." The doctor rolled Ani's limp body over to inspect the wound. "Go, Marquis de Collioure." He took Ani into his own lap. "Get out of here before I change my mind."

But Aubrey remained in place, squeezing his eyes tightly closed.

"Aubrey Beaumercy, goddamnit," the doctor said louder. He snapped his fingers in the marquis' face. "Get out of here. Go, now. Forget you ever saw her." Breauchard raised his gun and cocked the hammer.

The nobleman finally stood to his feet, looked dispassionately at the gun, backed away from the scene slowly, then turned and walked out as if suspended in air. The door slammed behind him.

Ani watched him until she could see him no more, then felt the doctor's arms lifting her. She broke down against his waistcoat, sticky with her blood, and she whispered with the little strength she had left, "I can't feel my legs."

CHAPTER THIRTEEN

EIGHT HUNDRED AND FORTY-ONE

Courage isn't having the strength to go on—
it's going on when you don't have strength.

—Napoleon Bonaparte

Ani yelped at a prick of pain in her left thigh. She opened her eyes to Dr. Breauchard staring into them. The stall-sized room was packed tight with labeled cases messily strewn on shelves. Such disorganization was uncharacteristic of him.

"Where am I?" she asked.

"If you hadn't led the Marquis de Collioure to Boutique de l'aquatinte, then you'd know where you were."

She felt another poke at her upper leg and looked down to see herself exposed to her thighs. A towel draped over her tender parts, and a bayan robed the upper half of her body. The latter lay unfastened and parted at her ribcage beneath her breasts and hung open onto the cot, leaving most of the lower half of her body bared. This wouldn't have been so alarming if Breauchard were the only one in the room. But the realization that three other men were also present scarleted her cheeks. They all knew that she'd led the marquis to the doctor's secret workroom.

"You don't needs to know where you is." The voice of Évard Pinsonnault was like bass notes on a pipe organ. "I'm sure the marquis has men tearing apart the printshop right now, but they willna find nothing."

Ani hated coming face to face with Évard Pinsonnault. He was an old medical colleague of Breauchard's, always angry about something. A man in his early thirties, rugged good looks soured by a permanent scowl. He was, in all endeavors, a man in charge, though he remained poorly dressed, and that satisfied him, his hair tousled without encasement, his fingernails always dirty. The changing political powers left tension between Jacques Breauchard and him, and their friendship increasingly gapped. Flippantly moving from less-extreme faction to more-extreme faction, Évard gathered documents and evidence that he could present against the men he deemed guilty, according to whoever was paying. The guilty men now were the ones who'd lost at the Tuileries. The King's Guard, the Swiss, the foreign alliances. The men of the Legislative Assembly and former National Guard who still remained royalists, now being replaced by the National Convention. Noble families with great wealth. If you had wealth, the poor, who once merely coveted it, now demanded it.

Among those wealthy families were the ill-fated Beaumercys, noblemen cast from an ancient mold who hoarded money from the masses; conducted deputies who extolled intolerably high taxes from peasantry, by force as often as not; purchased detained children to slave in their factories and mines; and embezzled their noble share off the top with cooked accounting books. Even though Ani had never found documentation supporting Aubrey's personal role in this, his name was Beaumercy. He was as guilty as the rest.

"What was I supposed to do?" she asked. "He wouldn't leave me. He was the only reason I reached you alive, Christ." She paused and pictured him crossing himself. "And I'd just killed his father, so I couldn't go back."

Breauchard froze, and Évard's hands tightened to fists. The room crackled.

"You done what?" Évard said. "Is this what happens when I sends a girl to do a job?"

"Ani, that wasn't the plan," another voice weighed in. Pere Dinaultbriand, the lamp-carrying galibot from Nord-Pas-de-Calais.

It was my plan, Ani thought to herself.

"We's bringing down the Second Estate's entire operation," Pere said. "It's more than your own vendetta."

"He choked on a glass with his fat fingers shoved inside me," Ani shot back. "Was I supposed to let him rape me?"

"Yes," Évard said.

"No!" Breauchard waved an acupuncture-style poking tool in the air at Évard. "What's the matter with you? Don't tell her to let some redcock rape her just so you can have one more bit of evidence against him, you sick bastard."

"Should I instead castigate the man who no doubt armed her with cyanide glass?"

"You're goddamn right I did! Any man tries to rape a virgin girl deserves to choke on some fucking poison."

"Is she still a virgin? How can you know?"

"Évard, you've missed the point."

"She was awful companioning with our marquis friend."

"I swear to God—"

"Let's hope we got what we needs to incriminate the marquisates and countships beneath Collioure. A dead man can't sign no confessions," Évard said.

Pere added, "We got what we needs from the marquis. Once he signs the confession that spells out his foreign alliances, you can choke him with a glass, too."

Ani visibly blanched. "I can't do that."

Pere grunted. "We sended you there to spy on him, not care for him."

"You sent me there to spy on the Marquis de Lourmarin!" Ani said. "How could you all have been so wrong? We know Lourmarin's ties, we know what he's done, but I wasn't prepared for—"

"Eh, one Beaumercy is shitheeled as another," Évard said.

"Don't forget he be's a treasonous King's Guardsman," Pere said. "Ain't no one to care about."

"I didn't say I cared," Ani said.

"Just cared enough to take his bullet for him," Breauchard said.

Ani closed her eyes and squeezed them tight. "I was...running."

"Well, you won't be running anywhere now." The doctor put down his tools and rested his hands in defeat on the edge of Ani's cot. "You haven't felt any of my pins sticking you for the last ten minutes, have you."

"I wasn't aware you were sticking pins in me."

He looked down at the floor when he spoke. "The bullet is lodged in your spine, and if I take it out, it will do more harm than good." He took a deep breath. "You are paralyzed, Ani. Partial monoplectia. Your right leg seems dead to you, including, I believe, the inside. Bladder, maybe uterus, maybe other things, as well. That isn't my area of exper-tise. I don't know how anything will function."

"Will I feel when I have to, um..."

"Hard to tell." He shrugged. "I'll bring in Dr. Tellier. It's not a clean entry. Wear a rag until you know for sure. The left side is not as bad. You can feel the whole outer the length of it, but not the inner." He indicated each area with a squeeze of his hands. "I admit I don't know much about the nerve system. Tellier will know more. I went for a copy of *Cerebri Anatome*, but my access to the nuerologie cabinet was denied." He glared at Évard—Évard was in with the men responsible for that. "They aren't allowing any higher texts to leave the cabinet, not even the Daniel Duncan texts they've lended me a dozen times." He bunched his brows. "You've got a tiny range of motion, but that's it." He brushed his fingers along the top of her outer left thigh. "Feel that?"

"Yes," she said. A shiver ran through her.

He squeezed his hand hard over her right kneecap. "Feel that?"

She waited for a moment to feel what she imagined she was supposed to feel. "No."

"I do commend you for the correspondence you acquired," Évard said, apologetically, quieter now. "It helped us overturn the National Guard at the Tuileries."

Ani paled, but heat fanned her chest. "That wasn't my intention."

"Don't worry about intention," said the fourth man in the room, a cohort of Évard's whom Ani didn't know. "You do what you do best. And we'll do what's best with it."

"Lafayette is in the National Guard."

"Fayette had his run. He runned too damn slow, so he's done now. Things has changed. Speeded up. The king's recent veto of new Parisian troops has showed he's not with The People. He nay wants Paris defended."

"That's not why he did it."

Breauchard pinched her arm.

The unknown man continued, "The king and his Austrian whore has been taked to the Temple. The Legislative Assembly that you were supporting—and once, even I…Jacques, Évard, Pere, was supporting," he motioned to each, "it is gone. The Insurrectional Commune be in power now, demanding a Révolutionary Tribunal for the guilty, and we's part of that now. Minister of Justice Danton drafted a proscription list—eight hundred forty-one members of those still in favor of the royalist Assembly and opposed to the Révolution."

"But I—" Ani started, but Breauchard shushed her.

"You added a considerable number to the list. That makes you a Conventionalist now." The unknown man handed her a rolled parchment, containing a list of names, and watched her reaction carefully as she read it.

"Eight hundred and forty-one members proscribed for treason," she read. "Priests and…Feuillants?" She swallowed. "The Congregation of the Mission; the Oratorians; the Priests of Christian Doctrine; the Eudists; the Congregation of the Holy Spirit; the Priests of Saint Sulpice; moderates, royalists, and those associating with foreign militaries." Her eyes fell to choice names of men she'd admired for their roles in drafting the Constitution. "Alexandre-Théodore-Victor, Comte de Lameth; Antoine Barnave; Adrien Duport; Charles Malo François Lameth; Lacretelle le jeune; Viénot-Vaublanc; Marquis de Sade." Her heart sank: "Marquis de Lafayette?" She looked to Breauchard for confirmation, and to her surprise, he nodded. "And the imprisonment of all non-juring clergy to La Conciergerie, Bernardins, Saint-Firmin, Carmelites, and l'Abbaye. They're turning churches to prisons?"

"And why not?" Évard said. "The government is bankrupt, and the church is rich."

"The church isn't rich anymore," she said. "Their property was taken for assignat bonds. It's not worth a cent—"

Breauchard shushed her and dangled the pendant of lilies upon the cross—that symbol of a lost united France—in front of her and watched her expression change. "Found it tied inside your nightgown. I assume it wasn't there for good luck." Opening her palm, he laid the necklace in the center and folded her fingers around it. He squeezed her fist and laid her closed hand over her heart. "Don't forget who these men are, Allyriane."

Angrily, she thought of them. Their faces. Her mother's face that she could no longer remember with fidelity. Aubrey's words as he put the necklace on her, this *trinket*. This possession. *Give it a better future than its past.* To the men in the room, she choked out, "You can add Baroness Annette Butte to the list, too. That woman is intolerable."

"Noted," Évard said.

Breauchard cut in, "I think you've said enough for now." He shooed the men toward the door to free up air in the tight space. "Give her some time to adjust. She's not going to walk again, for godsake." The realization set in with those words. The men looked embarrassed and left with their heads down, and Breauchard closed the door on them and turned to face her.

"Yes, I will," she said.

He sighed and came to her bedside. He sat, and the quiet yawned around them.

"You let Aubrey go," she finally whispered.

"You asked me to."

"They'll arrest him."

"If they can catch him, yes."

"He'll go to prison."

"Perhaps."

"Is he going to die?"

"No, he won't die." The doctor patted her arm. "They can't just kill them all. But he'll be arrested, yes. Face a tribunal, then imprisonment if he is charged."

"Charged with what?"

"Treason. Crimes against the Republic. If you fight against Paris, you fight against France."

"But that's absurd." Ani jerked her arm away from the doctor's consolation. "The insurgents fought against Paris at the Tuileries not a fortnight ago, and now suddenly they speak for us all? Aubrey loves France. He bleeds it and would die for it and has every bit of Paris in his heart. Why should he be arrested for loving his country? And Lafayette, too?—the Constitution is his!"

"This is an opinion best kept quiet now."

"That's not opinion. That's a fact that can't just be erased."

"There are new laws, new *facts*. These men who own everything—"

"These men? You mean men like Aubrey. He sends gift baskets to his soldiers' children on their birthdays. I saw his books; his men's solde are double what other guardsmen are paid, and it comes from his pocket. Everything is accounted for."

Breauchard patted her hand and stood. "All men will fight tooth and nail for their family name. Marquis de Collioure is no different. When his family comes into question, you will see: he will not denounce them." He began to tie her robe from the ribcage down. "I have to ask, in case of medical necessity." He slowed his tying. "How far did the duke get?"

"Only fingers." She shuddered.

"Thank God that's all." He squeezed the rail of the cot. "And. And. The marquis. Did he…"

"No." Ani felt the room sit on her chest. She laid her hand over the top of the doctor's and squeezed his fingers. "Jacques," she whispered, "he asked me to marry him."

"Did he?" A long pause. "And how did you answer?"

"You know how I answered. But it makes the betrayal harder."

"I see. Was he not who he is, how would you have answered?"

She shook her head and broke eye contact. "How can I separate him from who he is?"

"And you swear he didn't." He nodded quickly toward her thighs and reddened.

"I swear it."

"Listen. What you say to Évard and Jean Crissot—"

"That's his name, that other fellow? Jean Crissot?"

Breauchard nodded. "Be careful what you say to them. They're confiscating his garrison before it can be moved. If the king's foreign armies are marching on Paris to take down the Republic and the Constitution, then they must be stopped, and anyone who fights with them must be stopped, as well, or The People will never prevail. Put the marquis behind you." He sighed. "I regret that he showed you kindness. Had it been Lourmarin—"

"How could they have been so wrong about that? We've never been wrong like that before."

"Things are messy," Breauchard said. "Everyone's getting sloppy."

She nodded.

"I'm going to fashion you a chair."

"I don't want a chair."

"Allyriane, you won't—"

"I will," she said. "I will walk again. With or without you. Help me walk again; don't put me in some chair to rot that way. You know what happens to people in chairs. They get put in asylums." She looked down at her broken body, feeling far too little of it, and wiggled her left toes to convince herself that control was still hers. She would walk. She would walk right out of this place.

৯

The initial week of recovery proved hardest. The first challenge was simply lifting her legs over the side of the bed. Achieving a kick with the left foot into the right, she eventually managed to shift herself over the edge and drag herself back up more times than not, ending up on the floor only a fraction of the time. Little pain stemmed from the source, most of the nerves having been severed around the bullet, but muscle aches brought new agonies and spasms. Her arms felt no sturdier than puffed pastry, though she'd always had strength in them. The edge of her bed became a pull-up bar, and she heaved the weight of her legs with her arms until it made her cry, doing repetitions each time her body could go again, then collapsing wherever she lay spent. Sometimes she just fell asleep there, only to wake and try it again, again. All she did, minute after minute, was try it again, again. She'd waste no waking moment on rest or weariness, depression or disappointment.

Breauchard came and went day after day in the tiny room, applying fresh dressings to the wound, helping Ani for hours at a time to master a few steps in his embrace until his arms tired. She needed ample food to keep her energy, and Breauchard made sure she had it, though he never mentioned from whence the food came. They studied the severity of the nerve damage to tailor her therapy to her needs, and Breauchard invited in experts, Dr. Tellier, specialized doctors. The advantage of communication with her left side helped her land more easily on her left leg and drag her unresponsive right leg to meet the other. She'd quickly stabilize herself with the left before she lost her balance. The challenge was less about feeling than it was about balance—just staying upright.

In that first week, Breauchard fashioned lightweight copper braces that utilized the motion available to her hips and maintained stiffness at the knees with the aid of appropriated carriage springs. This allowed her to put her entire weight on either leg without collapse. The braces extended down to boots that covered the back portion of her heels and slipped over her shoes with copper frames and leather straps underneath. Each step produced a metallic clink that marked her progress.

With the braces, she relearned her steps, first with Breauchard's aid, then independently with the help of wooden crutches, slowly, unsteadily. Under the watchful eye of the doctor, hour upon hour, Ani walked from one wall of the room to the next on her crutches, kicking her right leg out from the hip and dragging it to meet the steadier left leg. Over and over, back and forth, wall to wall, hundreds, thousands of times, faster and faster and more competently with each lap. As she gained fortitude, she practiced controlled tumbling and initiated a regimen of strength-building calisthenics. She would use her arms to tuck in her legs for a roll, then push herself up from the ground with sufficient force to regain a standing position. It was slow, but she achieved it again and again, though not always consecutively, and sometimes not always at all. It was unpredictable at best, but she wouldn't give up until she had it.

At Ani's request, the doctor constructed leather sheaths on the braces to fit the knife and gun she'd obtained from the Beaumercys. She threw the knife at targets affixed to the walls, objects placed on shelves. Gradually, the room felt smaller and smaller. While the news of the overflowing prison population following the arrests of clergy and moderates filtered in on the lips of the doctor and the others who now identified more safely as Girondins, her stir-crazy reclusiveness reached a fever pitch, and she began a new phase of recuperation: running to build up her leg muscles.

It wasn't running, of course, but nor was it limping. At first, she'd fallen on most of her attempts. Eventually, she came to know the feel of her legs' motions in the top half of her body, and the rhythm be-came a new nature, the spastic impulses that she learned not to fight. When Breauchard returned this time, along with Évard Pinsonnault, both men stared, jaws slack, to see her walking across the floor, back and forth, with no crutches at all, using the wall to balance.

She was out of her mind with claustrophobia, needing to leave the tiny space, to breathe real air, even if it was only the filthy factory smoke of Industrial Paris. There'd be so much more recovery to come, but she had to move, *move now*. Get out *now*. She turned to Évard with eager eyes. "Whose documents do we need next?"

Chapter Fourteen

A change of plans

Uncertainty is an uncomfortable position.
But certainty is an absurd one.

—Voltaire

On the first day of September, the floor of Ani's boarded-up Saint-Marcel cellar was damp from a heavy rain. She sat on the driest part of the ground with her legs out before her, reading a book, whilst Grietje and Béatrice paced back and forth. Isabeau rarely made an appearance anymore after going off to join a radical women's faction, the Mothers of the Nation, in the cellar of the wineshop that fronted for the group.

Béatrice sidled up to Ani and said quietly, "Maybe they's treating him all right?"

She was speaking of Lafayette. He had been the founder of the revolution, and now he perched in precarious balance: proscribed by his own new government for being too moderate and a proponent of the king, while outside France he was deemed an insurrectionist who'd started it all, an enemy to foreign governments. He'd been arrested fleeing to the Dutch Republic and was imprisoned in the Prussian fortress at Westphalia.

Grietje didn't care; it had all moved too quickly for her, and she didn't understand it. She was resigned to being a mouthpiece for whoever was feeding her from day to day. But Béatrice had been a Constitutionalist moderate Feuillant with Ani since the beginning. It didn't seem so complicated to either of them: it was an injustice for the man who penned the Constitution to be an enemy of those claiming to uphold the very Constitution he created. There was just one hangup with the Constitution he created: it required a monarchical head in order to enact the votes of the people, and under the new government, any utterance of pro-monarchical sentiment was outlawed.

"Why knives?" Grietje asked, turning a poorly crafted, stolen stiletto in her hand. "You're the only one who's good with them."

"Knives are silent," Ani said. "I don't anticipate we'll need them, but I'm taking no chances." She nodded toward the targets drawn on the wall with charcoal. "Why don't you practice some more."

"Easy for you to say; you got all your fingers. I can't throw the damn thing right."

"Use your other hand."

"That's not the hand I use."

Ani glared hard at her but shut her mouth. At some unmarked juncture, the tension between them had become palpable.

"We don't all get to go on daring adventures in palaces," Grietje said beneath her breath, though her deafness meant it came out louder than she thought.

"It wasn't my choice. That grievance is with Évard, not me."

"He says to call him Citizen Pinsonnault." Grietje threw a knife, and it missed its mark by a wide margin. "You getted to eat like a king there."

"A king for a day is no king at all."

Béatrice snapped, "You eated like a king off her all that time, too, Gret. She didna have to send us provisions. That wasn't no part of it. But she did, so hush up, ya snivelwit. You never went hungry." She tugged on Ani's sleeve. Béatrice, rolling in fidgety fingers the passport paper that Ani had procured, whispered, "What if I'm in-cepted before I get to him in Westphalia?"

The Duke of Brunswick's Prussian armies were somewhere outside of Verdun, and that's all they knew. Béatrice would have to travel thereabouts in order to cross the border. Ani's mouth curved into a frown. She wished she still had access to Aubrey's knowledge of troop movement, the maps with colored inks and arrows he'd sprawled across tables. What she wouldn't give to know where the troops were now like she'd known with him. "Bet, you've done this before. You know what to do. Keep your head. You have papers. If anything happens, just make up something."

"You should not be planning to break out Lafayette," Grietje said. She was Dutch. What did she know.

"That's what you's whispering, inn't? That you's breaking out Lafayette? Citizen Pinsonnault would be furious if he found out. You know you'd be proscribed."

Ani tightened the brace straps around her right leg. "Are you going to tell him, Gret?"

She scratched at her arm with the tip of the knife blade. "No."

"Then he's not going to find out."

Grietje threw her knife at the charcoal target but missed. "What is it we's actually supposed to do? Because it's not breaking out Lafayette. That much I do know."

"Forget what you think you know. We're going after a rich man's books. Émilien Gagnon. He bribed statesmen to keep quiet while he stocked factories with girls like you." Ani corrected quickly, "Like us."

One effect of the revolution in their favor was that the orphan trafficking trade was dwindling rapidly, but they'd all been through enough in their lives to carry the trauma with them forever. It was easy to groom traumatized girls to fight back against the whips that scarred them. Grietje flung another round at the target before skipping over to retrieve her knife.

"I'm told there's a double-set of accounting ledgers," Ani said. "I have to retrieve them for Évard to condemn some bastard in a tribunal."

"You mean Citizen Pinsonnault."

"Citizen Pinsonnault," Ani grunted and watched Grietje's indifference with dismay. "All you have to do is cover me. Nothing more. Keep practicing."

The old planks rattled with the knock at the door, and Béatrice lent a hand to help Ani from the ground and toward the door slowly. Ani could move, but it was slow—ungodly slow to her. She opened the door to see Jean Crissot—Évard Pinsonnault's newest henchman. His chest puffed like a mating Bantam. He glanced repeatedly over his shoulder.

"Citizen Pardieu."

Ani sighed. How ridiculous. "Citizen Crissot." She nodded and took from him the papers that he administered, one of them being a floor plan for the mansion in which was housed Émilien Gagnon's offices.

He pointed to a room on the map and added his instructions: "We has reason to believe the accounting ledgers be located here, the master study. Monsieur Gagnon has many workers in the building, so take care. There be a back way what leads to the cellar and takes you up some stairs right here," he indicated, "bringing you out in front of the master study, here. Don't harm Gagnon; we need him for confessions. Don't engage with no one. In and out. Drop the books where we discussed. Citizen Pinsonnault says you requested a carriage because of your," he waved his hand at her, "uh, condition, so your carriage has arrived with mine. Remember: both ledgers."

He walked out, got in his carriage, and that was that. Ani looked down at her feet to see a small basket filled with apricots, cherries, and wax-covered cheese. A card protruded from it that simply read "V." She watched Crissot go until she could see him no more, and she turned to Béatrice. It was time to implement their true intentions with the carriage.

"Be so, so careful, Bet," Ani whispered, picking up the basket and putting it in Béatrice's hand.

"Bless that Valéry," Béatrice said as she took the basket.

"Stick to the plan: Investigate what we don't know about the prison layout, especially where the stations are. Get word to Lafayette that there are American representatives from the States who are working to secure his release." She placed a coin pouch of bribery money into Béatrice's hand. "I'll work on the Americans and the papers, but we need a full sketch of the prison floors and exits. And remember, not a word of this to The Citizens." Ani kissed Béatrice on the forehead and lingered there briefly. "Luck speed you, Bet." She kissed her again, and her eyes misted.

Ani watched Béatrice get into the carriage and exchanged an understood nod with the driver—Café de Foy's bartender, Henri Sault. The big man winked, cupped his balls, blew a kiss at Ani, and kicked the carriage into motion. When it took off, headed toward the countryside, Ani closed the door to block out the chaotic sounds from the street.

"That was wrong of you to do," Grietje said, standing too close over Ani's shoulder. "It's treasonous. Lafayette be a enemy of the Assembly now, a émigré."

"I hate that word," Ani muttered. "How can he be an enemy when he has been imprisoned by our enemies? Is not an enemy of our enemies an ally? Émilien Gagnon is the enemy. He's your concern. Don't pay such close attention to mine." She smacked the floor plans of the Gagnon offices against Grietje's chest. "You'll feel better once you've brought down an actually corrupt aristocrat."

It was a slow-go to the mansion, but Ani couldn't have asked for a second carriage, or it would arouse suspicion. Her wool skirt covered her braces, but even without the petticoats she could no longer wear, she felt like she were lifting her legs against rushing floodwaters. Grietje wasn't the supportive helper that Béatrice was, and Ani had to lean constantly on fences and building walls to keep her strength. Finally standing before the mansion on rue de Vaugirard, the two girls breathed in unison and squeezed through a partition in the gates. They headed toward the back entrance, hugging the building beneath the overlooking fanlight windows. The back way was dim, and in the way of all mansions, the entry took a person down to go up, then up to go back down. *Stairs.*

She sighed heavily and ushered Grietje through first. Huddled against the iron railing, Ani made it down the first small flight. Up was harder. Dragging herself upward put her off-balance and rested all her weight on a part of her body that couldn't feel it. If no one were around, she could scoot faster up stairs on her butt, but she couldn't be alert in that state, so it wasn't an option now. It took several minutes to reach the top of the insignificant flight, but once she'd done it, she smiled to herself. Grietje had gone on ahead, growing impatient.

Ani peered around the doorframe at the top, seeing Grietje crouched with her knife at the ready in a hidden corridor. Ahead was the heavy oak door of the master study. Ani waited while some errant bodies moved languidly through the hallway, then she stepped out of the stairwell to position herself across from the door. Her braces clicked against the floor with each step. The ticking of a clock. The cocking of a gun. Click. Click.

Through the glass, she could see the master study was occupied. She ducked behind the nook of a curved fountain across from the room's frosted-glass windows and tried to make out the unfortunate figure of Émilien Gagnon. Who was he? What did he look like? She crouched there for nearly half an hour, the one instance in which her numbness came to an advantage.

The financier finally emerged from his study. When the light hit his face, Ani's breath caught. *She knew that face.* She'd seen Émilien Gagnon. At Palais d'honneur. With Aubrey. They'd spoken gaily as old friends. Her heart thudded. She no longer wanted to know whose names were in those accounting books. She'd find Aubrey's name there now, she was sure. All the times there'd been nothing, nothing—how aboveboard he'd seemed—his name would be there now. He was friends with a man whose fortune was built upon the exploitation of the poor, the very type of man who'd sent the girls to mines time and again, each instance they were snatched from the streets. Her resolve plummeted. It was one thing when it was a father; fathers weren't a son's choice. But a friend was a choice. An associate, a partner, an acquaintance, a choice. Citizen Pinsonnault and Pere—or Citizen Dinaultbriand, as she was now expected to call him—had been right. She swallowed hard. For every lie she'd told, she'd been blindsided by one in return. She shook her head from side to side as if to loose the thought. It didn't matter now. It couldn't be helped. It couldn't be undone. Whoever's names were in that ledger—it couldn't be undone.

Gagnon walked down the hallway, leaving the door cracked. Ani steeled herself. A few clicks of copper on tile, and she was inside the study, taking in the beauty of a rich man's world: tall bookshelves and dark mahogany and superior craftsmanship apparent in everything from the carved balustrade to the crafted chairback. The bookshelves held scholarly books, literary classics, notebooks, obsessively ordered—categorized by subject, alphabetized by author, matched heights by binding. She admired the organization, then pulled each one down and leafed its pages. No drawer went unsearched, no stack unturned. She felt along the bottom of the desk, the sides of it, all along the wall around the fireplace, the mantel overhang. But the ledgers didn't present themselves.

The lock twisted on the door, and Ani ducked behind the desk where she stood. The preamble of panic clawed at her. She held her breath.

"Sir, if I may—" the man began, then stopped when he realized he was talking to nothing but some tobacco-scented air. Turning back toward the hallway, the young male paused before the hook could catch.

Ani tucked herself underneath the desk, holding her breath, counting seconds, her knife newly drawn in one white-knuckled fist. She imagined he saw the books on the floor, items upended, and she was listening to the movements of the man when her head touched a façade that shifted beneath the desk. Nothing was visible to the eye, but there was some kind of hidden compartment. She waited until the man was gone, knocked softly for the hollow space, and pinpointed the disguised door that contained two narrow accounting ledgers and a thick wad of uncirculated assignats. She smiled, then quietly pulled the two accounting books from the façade and tucked them under her skirt and into the tight drawstring of her undergarments. She left the assignats—that currency was worthless now. Her leg twitched involuntarily, and the copper brace clicked against the floor.

"Who's there?"

Ani stilled and heard the shuffling of someone in the room. The man had been suspicious enough to return. He ran quickly around the desk and tripped over her brace extended in front of him and went down hard. Before he could move, she put her finger to her lips, but he yelled out. She cringed at the wail he made, and it left her no choice.

She stabbed the blade into the man's throat, spilling his last sounds over imported tile.

But it was too late. Passersby had heard the strangled cry. Two other men rushed into the study following the howl of the slain man. Swiftly, Ani hoisted herself from the floor behind the desk up onto the top of it, and let the momentum carry her leg into the air. Her brace flew against the second man's face as he lunged forward, and cut a deep slice across his cheek, knocking him to the floor. She brought her brace down hard on his jaw and threw her dagger across the room and into the third man's lung. Air whooshed out of him, and he went down beside the other men with a look of astonishment on his face. One more dead; one just wishing he were.

"Gret!" she called. No answer.

Ani slid from the desk and limped toward the door, balancing on a table and retrieving her knife from the third man's chest. Blood bubbled out of the opening it left. She wiped it hastily on the dying man's shirt, then sheathed the knife and peered around the doorframe, her heart pounding. Grietje wasn't there. Ani made for the door to the stairway before Émilien Gagnon could return to discover her among the carnage.

She moved down and then up the devastating stairs on her butt, cutting the time in half, though the position left her prone. Midway through the second flight, voices mounted behind her. The hem of her skirt trailed a line of blood leading right to her. She cursed, but within a few more steps, she was finally outside, gasping for breath. There stood Grietje, plain as day, past the gate and well down the street. She didn't look like she cared. That stung. Ani hid among trees and buildings as she hobbled after Grietje, using every available object for balance.

"Shit. Shit, shit, shit," Ani said when she reached her. "Move. Go, go."

"Where is the books?" Grietje asked, eying the blood on Ani's skirt and sleeves.

Ani had other questions. Bile rose in her throat with each slow step. "I couldn't find them. They weren't there." She stopped. "And neither were you." What just transpired could not be reversed. "Why didn't you cover me? You left your post and let three men walk in on me without a warning."

"Ja, I was bored stiff. You sat there for half a hour without moving. I got hungry and left. You don't need me to cover you; you're good at this stuff. That wasn't even a hard situation."

"Gret, I don't move like I did."

"You shouldn't have gone after Lafayette." The words slipped out fast and loose. Grietje pivoted around to face Ani. "I don't cover traitors. Citizens Pinsonnault and Crissot say that Lafayette is a traitor."

"You once followed him with me. He's not the one who changed. The Citizens changed." Ani thought better of continuing her explanation. She stepped toward Grietje, her brace clicking emphatically on the road. She tapped the younger girl's sternum. "If you breathe a word of this, then you're the true traitor."

A beat passed, then Grietje turned and walked away without a word or a glance back. Ani had never felt more alone, and the loneliness suffocated. She'd wanted to save her father. She'd wanted the girls to stay safe. She'd even somehow wanted Aubrey to be innocent. All these wants that amounted to nothing. Tree stumps lined the rue where all the lumber had been stripped, and blight choked a lavender bush. Famine loosened the worthless soil, and dust kicked up from seemingly nowhere. She checked over her shoulder, fought back her deflated sense of security, and headed toward the location she'd been given to deliver the ledgers. The rest would be on her own, she knew. Maybe everything would be that way. Maybe it truly always had been.

The safe house was nearly two miles away. She was sweating. Tired. Bloodstained. A cramp shot into one hip. As she shuffled toward the address where she was to deliver the books, her brain reeled in a deadlock of moral quandary. Aubrey knew Émilien Gagnon. How? Was the marquis' name really in the books? Did she want to know? Had he lied to her deeper than she could have imagined, hidden it all, kept it out of the documents she'd taken? Were there documents somewhere else in his palace she hadn't searched, hadn't found? She'd been so thorough— but then, he was careful and clever. With every step, she fought to keep to task, but her task was swiftly changing. She realized she wanted to hear his voice. No matter what he'd done, to hear the orchestration of his laugh again. She had to know.

Near her destination, she ducked into a secluded alleyway. She cracked open the binding of the first account book and, without focusing on any other names present, she skimmed for banknotes made out to Beaumercy, to anyone Beaumercy at all. Anyone who might have even been close to Aubrey in name would be enough for her to condemn him without remorse. She scanned every page, but nothing. Nothing, nothing, nothing. Page after page. Back and forth between books. She tried Collioure, then the maiden name, Montchamb. Then Lourmarin. Nothing. Not even the bastard duke had taken or made bribes from or to this Gagnon financier fellow as Évard Pinsonnault had sworn he had. Évard had sworn to her that every name in these ledgers was a briber, that Beaumercy would be in there. What was she doing with these books? She'd combed both volumes and had come across no Beaumercy or Collioure. Then, with a glance that made her almost physically retch, she encountered another name she wished she'd never seen.

Simon Pardieu. *Her father.*

Her lungs flailed in arrhythmic thudding, and she heaved wet coughs that clung to her insides like algae. Her unsteady legs gave way. She crumpled against the alley wall like a ragdoll. She felt along her waistline pouch, but she had forgotten her inhaler, the insufferable pain making her think only one thought too vibrant to push away: Aubrey would not have forgotten it.

She put her head against the wall, catching her breath, blinking through the hazy spell until the pain subsided. Seeing there, the very rowhouse across the street where her delivery was to be made. Why was her father's name in that ledger? She shook her head. Again. Again. But the question remained. *Why? Why he?* She closed her eyes and rose with great effort to her feet. She tucked the books back into her undergarments and turned away toward her Saint-Marcel cellar without making the delivery drop.

Chapter Fifteen

The slaughterhouses of September

*Those who can make you believe absurdities,
can make you commit atrocities.*

—Voltaire

The stench of the city morgue permeated the streets outside the stronghold Grand Châtelet, the fortress that had held Ani's father for the last years of his life, once the Bastille had been emptied of prisoners. Coffee in hand, she now sat at a picture window with a view far more grotesque than picturesque. The area suffered from the odors of the dried blood and carcasses of the nearby slaughterhouses and the sewage that penetrated the contaminated waters of the Seine to the south over the Pont au Change—where one could find as many as fifteen floating bodies a night since the sixteenth century. On this day in early September, it would bear a great deal more.

Ani watched as a mob of commoners at the gates of the prison severed limbs from bodies of massacred prisoners. Right there in the open street at the stronghold's gate, a pile of body parts a story high. She still felt the guttering pang of violent deaths, the fear in a man's eyes, but the grim reality was that it got easier. A numbness came of the repetition. She felt the humanity inside herself drifting away. The ransacked Palais d'honneur came to mind: how The Citizens and their minions had emptied it of its art, munitions, and fancy furniture. Numbness. Ani tried not to care. There, before her, a man bludgeoned another with a stone. Four men surrounded a clergyman, yelling something Ani couldn't hear, before driving a pike into him. Small boys played with human heads like bowling balls. Ani tried not to care. Numbness. A young woman's breasts were cut from her while she was still screaming, and after she'd lost consciousness, her feet were nailed spreadeagled to the ground and a bonfire lit between her legs. Cries came from a tangle of bodies against the wall, and Ani turned away, finally shocked at how serene the café was by comparison, how these worlds could exist side by side.

The stench of the magistrate chambers, above the morgue in the fortress' western wing, may have stunk more than the bodies pulled from the Seine this day, the chambers in the process of becoming a site of mock tribunals with blood-covered, tattooed tradesmen for judges and women with severed ears pinned to their skirts handing out death sentences to what would end up being two hundred sixteen of the two hundred sixty-nine prisoners held there. Some were freed because they knew someone with influence; others, from the tears of daughters pleading for mercy. The rest were slaughtered, like the hogs in the surrounding factories, by septembriseurs drinking brandy mixed with gunpowder to keep their vigor.

The fortress had a reputation for housing serious offenders and making them pay daily jail fines for the privilege of a night's stay in the damp Grand Châtelet. Extra if a man wanted a bed beneath him. A pile of hay for the lesser man. Nothing at all for the least among them. Most here were prisoners of the worst kind—murderers, thieves, rapists—who thought they might be freed in the chaos brought on by the tocsin bell alerting that the Duke of Brunswick's foreign armies had captured Verdun and now marched toward Paris to liberate the imprisoned king and queen. But at nearly seven of the evening, the story had changed. The prisoners' collective hope of release was a ship upon rocks, for nowhere had the insurrectionists been more ruthless than against the prisoners of Châtelet.

Had Ani's father not already lost his head those several months ago, he would have lost it today. The commoners were fueled by fear of traitors in their city jail cells, traitors who could effect a counterrevolution with the enemies of France, traitors who could escape and rally to the now-deposed king and the foreigners creeping across the countryside. Without evidence, without reason, without permission or jurisdiction granted by the collapsing government, the commoners took matters into their own hands and massacred the prisoners, before the prisoners could massacre them. It was the desperate logic of a panic-stricken populace.

A ricocheting musketball blasted through the glass window above Ani and rained a sprinkling of shards over her table. Glass fell into her coffee cup and clicked against the copper of her holster that protruded from the reinforced hole she had cut and sewn into a pair of her father's pants. She shrieked and ducked, her heart pounding when the bartender screamed for everyone to get down or get out. She got out. Dr. Breauchard's current hideout with The Citizens in the basement of a slaughterhouse resided only a few alleys away, and even that smelled better than the alternative right now.

As she rounded the first alley, she was nearly knocked to the ground by dozens of horses headed out of the city, toward Verdun. Soldiers on foot followed in homespun jackets, and then three more men on horseback. They were dressed in the blue, red, and white uniform of the National Guard, although which National Guard was anyone's guess, as that entity had been split into as many factions as had the new Jacobin party that assumed governmental control. The riders rounded another alley, then one suddenly wheeled about on his horse and walked Ani back against the wall. Her heart dropped. The blood in her veins slowed to molasses, her legs, what she could feel of them, to stone. The other two riders turned, and the three horses stood from left to right carrying none other than Aubrey Beaumercy; his key strategist, Yves Lenoir; and the Baron René-Gervais d'Egrenant.

Aubrey's horse whinnied and reared before he could settle it down. Ani's blue eyes shot through him like electricity. She was alive. And standing. A bullet to the back had not ended her. He silently thanked his God for that, though he remembered painfully what she had cost him.

"Please, keep still," she spoke low, barely heard against the backdrop of the city's screams. "Stay quiet, Marquis de Collioure, sir."

"*Marquis de Collioure, sir?*" Aubrey said with disappointment. The umbrage of her estrangement overtook his militaristic inclinations. He drew his pistol from his belt and held it on her, cocking the hammer in response to her renunciation of their bond that he'd once considered precious. "She is a spy." The words came from his mouth, but it was someone else who said them.

"You fool," she said and made no motion of surprise as Lenoir and d'Egrenant, instead of aiding in her capture, both pulled their guns on Aubrey. Had that been what was about to occur before she got here? Could she have avoided being a witness, save for one misplaced musketball and rains of glass over her head?

"All of you? You are all together?" Aubrey said, glancing slackjawed at the guns pointed at him. "You, Yves?" Aubrey jammed his lips into a thin line when the men returned only stares.

Lenoir brought his horse in closer to relieve the marquis of the gun still drawn on Ani. "Dismount," he ordered, alleviating the marquis of two pistols, a saber, and the reins of his horse.

Aubrey reluctantly dismounted and stood before Ani. Lenoir's pistol remained fixed on the marquis' head. Lenoir alighted in turn, and d'Egrenant gathered the reins of both unmounted animals and led the stallions out of the alley, out of sight.

"You know everything there is to know about me," Aubrey said.

"Vive la Révolution," Ani said.

"Vive la Révolution," Lenoir echoed, shoving the tip of his pistol into Aubrey's back. "Put your hands on your head and start walking."

As Lenoir ushered Aubrey toward the direction of the slaughter-house cellar, the marquis brushed against Ani, and she fell over with such ease that he thought she'd fainted, until her braces clinked the rocks. He looked back at her, and his chest tightened. Lenoir pushed the gun harder into the marquis' back, but Aubrey knocked it to the side and watched Ani. She rolled on the ground to get her legs under her.

"Keep your gun off me," Aubrey grunted. "I'm not going anywhere." He walked back to Ani and extended his hand down to her.

She shrugged him off.

Squatting before her, he lifted one of her pantlegs to midcalf, show-casing the copper brace. He lowered it and stood, most of his anger succumbing to an unsolicited wave of pity. That bullet had been intend-ed for him. She was injured because of the uniform he wore, paralyzed because she'd pushed him out of the way of harm. He held out his hand for her again. With a well-practiced tumble, she gained her feet on her own.

Lenoir urged the marquis forward at gunpoint, and the three of them turned down another alley. The stench of slaughter became so prominent that Ani could hardly breathe, which meant they were close. Aubrey gagged twice before having to move one of his arms from the back of his head to clip his nose. The door to the cellar awaited only steps further, and Lenoir pushed Aubrey through it, Ani trailing behind. Stairs. Always stairs. They led down, and she took each one in careful stride, holding herself upright on a slippery wall coated in grease and pig fat. At the bottom of the stairs abided The Citizens. Aubrey was directed past them without ceremony, thrown into a chair, and tied to it. He found himself sitting in front of a narrow table too rough-hewn to have ever graced his palace. Ani was certain that he noticed the ale rings and nicks in the unpolished table's surface before he noticed the knot clumsily tied at his wrists.

"*My lord general,*" Yves Lenoir addressed first. "We's well acquainted, me and you." He swept his arm around the room. "I'll introduce Citizens Pinsonnault, Crissot, and Dinaultbriand." Lenoir unrolled a long piece of paper in front of Aubrey, weighting its edges with beansacks, and sliding a pot and pen toward the marquis. "Alas we come to this. We was trying to squeeze a bit more of your military knowledge out of you," he glared at Ani, "but here we are. It's been grand help knowing your movements, but we don't really need them no more. We just be interested in one last thing from you: your signature on this condemnation. We'll untie you once you've complied."

Aubrey skimmed the document. "No."

Before Aubrey reached the end of the syllable, Lenoir smashed the butt of a pistol against the marquis' cheek, letting a spot of blood. Ani winced.

"Sign it, Marquis, and I will clear your name."

"But you cannot clear my conscience, Yves—"

"Citizen Lenoir."

"Heh, Citizen Lenoir," Aubrey grunted.

Évard Pinsonnault stepped forward and added a matching mark to the marquis' other cheek.

Aubrey shook the momentary dizziness away and spat blood onto the parchment. "My apologies, Citizen Pinsonnault, if my face has rendered any damage to your pistol." The marquis looked at Ani, who couldn't return his gaze. "So it was all planned, all along." He spoke to the side of her head. "You didn't need a job, didn't need to beg me for anything. False tears, false identity."

She studied her shoes, and her skin burned hot with embarrassment.

Évard slammed a finger on the letter of condemnation. "Sign it."

"Absolutely not, no matter what you do to me." Two more fists landed hard across his face, first from Lenoir, then from Évard.

Ani peeped mousily, "Please stop hitting him," and the men turned to look at her. She was shaking. "That's not the way to get it from him."

"And you'd know how to 'get it from him,' wouldn't you," Lenoir snarled.

Aubrey glanced groggily back and forth between the men. "Citizens Lenoir, Pinsonnault, Crissot, and Dinaultbriand," he recalled, nodding to each man in succession. "I seem to be missing one." His eyes fell on Ani. "Who are you?"

She took in a deep breath and exhaled like a horse. "Allyriane Bysshe Pardieu."

"Pardieu?" Aubrey said. "Of Simon Pardieu?" He clucked his tongue. "That explains more than you want it to."

"My father was taken from me when I was only eight to go rot in the Bastille and Châtelet before losing his head unjustly right before my eyes. He was detained without charge and put to death without charge by your own father." She extended her finger toward Aubrey.

"Your father was an infamous dissentient of the wine tax," the marquis said. "Stole barrels of wine for his own means, bribery mostly. Held up the roads through the Provence for the king's ransom. He was a glorified highwayman, no less a criminal than my own father—whose life's work, you might remember, I don't condone."

"That is a lie." She balled her hands into fists. "Your father was a murderer!"

"So, all right, my father was a murderer. And he paid the price at the hands of another murderer, didn't he. Can't take anything more from a man than his own life."

"See this?" Ani grappled for the pendant of court lilies she'd taken from Aubrey's guestroom. "This...this *trinket*, I believe you called it? Taken from a woman at, oh, where was it? Sainte-Pélagie? Hard to remember because there were so many prisons, so many women?" In her acrimony she nearly tore the pendant from her neck. "I'll tell you. For-l'Évêque, cell thirteen, second floor of the west tower. A woman arrested by your father's deputies for resisting the gabelle, for leading other women in resistance who were forced to pay salt taxes when they only had two livres a week." She was seething now. "A woman taken from her husband and two-year-old daughter to be imprisoned and raped. Raped! Over and over. Until she did not get back up and was left there to die on the filthy floor. And after *your father* had his way with her, she was dumped like rubbage into a pile of bodies in the courtyard." She felt the pain leaving her at the confession, replaced by something much darker. She stiffened and stared Aubrey down. "I'd once only been able to guess it was your father. Until I found this." She grabbed again at the necklace. "This...*trinket*, this..." she paused, choked, "was my mother. It's all that's left of her."

Aubrey remained silent, his eyes glassy wet.

"Say something!"

"What do you want me to say?"

"Apologize," she whispered.

"I didn't assault or kill your mother, Ani. I'm deeply moved, ago-nized, ribboned by your pain. But I didn't cause it."

Another fist landed across his face. "Sign it!" Évard shouted.

"No, I won't. Let me talk to Ani alone."

"She is Citizen Pardieu to you."

"She'll never be Citizen Pardieu to me."

Jean Crissot struck him this time. "We know you was headed to Ver-dun and Valmy to assist Brunswick's troops. That's treason. Generals Dumouriez and Kellermann have been sent with troops to stop Bruns-wick."

"We's got something you king boys don't got," young Pere Dinault-briand added. "Patriotism."

"Oh, hell, why not?" Aubrey laughed, a trickle of blood leaving his mouth. "It worked for the American colonists; it can work for you, right?"

Aubrey kept laughing, even after another pistol butt hit him at the temple. Ani winced again. Another and another and another blow land-ed against his face.

"Stop hitting him!" she cried. "That is not the way to do this."

Lenoir snapped back, "Surely all the times he escorted we officers out of the boardroom to put a hand up your skirt hasn't softened your heart for him, have they, Citizen Pardieu?" A corner of his lip rose. He stalked toward her. "Or perhaps you getted soft for the Beaumercys when Duke Collioure went up your skirt next? Is that it?"

Aubrey growled deep in his throat.

"I'm warning you, Yves," Ani said, her hand indicating the knife at her thigh.

"Citizen Lenoir," he corrected.

"Citizen fucking Lenoir!" Some of the spit from her words landed on his face, and it took nothing at all for him to knock her to the floor.

"What's the matter with you?" Aubrey said, struggling against his bonds, loosening the poorly tied knot at his wrists that was coated in slippery pig fat. "Big man you are! A crippled woman."

Lenoir, seeing the marquis' reaction, kicked his foot against Ani's brace as she lifted herself, sending her sprawling back to the floor. Au-brey stood, chair and all, and slammed the crude piece against the sup-port pillar, then shook out of the loosened rope. He scaled the width of the table in one bound. His hand came down onto Lenoir's throat and pulled the man to the ground. As the other stunned men reacted too slowly to pull the two apart, Lenoir reached for his gun and raised it toward Aubrey. Both men endeavored to aim it into the air or at the other, but Aubrey succeeded. He pulled the trigger, and the bullet fired into Lenoir's gut. Bits of intestine splattered out behind him, and he screamed. The other men ripped the marquis from the fray and threw him aside to tend to Lenoir. Aubrey recovered his awareness to find his face at the end of Évard's gun, as Crissot and Pere lifted the cursing, bleeding Lenoir by the arms and legs and marched him up the stairs for help. It was over as quickly as it had begun.

"Sit down, Marquis," Évard ordered, breathing raggedly. He nodded toward the table and kicked another chair in place of the now-broken one.

Aubrey muttered, and Ani wondered if it had been a prayer or an oath. He hadn't crossed himself, but then, maybe he didn't these days. God clearly wasn't answering. Aubrey looked back at her, sitting on the floor where she had remained, her face reflecting the shock of every-thing that just passed. He walked around the table and sat down. He put both hands flat on the tabletop and stared at the document in front of him, giving attention to the details this time.

Sliding the gun back in his belt, Évard walked over to Ani, but she waved him away and stood on her own. "You all right, girl?" he asked, tilting her chin. "Did Citizen Lenoir hurt you? He can be brash."

She twisted her chin out of his hand and looked back at Aubrey.

Évard followed her eyes to the marquis and sighed, then cracked his knuckles and called out to him, "If Citizen Lenoir dies, understand that you will, as good."

"I imagine I'll die either way," Aubrey replied.

"Sign the damn thing and be done with it."

"I will sign this confession," the marquis said, "if you'll allow me speak to Allyriane alone. Ten minutes. That's all I ask."

Évard eyed Ani, who lowered her head and tapped her brace. "Ten minutes," he agreed.

Aubrey waited until the last echo of Évard's boot heels died away before he spoke, shakily. "You know what you ask of me now, don't you? You know that if I sign this, it makes me look a traitor to France and a foreign spy and myriad other untrue things written in the slant of your Révolution?"

"Yes," she said, unable to look at his face.

He lifted the paper toward her, waving it, wanting her to see it as an actual physical thing. "Have you seen the list of offenses?" he asked, scanning the page. "Refusal to wear compulsory tricolor cockade. Illegally emigrated from Paris to London. Sold secrets to British troops during the Colonial Revolution?" A laugh escaped him. "Colonial Revolution? Ani, I was six years old. The only secret I knew was how to sneak jars of preserves from the pantry without getting caught." He looked back to the paper, and his smile faded. "Stole a man's horse? Was nothing sacred between us?"

"Since when is stealing a man's horse sacred."

"You stole mine not part of an hour ago! Nothing was withheld, was it? The garrison, the plans, the iron maiden, the lockbox, nothing. Asking you to marry me. They know it all, don't they."

"Yes."

"What cognac I drink. When I wake in the morning. Where my men are stationed. My involvement with foreign troops. My love for d'Alayrac's operas."

Her lip quivered. "Yes."

"Did you know, when you were gathering this, that you were putting me to my death?"

She looked down. "You won't die."

"I will. I'll be a body in a courtyard. Like your mother."

She inhaled.

"My signature to this sends hundreds of men to prison, to their deaths if what's going on out there is to be repeated." He gestured toward the street. "Good men. Women, children. My family, their families. My counts and barons, my mercenaries, my Swiss Guard, my soldiers. The same men are making these demands who put away your Feuillants, imprisoned Lafayette and his moderates. Did you even read this? Do you see what I am to admit here?" He held the paper toward her face again. "But how could you care, right? You killed my father; you killed two of my Swiss Guard. Of the same outfit who'd protected you with their lives at my palace, who would have died in their boots for your safety. Two men with families. One, the father of eight girls—Agnes, Perreta, Marie, Barbara, Anna, Magdalena, Catherine, and Claudia; I know all their names—who touted proudly that his wife, Johanna, was finally pregnant with their first boy, he was sure of it. A boy who will never know his father. Less than you ever knew yours. These are men, Ani. Fallible creatures of God. But you don't care, do you? Human life is cheap; how could you care?"

Tears threatened, but she choked down her own self-pity like a bitter pill. "I do care, Marquis. But I can do nothing about it."

"Yes, you can, you coward. You can tell them no. You can be the general that men would want to follow into battle." He took a sharp breath. "Did you even care anything for me?" He waved it off. "No, don't answer that. I don't want to know."

There arose a silence on the air that could breathe on its own, so full of life that it was downright suffocating. She whispered, hardly audible, "Yes."

"Yes," he echoed, listlessly, unmoved. "Was I easy for you to betray?"

Tears finally stung her eyes. "No."

"Don't waste your tears. No one else can see you, and I'm certain they are not for me." He picked up the fountain pen and dipped it in the ink twice, taking care to catch the drip and to move it quickly to the paper for a good, clean signature. If it had to be there, then by God, it was going to look good.

Ani blurted, "Don't sign it, Marquis."

He scratched on his elegant A, and snapped, "Stop calling me marquis! Don't insult me. Let something remain pure, for fucksake." He calmed, didn't bother crossing himself, and dipped his pen back into the jar. "I gave my word that I would sign it if I could speak to you alone, and here we are, speaking alone. Some people still keep their word."

She watched him sign with his careful hand, decorating the hanging Y's and making extra loops on his fancy B, just to drag out the moment longer.

"But now you listen to me," he finally said. "If I am to die, then it had better be by your hand. You'd better have the guts to finish what you started." He set the fountain pen delicately into the jar.

"Marquis, please understa—"

"Ecchh, marquis. Stop with the marquis. I understand—I do—perfectly well. Better than you understand it, I'll wager." He cut off her protest before it could begin. "How you've broken me is not a secret that anyone will buy from you. I politely request that you don't make me watch my friends and family die first, and please, God please," he crossed himself this time and put his hands together in front of his mouth in prayer, "if there's anything that you did leave out, I beg you, let it be left." He put up a finger to stop her from interjecting. "Don't. Just let me be." He held up his hands. "You've won. I surrender to you, as I did from the first."

After a stretch of silence, Évard Pinsonnault opened the latch to the door with a hearty "Ten minutes up," and he strolled to the table and lifted the paper. "There, now that wasn't so hard, was it?"

"No, Citizen," Aubrey said. "I can be a scum-heeled lout, too, same as you."

"Splendid." Évard looked over the signature, rolled the paper, and pulled from his pocket the marquis' stolen pewter insignia ring. "Now for the closing act of this d'Alayrac opera." He chuckled, waving the ring in Aubrey's view before heating wax over the candle, dripping it onto the document, and pressing the marquis' insignia into it.

Aubrey glared at Ani and shook his head. "That's a well-played card."

"You think that's some impressive thievery?" Évard grinned slyly. "Why don't you tell him about the documents you stole from him, Citizen Pardieu—the foreign correspondence, the letters to Brunswick?" He smiled with delight as Aubrey shot a horrified look at Ani. "Oh yes, those letters."

"That's enough, Évard," Ani begged, so tense in her stomach that she almost threw up. "He doesn't need to know."

"It's Citizen Pinsonnault. And yes, I think he'd like to know how he murdered Baronet Chicoine in his parlor for crimes you committed, Citizen Pardieu, based on false evidence from men you, yourself, paid." He laughed coldly, and Aubrey gasped, hung his head. "But alas, the baronet received a good funeral. You just shot the wrong spy, Marquis." Évard shrugged indifferently, figured he'd said enough to avenge Lenoir, and let the tension linger.

"Please don't take him to l'Abbaye," Ani said, after a bout of silence between them. "Not tonight. Not how it is out there."

"Aw, see?" Évard smiled. "She's not all bad, that one." He nodded at her. "No mob justice for you tonight, it looks. You earned yourself a nice set of manacles until the cleansing subsides." Évard retrieved grease-coated shackles from a shelf and tossed them to Ani. "He's all yours."

She stared at the iron shackles and the skeleton key protruding from the lock in her hand and walked toward Aubrey, dragging her right leg more than usual after a tiring day. When she got to him, he stood and put his hands out, allowing her to snap the manacles around one wrist without resistance and then following her lead, patiently, over to the support pillar to shackle the second one around it.

"Why do you let these men walk on you?" he whispered, her face finally so close he could smell her hair over the stench of the slaughter-house. Blood dripped from his mouth onto his raised hands.

"They'll calm down. They've waited quite a while to shout at you, my lord."

"Please say Aubrey."

"You mean you don't want to be Citizen Beaumercy?"

He wrinkled his nose. "If those are my choices, then I'll stick with lord, thanks." He sighed. "Before you chain me up, any chance a man could relieve himself somewhere abouts?"

"You have to go?"

He cocked an eyebrow and made a face of obvious affirmation.

She called out to Évard, "He has to make water."

"He can piss his damn self."

"Évard."

"Citizen Pinsonnault."

She took a long breath. "Citizen Pinsonnault, that's not very humane."

"Then take him up for a piss."

"Me?"

"You're the one concerned about it. We got his confession—I don't care about his fate. He can piss his damn self."

She glared. "All right, come on." She closed the shackles over Aubrey's wrists behind his back and pushed him toward the stairs. "Don't try anything. I have a gun at your back."

"Yes, I recognize the gun."

He moved to the stairs in front of her at her pace. When he set his foot on the first step, he heard a noise leave her like a deflating windbag. The stairs. He took four of the steps with guilty ease and heard the clink of her copper boot landing on the first one. She put her hands on the stairs in front of her and pulled her weight up to meet one foot with the other.

"If you unshackle me," he offered, "I will carry you."

"No one carries me."

She picked up her next step and her next and made it to the top of the stairs faster than she'd ever made it before. Neither admitted how easily he could have outrun her and fled, even shackled. Once outside the cellar door, a light cough left her lungs, but at the end of it, she was still standing.

Aubrey faced away from her in the dark alley. "I can't do much unless you unshackle me." He indicated toward his buttoned fallfront fly. "Or unbutton me."

She glanced at his buttons, blushed, then grappled with the skeleton key at the shackle lock.

"I thought for a second there you might unbutton me." He smirked, turning his back to her and adjusting. "Sweet relief! It's almost enough to make me forget you deceived me into killing my own innocent man."

"He wasn't innocent."

"Ah, cabinet talk! Do tell."

"Put your hands on the back of your head."

"I can't very well do that without wetting myself," he said. "I need at least one of those hands for my other head."

"All right, one hand, then." She prodded the gun into his back until he raised one hand to the back of his neck. "Baronet Chicoine might not have stole the correspondence you thought he stole, but he," she paused, "did other things." Another pause.

"Such as?"

"I can't tell you."

"You can't leave a man in suspense like that. Shouldn't I at least get to know what you have on me to help build my defense? I won't be offered a fair trial, and I'm sure I'll have to be my own lawyer, so what does it hurt? It isn't like my opinion of you can lessen." A part of him felt shame for giving in to the desire to hurt her as she'd hurt him. She was clearly being used as a pawn in someone else's game.

"All right," she conceded, "but only in exchange for one more piece of information from you."

"Deal."

"Two pieces of information."

"Aht-aht, you already said one, and I agreed. You can't change it now."

"Two," she said. "I need two."

"All right. Two. You first."

"Baronet Chicoine sold the names of the ten men you met with in London."

Aubrey sputtered, "What? How? How do you know this?"

"He had you followed, and I know because," she hesitated, "because I bought the names from him. Well…you bought them. With your own money, out of your own safe."

"Oh, Allyriane," he sighed with disappointment. He had unwittingly placed those men in danger—British men who were helping French no-blemen and their families escape France safely. "God, how you betrayed me." He moved his hand from behind his head to cross himself, and she stuck the gun into his back. "Please tell me the Brits are still alive."

"I don't know."

He finished relieving himself, shook it off, tucked it in, and moved his hand up to join the other at the back of his neck, leaving himself unbuttoned. "All right," he whispered. "What is the first piece of infor-mation you want?"

"How do you know Émilien Gagnon?"

"Huh," he grunted. That name was not expected. "Tell me I'm not incriminating him, and I'll answer."

"We had a deal. Answer."

"Ani, please."

"Answer."

He took a steadying breath. "Émil is a very close friend. We were classmates at Lycée Louis-le-Grand. I've known him for, I don't know, eight years. He is a good man, Ani. Up to snuff, and a pinch above it. Good businessman, husband, father. Please don't involve him in this."

"Good businessman?" she said. "Do you know he sells orphans into industrial slavery to get a percentage return on the goods they produce?"

He groaned. "It sounds like that's what you think you know, but that doesn't hold one ounce of water with me. Where did you hear that? Did you question it? Investigate it?"

"I was an orphan sold into slavery."

"By Émil?"

"No," she replied sharply. "By your father."

"That sounds more like it," he said with ironic approval. "That I will not refute. But don't condemn men until you know the truth. That's how we've arrived at this mess." His voice softened. "Émil is probably the best friend I have. A father of two boys and three girls he asked me to godfather. A kind, loving husband to a teaching instructor for the deaf-mute. He lives on land I gave them as a wedding gift. He would not enslave children lest his own should become enslaved."

"You're wrong. I have his accounting books."

Aubrey brayed like a donkey. "Well. Don't I stand corrected, then! Surely you know exactly how to interpret the intricate shorthand cipher in a man's accounting books. I'm sure a veritable codex is stamped in the inside flap, along with a convenient summary and a table of contents. 'Dear revolutionaries, please see enclosed enslavement-of-children profits on page nineteen. Your humble and obedient,' right? And whysoever might anyone dare to fabricate such conclusions? I mean, someone told you what it was, and no one would ever lie to you, would they?"

"Enough. I'm sparing your life by not letting you get massacred at l'Abbaye right now."

"My, thank you, your gracious majesty. I hope you're not terribly insulted when I tell you that I'd rather be massacred and have my body thrown from the Pont au Change than be at the mercy of Jacobins signing false confessions that will imprison every miserable sap who has had the misfortune of knowing me."

"They're Girondins."

"No. They're not," he said without comedy. "Maybe they once were, but they're not now."

"You don't know them."

"I don't care to. Those sons of bitches hurt my face." He winced as he said it and mentally crossed himself. "You were once a Constitutional monarchist—what happened? You traded in your common sense for common men. They don't want *the people* to control anything; they want to control it themselves, to be their own king." A few seconds of quiet passed between them. Aubrey cleared his throat. He couldn't hide his disappointment. "What was the second piece of information you wanted?"

She tensed. Were it not for the springs, her knees would have buckled. It was something she wanted to know as much as not know, hear as much as not hear, unsure if she wanted her ignorance to remain as it was, or if she could stand to hear the answer without collapsing. Finally, she mustered, "Did you know my father?"

"Do you mean Monsieur Pardieu?"

"Yes, of course," she said, "who else would I mean."

The answer came slowly. "I only knew of him," he said softly. "He gave great grievance to our departments."

"Did he deserve to be imprisoned?"

"Probably. I wasn't in his court."

"He never went to court. He was never tried or charged, just locked up and killed."

"I only know stories," he said.

"Tell them."

"I was maybe fourteen when he was first imprisoned at the Bastille, but his rebellious legacy lived long after that. I knew the men charged with moving him later to Châtelet, and they'll tell you he was no gentleman. He was not one of the pailleux on straw beds; he could buy and sell whatever he wanted. Would that he had spent a little more of that money on your care, and I might think that much higher of him, but he spent it on his own comforts and desires. Did he deserve to be imprisoned? I don't know. I want to shout yes, Ani, but I swear I don't want to hurt you. He knew what he was doing, and he knew the risks. He repeatedly stole and damaged the king's property, the least of his offenses being bootlegging the king's wine."

"The king's wine?"

"Yes. Simon Pardieu was a thief. Highwayman, robber, bootlegger, you name it. But more unforgiveable, he abandoned you to a wasted, lonely life for a bag of the king's gold. For that alone he deserved to be imprisoned." The cocking of the gun behind his head told him his words cut deep.

After a slew of curses, Ani spat, "I wish I could kill you right now."

"Why can't you?"

"Because I believe you're telling the truth." She sniffled, took a deep breath that caught repeatedly in her diaphragm, and Aubrey didn't need to look at her to know she was crying and that the tears were real this time. She shoved the gun into the small of his back. "And because they might need you to back that confession. Now turn around."

"I won't back it. I will contest that it was coerced." He moved his hands from his head and slowly lowered them out to his sides with his palms up and his fingers spread. "May I at least button my front?"

He took extra long adjusting his carriage, restuffing, and fastening each button, letting her wallow in the silence and the stench of the slaughterhouses, before turning to face her. Ani's gun hung weakly limp before him, extended half-heartedly. Her face was blank. She was spent. Physically, emotionally, mentally. He held his hands out, the shackle loosely dangling around one wrist, and he came within inches of touching her skin, her arms. So close, she felt his warmth rising off his body, almost visible like steam, as he pressed his stomach into the tip of her gun, unafraid of anything she could do to him now. She uncocked it.

"Run away," she whispered.

He gave a half-smile. "You'd better shackle me up." He wiggled his outstretched hands.

He was warmer than the September night when she pulled from him, lowering the gun. She stepped away, and he stepped away. The stairs were slow, but she managed them, and he took each slow step with her, and at the bottom, he helped her stand upright, her lungs again exploding in fire inside her. When she faced him, her eyes were moist. He came forward and pulled her into him, and she released an emptying, silent stream of tears against his chest. He waited until her shaking stopped, and he moved her away, balancing her at the wall. She rubbed the wetness from her eyes to avoid Évard's impending judgment.

"No more of that now." Aubrey lifted her limp hand with the gun, extended it outright, and turned his back to the barrel, walking through the door ahead of her and back to the pillar, shackling his own wrists around the post. "Have you got any whisky?" he whispered with a smile that didn't meet his eyes.

"Your hands are not idle enough for whisky," she replied, wiping her cheeks with her sleeve, "but I got some coffee."

The smile met his eyes. "A mercifully swift death."

Chapter Sixteen

The inevitable death

Pity is treason.

—Maximilien Robespierre

The September Massacres, as they came to be called, lasted only a handful of days, leaving nearly three thousand prisoners dead in prison cells and abbey courtyards, thrown into the mass graves of the catacombs at the city's walls, or used as breaker bags along the Seine's shores, the stench of rotting bodies adding to that of the sewage. As the weeks passed, the Legislative Assembly became powerless, and the government was turned over to extremists set on destroying the last royalist threads of the Assembly. The new National Convention finally and fully reared its head and swallowed whole any hope of moderation. It crushed in totality the Feuillants, the royalists, the moderates, the clergy, the foreigners, and all who stood with any of these.

Ani paced the floor of the slaughterhouse cellar, click, click, until the door opened, and in walked Évard, disheveled and unkempt, stubble speckling his stiff, tight jaw—yet dressed in a new tailored outfit. Ani wondered how he had the money to afford it; she certainly wasn't getting rich off giving him her information. Spent and seething, he skulked around the quarters.

"You look like the bottom of a boot, Citizen Pinsonnault," Ani said. "What happened?"

A bitter crinkle creased his face like he'd licked a lime. "Citizen Lenoir didn't make it," he said. "Succumbed to the fever."

She drew her lips taut. Shit. Shit, shit, shit. "If I had shut my mouth, he'd never have got shot."

"No, it's that goddamn marquis' fault." He scratched at his chin hairs, and dry flakes fell from his skin onto the sleeves of his new overcoat. "I warned him he'd pay. Laurent is on graveyard. He'll gain me the marquis' cell for a humble fee."

Aubrey had been detained in the damp, medieval galleys at Prison de l'Abbaye for thirteen days without trial or charge, while Lenoir slowly died in a neighboring slaughterhouse converted into a makeshift hospital. It didn't seem to Ani like a good way for either one of them to go, but one was more fitting to her than the other, and not the way-around it should have been from The Citizens' point of view.

"It's good to know folks in the right places, Citizen Pardieu," Évard finished with a sadistic grin.

Ani said, "Don't you need the marquis to confess before a tribunal?"

"If he's nay alive, no tribunal be necessary for him."

"The tribunal is not for the marquis, but to condemn a whole ring of corrupt noblesse, remember? The whole Beaumercy empire, the foreign alliance, the Swiss Guard, all the aristocracy. The confession will incriminate hundreds in their tangled web. Are you willing to give that up?"

"I don't care," Évard brushed it off. "It's not about that now, Citizen. The rich think they can do whatever they please, own whatever falls beneath their slippers, and it don't matter what they crush in the process. It's time to show them that's nay true no more. Citizen Lenoir paid his price for insurrection. Now it's time for the marquis to pay the price for treason."

Ani picked a loose shaving of brown paint from the tabletop where she had plopped herself as she studied Évard's determined face, too close to hers. She could smell the rot of his brown teeth. If he murdered Aubrey, it would not be quick or painless or humane, but a butchery as intense as any in the past weeks. Aubrey would be slowly mutilated and would suffer immensely. One limb would be left by the river, three limbs in the courtyard, his torso off the Pont au Change, his head atop a pike. She shuddered.

"If it must be done, then let me do it," she finally said, unsure she'd heard herself correctly. "It was my provoking what led to the marquis attacking Citizen Lenoir. At least let me make up for it." She could sense his hesitation. He put a hand on her knee, and she was thankful she couldn't feel it. She nodded to her unresponsive leg. "I'm expendable. I can't do much now, but I can do this, and you know I can. I'll pay Laurent. Save your bribe money and get an ale instead, bury your friend, grieve like you should."

"I could use an ale." He laughed uneasily. He touched the tip of her nose with his forefinger, and it didn't feel as much like rifled steel as she thought it would. "You'll make it hurt, won't you?"

"His family killed mine," she said.

He smiled briefly before he walked out, much calmer than when he'd walked in. From the top of the stairs, he yelled back down to her, "Make it hurt!"

ఴ

The hours passed and a small horloge struck nine. The gallery of prisoners sat near the back of the Prison de l'Abbaye, and the rest of it lay quiet. Eerie vacancy washed over the newly emptied abbey and played a creepy accompaniment to the smell of rotting flesh from the discarded. Moving down the narrow corridor of cells, Ani scanned the layout for deviations from the floor plans she knew well. The sound of her clicking copper cut through the halls with metronomic rhythm. She wore a dark forest-green cloak pulled over her hair and face, clasped around men's pants—but no longer her father's.

From the end of the hall, even Aubrey could hear her drag and click. Drag and click. Drag and click. Mixed with the clanking keys of the guard, Laurent—a man riddled with prurigo skin disease who galumphed like an obese cat searching for slow-moving rats—the two were an ominous pair, and Aubrey could hear death walking with them.

Ani knew that seeing his eyes would be the hardest part. They'd hold no sign of censure. They'd shine instead with that pathetic glimmer of joy to see her, however fleeting. And when he was finally gone, that would be the image to haunt her forever, to replace her father at the guillotine, her mother's apron on the last day she'd seen her alive, all she still remembered of that day. The lilies. Dr. Breauchard's broken heart. Allowances of imagination stole through her: Aubrey's solitude, the loneliness of a cell, the beard he must have by now, the fear that might flicker across his face, tension in his jaw, sadness of succumbing to frailty and fallibility as all things must. Would he passively let her do it? Would he struggle? She jerked her hand upward in a thrusting motion repeatedly, involuntarily. It would have to be rote muscle memory to preclude the chance of failure from mental laxity. His face would draw out weakness in her. But she brought him mercy; she consoled herself with this.

The clanking of keys stopped, and the clicking of metal stopped, and Ani pushed back her fear as she looked into the cell. She still felt unprepared, but there he was. Sitting in profile, surprisingly clean-shaven, on the edge of a comfortable bed wedged in between a table with an oil lamp and a couple of books and a chair, staring at a painting on the wall. Ani couldn't see it from her angle, but it certainly mesmerized him.

"That's the one," she said to Laurent. Aubrey sat motionless, not turning to face her.

Laurent hissed, "So this be the prattle-toothed scum what killed Yves, eh?" He looked Aubrey up and down with a twitching, wrinkled nose like a rodent sniffing offal in a sewer. "Don't look none scary to me."

When Aubrey spoke, his voice was sure and steady. "Did he die then, the sorry swine?" He finally looked at Ani. "Guess he won't be hitting you again."

The guard fumbled with the ring and opened the wrought-iron gate, its creaking moan a warning. Ani looked down at the chalk mark on the floor, the indication that Aubrey was to die without appearing before the tribunal to defend himself, and she rubbed the edge of her shoe back and forth over the mark until it was ground into the stone, then fought her obstinate legs to step over the gate's lower threshold. Aubrey slid off the bed to his feet and awaited her approach. Her cloak obscured her eyes, chin bent nearly to her chest.

"At least it's you," Aubrey said, and waited until she lifted her chin into the lamp's light. "You look terrified. Do you need me to provoke you, to give you reason to go through with it?"

She tilted her head toward the portrait that hung above eye level on a suicide hook, and she made a small moan. It was she. The portrait for which she'd posed, holding cups of imported tea. The flames of the Bastille rose over her shoulder in the background. Her face, turned to it as if looking to the fires for answers.

"There's your reason," Aubrey whispered. "Monsieur Lethière's messenger brought it to me just yesterday, and I haven't taken my eyes from it since. I call it *The Betrayal.*"

Ani's shoulders slumped.

"The look in your eyes, the flames snapping like an aristocrat's neck. Didn't think he'd actually paint them in, but there they are. I know now what you were thinking: Your father. Your mother. Everything taken from you in my name. I look at it and think of how I didn't know that then. Look at the pain in those eyes. Doesn't it make you angry enough to kill a man for being his father's son?"

Laurent stepped in and separated the two. "We inn't here for no social chat. Slit his throat and get it on with."

"Don't rush me," Ani said, shaking. "Marquis—Aubrey—I do not aim to make this torturous. I come in Évard's place—"

"I believe you mean Citizen Pinsonnault," Aubrey said.

"—because I could not bear what he'd do to you."

"Thank you for that consideration," he replied in earnest. "Grant me a prayer first, if my time is short: O God, great and omnipotent Judge of the living and the dead, I am to appear now before Thee after this short life to render an account of my works—"

"Oh, for god fuckin' sake on a shitpile, what be this, church?" Laurent blurted, spraying spit on his audience. "Get it on with!"

Ani said, "Let him finish."

Aubrey stared at her, not bowing his head or kneeling, just staring. The prayer was not for God. "Give me the grace to prepare for my last hour by knowing I led a devout and holy life, and protect me against a sudden and unprovided death, forgiving those, I ask Thee, who would provide that death unto me. Let us all abiding here remember our frailty and mortality, that we may always live in the ways of Your Commandments. If this is to be the last of my earthly trials before Thee, then help me face it with courage, mercy, and forgiveness of those who would inflict pain and finality upon one of Your children. Teach me that when Your summons comes for my departure from this world, I may go forth to meet Thee, experience a merciful judgment, and rejoice in everlasting happiness. I ask this through Christ, my Lord. Amen." His voice was soft, and he nodded assurance of his submission, crossing himself slowly, his gaze into her eyes unfaltering. "Thank you for that, Allyriane."

She choked down the lump in her throat. "Anything else you'd like to say, speak now."

After a pause, he said, "I would have built a fire for you every day in French Canada."

The words crippled her more than her legs ever could. The knife shook in her hand beneath her cloak and rattled against her brace. "I will make this swift and painless, absolving you of any crimes that I cannot withdraw from your name," she promised, her lip quivering to match the rattling of the knife at her side. "Do you have any request for how you'd like to," she choked, "die?"

"Yes," he chuckled. "Old age, maybe another fifty years, warm in my bed, lying next to a loving wife, dog curled at my feet, fire in the hearth, hot whisky in my belly." From beneath her cloak, Ani drew the glinting blade, and Aubrey's eyebrows went up. "Ah, my father's knife. How appropriate. Maybe not the throat, then, so I can still look handsome in my coffin. If I'm allotted one, of course. A stab to the heart will do fine. I already know how that feels." He paused, seeing the torture Ani was enduring at her unfortunate task, but then added pointedly, "One more request." He stepped toward her. "When you drive the blade in my heart, look deep into my eyes and watch the life go out of them. I want you to never forget that look. Because that, my girl, is the true look of a revolution."

"Jesus, no more requests!" Laurent finally squealed. "He don't get no more requests. Gut the bastard like a bloody screaming pig, give me my livres, and get done with it."

"Be respectful of a man's last breath," Ani shushed. "You will get your money when he is dead." She moved the tip of her knife to Aubrey's gut, just above the stomach, aimed upward to pass beneath the ribcage and into his heart. She steadied her shaking hands for the awful thing. "If there truly is a god in heaven," she whispered, "do not forgive what I do." Tears streamed down her cheeks as she turned, drew her hand back swiftly, and fiercely drove the blade home, the deadly point finding its way into his gut, tearing through the aorta in a quick twist up to her knuckles, and the thing was done. The body dropped before her on the ground without having even uttered in pain. She bent and retrieved the knife. It was red all the way to the hilt like a prong of the devil's trident. She breathed hard. It was done. Her decision had been made.

"You've got to admit that pilgarlic deserved it more than I did." Aubrey's voice cut through the air as he stood over Laurent's body.

"He had a family, a wife, a little boy," she said. "I even know his son's name."

"Oh, don't you use my tactics on me. He was a filthy louse." He paused. "Do you really know his son's name?"

"Don't even know if he actually had one. Just made that up."

She bent slowly again and lifted the keys from Laurent's fingers, carefully balancing on her uncooperative knees. As she drew back her cloak, Aubrey saw that she carried the white satchel of the old Constitutional revolutionary soldier garb slung over her shoulder. A military scabbard hung about her waist displaying the hilt of a displanted National Guardsman, bearing Lafayette's cameo insignia forged into the custom knuckle branches. She placed the key ring into her satchel and reached out to Aubrey, both for her own stability and to pull him along with her.

"That was a really longwinded prayer," she said. "One might think your god is not wont to be merciful to someone who loves so much to hear himself talk." She stepped over Laurent's body. "Come on with me, quick."

Aubrey kicked the chair along the wall, stepped up onto it, and pulled down the large painting of Ani.

"Leave the portrait. What're you doing?"

"Are you touched?" he said. "Do you know how much this cost me? What it's worth? This is an original Guillon-Lethière! No chance I'm leaving it behind. It gave me wild premonitions all through the night, and then today you arrive. You can't fiddle with that intervention. It's the reason I recite long prayers."

"You don't suppose you could've commissioned a miniature?"

"Pah, miniatures are for gentry." He set the portrait on the bed, took the knife from Ani's hand, and slit the edges of the canvas along the inside of the frame. Once the canvas separated from the ornate wood, he rolled the painting carefully and tucked it beneath his arm.

She led him out of the cell and toward the series of tunnels that curved under the Chemin de Ronde and came out beneath the rue Sainte-Marguerite. The tunnels were ink black save for small spots of light that flittered from a few errant oil lamps. Aubrey marveled at how quickly she moved. Her unbalanced drag and limp seemed nothing worse than the gait of an average drunkard.

"You were really going to kill me, weren't you," he whispered, his mind still staggering with the thought of it.

"I don't think so."

"So, there's a chance you were?"

"I don't know," she admitted. "I didn't; that's all that matters. But I'm in a hell of a stew now. Stay right with me. There's a blind turn here soon."

"Do you know your way everywhere?" he asked, surprised at how far his echo carried.

"Everywhere you've been."

When they neared the brightest portion of the last turn, she stopped to utilize what light was available. Billows of smoke came down the hall from winds uttering through an antiquated chimney. She reached into her satchel and drew from it the rolled confession he'd signed accusing hundreds of treason, of corresponding with foreign troops, and of stealing money from peasants.

"Burn it," she said, handing it to him. "Only the men in that room know of your signature to this condemnation. One of them is dead; the rest of them now think you are. They think this has gone to the minister of justice. Someone will figure it out, but we bought ourselves a little time, and if they want it, they'll have to start over for it. So burn it, and your family is clean. I will wipe them from any lists I find and contest that I don't know what happened to the confession, but in exchange, you must—look at me—you must stay dead. If they find you alive, then I can't do a thing for you. And there is more." She pulled the two small accounting ledgers of Émilien Gagnon's from the satchel and placed them in Aubrey's hands. "Keep these safe. You'll know what to do with them when the time arrives. Now you must go. Straight down this tunnel, and then there is a ladder that leads to a back exit to rue Sainte-Marguerite. There's a carriage just above it, disguised as a doctor cart. It's headed over the Pont au Change toward Switzerland to ride through the night. They will make room for one more. Get in it. No questions. Go now." She pushed his shoulder toward the exit, but he turned back around to face her.

"You're not coming with me?" he asked, tucking the confession and thin ledgers into his inside jacket pocket with difficulty until a seam ripped.

"No, go now. Do not join in battles; do not let anyone know you're alive. Just save yourself from this. I risked everything. Don't disrespect that sacrifice."

Even the tunnel's darkness could not hide his despondency. "But what of later? You'll not come later?"

"There is work to do here."

"Ani, run with me—to England, to America, to Canada. There are places we could go. To the Dutch Republic—anywhere. I'll pledge myself to you."

She clanked the metal of her boot brace against the ground. "I cannot run anywhere with you."

"I will carry you."

"I told you no one carries me."

"I carried you before." He stepped closer. "You were shot and scared, and I carried you. You were betraying me, and I still carried you. I carried you to my death, knowing it would be my death, so that it wouldn't be yours." He put his hand against her cheek and searched for her nearly invisible eyes in the dark, moving his mouth close to her temple. "Must we do it this way?" he whispered. "I'll come to terms with this immense confliction, I swear it—just give me time. But let me in. I'm not a coward. I won't leave you behind."

"Aubrey." His breath was so warm she thought she might dissolve into it. "People will die because of me. I must fix it. I can no longer stand still in this hole of humanity feeding on itself."

"And I get to be no part of that because of my name? Let me help you. We've all done wrong. I'm a general, for God's sake. I've killed my own countrymen! I have to believe something better is coming." He pressed his mouth against her forehead. "Either let me stay, or come with me now." His mouth grazed her temple, her cheek. "Don't condemn me never to know what's become of you." He leaned the rolled portrait against the wall, and pressed his hands into her back, pushing into her, her to him, lifting her into his chest without resistance as she nuzzled her nose into the crook of his shoulder. His mouth touched the corner of her eye when he spoke: "I need to teach you how to waltz with your braces on." He moved his hands down her back.

She crumpled against him, the darkness enhancing her vertigo state. "Will I stand on your toes?"

"Would that be different than usual?"

He pulled her toward him as if to kiss her, caressing lightly across her hip, tracing the outline of her body along her outer thigh, touching the edge of her metal brace through her pants' thin fabric. He brushed his mouth against hers, and she responded to his lips and held them in her own, and he moaned. She suddenly took hold of his arms, pushed him back, and gasped like a beached fish.

"I'm sorry," he said. "I went too far."

"You're a fairytale. You are not in my world." She lifted the portrait from the wall where it leaned at her side, and placed it in his hands, dismissing the pain that flashed in his expression. "I need to know that you're gone from here, and that's all I need to know." She slid out from beneath the light and pulled her cloak back over her hair, drawing from around her middle the belt that held the scabbard that held the saber that held Lafayette's once-revolutionary likeness. She placed it around the marquis' waist and secured the buckle. "You might need this on your way out of France," she said flatly, and reemphasized, "*out* of France."

Before he could protest, she turned from him with a swish of her cloak and disappeared in the darkness back toward the center of the prison, the clicking of her brace and her taste still upon his lips the only proof she had existed there at all.

Chapter Seventeen

The carriageway to Switzerland

*There are only two
forces that unite men:
fear and interest.*

—Napoleon Bonaparte

Aubrey felt his way through the last stretch of the dark tunnel until a stream of light came in around a large drain cover. It slid open to spit him out into the gutter of rue Sainte-Marguerite, shadowed overhead by the underbelly of a carriage. He squeezed himself through the opening, portrait and all, still wearing his lieutenant-general uniform, weeks now without wash. He caught a whiff of himself and grimaced. Crawling out from beneath the carriage, he saw on its side the insignia of a doctor cart—an oversized conveyance to transport the injured, complete with a fat driver wheezing like he should have been inside it instead. For a brief flash, Aubrey thought he recognized the driver, but there was no time to ponder it. The marquis rapped against the side of the drawn window shade. The door opened without hesitation. He couldn't make out the shadowy figure that occupied the carriage, but he took a deep breath, stepped in, and jerked back.

"Dr. Breauchard." Aubrey gripped the sword at his hip. "Is this another trap?"

"Sit down," Breauchard replied. "Hurry up. Shut your mouth." The doctor draped a blanket around Aubrey's shoulders while the marquis seated himself, pulling it taut around the chest to conceal the noble general outfit. "So it was you she saved. I hope you realize the danger you've put her in. To hell with whatever you said to her that's got her muddled so." A brisk pause, and he added, "If the carriage gets stopped for any reason, act sick or injured. And keep that uniform covered."

Studying the doctor, Aubrey asked, "Why are you helping me? Aren't you a Girondin?"

"Yes."

"Why not turn me in?"

"We Girondins are a dying breed now, too." He shrugged, pulled at a loose thread on his sleeve. "Allyriane told me to wait for someone. She tells me to wait, I wait." The doctor knocked on the wood paneling behind his head, and the carriage lurched forward.

Aubrey adjusted the portrait such that it leaned against the side of the bench between his feet and the door, but the doctor lifted it into his own lap and unrolled the canvas.

"You had her painted? Is this the signature of Guillaume Guillon-Lethière?"

"Yes."

"It's beautiful."

"Helps to have a beautiful subject."

The doctor looked at the portrait. "The Bastille. I'm sure she appreciated that." He cocked a brow. "Her crooked teeth. Her pointed nose. Most men would not call her beautiful."

"Most men are fools, Doctor. Or is it Citizen Breauchard?"

"Jacques," he allowed. "I'd kiss your hand, but you're filthy." He rolled the portrait and set it back along the inside of the carriage door.

"Will you bring her to me so I can keep her safe?"

"Stay far away from her."

"Then let me out right here."

"No." Breauchard considered the marquis' disappointed expression. "Do you still believe she cared for you?"

"Yes."

The doctor looked out the window, the shade raised as they crossed the Pont au Change and headed toward the charred remains of the Bastille—still in ruins three years after its demise—then on to the stretching faubourgs and countryside. "I doubt she remembers that she was a happy child," he finally said, "that she played with marbles and paper dolls, recited poetry. Drew still-lifes of vegetables and ewers, wanted to be a painter at one time. Used to read innocent children's stories that were not the words of Thomas Paine and that Hamilton fellow."

"Are you really taking me to Switzerland, or are you going to put lead in me in some dark countryside?"

Breauchard chuckled. "If I did that, she'd know. I've never been much good at lying to her."

"I'd say you've been quite good."

Breauchard narrowed his eyes at the marquis.

"When are you going to tell her?" He paused. "Don't you think she'd like to know she's your daughter?" Aubrey watched Breauchard deflate. "The second I saw your matching eyes in that printshop, I knew. Your hair, your nose. The reason I was permitted to walk away from that shop with my life. It's why you're sitting here right now, and I'm still not dead. Even your dimples hollow the same. She'll figure it out eventually, and you know it. Shouldn't she hear it from you before she hears it from a mirror?"

"I will tell you a story," the doctor said. "Maybe someone should hear it. It's no secret you're only here because of Ani. I have no regard for you. I despise your family tree right down to every last bastard child in the deepest of the roots or the thinnest of the branches."

"Yes, yes, I'm abhorrent. Just tell it."

Breauchard swallowed. "I loved her mother. Marie Pardieu, I loved her. The affair lasted three years before the inevitable happened, but she was married to Simon." He held up his palms and shrugged. "Deputies imprisoned her for being among a group of women who stole two ounces of sugar from an apothecary shop, and at For-l'Évêque, your father became obsessed with her. Helped himself, as did the guards. She's in an unmarked hole in a courtyard." He rubbed his eye. "She wouldn't have wanted Ani to know, but I cannot help rogue tongues from telling what they hear." His tone turned from melancholy to angered. "I couldn't protect Marie, but I can protect Ani. I know you asked it of her, but she'll never be a Beaumercy."

Aubrey picked at the edge of the portrait. "Simon knew."

"He did. No one had to guess where those blue eyes came from."

"Does she know that she's not from lower class?"

"She may remember some fragments," Breauchard said, "but I don't think she's ever entirely pieced it together, no. Simon was not a good father—absent, abusive. She misses the idea of him more than she misses the man himself."

"He was more than a poor father—Simon was a scapegrace, and Ani mistakenly thinks him a saint. I wonder where she got that impression?"

"What harm is there in a child honoring her parents? Is that not one of your commandments?" Breauchard smirked.

"So is not committing adultery," Aubrey said sharply, then sighed. "Why did you tell me? You know I will tell her."

"No, my lord, I believe you won't. You'll let things lay as they fall." He pulled a tin out of his pocket and slid the cover open between thumb and forefinger, dabbing a pinky into the ground powder inside, then extending the tin to Aubrey. "Snuff?"

"Unadulterated?"

"Do I strike you as a fraud?"

Aubrey grunted. He dabbed a pinky and a thumb into the tin. With his pinky against his nose and his thumb in his mouth, he breathed in quickly. "Whew, that's some stuff. That's more than just tobacco, there."

"It may or may not contain a sprinkle of nightshade and dried opium milk." Breauchard smiled.

"Well, thank you for the warning." He laughed. "I suppose the night couldn't suffer from a few falling stars."

The wood paneling pressed Aubrey's head as he pondered what Breauchard had told him and slipped the signed confession out of his pocket. He unfolded the document and read it over, solemnly. Breauchard watched him without interjecting. Aubrey curled the parchment into a tight roll and held it toward the carriage lamp. He lifted a hot glass pane and inserted the paper into the lampfire, shielding the burning end from the breeze. Errant sparks crackled from the flame as the document ashed off into the meadows, chars of Aubrey's crimes swallowed by the sheep's fescue thriving through the drought.

Evening air quieted around them by the time they wended deeper into the countryside. They would go north as far as they could before turning east; troops had been crossing the frontier from Austria, heading westward. Questions weighed heavily on the marquis, even with hallucinogens keeping his mind clearer of troubled thought. He wiggled the accounting books loose of his inside pocket and extended them to the doctor.

"God, she did find the ledgers!" Breauchard said, cracking the first one open and leafing through the pages. "She said she'd been unable to retrieve them from Gagnon's. That girl."

"Émilien Gagnon?" Aubrey watched the doctor's face carefully.

Breauchard flipped through the pages. A guttural sound escaped him as he snapped the first book shut and handed them both with a worried glance back to the marquis. "Does she know what those ledgers truly are?"

"I believe she thinks she does, yes. Do you?"

The doctor didn't answer and remained silent until the carriage rolled to a stop. The marquis pulled up the shade of the window across the far side of the bench. A smallish, gangly man appeared—middle-aged, spectacles resting on the tip of his nose. Aubrey felt the weight of the man's satchel as it dropped onto the footman's rest at the back of the carriage, and next arose the same timid rap at the door that the marquis had made outside l'Abbaye. Breauchard opened the door and ushered the lavishly dressed man inside to sit beside the marquis.

Aubrey asked with surprise, "You are a nobleman?"

"Heh," the man muttered, "is anybody noble anymore?" He turned to the doctor and gushed, "Please, thank Ani for me, Monsieur Breauchard. I am forever in her debt."

Aubrey creased his brow but kept his mouth shut. Breauchard hand-ed the new passenger a blanket and instructed him in acting injured should the carriage be stopped. The men rode for the next quarter of an hour, and the carriage stopped again, this time at a well-lit, large home. The passengers felt the jostle of a heavy bag dropped onto the backend and waited for the faint rap of an unsure fist upon the shutter. When the doctor opened the door, another man entered the carriage and positioned himself beside Breauchard. The marquis recognized the downturned brow, thin pouty lips, powdered and curled hair, and cleft chin, and was recognized in return.

"Marquis de Collioure," the new passenger acknowledged. "You look like you've already died a few times over."

Aubrey nodded. "Monsieur Duport, lovely to see you, too."

"I would not have thought Ani would have bargained for your res-cue," Duport said with a smirk. "Was I a better lawyer, I would have shut the Collioure empire down after what you did to her family." The snide man took the blanket Breauchard offered. "Thank Ani for pro-curing my paper, would you?"

"I believe it is only of late that you've found yourself in the business of defending peasants, Adrien," Aubrey replied. "Were you a better law-yer, you might have saved us a king."

Duport grunted, and Breauchard laughed. "Both of you and your fathers are bastards," Breauchard said. "But Monsieur Duport is a Feuil-lant, Marquis, so need I say more?" He glanced back and forth between the two.

"Worst decision of my life to defend the king's flight to Varennes," Duport muttered. "Such a farce! Imagine! You ever try defending a *king* against treason?"

"There was a time I would have called your Committee of Thirty treason," Aubrey said. "Seems definitions change with the crowd."

Duport snapped his mouth shut.

Breauchard said, "Monsieur Duport was arrested after the massacre of the Tuileries and is fleeing to Switzerland to escape imprisonment, same as everyone else here." The doctor swept his hand around the carriage.

A smile played across Aubrey's face. "So this is what Ani is doing with the lists. The eight hundred forty-one proscribed. Freeing them. Helping noblemen escape France. How many have there been?"

"Twenty-three, if you all make it out alive tonight." The doctor was pleased with the queasy expressions his words elicited. He wanted them to remember they were in grave danger.

※

Almost three quarters of an hour out of Paris, the carriage rolled to a stop, and Aubrey recognized the land. Soft lamplights lit the large townhouse down the drive. Two shadows approached the carriage. The door opened, and in climbed an eight-year-old boy, tired-eyed but newly awakened when he saw the marquis.

"Uncle Aubrey!" the boy shouted and laughed a happy childish laugh, then pulled himself into Aubrey's embrace.

"Grégoire, you get bigger every time I see you, big man," the marquis said, cradling the boy inside the blanket against his uniform and kissing Grégoire's small forehead. The marquis looked up at the young boy's father, Émilien Gagnon, with surprise and confusion, but accepted the cheek kisses of his longtime friend.

"So you're the reason I'm here," Émilien said with relief as he took a seat across from Aubrey.

"I had nothing to do with it," Aubrey said, "save maybe a few words in your favor, in what was apparently the right ear."

After Aubrey looked at Grégoire's new wooden toy boat and heard from the young boy how he had passed his latest tutoring lessons and was learning to use a sword and had started using the heavier broad ax to chop wood now that he was stronger, and had begun learning German and helping his papa file papers in the office, Aubrey finally got a word in with the boy's father. The other noblemen nodded off, and the youngster drifted to sleep in the embrace of his godfather.

"I think you have some explaining to do, old friend," Aubrey said.

"To be candid, chap, I landed myself in a stew that no right man would want to sip. You'll be so sore at me that I'm loath to tell it."

"Émil." It sounded like a parent scolding his child.

"I was bought out." Émilien paused when he heard Aubrey's disappointed sigh.

The marquis reached into his pocket and retrieved the ledgers, hearing his inside pocket rip. For a brief moment, he thought of Josephine, who would have sewn the hole for him. Her fate now rested in the hands of the revealed Brits who'd been providing safe passage for the ostracized French nobility. Silently, he prayed for her.

"I believe these are yours," Aubrey whispered, careful not to wake the child sleeping in his lap. He ignored Breauchard's startled sound and handed the accounting books back to their rightful owner.

Émilien took the books from the marquis' hand, but he seemed displeased to have them back. "Men died for these accounts."

Aubrey nodded. "Ani told me I'd know what to do with them when the moment arose, and I believe this is what she meant, to return them to you."

"Ani," Émilien said, wistfully. "That is the second time I've heard that name. Who is she?"

No one answered. Each answer would have been different.

"These books. These forsaken books," Émilien cried, and crossed himself, holding his thumb to his mouth as a dam.

"Émil, look at me." Aubrey waited until he looked up. "I have vouched for you, so tell me true. Did you purchase orphans from detention halls for use in your factories?"

"Did I what? That's risible preposterousness. Heavens, no." He crossed himself again. "I have redder blood than that on my hands—I funded the Jacobin Club."

"You didn't."

"I did. I had to. The New Convention needed money for their military and election campaigns. Turns out political campaigns are very expensive; who knew? Also turns out some men can be easily blackmailed, and you're looking at one of them." In response to the marquis' horrified face, Émilien added, "I was instructed to write bills of pay to persons in the Club from the money earned in my factories. It would have been quite a dent, and as you can imagine, I refused to do it."

"What would they have on you to blackmail?"

"Ah, it gets sticky. Seems some of the men I employed at the textile factories to manage and disburse the payroll were not trustworthy chaps. They took cuts from the workers, sent employees home without pay, continued 'paying' workers who'd been fired or never even hired in the first place, and that money went in their own pockets. I didn't know. Ghost payments." He shrugged. "Perhaps some of those without pay were orphans. That I don't know, either."

Aubrey's brow creased. "But someone claimed you did."

"Someone had been investigating this privately."

"Citizen Pinsonnault?" Aubrey said to Breauchard, and the doctor looked out the window, silent.

"If my factories had been exposed, burned, shut down, looted—I have children. What if I'd been arrested? Jailed? How could I support my family? Christ, what if I'd lost my head?" He crossed himself. "So, I did it. I wrote banknotes for three-quarters of my income, to support a violent cause that's murdered my friends and mentors. You know they've killed our mentors from le-Grand?"

Aubrey looked at the child in his lap and visibly fidgeted. "Then why are you here? Are you not the Convention's darling?"

Émilien turned the accounting books over in his hand. "Georges Danton learned of the double ledgers. He didn't like the paper trail."

"You dealt with Minister Danton directly?"

"I did. His name is in here."

"That fat stuffed turbot," Aubrey said beneath his breath.

"When he demanded the ledgers be handed over and burned, the damned ledgers—these cursed things!—they disappeared." Émilien crossed himself. "Someone stole them, and I suppose earned quite the bag of gold. I had to tell Danton that the books were gone. That conversation went the way you'd imagine it would go, and he said I'd be discredited if word got out. He's had to be more careful since he became minister of justice. At first, I thought it was nonsense. Utter harebrained ludicrosity. Then, someone burned my Picardie textile mill to the ground and looted my wineshop on rue Saint-Victor—I mean, emptied the place clean out. I wouldn't be surprised if they pinned all manner of lies and misdeeds on me. It was then I received the memorandum."

Aubrey cocked his head. "Extremists are resorting to letterheads?"

"It was not from the Convention. It was private. Something I was not supposed to see, not meant for me. A memo from some Jacobin group, Citizens or some trifle like that. It had my entire family on a proscription list, stating that we were all to be imprisoned for treason. Even my daughters were on it. Little Antoinette, even—a baby guilty of treason, imagine! That's where I heard that name, *Ani*, for the first time. She intercepted this memo and sent it to me. In the envelope were two passport papers, one in my name and one in Grégoire's, with the promise that the rest would come, and that my youngest boy and three girls and my wife—oh, God, deliver me, my innocent Lorraine. What I've done to that woman!" he crossed himself, "—would follow as soon as papers could be procured. I'm so desperate."

The marquis looked to Breauchard and said quietly, "The Citizens are in those ledgers, too, aren't they, Jacques. That's what she knows. That's why they sent her to collect them. They took blackmail money to get the Convention elected, and now they want to hush it up so the masses don't turn on them. They lied to you to get those books, lied about what was in them. Lied to her. And she was expendable. If she'd gotten caught or killed, they'd have claimed no knowledge, yes?"

The doctor looked as if he were about to say something but didn't.

"You let her be expendable."

Breauchard winced. "I didn't *know*. They kept it from me, too."

"Simon's name was also in there, wasn't it," Aubrey said. It wasn't a question. "She doesn't know about him."

"She doesn't know," Breauchard confirmed quietly. "Simon was a corrupt rat, active in the orchestrations of the Club even from his cell at Châtelet. He hated the monarchy. When he went away, I had to tell her *something*. It's far easier to tell a child that her father is a good man than a despicable one."

"Her father is a despicable one," Aubrey said markedly.

Breauchard scowled at the slight and pulled out two folded papers, handing one of them to the small, gangly man and the other to Adrien Duport, waking them both. "Ani could not procure papers for you in time, Marquis," he said to Aubrey. "You weren't part of the plan. The rest of you, keep them on you at all times."

Aubrey grinned a little. "How did she do it?"

"Well, sir," the doctor said, "you did it." The marquis raised an eyebrow, and Breauchard smirked. "*Candide*."

Aubrey laid his head back against the wood paneling, careful not to wake his sleeping godson, and stifled a laugh. It was the first genuine burst of joy he'd felt in weeks. "I can't think of a better way to spend it. You won't need a paper for me, though. Drop me off as close to Valmy as possible."

"No, sir. I have explicit instructions that my passengers are to be taken over the border."

"Just tell her I've gone safely to Switzerland. No need to alarm her. But in that tunnel under l'Abbaye, she let go of me. I gave her one last chance to say what becomes of me, and she refused to say it. So now, it's no longer up to her. Or you."

The doctor refuted, "I cannot allow you to go anywhere near this war."

"All due respect, Jacques," Aubrey grinned, "only death can keep me from it."

PART III

What Comes After

Chapter Eighteen

Le Capot: The Hood

*A revolution can be
neither made nor stopped.
The only thing that can be done
is for one of several of its children
to give it a direction
by dint of victories.*

—Napoleon Bonaparte

Autumn and winter and spring and summer passed like this, well into 1793, an electric chaos to every step, a prayer to every breath. The tip of Ani's cane struck the ground in rhythm with her braces as she walked among the crowds of rue Montmartre. With her cloak pulled over her head, she kept her eyes low. She carried a dead duke's dagger and a liberated marquis' gun on either side of her, and an old National Guard satchel containing documents that could send her to the gallows without even the ruse of a trial. She headed toward a newly painted doctor cart with a different insignia than it had touted the week before, and the week before that, and the week before that.

She leaned against the shutter at the door of the coach, tapped a predetermined rhythm with the handle of her cane, and called out to a passerby, "Would you get a whiff of that air today? It smells ripe as a First French Republic, wouldn't you say, monsieur?" She chuckled uncomfortably as the door opened a crack.

"Not terribly inconspicuous," Dr. Breauchard admonished from inside the carriage.

"Good day, gentlemen," Ani said too calmly, leaning against the coach interior. She produced a set of documents and read names from them as if calling roll to leisurely traveling tourists. "Monsieur Antoine François de Bertrand de Molleville, paper for London for you, sir." She handed him his border document. "Monsieur Louis Lebègue Duportail, welcome out of hiding, sir, and enjoy your travels to America via the beautiful Dutch Republic." In turn, she handed Duportail his document, and turned to the final passenger in the carriage. "And last but certainly not least, Monsieur Louis Hardouin Tarbé. Enjoy your freedom, sir." She looked at Breauchard. "You'll be traveling sans one, as I was unsuccessful in releasing Marguerite-Louis-François Duport-Dutertre, and his bribe near cost me my head." She smiled rigidly, trying not to alarm the passengers.

"Goddamnit," the doctor said beneath his breath. "La Conciergerie is no place for a bribe to go bad."

"And way up in the Tower of Caesar, no less. What fitting location for betrayal." She raised her brows and clucked her tongue. "Alas, I have to be returning to La Conciergerie for a few more, but this first for you." She held forth four documents and a satchel of money in a crudely stitched cloth purse. "Passport papers for the three daughters and remaining son of Émilien Gagnon. Once you reach London, Sir Edward Brighton will take the children from you, along with this money, if you mention the name of a certain marquis," she raised her brows again, but there was also a hint of sadness, "who has established relations with this certain knighted dandy some time ago. Sir Brighton has arranged for the children to join Émilien in hiding, and everything will be handled from there. Please tell Lorraine that I swear I will reunite them all, but I'm still one paper short, so the children must go first, and she must wait. She will protest, but don't let her refuse. Take care of them, Jacques, and enjoy your pleasant stay in London." She winked at the doctor, knocked hard with her cane on the outside of the carriage signaling for it to go, and held up her two forefingers in an inverted V, mocking the scurrilous salute of their final destination.

Breauchard shook his head at her, and Louis Duportail said confidentially, "Your daughter is incredible, Doctor."

"My dau—?" Breauchard stopped himself. "Yes, she is." He nodded, and she waved, and he drew the shades for another tense and unpredictable journey.

❧

The winter had killed the last of Paris' innocence, and the spring had brought the Jacobins. The Armoire de fer, a hidden chest of the king's correspondences, had been exposed, and its decidedly treasonous contents, along with a bitter November of starvation, meant the deposition of anything monarchical that had remained. December's cold lowland winds blew King Louis XVI to trial amidst the cries of revolution's loudest sentiment: *Louis must die so that the country may live.*

Ani's hope could last no longer than her eighteenth birthday. As she marked another year at the foot of the National Razor, the metal beast stood as proud as a monarch itself, yet swung low that day of January twenty-first, 1793. The vision of the Place de la Révolution blurred into the bloody memories of the past. Instead of eating her cake, she watched the blade come down over Citoyen Louis Capet, a once mighty, peaceful, and untouchable king, reduced to a burlap sack and a death gown. The drums of the National Guard rolled over the top of his final words, leaving no chance for martyrs. Ani whispered a different kind of birthday wish, pulling her hood over her eyes and turning from the bloody scene with a newfound fear for its insistence.

The spring of 1793 that followed ushered in the last of the moderates, then out the last of the moderates. The war in the Vendée pitted royalist against revolutionary, clergy against atheist, Frenchman against Frenchman, and killed thousands in the monarchy's struggle for a final breath before she was inevitably strangled of it. Monarchy was over. Moderation was the losing man's burden to mourn and bury, or to be buried alongside. Lafayette's Constitution was overruled, the Revolutionary Tribunal was erected to try all unjust men unjustly, and the newly formed Committee of Public Safety outfitted itself for one unfathomably awesome word: *Terror.*

June found the Jacobins in control a year after Ani had first landed on Aubrey's doorstep. A violent extremism permeated the air, and Paris teetered in its winds like a house of cards. The Girondins and their deputies, no longer extreme enough, suddenly came under arrest, first one by one, then by the hundreds. The risks mounted for Ani to help the proscribed revolutionaries as security in the countryside and along the borders tightened. Twelve died. Eight had been sent to the guillotine; one had been hanged; one had been quartered; two had been shot. Another nine were caught and sent back to prison, four of them locked into worse fortresses than those they had fled.

But despite the failures, seventy-one had been saved by the traveling doctor carts, and another two hundred thirteen had been matched up with other safe passages, other covered carriage carts carrying saltpeter and coal boxes and barrels containing hidden émigrés, or were simply granted their papers and bid *bon courage* with a slap on the back. Another thirty-two had been saved by the ten British gentlemen—bearing the

insignia of a red flower—whom the Marquis de Collioure had first employed to assist in rescuing their French noble counterparts. There was
a whole network of rescuers now, and Ani was only one among them,
but her willingness to be daring, to go where others wouldn't go, set her
apart.

As Ani weaved through the marketplace off rue Saint-Antoine near
the Hôtel de Ville, she watched rioters break into a candleshop and
pilfer tallow sticks and lanterns. A line of men stood against a wall with
a mob surrounding them, throwing small bags filled with rotten beans.
Crowds bought biscuits and wine from hawkers and watched the chaos
as if it were theater. From her left, Ani's shoulder got clipped by a
woman fleeing from something unseen. Ani clutched the wooden cane
for balance.

The woman stopped and helped steady her. "Forgive my haste. I'm
so—" She at once looked relieved and lowered her voice. "You're La
Capot."

"The what?" Ani said, but two running men—Committeemen, now
all calling themselves Citizens like an infectious pandemic—entered the
market. Ani instinctually lifted one side of her cloak, obscuring the fleeing woman from view as the men passed. "How do you think you know
me?" Ani pushed the woman toward the closest wall.

"I saw you once. You tried to help my husband escape."

"Your husband?"

The distraught woman's lips quivered to say his name. "Jacques Brissot de Warville."

"Brissot?" Ani's face split into a frown. "What do you mean 'tried'?
He was sent in disguise to—"

"He was caught at Moulins. He was arrested and imprisoned."

Ani stared, and the woman's face reddened. The Brissotin Girondin
movement, once an extreme contingent under the moderate Legislative
Assembly of nearly a year prior, had become the conservative voice of
the National Convention, and was now being replaced. Not merely replaced, but arrested on the accusation of royalism by the newly installed
Jacobins of the First French Republic.

"I'm sorry, Madame de Warville. Where is he now?"

"At La Force Prison. With other Girondins proscribed."

"La Force." Ani sighed. "La Force is heavily guarded, madame. I
don't know if I can help him."

"Call me Félicité, please. Listen, I do not plead for my husband, nor for myself. But I've been looking for you. Please, we have three children," Félicité rasped. She wiped at her eyes with her cuff. "The Committee came for us this morning, all of us, but I hid my babies away and ran. We have friends in America. I cannot orchestrate that escape, but you can. I know you can. I believe you can. I must believe it. Please, please, take our children. Get them safely to the United States. I beg you." Félicité unslung the tiny change purse from around her neck and shoved it into Ani's hand so there was no chance of refusal. "Take this. I have more. There will be more money; I swear it. Whatever it takes."

Félicité's breath stopped short at a hand landing on her shoulder. The Committeeman who'd been chasing her had caught up to her. Ani lifted one side of her cloak with her cane to hide her other hand lifting forward, upward, and past Félicité by narrow inches. The dagger slid effortlessly into the stomach of the Citizen. Ani drove the surprised man back into the wall with carefully balanced steps, then inched him down to a slumped position beneath the cover of her cloak and covered his mouth as he gasped for air.

"Go quick," Ani whispered to Félicité. "Boutique de l'aquatinte. Honoré. Names and location of the children and your American friends. I will do what I can."

Ani pulled her cloak away from the slumped man and turned from the scene, leaving Félicité shocked in place, the woman looking down at her own shaking fingers to see the coin purse that Ani had given back. Through the crowded marketplace, Ani made out a familiar face. Familiar, but she couldn't quite place it, and every face was familiar these days, all haunting her and returning again and again. Her patterns were too obvious, she feared. She ducked between an overhang and a potato cart and positioned herself for a clearer view. She briefly studied the intricacies of the potato, this strange new foodstuff introduced by the North Americans, then it clicked. *Aubrey's bullet.* An unfashionable hat. The man who'd taken her legs. That gun, that smoke-filled street rushed back to her like a wave. Aubrey's arms, his hands all that were warm. The sound of his change purse in the carriage, his trembling against her. How scared he'd been, and she'd been the one to put that fear in him. She blinked it away.

The man stood there. The coward who'd once run now stood there openly. She eyed him like prey and sneaked a potato from the cart, slid it into her satchel. She'd wait for him to step away, into an alley. Another few moments of watching, and something entirely other was made plain. From the gunman's right strode Citizens Évard Pinsonnault and Jean Crissot, looking over their shoulders in unison, scanning, then nodding to the gunman. Before she had time to contemplate the obvious acquaintance of these men, a scream arose behind her, and a group of women gathered about the slumped Committeeman propped against the wall.

"This man is dead!" a shrieking voice pierced the air. "Dead! Who did it?"

Frantic men blew tin whistles and grabbed elbows of onlookers in the vicinity. Red caps waved through the air like banners. Ani hunched her back and hobbled away. As a hand seized her arm, she hissed and wheezed beneath her hood, shielded her face, and waved her cane at the man.

"Would ye touch a syphilitic leper?" she growled in a scratchy voice.

"Have mercy!" the man said, flinging her away and wiping his hands down the front of his jerkin. "Get from me, you hag."

She caught her balance on her cane and wobbled off, righting her faux hunch once she'd gotten far enough from the market to be rid of its mess. She hoped that man did catch her imaginary syphilis. When she looked back to the spot where the gunman and Citizens had been, they were gone.

Days had passed since Breauchard last left with the carriage, and Ani heard through the lineage of rumors that he'd returned, stationed with his doctor's cot back at the printshop. The danger of imprisonment now hovered over him were someone to suspect he harbored Girondist sympathies. He was, by virtue of his trade, still more valued than despised, but the risk came ever closer. He hardly spoke a word these days for fear of it being the wrong one.

When Ani entered the Boutique de l'aquatinte, she found Grietje sitting at the front counter, flipping a copper two-sol coin into the air and trying to catch it on her eye. Grietje turned to Ani, the coin pinched in one eye, and scowled. The girl opened her mouth to speak, but instead went back to flipping the coin. Ani choked it down for Breauchard's sake since he still tended to both young women, but nothing had ever been repaired between them. The gap didn't widen, but nor had it closed; it just loomed open like a pit.

"Gret. Is Jacques with a patient?" Ani asked, and Grietje nodded without looking away from the coin. Ani reached into her satchel and pulled out the potato she'd stolen, tossing it to Grietje. "Here, I brought you an American potato."

"A potato? What do I do with it?"

Ani shrugged. "Bite into it." She walked to the back of the shop.

Grietje whined from the counter, "Ow! It's hard as rock. I think I breaked my tooth."

Ani knocked her cane against the hidden door's painted mural at the back wall. "Dr. Breauchard?" She stood there until he opened it.

"Allyriane, you and I need to have a little talk." The doctor wiped his bloody hands on a once-white cloth and down the front of his once-matching apron. "You were specifically told to leave Lafayette stuck where he got himself. How could you send Béatrice in there after him?"

Her heart thumped. It had been months since she'd heard word that Béatrice was safe and working out details of an elaborate plan. "You heard from her?"

"No! A prison in a foreign—" A male voice caterwauled from the doctor's room, and Breauchard whirled out of sight midsentence to tend to his bleeding patient.

Ani spun, her finger pointing. "Grietje Hindriks. How could you tell him? You could betray Bet, just like that?"

"I didna tell him a damn thing, although I should've, you royalist," Grietje said, and the doctor stepped back through the door before the girls could dig into each other.

"Grietje," he said, motioning for her to exit, "I need to speak to Allyriane alone. Take that two-sol and get something to eat. And pay for it; don't steal it." When Grietje had gone, Breauchard turned to Ani. "What you did was not right. I don't know what you have planned, but this is the result." He reached into his pocket, pulled out a folded letter, and opened it before her.

She took it from his hands and read: "Dearest Jacques, It has come to my attention with some urgency that a young girl acting under Allyriane's name, going by the name of Béatrice Meschinot herself, has been taken into captivity at Olmütz for orchestrating an escape of the Marquis de La Fayette during his prison transfer. I've no extensive details, but someone ought notify her family." Ani's voice trailed as she grunted, "Hmph, family," and scanned quickly down the letter before the doctor could pull it from her hands. She caught the signature that she knew right down to the perfectly crossed A and swooped Y. "Yours, Aubrey?" At once, it was no longer about Béatrice's predicament. Ani felt the ground fall from beneath her. She put her hand on the doorframe to steady herself, clung to it like a liferaft.

Breauchard jerked the letter from her grasp. "I've gone along with everything you've requested, but you didn't tell me it involved getting my girls locked up for a royalist."

"Dearest Jacques? Yours, Aubrey? How long have you been corresponding with him?" Her voiced cracked.

He winced. "Since I dropped him off. In Switzerland."

Her eyes narrowed. "You didn't drop him off in Switzerland, did you." Her lips thinned into a tight line. "Did he ask about me?"

"You're all he asks about. He requests I write him how you are."

"Requests?" Ani said, ripping the letter from the doctor's hands. "I'm never to see him again, and you're playing fountain mates?" She skimmed the letter as she held it away from the doctor's reach, her lips mouthing along with the words her eyes scanned. "…Fighting in Lyon?" she read aloud, then, "Someday this land could be my beloved France again, even if she is not to share its restored Glory with me." Ani choked, then glared at the doctor. "You can say what you want about my betrayal with Bet, but you betrayed me with this. I'll find a way to get Bet out of there, but this, Jacques. This. How could you? All this time." She wadded the letter in a fist and pounded it against his chest. "Switzerland! Switzerland. You had one order. One. A child could've done it! It was still an unsecured border." She pounded the letter a second time against his chest until he took it from her clenched fingers. "So if he's safe in Switzerland, then tell me how is he fighting in Lyon?" She made a grunting sound, and her lungs heaved and filled, then released a painful cough from which it took several seconds to recoup with any dignity. When she'd righted herself, her tears fell, and her glare held a new distrust that Jacques had never seen before. She whispered, "Do you know who shot me?"

"What? No! If I knew that, the bastard'd be dead."

An uncomfortable pause squeezed its way between them. "Was your name in Gagnon's ledger?"

"Absolutely not," Breauchard said. "Why? Is there a connection?"

"You tell me."

"I don't know. I swear it." His voice sounded desperate.

"Some liar must know something. You're a liar, Jacques, so tell me who's lying here."

"All right, I lied about taking the marquis to Switzerland. He asked to go to Valmy, and I complied because..." He paused. "Damnit, Ani, if you had seen his face. He was a broken man. He needed purpose."

"Valmy?"

"So what! So he wanted to join the war. Is that so bad? He's a general. He's a monarchist and the cousin of a beheaded king, and man-to-man, that's what he asked of me, what he wanted. So yes, Valmy. Where he was defeated, then defeated again in the Vendée where he had to withdraw troops. Now he is fighting in Lyon, where he will be defeated because they are outnumbered. All right, I admit it, and, yes, I knew it all along. But I know nothing about Gagnon's ledger except that I'm not in it. I've never accepted or demanded a bribe from anyone for any reason."

Ani stood motionless before him, her stare boring through his very core, her jaw as tight as a carriage spring. "I don't believe you."

"Ani..." He moved to touch her, but she stepped back, righted herself on the wall.

"I don't believe anyone. You're all liars. The monarchy, the Republic, The Citizens, the Beaumercys, you, my father. You're all self-serving liars. Once I was, too, but I'll be no more." A tear left her eye, and she felt Aubrey's cognac breath on her cheek, the darkness of his eyes in a prison tunnel, the vacancy he'd left behind. "I thought so much higher of you." She swung around on her cane and moved as quickly as she could, letting the click of her brace make her final statements for her.

"Don't say that," he yelled behind her, rooted in place by a dying patient in the next room, but pierced by the finality of Ani's words. "I've loved you all your life; don't turn from me!" His voice echoed around the room unreturned as her hand hit the door handle. "Allyriane, don't you do this."

The door slammed.

Chapter Nineteen

The Law of Suspects

*True Republicanism is the
sovereignty of the people.
There are natural and
imprescriptible rights
which an entire nation
has no right to violate.*

—Marquis de Lafayette

The weeks passed, and the lists of suspected men, women, their children and housekeepers, Girondins, clergy, their parents, brothers and sisters, and even their pets, grew innumerable. The names were collected by the Watch Committees of the respective city departments to turn over to the Committee of General Security to turn over to the Committee of Public Safety to turn over to the National Convention. An elaborate hierarchy of power and fear. The people who felt the most empowered were the ones who feared the most. The ones most blinded with compliance were the ones who would most feel its wrath.

The Law of Suspects managed to be extensive and explicit while remaining frighteningly vague. Those who had shown themselves partisans of tyranny or federalism and enemies of liberty, by their conduct, associations, talk, or writings; those who were unable to justify their means of existence and the performance of their civic duties; those to whom certificates of patriotism had been refused; public functionaries suspended or dismissed from their positions by the National Convention or by its commissioners, and not reinstated; those former nobles, husbands, wives, fathers, mothers, sons or daughters, brothers or sisters, and agents of the émigrés, who had not steadily manifested their devotion to the revolution; those who had emigrated during the interval between July 1789 and the declaration of war, April 1792, even though they may have returned to France within the period established. Anyone was suspect who was suspected by anyone else who might be suspect if he didn't suspect the other suspect first.

By the end of the autumn of 1793, one in five on these lists would survive. Of those survivors, another fifth would live only to become listed again and not find themselves so lucky the second time. The rest would remain in prison uncharged and without trial, forgotten in the increasingly numbered cells of converted churches and reinstated medieval dungeons. These prisoners were crammed into crowded prison courtyards and dank rooms so filthy and sickening, that it was considered lucky instead to be among the tumbrels carted from La Conciergerie to the Place de la Révolution, Madame Guillotine's proud monumental ground—the site where Ani had watched her father die almost a year and a half earlier. She couldn't complete that thought without remembering the fated introduction with Aubrey only a month later, and how that was now nearing a year and a half ago, as well. Time that had been kind to so few.

Ani walked along the back walls of the Place de la Révolution, her cloak pulled over her head. Her features filled in as she neared nineteen years, but she was still a nondescript thing, easily coming and going unnoticed. She interacted with few in Paris save solitude and guilt, persistent companions. She dropped her surname, any attachment toward it gone. Once, she thought she'd take Breauchard, but they hadn't spoken in so long that it seemed vacant, a lie, as they continued operations from separate sides of a tiny universe now so overcrowded and dense that their paths might have gone on to separate worlds before ever crossing again in this one.

She steadied herself along the wall as inconspicuously as her legs allowed, keeping her eyes from the guillotine. Masses of people gathered daily to witness the executions—ten deaths per day, a modest taste of what would follow. A group of women met to knit along the front line, seated in crude chairs, alternating between sour and rapturous faces. Children made up the largest portion of the onlookers—their curious, impressionable minds forever marred.

Ani stopped abruptly and took a few steps back to read a flier pasted to the wall. *Le Capot*. Christ, the fliers were everywhere now. This silly name she'd been given—who thought it up? She stared into the misshapen attempt at a face peeking from beneath a squiggly cloak and read the inscription: *Cloaked Man. Sways as if drunkened. If seen, report immediately to Committee.* True to the chauvinistic Jacobins' underestimation of a female, this faceless and shapeless cloaked monster—The Hood—whose illustration had recently come to be the muse of etchings and pamphlets, was being billed as a man, and not to any of their credit if they thought a drunken man could orchestrate her entire year's work. She scanned around her, then ripped the poster from the wall and tucked it into her satchel. She wanted them gone.

"You're quite late," Pere Dinaultbriand said to Ani, when she'd made her way across the Pont au Change to Île du Palais. "I had to empty them barrels myself."

"I'm a slow walker. You might not have noticed," she said, meeting him nervously before La Conciergerie, the medieval palace-cum-revolutionary prison that also housed the heartbeat of extremism: the Revolutionary Tribunal. This was as close as she could get to death without dying.

The year had left Pere as conflicted as Ani. Afraid of the revolution's bloody turn, he'd become distrusting of everyone but this woman. Her convictions had remained true and strengthened him. While the revolution destroyed everyone it reached, it somehow managed to make her shine. Pere saw her plainly, who she was, and for that rare honesty, he didn't let her down. They straddled a dangerous line between keeping out of the reticle of the same extremists who had once brought the two orphans under revolutionary wing, and helping the condemned who had once been too extreme for even Ani's taste. The condemned, mostly noblemen, at least deserved the fair trial that Lafayette had fought so hard for them to have—the trial that no longer existed.

"I see that I've still beat the saltpeter wagon, though," Ani said, nodding to the barrels across the street.

Pere lifted a battered pocketwatch by the fob and looked at it for the third time since she'd arrived. "Yes. Much later than expected."

The two stood straight as soldiers along the Tour de l'Horloge clock tower where rue Saint-Barthélemy met with rue de la Barillerie between the street markets of the Old Drapery and lines of merchant barrels that gave la Barillerie its name. To the left, they looked over the intersection of Quai de l'Horloge and Pont au Change; to the right, they looked over Pont Saint-Michel; and straight ahead, they saw crowds of people passing along the roads in front of hundreds of barrels and portly kegs.

Pere fidgeted and looked up at the Tour de l'Horloge to be sure his pocketwatch was correct. The magnificent beast, Paris' first public clock, with its multicolored face and framed design featuring Latin inscriptions and bas-reliefs of personified allegories of Law and Justice, wagged its mocking fingers back at Pere. Yes, everything was running late.

"You don't have to do this," he said. "Not this time. Not here. I's a bad feeling about it. La Conciergerie is too risky now, and these men…"

"I must do this. No one else will."

"You can't bestride this line forever. If Citizen Pinsonnault finds out, then you might as well walk in there and lock yourself in one of them cells your damn self. Committeemen is starting to interrogate and imprison anyone wearing cloaks. You's terrified them. We can't hide this much longer."

"You can go back to the printshop if you don't want to be part of this, Pere. I'll never hold you to it."

He checked his pocketwatch again and frowned. "Just come back out; that's the only thing I'm holding you to."

Across the street, the figure of a familiar fat man meandered inconspicuously toward the saltpeter barrels.

"There's Henri," Pere and Ani said in unison and exchanged uneasy smiles.

"And there's the food carts." Pere nodded. "Of course they would be early when everything else is late." He grunted and shifted his weight back and forth from foot to foot and eyed the gilt-iron railings that separated the rue de la Barillerie from the courtyard. "You better change and go in."

He stood tall over her, keeping a lookout, shielding her from view. Ani dropped her cloak to the ground to reveal a plain gray shirtwaist and matching skirt uniform. She slung her satchel around in front of her, then tucked it beneath the ties of her white apron. She lifted the cloak into Pere's outstretched hand and gazed down at her pedestrian outfit of servitude.

"I'm ready," she whispered, and she turned toward the Quai de l'Horloge to round the clock tower for the kitchen entrance.

"Make it fast," Pere said, grabbing her sleeve one last time. "I'm praying for you."

"You might rather pray for the saltpeter wagon."

With a head nod toward Henri and a quick squeeze of Pere's hand, Ani ducked around the corner and rounded La Conciergerie's walls to the kitchen. Every area in this prison was guarded with so many gendarmes that no one could walk in and out undetected, but the kitchen loaded in full carts of food multiple times a day and loaded those same empty carts back out as many times a day. The deliveries were made from the river or from wagons in the adjacent street that filtered in among other wagons, crowds of people, and kegs. Once out into the street, one could disappear easily among the numerous merchants and barrels.

As the food wagons rolled to a stop in front of the kitchen entrance, strong hands unloaded crates and boxes and small carts full of produce, fresh meat—catered meals that only the pistoliers and noblemen could afford to buy inside the prison walls. When the kitchen entrance flew open to admit the staples, Ani grabbed a small crate and fell in line with the deliverers, briskly walking into the kitchen. She ducked near a stew pot in one corner and inspected whether her apron and dress fit in with the kitchen staff. To her relief, they still did. She clutched a salt block to her breast and lifted the closest spoon to stir the pot.

The Cuisines Saint-Louis kitchen was enormous, just one level of a once-multilevel square kitchen pavilion with a vaulted ceiling of intersecting transverse ribs, arches that curved into Gothic ogives. The stonework continued the curve down the wall, ending with a substantial fireplace in each of the four corners, each fireplace in turn being designated a cooking task: one for poultry and meats, one for broths and stews, and the other two indistinguishable to Ani where she stood with her back to them. She listened intently to the commotion of the kitchen servants until she surmised that the loading of the noble catering carts was underway, and she stepped toward the nearest one with her hand extended. Another hand clasped with hers around the cart's pushbar. Ani cleared her throat and made reluctant eye contact with the woman decidedly in charge of the cart.

"I getted this one," Ani said, forcing the quaver from her voice and slipping into common lowborn speech.

"Um, this one is…" the stout woman started, but clipped her words. "All right. It's going to the—"

"I know. Back toward the king's oratory."

"No, toward the pailleux. Don't let no one hear you say king's oratory no more. Now it's just a cell."

Ani's eyes widened, and she stammered for an excuse. "I done the pailleux last time. Those men is so depressing on them piles of straw. Please, it would raise my heart to attend the nobles, instead."

The woman pondered this, shrugged. "It don't matter to me, but that's Justine's route, so you gotta talk it with her if she'll take the pail-leux. Load it up." The woman whirled toward a young girl and hollered, "Justine, will you take the straw-men?"

Ani pretended not to hear the young girl's complaints and threw two table linens over the top of the large wooden pushcart, letting the cloth hang down to the squeaky wheels, completely covering the hollow, boxlike serving cart. Tin plates were handed down the line of cooks, and Ani scooped stew into one of the rounded slots next to a generous portion of poultry. Her stomach growled. How long had it been since she'd eaten? She couldn't honestly remember the last time she'd even had an appetite. She didn't wait for Justine's reply. When the woman's back was turned, Ani stacked four plates on top of the cart and pushed forward quickly toward La Salle des Gens d'Armes, the great chamber leading westward through the palace prison to the cells of the Galerie des Prisonniers. She nodded to the guard to let her through.

La Salle des Gens d'Armes was a sight to see. Upon entrance, the room swallowed Ani whole. Secular-Gothic architecture swept over-head in curves of ogival arches set in light stone bricks that rainbowed down into columns big enough to hide behind, then shot back up into four rib-vaulted vertical naves even taller at the keystone than the room was wide. Arch after arch of stonework spilled into column after col-umn of marbled obstacles that Ani had to swerve around. Four large fireplaces heated the room, and spiral staircases led to a second level. Echoing above were the stomping feet and screaming voices of the Revolutionary Tribunal, stationed overhead in the Great Hall, or Salle Haute, a vast chamber that once housed the former courtrooms of the recently abolished Parlement de Paris. Although she couldn't see it clearly, she knew the Salle Haute stood equally as glamorous as the hall below, supported by a line of pillars that divided the room into two long naves covered at the top with paneled arches. They were courtrooms of a different kind now. As Ani traveled through the hall below the Revolu-tionary Tribunal, she held her breath despite the room's attempts to rip it from her. Panting breathlessly would give her away. La Salle des Gens d'Armes might have been the most august room she had ever seen, yet there before her, spoiling every luxury, were well over a hundred prisoners, walking through the magnificent hall that had become a cage for the condemned.

Eyes averted, she approached a stoic man listing his way from one end of the hall to the other. "Antoine Barnave?" she asked tenuously.

The man shrugged and turned away, and Ani put her hands again on the cart. Suddenly, stiffened fingers grabbed her own, and she turned to see the same stoic man eying her intently. *He knew.* Her fingers tightened around the bar. She reached for her knife. But the man tilted his chin to the right and nodded to the gates at the other end of the hall. Ani traced his nod to the Rue de Paris, the wide corridor that stretched from the Salle des Gardes out to the prisoners gallery, ominously named for the city executioner, Monsieur de Paris. The Guardsroom, the Rue de Paris corridor, and the Galerie des Prissoniers were all packed with miserable bodies. Ani swallowed audibly and nodded back.

"Jean-Baptiste Louvet de Couvrai?" she asked him quietly. "René Legrand de Saint-René?"

"You've lost your mind, girl," came his reply, but he nodded again toward the iron-gated corridor. "Godspeed." He released his grip on her arm, crossed himself, then held his thumb to his lips and stayed rooted in place, murmuring a prayer for her.

Ani pushed her cart through the exquisite hall toward the darkened corridor. To her left, glimpses of the planted trees of the Cour de Mai shown sporadically through the generous windows, until she had to battle with the wooden wheels of her cart to take the incline where the level of the floor had been raised in the fifteenth century. At the end of the incline was the Rue de Paris. The pailleux were there—men who could afford no beds and were shoved by the hundreds onto piles of straw. Rodents ran at her feet. The coughs of sick and dehydrated men pealed through the halls in tintinnabulous fits. Ani's resolve galvanized at witnessing their abhorrent condition; these men had to pay a tax for their own sentence in these unsanitary surroundings. Those who could not pay, lost personal possessions and slept on straw. Those who could afford to pay a few pistoles to the concierge or the guardsmen, could get beds or mattresses in exchange for the bribes. The pistoliers and high-class guests could afford individual cells, with individual beds, some modest furniture, coat racks, writing parchment, oil lamps, books, blankets, chess boards, and catered meals.

Two gendarmes stood at the gate to the dreary corridor. Their long navy-blue tailcoats crossed with the white Xs of shoulder satchels, and their stiff red collars rose up their uniformed throats to squish their scrawny faces between straight necks and dark, French-cocked bicornes. As she neared, one of the men put his hand against her breast.

"Where's my Justine?" he asked.

"She, uh. We switched this time," Ani stammered. "I—I didna want to—"

"Aw, give her my love for me, will ya?" He winked and fiddled with his pocket where he drew out a peppermint and put it in his mouth. "I'll be ready for you on the way out, dove." He winked again, unlocked the gate, and helped her ease the cart across the threshold.

Ani was thankful that she couldn't feel the butt pat she assumed she'd received. Her thoughts flew to Justine. The poor girl couldn't have been but twelve.

"I's going to have to make two trips," she said.

"Wouldn't have to if you'd piled them plates up better on that cart, girl. You must be new here, or else hankering for what happens when you come back through this gate."

Ani hoped she misunderstood. "What happens when I come back through the gate?"

Both guards cocked greasy smiles, and Ani felt a lump harden in her throat. Poor Justine. The man was in desperate need of a bath. She guessed that wool uniform hadn't been peeled off his body in months.

She moved quickly past the Rue de Paris corridor, the oubliettes of moaning men, and into the prisoners' main thoroughfare, where suspects wandered freely. The gallery held only men. Ani could see the women sectioned off in another gated corridor and out in the Women's Courtyard through another set of gates and windows. A fountain brimmed with spent water in the center of the courtyard. Two stories of prison cells rose around the yard like stone colossi, and the Corner of the Twelve sat passively between the courtyard and the Cour de Mai, so men and women could make their last goodbyes to each unlucky dozen carted off to the guillotine daily.

Ani treaded softly to avoid her heel clicking as she passed the Clerk's Office where they registered prisoners' names. The wickets that led out to the Cour de Mai where the guilty awaited their deaths; the office of the concierge who held charge of the prisoners; the Grooming Room, where guillotine-bound prisoners were stripped of their belongings before traveling by tumbrel to their executions. Between the men's and women's gates, a dowdy dame pressed herself into the bars, into the chest of a nicely dressed pistolier on the other side. Her hand was tucked beneath his open overcoat, and the expression on his face denoted that her servicing fingers worked sufficiently. Ani tried not to stare as the man audibly moaned; relationships were brisk and heartless here.

Privacy could not be bought. She thought of what might be required of her to exit back through the gates into La Salle des Gens d'Armes to get to the Cuisines Saint-Louis, and she cringed.

She caught a slow-moving, well-dressed man by the sleeve and whispered, "Jean-Baptiste Louvet de—"

"In the red weskit." The man pointed before she finished. His eyes were canyoned, and he didn't look at her, just walked away.

Ani dug her hand into her satchel, lifted a piece of parchment, then pushed her food cart to one end of the long gallery. When the small, awkward man in the red waistcoat made his way toward her, she stepped in front of him and surreptitiously laid the parchment into a palm as thin as a monkey's. "Jean-Baptiste Louvet de Couvrai," she said, as he studied the passport in his hand, "I have your wife, Lodoiska, in safety in Switzerland, and I will lead you with other Girondins who are fleeing."

His lip trembled in want for words. "Lo—Lo—Lodoiska," he echoed longingly and followed Ani like a pacified sheep in the direction of the food cart.

She lifted one edge of the linen so he could see that the cart was empty beneath, and he nodded. "First, you must help me, monsieur. Is Gui-Jean-Baptiste Target in this room?"

Louvet didn't need much time to look around before he shook his head. "You will know if he is in the room. There will be no more space left for you to stand in it." A smirk tugged at his lip. "I hate to inform you, mademoiselle, but if you have come for Target, you will need a bigger cart."

Ani mulled this over, but she could do nothing about it now. "How about René Legrand de Saint-René?"

Louvet's eyes scanned the room until they rested on Legrand. "He is near the courtyard of the women, of course." He indicated with a tilt of his head that caught Legrand's eye. "In the brown tailcoat with his hair queued perfectly. I have not seen his hair imperfect since he arrived. I got his attention; he is walking this way as we speak."

"And Baron Honoré-Nicolas-Marie Duveyrier?"

"Baron Duveyrier is a lazy bastard. He might not be walking around thi—" Louvet reneged, "He is that one in the middle of that group of three over there. With the fancy boot buckles, the show-off."

"And Antoine Barnave?"

Louvet locked a dark gaze on Ani and growled, "The Feuillant? What do you want with him? He's what landed us all here."

"Don't you think that's a little unfair at this point? We're all in this now. The only way out is to help each other."

"He is celled up. Doesn't get to wander. He's a great catch for the tribunal, and there is a price on his head should he run."

She scowled at the words but didn't have long to think on them. A tap landed on her shoulder, and she turned. "René Legrand de Saint-René," she said, "your brother is waiting for you in a cavalry regiment in the Army of the Rhine. He has a safe place for you." She again lifted the linen, and Legrand eyed it with a cheerful smile.

"You will not have to tell me twice," he replied and kissed her on both cheeks. Looking over his shoulder, he espied no guardsmen present and quickly ducked beneath the linen and tucked his knees up to his chin.

"You, too, Monsieur Louvet." She motioned, and he followed Legrand's lead. "You will have to make room for one more. Be perfectly still and silent. Hold on to the cart no matter what," she whispered through the linen. "I will handle any situation that arises, but you will be a heavy load on the uneven floor, so hold tight."

Within moments, she had nabbed the Baron Duveyrier, as well, and he joined the men in the cramped lower space of the wooden cart, while Ani handed out her remaining plates to any man who looked hungry enough to need one. She turned the pushcart back through the Galerie des Prissoniers, past the wickets, and around the bend of the Rue de Paris corridor. She cursed the gendarmes at the gate. Heaven help her, but she'd have to take them on.

"There's our girl," said the first guard, while he fussed with the buttons of his uniform and resituated his musket. "How are you planning to pay to get back through this gate?" There was that greasy smile again, but he surprisingly had a full set of teeth.

"I—I's got a few coins," she replied, fishing through her satchel.

He sneered. "I didn't waste a peppermint for some coins."

The guard latched onto her wrist and directed her hand to the bulge in his pants, and she gasped. He rubbed her hand briskly over his trousers, and she bore it stiffly when he pulled her up to the bars and closed his mouth over hers. A rush of peppermint wafted over her, but she remained still. His grip tightened on her wilting, noncompliant hand. Then he let go, unamused.

"Ugh, maybe I did waste a peppermint." He brushed the back of his sleeve against his mouth. "Like a limp dishrag. Tell Justine this is the last time she switches on my post."

Before Ani could reply, the second guard, undeterred by her previous lack of performance, stepped up for his turn, but the peppermint man pressed on his fellow gendarme's sternum and swatted his hand away from the front of his trousers.

"She's new here. Don't scare her off yet," Monsieur Peppermint said, grinning. "She's probably a virgin." He turned to Ani and scratched at body lice on his chest and arms. "Looks like we'll be taking them coins, virgin." His fingers reached through the bars, and Ani placed in his palm the coins she was still white-knuckling. "But listen here: you'll be expected to improve that haughty nature next time through, or we'll leave you in there and let them pailleux have at you. They's some desperate men."

He unlocked the gate, and she took careful notice of the key as it passed through the lock. Smoothing her ruffled dress, she grabbed hold of the cart, forcing an effortless motion as she fumbled through the threshold, then down the incline, the rude murmurs of the gendarmes fading behind her. She cursed silently.

The Salle des Gens d'Armes and the Cuisines Saint-Louis whirred by in a fog. She entered then exited the kitchen with her cart of human contraband, headed toward the loading dock, then veered to the right at the clock tower. Pere was there to intercept the cart, and no sooner had she handed over her charge than she turned back and reentered the kitchen, grabbed another full cart without making any eye contact, and headed back down the corridor to the Salle des Gens d'Armes before anyone could suspect anything amiss. The peppermint guard at the Rue de Paris laughed at her approach.

"Didn't learn nothing the first time through?" he asked. "I think you has even less trays than last time. Learn to stack them, and you'll save some coin and crotchfire." His eyes lit up, and he elbowed her. "Jean here has the red creepers on his toddy. Your mouth is going to be burning for a week on your way back through. That'll teach you to stack your trays—save you some lumbering on that bum leg of yours, too."

The key hit the lock on the gate, and she heard the second guardsman, Jean, grunt like a caveman while he scratched his fiery balls. She didn't breathe a sigh of relief until she heard the lock plink closed behind her, and she was already well on her way to the gallery of pistoliers and noblemen, finding it ironic that she felt safer on this side of the locked gate than on the other. She found dark amusement in the fact that if Jean gave her crotchfire, she wouldn't feel it. Mouthfire, however, was a different story.

This time around, Gui-Jean-Baptiste Target wasn't hard to spot. His girth was that of a pony; but like a pony, too, he was thankfully squat, so at least ducking beneath the cart wouldn't be a severe issue. Upon introduction, he wasn't taken with the idea of squeezing into the underbelly of a cart but became more amenable after Ani starkly reminded him of his alternative. To both their chagrin, she still had one more man to cram onto it—the most important of all her charges: Antoine Barnave, one of the fathers of the Feuillants alongside Lafayette. Antoine Barnave, the leader of the Constitutional monarchists. If she could free him, he could regroup his men, join with Lafayette, and take control of this bloody revolution again. Or so she hoped. Oh, how she hoped.

Target required quite a bit of stuffing and prodding, but he was finally secure in the cart as inconspicuously as could be expected for a man in his unfortunate condition. Unstuffing him might prove to be more difficult. Getting him into a saltpeter barrel? She didn't even want to think about that impossible task—she'd let Henri and Pere handle that. She was sweating by the time she pushed the cart down to the end of the gallery where the prized noblemen were locked in their cells. She had the advantage this time of knowing what her next prisoner looked like; he'd spoken before enough crowds at the Palais-Royal that she could have drawn his face from memory.

"Antoine Pierre Joseph Marie Barnave," she said as she crept up to his cell, realizing with disappointment that the padlock staring back at her was not the type she had expected.

Barnave stepped away from his cellmates and replied, "Have you come for me a day early, then?" When he pivoted and his eyes found hers, his brows arched in surprise. "Ah, dinner! Not death. That's much kinder."

Antoine Barnave looked good for a man who'd spent fifteen months locked in three separate prisons. He had a high, stern forehead with devilishly curved eyebrows; a strong jawline that came to a charming cleft dimple below plump, naturally puckered lips; a long nose of full, rounded nostrils; wide eyes, too far apart; and hair fetchingly pulled into an unmarred queue, with straggling ringlets at his ears. A white scarf wrapped around and around and around his neck, the ends frilly and loose at his chest and spilling into a tight, fitted waistcoat that spilled into high-waisted fallfront breeches that spilled into tall, decorated boots. Fitting as snugly as cloth ever could on a man, was a brown, high-collared cutaway tailcoat of fine silk and cotton weave and silk satin stripes that hung to the backs of his thighs and ran down lanky arms to white, ruffled lace at the wrists. He stepped forward from the meager cell furnishings of a wooden table, two beds and two floor mattresses, a straight-backed chair for each prisoner, a coat rack, a chess set, an oil lamp, and a metal funneled urine collector. Despite his predicament, he managed a smile when he approached the bars. It seemed that, as far as Feuillants went, visitors were rare.

"You don't look like you've come to bring me dinner, throwing around my middle names like that," Barnave said. "I'm generally lucky to get 'Hey, squatbucket.'"

Ani lifted the corner of the linen on her cart where a red-faced Monsieur Target was desperately attempting to keep from spilling over the sides. "Hurry, Monsieur Barnave," she replied. "There isn't time to waste." She peered around the edge of the corridor to where a few men walked freely, one of them a guard under the care of the concierge, in charge of maintaining order in the cells. There on his hip, Ani could see his jangling keys. "Monsieur, come smart!" she called to the guard. "Godspeed, sir. This man be sick." Ani pointed frantically to Barnave. "Please, sir, you must come have a look at him."

The man rounded the corner of the gallery quickly and arrived before Barnave's cell. "He looks right as rain to me," the guard stated.

Ani furrowed her brow at the prisoner, and Barnave coughed gingerly, putting on a sour face for the guard. "Look!" she said. "Look sharp. See, he be sickly and needs care. Please, just go in and check on him before he infects us all."

The guard sighed with annoyance and removed the keys from his belt, thumbing through them slowly. There must have been a hundred. Ani rocked on her brace while he found the key, but as he reached for the lock, Target shook a cramped arm beneath the linen of the cart, and the cloth moved several inches.

"What the—" the guard said, looking quickly from the cart to Ani.

She sucked in a surprised breath, and it gave her away. The gendarme drew his saber, and she ducked out of the way, hiked her skirt, and extracted the knife from her brace's sheath. Before the guard could take his swing, Ani drove her blade clumsily into the man's side. He cried out and dropped the ring of keys onto the marble floor, and she had to stick him a second time to finish the job. Her hand leaped to his mouth as she eased him to the ground, but the damage had been done. Monsieur Target shrieked, Antoine Barnave cursed louder than a sailor, and Ani stared at the key ring lying in a pile of jumbled metal and blood.

"Shit!" she hissed.

"In the name of the God of Peace!" Target shrieked.

Ani put her hands against the bars and walked herself down to retrieve the key ring, then inched her way back up the bars. "Shit, shit, shit." It would take her minutes upon minutes to try every key, and there wasn't enough time.

"You have to go, mademoiselle," Barnave said when Ani settled on her first key and systematically jammed each one against the padlock keyhole. "You have to save yourself." His eyes darted in the direction of shuffling feet and mounting cries, and he saw the guards coming down the gallery. "They're coming. Go!"

"No, Monsieur Barnave. I came here for you, and I will not go without you."

But her frantic search for the right key was interrupted by the commanding shouts of two guardsmen, and she whirled to face the same two gendarmes who had been stationed at the closest gate: Jean the Red Creeper and Monsieur Peppermint. The men's steps faltered when they saw Ani standing over a dead body, fumbling with the keys to Barnave's cell. When the realization sank in, they shouted and bolted for her, lifting their bayoneted muskets toward the treasonous woman. Monsieur Peppermint fired, and it hit the bars and ricocheted into nothing. Barnave ducked.

"Stop her!" Jean called out, approaching first.

Ani sidestepped his charge and walloped her brace against his shin. The unexpected impact took the footing from the guard and sent him lurching forward, his musket flailing. Ani grabbed the barrel and directed the bayonet into the man's neck as he fell. The sharp tip pierced through his neck and into his throat, and Jean slumped to the ground just as the other guard reached her. The two dead men put a quick barrier between the approaching guard and Ani.

Monsieur Peppermint dodged, avoiding Ani's dagger, and he lunged with his bayonet. She deflected, and it struck too low, jamming into her brace, the impact taking them both off-balance. His foot landed in a spreading pool of Jean's blood, and he skidded one leg apart from the other, toward the iron bars. Antoine Barnave reached both hands through the bars, took hold of the musket, and lifted it across the guard's neck, throttling the man with the barrel against the cell. The guard choked and spit and gasped for breath between curses, but Ani recovered her footing and drove her dagger into his heart. His mouth fell slack in surprise and stayed that way, a waft of peppermint leaving it.

"I'll tell Justine how your heart bleeds for her," she seethed, close to his face. Then she drew the dagger back out, sheathed it, and watched his eyelids flutter for a few seconds before blood trickled over his full set of straight teeth and out his languid mouth.

Barnave released one end of the bayonet, and Monsieur Peppermint fell to the floor in the heap of bodies. "Well, that was certainly something," Barnave said.

When Ani looked down, she saw the edge of the key ring sprawled on the floor beneath the guard. "Shit!" she spat out again and was thankful when Target reached from beneath the cart for the keys, so she didn't have to retrieve them. His fingers shook beneath the lifted linen cloth as he handed the ring to Ani. It was all she could do to keep from smacking him for the trouble he caused. More guards' voices echoed down the hall, but she ignored them, starting over with the keys and driving an arbitrary selection toward the padlock.

Barnave put his hands through the bars and around hers to still her movement. "Mademoiselle, you must go. You cannot fight them all. When those guards come around this corner, you are dead. There is no reason we must all die. Go now while the gate to the Salle is unmanned."

"No," Ani's voice cracked. She was about to cry. She stared at his hands around hers, and the skin was the soft, unworked skin of a no-bleman, skin like Aubr— "No. I will not fail you." She forced her hands from under his. "You are the Feuillant I came for. You're the voice of reason."

"I *was* the voice of reason. Now I am the voice silenced. Just one of the many. We've turned on our own; there is no reason any longer. There will never be again." He watched her hands flying through the keys, but there were too many. The voices got closer, and soon the three dead men slumped against the bars would be discovered. "You must go. Leave me. Save the man you have, or it will all be in vain."

Tears left her eyes now. She couldn't dam them. "No, Monsieur Barnave," she whispered through a parched throat. "I will not leave you behind." Her tears were such that she could no longer clearly see the differences in the keys, and she shook her head in frustration and cursed her trembling fingers. "I came for you! I came for you!"

He closed his hands again over hers. "What is your name?" His smile was calm and considerate.

A wave of comfort coursed through her. "Ani."

"Mademoiselle Ani." He smoothed her hair away from her face. "I have already gone before the tribunal. I have been sentenced to die tomorrow—"

"No!"

"—and I will die tomorrow."

"No," Ani repeated. "No, no, no." The voices of the approaching guards rang in her ears like warning bells.

"Do not cry, dear Ani." His voice was softer than a hush, the brush of a feather. "I do not wish to live if this is the France I must live in. I will die with my France, but this is not the revolution we started. What is born now of this Terror, I want no part of. You did your best, and I thank you. You did not fail. You have given me hope—hope that my written words might survive, that I touched someone with them enough to be remembered."

"I saw your speeches."

He smiled. "Tell your children how great they were. But go now before all our words are silenced forever."

Ani sniffed back her tears and cleared her throat. It was hopeless, and Barnave had resigned himself to it. She reached through the bars and laid the ring of keys in his palm, lingering until he had closed his fingers around the metal. "Keep trying them. One of them works." She ignored his soft chuckle. He still held the musket. "You can release yourself and the others."

His eyes gleamed with admiration for her tenacity. "All right."

The guards were at the end of the hall. Ani could finally see their shadows moving toward her. If they spotted her, she'd have no escape. There were too many of them. She looked at the keys in his hand as he slid them down his person and into his coat pocket.

"Please. Try." Her tears threatened again.

"I tried once." He smiled. "Death's not so bad. We all must do it. Better to do it principled than cowardly." He patted her hand. "But I have a game of piquet to win before I die."

He turned away from the bars so Ani wouldn't remain clinging to them, and she heard him mutter a little prayer for her safety. She bent to retrieve the small ring of keys around the peppermint man's belt. Thankfully, she knew the correct key this time.

She whispered through the bars, "I will avenge you."

He looked over his shoulder. "You already have."

She turned to the cart and gave its heft a mighty shove, pushing it from the scene of the crime and down the gallery toward the Rue de Paris, arriving with her key readied at the locked gates into La Salle des Gens d'Armes. She breathed easier when she saw that the dead guards had not been replaced at the post, but she could hear the swarm of gendarmes behind her who had discovered the bodies. Time was slipping away.

"Hold tight, Monsieur Target," she whispered through the linen cloth.

The gates opened and closed quickly, and she was headed down the incline and through the long, elaborate room of the Men at Arms. She was sweating profusely and nearly out of breath at the difficulty of plowing Target's bulk across the uneven floors. The guards' shouts were now clamoring through the Rue de Paris corridor, and she felt the tickle in her lungs. Ani didn't look back. She hauled the excessive cart into the kitchen and right out the loading door without speaking a word or sharing a glance with anyone.

When Ani finally made it outside, she was struggling to breathe full breaths, praying for her inhaler as she hovered on the verge of a black-lung attack from the winded flight. Her pulse leaped with relief to see the back of Pere leaned against the clock tower, one hand on the wall and the other hand holding the pocketwatch that he was completely engrossed in.

"Good to see you, stranger," she spoke suddenly, and Pere jumped.

"Godbloodyhelldamnit," he said. "Don't scare me like that." His eyes roamed her, and he instinctually moved to hold her upright. "You's having an attack."

"I think I'm better now." Her breath pounded out in uneven bursts.

"You're not." He shielded her from onlookers and held her by the elbows.

"I am."

"The wagon is not here yet." Deliberately, he avoided her eyes, knowing the panic he'd see there, but with his face so close to hers, something else caught his attention. "Why do you smell like peppermint?"

"I had a little run-in with a charming confectioner."

Pere's eyes narrowed. "Ought I be jealous?"

"Not anymore. He spilled his sweet syrup all over the floor."

Pere smirked. "I hope you didn't lick it from the boards." He picked up a chunk of poultry from the plates still on her food cart and bit into the morsel as he rolled the cart across rue Saint-Barthélemy toward Henri Sault and an array of barrels. "You seem relaxed as a humming-bird, woman."

"I ran into trouble. Serious trouble."

"I told you."

"We have to move now. You can tell me how you told me later."

"The wagon isn't here."

As they reached the other side of the road where the escapees were resting in empty saltpeter kegs, the scheduled delivery wagon came into view rolling over the Pont Saint-Michel—very, very late, but arriving, nonetheless.

"There it is," Ani, Pere, and Henri said together.

"Keep breathing, darling," Pere said to Ani, rubbing her back with his open palm to calm her. Pere lifted the linen of the cart and was surprised to find that the immense weight he had carted across the road belonged only to one man. "Where's Barnave?"

Ani's eyes dimmed, and she lowered them to the ground. "He was the trouble I ran into. I'll have to go back for him, but only after the smoke clears inside. I killed—"

"Stop right there. Don' say it o'loud," Henri said, taking hold of Ani's shoulders and pulling her from view of La Conciergerie, should anyone be looking for her outside the prison walls. "Ya can't go back for 'im now."

"He dies tomorrow."

"Then 'e dies t'morrow," Henri replied tersely, lifting a drumstick from a plate and tearing from the bone a larger bite than would fit in his mouth. "Get this fat man into a barrel." Food landed in Gui-Jean-Baptiste Target's hair.

"Excuse me, monsieur," Target said. "I'm a lordship. I'll have some respect."

"Ya just came out in a food cart, so yer dignity's done for, fat man. Yer 'arder t'shove into a barrel than even I would be, an' that's sayin' a lot." Henri helped Target into the largest barrel they could find and paid no attention to his cries of pain as the lid closed over the humiliated creature. "Serves 'em bloody right, the lot of 'em. Don't deserve t' lose a 'ead, but 'e damn deserves t' be shoved in a barrel."

The trio remained unnaturally still until the wagon came to a crawl before the barrels and rocked back and forth as it came to a stop. The sounds of dirt crunching beneath the driver's feet as he rounded the opposite side of the wagon echoed in Ani's brain, and Pere threw her cloak around her shoulders. He kissed her head, then covered it with the hood. She withdrew her knife and waited patiently, steeling herself against the portension of a lung attack. With the driver's final step around the rear of the wagon, Ani fell in line behind him and held her blade to his throat.

"Don't move, and don't call out," she spoke in his ear, and walked him toward Henri who waited to pound the scrawny pilot into a barrel. After Monsieur Target, this impish man took no effort.

With the driver in an airholed keg alongside the rest of the escapees, Henri climbed into the back of the wagon, unloaded five full barrels from the interior of the bed, and loaded in, with the help of Pere, the barrels filled with revolutionary suspects fleeing for their lives to waiting family members across friendlier borders.

"Pere, why don't you get in a barrel, too?" Ani directed, her insides still fluttering from the close call.

"And what about you?" he asked.

"I'm going after Bet and the Marquis de Lafayette."

"Always softening on marquises. Save a little of that heart for the salt of the earth, would ya?" He winked, but her face darkened. He watched her finger the wax-seal stamper ring around her thumb, and she glanced far off, in the direction of the Swiss border. "I wish you'd forget him."

"'ell," Henri said, coming back around the wagon, "I liked 'at sorry charmin' sot. Was sadder'n a funeral march when it turned out he was 'im, th' bastard."

"End of discussion," Ani said. "Get in a barrel, Pere, and save your own neck now. I care too much about you to drag you down with me."

"Sorry, darling, but I willna leave you like he did, to fight all this mess alone."

"He fought, too," she said sharply. "I said end of discussion." She walked around the edge of the wagon with Henri, who situated himself at the helm of a brace of horses. "You know the way. Luck speed you."

Henri lowered his mouth to her cheek and patted her on the head. "I love ya, girl. Be strong for yer ol' 'enri. My crotchety 'eart couldn't take it if'n I losed you."

She smiled and stepped away from the wagon, watching it roll over Pont au Change until it was too small to see. Her heart couldn't take losing him, either, any of them. No more. She turned abruptly to the sound of gendarmes charging through the wickets of La Conciergerie, looking for anyone who seemed suspiciously like she'd just killed three guards, and Ani's heart raced once more.

"Pere, go," she said.

"Where you going?"

She turned toward Pont au Change and clasped her cloak tight around her. "To end this brutality we started."

CHAPTER TWENTY

TIME RUNS OUT

I shall ask for the abolition
for the punishment of death
until I have the infallibility of
human judgment demonstrated to me.

—Marquis de Lafayette

Ani's eyes were red and swollen by the time she'd found her way back to the Place de la Révolution, fiddling with the lists that she had transferred from her discarded servant's uniform to the pockets of her trousers. Her mind raced with thoughts of Antoine Barnave, of all the prisoners she was unable to save, of the absolute end of reason. Another thought slithered through her brain like an asp: The extremists had killed the Constitution. If she couldn't get to Lafayette, there'd never be a chance of reviving it. *But she couldn't get to him.* The American ambassadors who'd been sent to retrieve him were stopped in Nantes, held up without papers. Without the papers to aid in the ambassadors' free rein to traverse the country unbothered, it would be impossible to negotiate a release for Lafayette.

She fingered the lists and dreaded them, their names gathered daily from the entertainment cart hawking programs next to the Madame's bloody feet, and she pulled her hood up and walked toward the office district in the direction of Chaillot—that old familiar path. How she'd reveled in traveling this road once, when it led to his palace, when he walked beside her. And now, she checked over her shoulder. Dried blood clotted in the cobblestone grout. She ducked inside an overhang of the old consulate building and pulled from her satchel a tiny tin case with a sliding lid that held a piece of chipped charcoal. Flipping through the pages of lists, she circled names with the highest priority, enough to fill only one packed carriage, then separated the lists with the circled names from the lists without, unsurprised now to find the anonymous

Le Capot on every list. She'd have to dye her cloak again and possibly cut off her hair.

She leaned against the wall and looked at the building's entrance, thankful the consular office was situated on the first floor. A groan escaped her as she ripped from the wall another flier of Le Capot and stepped inside the door, removing her hood and walking toward the office door unmolested. Putting her ear to the door, she listened for voices or any sort of surprise. None present. She lifted her gun from her side, pulled her cloak back over her head and face, and pushed open the door, ducking inside to stand before the consul.

"You know the routine," she spoke in a low, gravelly voice, keeping her face down. She approached him slowly, dropped the lists on his desk, and stuck her gun in front of his face.

"Dear God, not you again," the consul whined, staring at the barrel of her gun.

"The circled names. Passports to the Dutch Republic, generic descriptions, spaces for signatures, your stamp. Now."

"Wasn't it just my turn last week, boy? Why do you always pick on me? There are two dozen other consuls."

"They get theirs, Consul Leclaires," Ani said, pointing again to the lists, and the consul picked up a pen. "But your cheery face is my favorite." She watched him fill out the passports with careful script, and she read each word upside down as he wrote it, wary. "I also need one for Lorraine, two R's, surname G A G-N-O-N." She paused and waited for him to write it out, then breathed easier. "I have come here to you, since you asked, because there is this little rumor that you know the names of some North American statesmen who have come to negotiate a release for a one prestigious Marquis de Lafayette but are currently stuck in Nantes, unable to move eastward. You know something, Consul Leclaires, I would really like to have those American ambassadors' names, and passports for them to get into Prussia."

He winced. "Tell me who you are, and I'll give them to you."

"Ah, negotiations. How quaint." She cocked her gun. "I don't think you're in the place to negotiate. I have the gun."

"I have the names. You won't get them if I'm dead."

"Are Americans worth dying for?"

He curled a lip. "No."

"And if I don't get them from you, I will get them elsewhere."

"Then get them elsewhere."

"If I get them elsewhere," she reached into her satchel to retrieve a stack of bills, "then someone else gets the payoff." She slid the stack of money over to him and deliberately uncocked her gun, lowering it from his face. "We both want something: you want to live, and I want Lafayette to live."

He sighed heavily, then took the stack of money and slid it into his top drawer. "Lafayette is an enemy of the state and a slippery-skinned reprobate maggot."

She raised her gun to him again. "It seems to me that only one of us has actually met him, Consul."

His cheery face pruned. "You won't tell me who you are? Or just show me your eyes, boy?" She shook her head, and he sighed again. "Mister Thomas Mason, and United States Senator James Monroe."

"Papers," she insisted.

"I can't. I would be killed for it."

She cocked her gun, and with a whimper, he signed two more papers for the Americans to travel to Prussia, effective immediately. He put his stamp on the documents and slid them across the table to Ani, who picked them up and looked them over carefully. She glanced upward to see Leclaires staring directly at her, studying her, his hands folded across his belly as if wondering what next. The stacks of all the papers and the original lists were in a pile at the edge of his desk for her to take. He knew the procedure, and he made no effort to risk his neck to go after her as she reached for the papers, leaving behind no lists or names. She threw the lists into his fire, along with a wad of fliers, watched until they burned to nothing, then slowly, she inched toward the door.

"I will give you a clue," she said, opening the door and squeezing a foot through the crack. "You drank my father's wine."

The hall seemed to go on forever when she stepped into it. She went faster than her balance normally permitted to avoid being followed, detained with documents of such importance in tow. She made it outside and into a nook at the door to catch her breath. Her heart thumped in her neck, and her chest heaved, but she'd made it out without being followed. Rest was a required evil, or she'd go into a breathing attack that she couldn't afford. Ani leaned her head against the wall before daring to turn back toward the Place de la Révolution in necessity of crossing its awful sights one more time. Her gaze settled on yet another flier of Le Capot mounted next to her head, and she cursed aloud. The posters were becoming too frequent. There was just too much of everything now. No moderation, just too much. Taking a nervous breath, she tore down the flier, along with two others of random aristocratic profile illustrations, sparing two more lives, she hoped, in the process. Her chest felt tight. This was coming too close to home, and she hadn't been careful enough. Why had she given clues to Consul Leclaires? Her exhaustion made her sloppy and brash. Or she wanted him to know she knew his dark past as she knew her own, his dirty dealings with her father's thievery, how tangled the woven web. Or a bit of both. Or...*she just wanted out.* Some way out.

Three loud Tricoteuse women stood along the wall near her, touting knitting needles, their hair pulled beneath headkerchiefs, spinning ideas dangerous and violent. One of the women cooled herself with a paper fan colorfully depicting Bastille governor de Launay's head on a pike, his mouth shoved full of exaggerated nettles. The women discussed suspects, whom they'd seen do what to whom and when and why and how that whole Enlightenment thing had gone to hell in a handbasket. One of the women attempted to put a list into the pocket of her apron but, unbeknownst to herself, accidentally dropped the paper. Ani set her foot over the list and remained in place until the three women moved on toward the guillotine, the madness of the execution square. Ani walked her hands down the wall, lifting the list from the ground. It was long. She swore it must have been every person that woman had encountered in her entire life. An intake of breath and a double-take. Not in anonymous disguise, not Le Capot, not The Hood, but plain as she was born: *Allyriane Bysshe Pardieu.* Her name was on the list. And there below it, in solidarity: *Aubrey-Catherine Beaumercy, m d Col.*

She'd worked so hard to keep his name from the lists that she'd given no thought to the addition of her own. That it should appear. That someone should know it: first, middle, last. She looked back at the women. She didn't know the list's author. How had that woman known Ani's name—and Aubrey's, when everyone in the city believed him already dead?

The twisting pain grew tighter in her stomach. Something was coming. A passerby handed her a copy of *Le Père Duchesne,* and she took the extremist octavo pamphlet mechanically, not even contemplating what she read. Ribald, scabrous invective. Her eyes skimmed the descriptions of the "toads of the Marais" led by tumbrels "to sneeze in the bag" after "trying on Capet's necktie." She'd come from Le Marais once, another lifetime ago—her own family had been the toads of that rich, aristocratic swampland. Something terrifying rose inside her, a fire from abdomen to throat to cheeks. She turned the last corner to the crowded Place de la Révolution and threw up all over the ground, falling forward onto her hands and knees impulsively at the sight that registered in her gut before it found her mind. Nearly twenty men and women, wearing only thin red cloth gowns, stood with their hands bound and their spirits broken. There were too many of them. And there among them, the faces she'd feared to find. Two of Aubrey's brothers, matching palace portraits. The Marquis de Lourmarin, the brother who'd started her world spinning—the one who should have been Aubrey, but she thanked mercy that he wasn't. One of his sisters, the one replaced in the picture frame, every bit as pretty and proud in life as in oil, clutching one of Aubrey's bastard nephews to her deathgown. Maybe more Beaumercys Ani didn't recognize, but the worst of it was unmistakable. There in the line: the palace servants Valéry-Marie and Arnaud, side by side, chins thrust upward, and dearest Josephine, followed at the rear by a solemn Baroness Annette Butte.

Beautiful Josephine. Her hair cropped short and jagged. Her face, plain and unrouged. Eyes puffy from tears, loss of sleep. At the sight of Josephine's appearance, Ani vomited again. She struggled for breath at her own sober realization and tried to call out, but nothing came. They had been arrested on information she'd gathered. The entire household, down to every servant and seamstress. She, and she alone, had put them on that scaffold. Josephine, Valéry. In her carelessness and jealousy, even the Baroness Butte. That moment clutched at her, haunted—over a year ago, the name leaving her mouth. How doll-like the baroness looked now, compared with the revolution's violent women. Ani couldn't even get to her feet before the deed was done, collected with her regrets inside a burlap sack at one seventieth of a second per head.

The more she tried to look indifferent to the bloodshed, the more obvious she became to onlookers, to the men gathered in waves wielding clubs like gavels. Pikes, muskets, pitchforks, scythes. Her mind blanked, then filled with faces. The soldiers, the Swiss Guard, the foreigners. Everyone waltzing at the theater. In the end, the numbers she'd indirectly killed could be higher than the numbers she saved. Her body tensed, and she couldn't breathe. Couldn't breathe. She coughed, and blood came. Couldn't breathe. She fought to regain upright stature, balance, wits, to flee the courtyard without notice, her hands clutching onto her cloak, her satchel, the Hébert pamphlet, her cane, air. Whatever she had about her to grasp. Whatever sanity remained. She forced herself to face away, not to scream out. She couldn't scream out. More blood came with the next cough. She ignored it. There was work to do. She had to get to Lafayette. Her heart thumped hard.

She had to get to Dr. Breauchard.

The courtyard stretched on for what felt like miles as she neared the far wall, daring not to look back at the bloodthirsty Madame. In Ani's haste, she'd forgotten to become a revolutionary. She'd forgotten to embrace the Terror. She'd forgotten not to care, not to be horrified, not to cling to the Constitution when it burned. She wasn't these people. She hadn't changed with them, but away from them. Paris, in all its ephemeral glory, was no longer home, merely a suffocating shell no better than the coalmines of Nord-Pas-de-Calais. The wall braced her as she leaned her hands to it, grazing the leaf of another flier that she ripped down in disgust, her shaky mind teetering on the edge of a vast, dusky canyon.

Against her better judgment, she glanced back to the scene, to the pile of beheaded bodies stacked at the foot of the scaffold in all the cheapness of life, and her eyes fell on another sobering sight. Among the row of feminist women lining the front of the crowd in their red liberty caps, shouting for the blood of the noblesse, fists in the air, stood the young Isabeau Léandre, long-estranged from Ani since fleeing coalmines and cellars, impressionable, naïve, and wasted. Ani turned away, unable to empty any more emotions from the devastation of the scene. Isabeau had never had a chance. If Ani ever had to be reminded who the people of this revolution were, from whence they came and why, she need look no further than this depraved girl, guided by a mad desire for liberty without bothering with definitions or costs of it.

Ani shook herself to her senses and turned toward the printshop. Now was no time to crumble. The half-hour walk formed into a lumbering gait, as fast as she could go without losing her balance. Dr. Breauchard. Her only thought was falling against him, never leaving his safety again. It had been too long. What had she said to him? God, what were her last words? When she arrived at the door of the printshop The Citizens still used as a hub, she flung it open, and it smashed against the side of the building, nicking the wood.

"Dr. Breauchard!" she called into the silence. "Dr. Breauchard!" She pounded on the backroom door to no answer. "Jacques?" She peeked inside, but the room sat empty. Nothing out of order. A fine layer of dust covered the counters. The front door of the shop opened too conveniently, and she faced the sound. "Dr. Breauchard?"

A train of Citizens walked through it as if they'd been summonsed to a tribunal: Évard Pinsonnault, Pere Dinaultbriand, Jean Crissot, Grietje Hindriks, and Baron René-Gervais d'Egrenant. The Law of Suspects was complete. Ani went cold.

"Citizen Pardieu," Évard said cheerfully, "you have been hard to pin down these past months."

"Do not call me Citizen," Ani said, avoiding eye contact with Pere. "Where is Jacques?"

"He's not here, Citizen," Évard said. "He hasn't came around since you disowned him."

"Do not call me Citizen. I didn't disown him. I was angry." She balled her fists. Adrenaline crashed into her exhaustion. "Where is he?"

"Not here, Citizen."

"I said *do not call me Citizen*." She stepped toward Évard until they were toe to toe. "I'm no longer one of your Citizens."

"That's not very wise."

"What care have I to be wise? The wise ones lose their heads. It's not a good time to be smart." She tightened her fists. "No, on the contrary, Évard, it seems a good time to put the wise ones on a list, doesn't it?"

He breathed out loudly and looked at the questioning faces of the others. "What you talking about?"

"You put me on a list. You know my name, my identity." She raised her finger to his chest, despite how he towered over her. "That was worth a lot, wasn't it. Bought you another fancy coat, didn't it."

"Be careful what you accuse."

"I've accused greater men of lesser things." She paused. "Who shot me?" He tightened his lips, and she looked at Crissot. "Jean? I know you both know. I saw you in the marketplace. That bullet was not meant for Aubrey. You were following *me*. You *knew* where I'd be. I knew too much, got too close to him. That bullet didn't miss its target. You wanted me gone." The men did not respond, but she marked Évard's eyes narrowing to dangerous slits. "You have joined this Committee of Public Safety, haven't you."

Évard's fingers twitched.

"I know your names were both in Gagnon's ledgers. You took the bribes, same as my father. If the people know—"

He swiftly pulled a fifty-four-caliber Sea Service pistol from his jacket pocket and aimed the barrel into Ani's chest. "The People won't know." Pere inhaled, and Évard swung the gun toward him, then back to Ani. One of Aubrey's guns from his garrison, one that Ani had once helped procure. "Shoulda kept that to yourself, little girl," Évard spat and waved his gun again at Pere and Grietje, then back to Ani. "Shouldn't have lied to me. Shouldn't have freed Collioure. Shouldn't have stoled the ledgers for yourself. You shoulda listened to your old man."

"Citizen Pinsonnault," Pere said, "think about what you're doing."

"Shut up! Don't fucking talk!" Évard tapped the gun hard against Ani's sternum, and Pere cried out and took a step toward her. "I said shut up! Step back!" Évard cocked his pistol and pulled from a sheath a narrow bayonet that he locked into place at the pistol's tip with a click. "I needed you to retrieve documents for me, not dig for their meaning. They was supposed to burn. No trace. But you! You and your monarchists!" He laughed savagely, waved his gun around. "I should have did the job myself," he snapped, "starting with the witnesses."

He raised his gun and fired a shot point blank that hit Pere and nicked Grietje, and in a haze of black smoke, he brought the barrel across Grietje's temple, then jammed the thin blade into Baron d'Egrenant's throat. Ani screamed and went for her knife, but Crissot knocked it from her hand. Grietje and Pere slumped to the floor, and the baron swayed, holding his neck, trying to speak, blood seeping through his fingers, before he joined them on the ground. Évard was already muzzleloading as Ani ducked for the knife and came up beneath him and slashed it across his arm and chest. Jean Crissot grabbed her from behind and pinned her arms to her side, shifting her balance. For an instant, she floated, unsure which part of her touched the floor. Then her left foot caught, and she sensed the balance, and she swung into her hip, lifting her foot and jamming the jagged claw edge of her boot heel down on Crissot's shoe. The sharp copper piece stabbed through the soft leather and into the top of his foot. He howled and released her, and Évard's gun muzzle flew back around to her.

He pulled the trigger at Ani's chest, but the gun kicked back with a pop, and a plume of black blasted into his face. Blood spurted onto Ani, and his ruptured finger hit her cheek before falling to the floor with the pistol. He shrieked and lunged at her and latched his bloody hand around her wrist as she groped for her gun. He took her to the floor, dragging the hobbling Crissot down beneath them. The two rolled, with Crissot maneuvering out of the way when Évard finally pinned Ani to the floor, blood seeping through a gash in his arm. She could not command her legs to kick. With four hands on the gun, they pushed it into the air, out to the side. Her grasp on it slipped. He lifted her hands up over her head and restrained her beneath him, straddling her. Her fingernails clenched and forced his hand to squeeze around the trigger. He released a wild shot that burst through the air and into the jaw of Jean Crissot. With a crash, Crissot went off his feet backward, to the floor, limp. Évard grabbed Ani's head and slammed it into the ground. She bit through her lip and her teeth clicked and buzzed in her skull, and he immobilized her hands above her head, breathing hard over her heaving chest.

"Your name is on the list," he panted. "You'll join your marquis in a burlap sack."

Aubrey's face flashed before her eyes, a lifeless head rolling in the gutter like her father's, and she yelled out like a battlecry, headbutted Évard in the face, and his nose slid to one side. Blood fell into Ani's mouth and down her neck. He yelled and clutched his broken face, and she withdrew her dagger from its scabbard and drove it into his stomach. He screamed and struck her face and reached above her head for his gun. She shook her vision clear, blinked hard, and pulled her knife from his gut to drive it in a second time. His body tensed, then liquefied. She twisted her blade, and he dropped onto her chest, a rush of blood leaving his mouth and coating Ani's shoulder. She let out a strangled whimper and pushed him to the side, rolling out from beneath him. Withdrew her knife. Kicked the gun away. Crawled along the floor toward the others, coughing, her ears ringing. Grietje stirred, sat up, but Pere and d'Egrenant lay motionless.

"Pere," Ani whispered when she got to him, his stomach blown through with the gunshot, a ragged hole, eyes glassy. "Oh, Pere, Pere. I'm so sorry." She lifted his head into her arms. "I should've—"

"Forgive me," he whispered, his hands clasped over his stomach. He watched the red seep out as if it were not his body.

"Pere?" She tapped his cheek.

His eyes misted and unfocused. She rubbed her hands along his face. His breaths slowed, shallowed. Incoherent murmurs left his mouth, and he closed his eyes.

"Oh, Pere." She cradled him into the crook of her arm and pulled his face into her chest, whispered, "These are human lives. Look how easily they go." She cried against him and kissed his cheek and took his hand in hers until his fingers fell limp. "Shhh. Just breathe calm." Time dulled to a gray crawl. "Goddamnit!" she cursed. "God fucking damnit!" Her fists pounded impulsively, purblind, into his stilled body, then she stopped. Stared. At Baron d'Egrenant, his throat open and draining into the grout, and then to Grietje, sitting upright on the floor, holding her forearm wrapped in layers of her skirt.

"Gret, how bad is it?" Ani asked, slinking toward her.

"He got my arm. Hurts like…" Grietje loosened her apron and wound it around her arm. When she lifted her face, blood also came from her temple.

Ani winced and looked back at Pere. She dragged herself to her feet using the edge of the desk and shuffled about, looking for something, dazed.

"Ani," Grietje whimpered, tears streaming down her face, "what have we done?"

"Don't tell anyone what you saw or what you know."

"What have we done?" Grietje repeated quietly. She couldn't take her eyes off Pere's body. "What have we done, what have we done."

Ani moved about the room again, gathering items that had fallen out of her satchel, wiping at her eyes. "Keep that cloth around your arm, and apply pressure. Constant pressure. Jacques says don't remove the cloths, even when they get soaked through. Go find him. *Find him*." She leafed through the passports to separate the ones Breauchard would need for the doctor cart from the ones she would need for the American ambassadors in Nantes. She placed the documents for Breauchard in a hidden compartment of his medicine chest, tucked her satchel into his valise and her papers into her shirtwaist. She slid Aubrey's ring from her thumb, removed her mother's necklace. She'd take nothing, nothing else that could be taken from her. With one last long look at Pere's bloody body, she headed for the door. "Not a word of this, Gret. Not a word of any of this." Ani pointed her finger, gestured around the room, back to Grietje. "Do you understand me? Not a word of this to Jacques or anyone. When he asks, you don't know who did this. It was just some stranger. Understand? I was never here. Tell whatever story you like except the real one."

"Why would you protect Citizen Pinsonnault now?"

"I'm not protecting him. He'll go where they're all going." Ani set her hands against the door. "I'm protecting Jacques. And believe it or not, I'm protecting you." She hiked a thumb over her shoulder. "Tell him to check his medicine chest."

"You's just leaving them here?" Grietje indicated the bodies. "Where're you going?"

Ani sighed. "Nantes."

"How will you get there?"

She shoved open the door. "I'm stealing a horse."

CHAPTER TWENTY-ONE

NANTES

I have no need of hope
in order to undertake,
nor of success
in order to persevere.

—William III of Orange

Ani had ridden a horse enough times in her life to know how to maneuver a cart down an alleyway, but that was the extent. She'd never even set a free foot outside the city—discounting her stints in various mines and in the Bicêtre once when Dr. Breauchard had bailed her—let alone traversed any distance on her own. The black Mérens she unhooked from an unsupervised military post proved a poor choice as she took off through Saint-Honoré and toward dozens of tiny rivers and the outskirts of the Forest of Rambouillet. The beast chose to walk for most of the seven hours it took to reach Rambouillet, grazing endlessly, and his gait was surefooted on rough terrain, but ragged and bumpy elsewise; by the time she came to the confiscated Château and the ransacked Hôtel du Gouvernement, she was starving, and her torso felt as if it would snap in two. She traded the Mérens for another horse and a night's stay in the city, never sleeping so well in her life as she did that exhausted night, her coveted papers tucked into her layers of shirts, her anonymity a blessing. The new chestnut Norfolk Trotter made it to Chartres before noon the next day.

At Chartres, she traded the Trotter for another Trotter, and told the tradesman she didn't want to know the horse's name. She wanted no connection to anything, alive or dead, anything left behind. She didn't want to feel, and by the time she made it to a commune of which she also didn't bother to learn the name, she could feel nothing but her aching chest slumped over the horse's neck, pounding with his lazy trot, releasing bout after bout of endless coughing. The countryside was littered with patches of dead bodies, soldier relics piled in streambeds.

Remnants of a year of interminable war and the shots and screams of nearby skirmishes still raging. After trading the horse for a night in a cabin room, better directions, and a smaller horse with a preferable gait and a gentler saddle, she made it to Le Mans two nights later, Angers after getting lost two nights after that, then followed the Loire River through some light snow to Nantes by the end of the seventh or eighth night—she'd lost track—but she didn't think she had the strength even to climb out of the saddle when she arrived to the final rivermouth decimated by war. She had never been to Nantes; she had no idea where to go and no idea how Aubrey could have made that same ride in three days, those poor soldiers, no doubt marching all night, trading in their horses every twenty miles, even in the dark depths of a midnight.

At the dawn of the tenth day, she came upon the sight she'd prayed she wouldn't see. Bodies floated against the gabion of the Loire. The gaseous, decaying odor preluded the port, and the quay was teeming with moored barges of royalist prisoners, tied to one another, tied to the boats, tied to ratlines and posts. Stones pelted them from the fists of children. Priests in their robes were draped in heavy bricks, weights hanging from their necks. Guards stood by with bayoneted muskets. Bile came into Ani's throat, and she knew she couldn't ride a horse through this. She veered near the Mint where dislocated churchbells lined the front walkway to be melted into valueless coins, passed the endless murmur of muffled cries from the Prison du Bouffay and the garish red of the painted guillotine in the scaffold square, on to the closest horse corral.

Before she'd even slid sideways, a man wearing two tacky cockades from his liberty cap took hold of the reins, her fatigue immediately obvious.

"I need to sell it," she said, climbing down and steadying herself on her cane against the rump of the small Jennet.

"Fifty livres."

"That's all you'll give me?" she said. "That's robbery."

The man narrowed his eyes. "Where did you get this palfrey? It's ran to the glue. A hide for knackers."

Ani glared at him. A night's rest was all the animal needed to be sturdy as new.

"Where's your cockade? You's not from here, are ya?"

"Fifty livres is fair," Ani agreed and held out her palm.

The horse would fetch ten times that price easily, especially with soldiers in such desperate need of them, but she couldn't quibble about it with a wary revolutionary. She had plenty of time to decide how to leave, after she stopped Senator Monroe from sailing home to the United States without fulfilling the most important mission. She'd figure out a way to steal the horse back later. The man counted out the coins into her palm, but as she withdrew it, he suddenly grasped hold of her wrist, twisted her off-balance, and locked her neck in an armhold. The coins scattered to the floor. Her cane dropped.

"I asked you where were your cockade," he spat, and as Ani choked and strained against him, the man called for other men from the stable.

Another ostler lifted her legs, slicing himself on the metal and cursing, and she was dumped into a handcart, her gun taken from her, then her knife. They rummaged through her cloak and frisked her for identification, but she had none, never once thinking of her own need for papers, with the sacred documents buried deep in her clothing. She groped at the sides to pull herself up, but a farrier knocked her in the chest with a shoeing iron. The air left her. She heaved for breaths and coughed and fell back into the cart, still heaving as it rattled down the quay and onto rue de l'Entrepôt toward the quarry. Her mind blanked at the bright blue sky, the cold ocean wind that stung her. An overwhelming odor of coffee, so potent it was suffocating. The moldiness of water and fish and drying seaweed. Rushing slivers of the Chézine ran beside her, and the cart dipped and rebounded in marshy soil, then rolled past the wooden Duparc bridge. She was dumped in front of iron gates, the coffee smell so much stronger.

Within minutes, she found her senses coming back to her inside a locked gate, in a quadrangle enclosing a courtyard with thousands of roaming prisoners. The sign above her read: *la salle de Café de Dépôt*, which explained the smell of coffee that dominated the entire port. An enormous coffee warehouse converted into a prison. Women and children, infants in the arms of their sobbing mothers, priests and nuns and men in wigs, rebel soldiers from the Vendée still wearing white sashes, entire families huddled together, sickly men lying in puddles of their own blood and vomit, feces and rice mush piled everywhere. Men with spotty rashes erupting across their naked torsos, hacking, dry coughs that gave way to nothing. In one corner, dead bodies dragged through a gate by the arms and legs, and Ani marked it in her mind as a possible exit. She shuddered. *Typhus.* She removed one of her shirts, careful to keep the documents safe, and despite the new chill, she wrapped the cloth around her mouth and nose. Her chest still ached. She inched through the bodies smashed so close together she could hardly move forward, careful to touch as few as possible, thankful she'd layered several longsleeved shirts stolen from Aubrey's palace, so her skin was not exposed. The place was a veritable deathcamp.

She didn't know the plans to the layout; the walls were solid wood and granite with few openings in the enclosure. Each opening had a locked gate from ground to voussoir arch. Three floors of storage space and drying racks for coffee beans, dark wood towering above her in cavernous ceilings and stairwells. She learned quickly that there was no chain of command, no one in charge, that guards who were sent in died of dysentery and intestinal eruptions, so guards were hard to acquire. Food was only unwashed rice, and the water couldn't be consumed without sickness. No roster could be found; the place was understood to be a well-kept secret. She stayed away from the crowded populace, slept on a wooden ceiling beam, and ate coffee beans for days, her body jolting into tireless spasms. She caught snow and rainwater on her tongue and shirt, wringing the fabric into her mouth and rinsing her rice rations in the rain runoff. Then, before the week was out, she'd discovered Thomas Mason.

L'Américain. He stood sequestered in a warehouse drying closet, pacing, arrested for being a foreigner and for not disavowing his god. His French translator slumped on the floor next to him, hungry and tired. Mason's face was too plump, his chin slightly doubled. His thin mouth rested in an upturned line with miniscule indents at the top corners. His French was choppy, but between the translator and what broken words the men knew, Ani determined that she didn't much care for Thomas Mason beyond the knowledge that he'd been sent to argue Lafayette's dual United States citizenship to spare the general who had won their American war for them. But unable to move freely throughout France without the papers the government was no longer granting, Mason, and his suspiciously absent cohort Monroe, could not reach the Prussian prison where Lafayette was being held. Ani had the papers. But the documents wouldn't free Mason from this place, and now that she'd met him, she wasn't sure she wanted to relinquish them so blindly.

In part broken French and mostly Southern-twanged Virginian English, Mason whined like a child at his predicament as he paced the only private space he'd been able to find away from the mass of prisoners. "Y'all people are animals. Fuckin' animals to cage me in here. I never shoulda let James talk me into this. I'm only here 'cause I let James talk me into this. Well, and my father was go'n send me here on business in a counting house 'fore he died, but then he died, and now… Man, I got a kid on the way. My father was a founder of America. I run a ferry and have a plantation, for Chrissake, and hundreds of servants running it.…"

The translator paused and rendered it properly as "slaves," and Ani looked sharply at Mason before a wrenching cough took hold of her. She patted her pocket, then remembered that the bastard ostlers had taken her inhaler.

"You got the typhus?" Mason said. "Christ, everyone in here's got some disease or other. Hear 'em all screamin' and hollerin' all night, can't a man get no sleep. And I am a man what likes his sleep, I'll say. I am a Southern genteel, the son of a prosperous founder, and I'll not be treated like this by a bunch'a savages, I'll tell you, and we wouldn't treat a man this way in the grand ol' States, I'll say that, too. And all this for a constitution? Hell, my daddy was a founder, and he refused to sign our Constitution. He was a powerful man, my daddy, and we Virginians wasn't gettin' a fair shake in the Constitution, havin' to give 'knowledgment to our servants 'n' all. Had it been me, well, hell, I wouldn't'a signed it, neither."

Ani just stared at him disappointedly and sat down on the floor across from the translator, picturing in her mind the exits to the prison, calculating when the men came in and out to haul the dead bodies. Remembering how hard-won France's Constitution had been, what a feat it had achieved—*how painfully shortlived.* Women screamed and pleaded against assaults throughout the corridors, and Ani squeezed her legs together reflexively.

"Listen to that screamin'!" Mason rattled on, peering around the corner of his safe drying closet. "Hollerin' like that! My wife hollered like that, and I'd take a strop to her, I'll say, but then, Sarah wouldn't holler like that because she's a fine-bred Southern woman, not an animal." When another woman cried out, he said, "Columbia! What're they doin' to 'em?"

"Raping them," the translator answered indifferently.

Mason stared at the man, and then looked concerned at Ani.

"All martyrs must be innocents," Ani said, "so all virgins could become martyrs. The Committee can't have martyrs." She shrugged sadly, so drained of emotion she could hardly feel the anguish of it. "So they get rid of innocence." It was the same practice the guards had enacted in Paris' jails. She remembered anew why Joan of Arc wore men's clothing. Ani's lungs tickled, and she coughed again violently, gripping her neck.

"You got the typhus, don't you. I knew it. Get away from me with that typhus. Listen to 'em all vomiting from that disease! We're all go'n die from it. We'll just die here like animals from foul filth and despair and disease—"

"You'll die of a slit throat first," Ani muttered, and the translator laughed darkly.

"You think this is funny?" Mason said to him. "I'm only twenty-three years old; I ain't ready to die! I'm a son of the Virginia Dynasty! My Sarah is a new bride, and she's in the family way. She's due any day now, and I left her behind for this 'cause I let James drag me 'long, bein' told it'd just be a right quick-enough thing. All because he wants to be pleni… penliportiary…peniportenary.…"

"Plenipotentiary," Ani said.

"That's the one! I mean, Christ, I have a child on the way.…"

"Everyone has a child on the way," the Frenchman replied.

"Bunch'a animals." Mason paced. "Bunch'a rabid animals. You people are not Christians. You are not God-fearin' creatures.…"

The Frenchman and Ani met eyes, and the man kept his face expressionless, and Ani knew then that he was also an atheist. Probably a revolutionary, only here by dint of association with this pompous blowhard to feed his own family, probably also with a child on the way. She wasn't going to ask his name. She didn't want any attachments, didn't want to know a soul. Pere's graying face flashed in her mind, and she focused on the women's screams, the agony of moaning, sick men. She tried not to imagine Béatrice, trapped in a prison in Westphalia. What were the guards doing to her? Ani closed her eyes. Mason was still talking about gods and kings and animals. *Twenty-three years old.* She thought of someone else who would be twenty-three years old now, how different he was from this man, how much more stalwart and duty-bound. She wished he could trade places, wished she could be sure she were putting the sacred documents into the hands of a capable man.

"You kingless men do not understand," Ani said. "God has done a lot of bad things here for a long time through the tongues of many kings."

Mason stared at her and pieced together her words, and the translator grinned coldly.

"Hell," Mason said. "Well, hell. I mean, in Virginia, it's like we have a king, the way them Federalists keep tryin' to take our state declarations 'n' all. I mean, my father was a founder, and he was a powerful man. Served in the Virginia House of Delegates, but he wouldn't serve in no Continental Congress because that damn Treasury runs the country like it's its own damn bank, and we have to pay for it all from the labor of our servants, our own sweat and land goin' to damn New York who don't work its land...."

"What is 'Virginia'?" Ani asked the translator, as Mason kept talking.

"I believe they call it a 'state,'" the Frenchman replied. "Like our old provinces, perhaps?"

"Is it a governing seat?"

"No, it's where the rich people live. Like Le Marais...but with farmers. I think farmers in the States are rich. It doesn't make sense."

Mason cut in, "I don't like it when you two talk. I can't parse it that fast. And did you call me a farmer? I am highly offended by that. I am a planter, the son of a planter and a planter 'fore him, and my planter daddy was a founder."

The translator looked up at him, then down at his folded hands, tired and repulsed, and he shot another conspiratorial glance at Ani.

"Did he mention," Ani said to him, "that his father was a founder and a powerful man?"

The Frenchman laughed, and Mason made to speak again, but there was the sound of someone calling his name loudly through the corridors, and he shrieked.

"They've come for my head, the ghouls!" Mason crouched and hid behind the translator.

But Ani perked. The accent wasn't French. She climbed to her feet using the wall for balance, and the translator saw for the first time that her legs were injured. He stood quickly to help her, but she waved him off. She didn't want any human contact. No disease, no mites, no lice, no filthy hands, no errant spit. That's how people died in here. She moved toward the sound of Thomas Mason's name, and there were two well-dressed men walking with guards, covering their noses with handkerchiefs. They yelled Mason's name again, and Ani waved her arms.

"He's over here," she called back.

"You squeeze-crab critch!" Mason yelled from his squatting position.

"What?" Ani said, then turned back to the approaching men, waving them forward. "Over here."

The men looked nervous, as if they weren't sure what they would see when they rounded the corner to the drying racks, but when they reached Ani, Mason hollered again and leaped forward.

"James! Dear God!" he shouted and ran to the man, hauling on his arm. "Ya gotta get me outta here!"

Virginian Senator James Monroe brushed him off and turned to the French translator and to Ani, who was already digging through the layers of her shirts for the documents. Monroe's French was also Virginia-twanged but otherwise educationally precise, and Ani made quick time with introductions. His eyes were striking but vacant, and his long, straight nose wrinkled when he spoke, as if he had a cold. A high white scarf squeezed his neck into tall, stiff collar points, and his brown hair receded into a widow's peak. Ani thought he was either brave or dense to wear the nankeen silk culottes of an aristocrat in this place. She hoped for brave.

"James," Mason interrupted. "James!"

Ani lifted the documents toward Monroe, and he took them absently, then stared at them in disbelief, the realization coming to him slowly.

"You—" he stammered, "you procured these?"

Ani nodded.

"Legally?"

"Well." She looked down at her shoes. "They're legal. Let's leave it at that."

"You're from the city?"

She nodded again, and Mason hauled on Monroe's arm, shaking it like an aggrieved toddler.

Monroe bowed politely to Ani, held a hand to his heart, and pocketed the documents. "Excuse me, Miss Pardieu, Léger." He turned to Mason and in thick Southern English said, "You hapless nincompoop." He reached into his breast pocket, pulled out a white glove for his right hand, slid it on, and slapped Mason across the face. "Insolent, churlish pup." He slapped him again, almost gently, like a scolding father who didn't enjoy punishing a wayward child, and then he removed the glove and put it back in his breast pocket. "You do this." He crossed his index and middle finger and held them in the air. "And then this." Then he slid his crossed fingers behind his back. "And you say, 'I denounce God.' Simple as that."

"No, sir!" Mason cried, rubbing his slapped jaw. "I am a principled man!"

"You are no such thing," Monroe said, and he turned back to Ani. He pulled out the documents and studied them carefully, coming back to his pedantic French. "These are real? I must be careful. I may soon be an ambassador if I play the right cards." When Ani nodded, Monroe leaned forward and kissed her on the cheek, and she blushed and pulled back.

"Them's the documents we needed?" Mason asked.

Monroe ignored him and set one of the documents into the hand of the man next to him. "Barlow, you're now Thomas Mason. Look alive."

Mason shrieked. "Wait, what? *I'm* Thomas Mason!"

"Barlow?" Ani said to the man next to Monroe. "Barlow who sent hundreds of Frenchmen to America on fraudulent land deeds?"

"That's the one," Barlow replied, his Connecticut accent not so harsh as the Virginians'.

Ani looked disgusted, and the French translator rasped out a curse and spit on the ground, biting his thumb. Joel Barlow took a step back but held his ground. He was a wide man, corpulent in the way that only a man of wealth could be, with a widow's peak more prominent than Monroe's and a rounder face that was a few years older than his counterpart's. His fetched queue was messy, and Ani couldn't decide if it were a wig or just the unkempt circumstances of the moment.

Barlow studied the document. "Even if this paper is legal, James," he turned to Monroe pointedly, in quiet English, "the action is not."

"He is our Golden Boy," Monroe dismissed.

"Where is this outpouring for Rochambeau? Paine? Biron? d'Estaing? Destouches? All our golden boys are being locked up, and they're hardly boys anymore."

"It must stop somewhere, Joel. Hell, d'Estaing can rot in it, but Washington wants Lafayette out; I work for Washington. We go to Prussia. Now, I repeat, 'Look alive.'"

"Well," Barlow said. "Let's hope we stay that way."

Mason whimpered. Monroe stuck his hand out to Ani, but she didn't take it. No human contact. The cheek kiss had already been too much. He nodded and withdrew his palm.

"We'll get him out," he promised her quietly. He turned over the document. Scrawled in one corner in small print was: *Béatrice Meschinot.* He furrowed his brow but nodded again.

"Please," Ani said. "If you can find her."

"I will do what I can. I cannot be reckless."

"I know."

Mason squealed again, and Monroe said, "Good Lord," and covered an ear, and the two visitors turned and walked away abruptly, leaving Thomas Mason to be held back by the translator as the three of them remained in the prison. There was nothing the men could have done. They were diplomats escorted by guards and would have to go through the flawed and terrifying system. But Ani'd done what she'd come to do, and she wouldn't wait around for the system. Monroe had the papers. He sided with the revolutionaries, which kept him alive, but both Barlow and he were Americans first, loyal to George Washington and to the baby nation they'd helped create. He'd get Lafayette released if anyone could.

Ani stepped out from the drying closet and into the courtyard and looked up at the night sky. It had to be nearing five p.m., the early winter dark, the dwarfed piece of moon showing in the last stages of its last quarter. It would be a dark night. *Good.* She glanced around the packed courtyard for guards, but most of them were drunk out of their wits and preoccupied with the deflowering of young girls.

"You ought not stand out where they can see you," the translator said, stepping up behind her. "I can maybe fend off one, but not more."

Ani glanced at him. She had not wanted to know his name, but Monroe had called him Léger. And he *was* short, a little wiry man, lightweight as a wafer, so whether it were a surname or a nickname, Ani didn't know and didn't want to. She doubted he could fend off even one, though she didn't doubt he'd try.

"Do you want to leave tonight?" she asked.

"I didn't get farther than the top of that wall." Léger nodded to a quieter area beyond the noisy courtyard.

"Guards?"

"Everywhere. On the other side, dozens. The ones who won't come in here." He looked up at the last throes of twilight, saw what Ani saw. "But it will be a dark night. I'll give you cover."

"But you?"

"I have nowhere to go." He held up his hands. "My wife was killed when the Army of the West decided our peaceful commune was a good place to stop for the night. They burned my house, and that was all I had left. I'm not even a royalist."

"They stopped making distinctions long ago."

She still watched the guards, watched their movements, her stomach tightening as they swaggered from woman to woman to little girl. When the debauchers had no more stamina, they used bottles and gun barrels to break virgin hymens. Did she have anywhere to go, either? She didn't know. Were Grietje and Breauchard alive? Could she get back to them? She felt sick when she thought of Paris, of returning, of the sanctioned butchery that would defile them all. Could she find it in herself to return? And could she even get over the wall, through the gate? To a horse? She choked down the feeling of hopelessness and watched the stars come out blink by blink, the heavens winking to life. Her legs felt heavy. Her lungs, a deadweight inside her, falling through her body. She was tired. She had to sleep a little.

෧

Sleep came fast but stopped even faster by shouts from the courtyard, the movement of men like a herd of animals, hands coming down on her hard. Léger cried out, and hands were on him, too, and the malty grain stench of drunken guards filled the tiny space. Ani was dragged to her feet, and men consulted lists by ineffectual candles, wadded them onto the ground, grabbed prisoners at random. Ani and Léger were pushed along into a mass of hundreds of people. Bayonets stabbed refractory men who veered from the swarm. Pretty girls were pulled aside for the later satiation of profligate guards. Ani pulled her cloak over her head. She held her breath, tried to touch nothing, no one. Léger stood too close to her, stepping on her heels, but Thomas Mason had been left alone, left behind. No one wanted responsibility for the American; he might cause trouble, unwanted attention.

The night was dark, the sliver of moon as impotent as Ani had imagined. A wash of limbs and cloth through the courtyard, and then the bodies spilled out of the gates onto muddy rue de l'Entrepôt, pushed from behind in a clump. Ani regained her footing in marshwater, saw the Duparc bridge, thought she might reach it, but a bayonet swung in front of her face, and she was hustled forward into the dark night, the spots of lantern light flashing into her eyes like the lamps of the mine. Pere had held them once, and she shoved her hands forward, pushed to emerge through the claustrophobia that racked her, to part the march that led down the quay and to the Loire port. Then she stopped, though she was pushed from behind—dragged her leg, though she was nearly lifted by the crowd forthcoming. Léger held her arm and calmed her, but they could both see the boats.

With a wide aft like a fluyt and a rounded forenose, the galiotes looked ominous with their two unfurled masts blading the sky. The long, flat bottoms made shallow-river travel easy, and leeboards were deployed at the sides to stop drift. Over a dozen oar holes pocked the hull. Dutch flags flew out behind the mizzen. Commandeered from a naval blockade, Ani figured. Where were they going? But there was no time to ponder it.

"Ten Nivôse, Year II," a guard called out, and another recorded it, and then heads were counted into groups of ten, and the first ten were stripped of their clothing as they screamed and begged.

The night was frigid. Ani's breath haloed her face at the sudden shock of the cold against the naked bodies. She glanced away. She'd never even seen a naked man that wasn't a marble statue, and here were seven, all of them priests, being trussed at the wrist before everyone, cheap cloth and hemp binding man to woman, woman to man.

"Jesus!" Léger said, and he looked away from it for decency, hauling Ani back, but soldiers in red caps and wide-brimmed hats pushed the crowds forward with swords.

Flecks of snow fell on Ani's lashes. "Mercy," she whispered, her lips moving in disbelief, but no other sound exiting.

Dozens of men walked down the line, and one of the three women deemed pretty and young enough was relieved of her innocence before the swarm of onlooking prisoners. The next ten were shoved forward and stripped, the mechanics the same, and then Ani and Léger were thrust into the group with nuns and mothers and little boys. A guard tore the ties down the front of Léger's shirt and rent the fabric from him in one yank.

"Please don't hurt my wife!" Léger said, and tugged Ani behind him.

She gasped, but then she understood. She'd never known a wife married to a Frenchman who could call herself a virgin. Léger might not be able to fend them off, as he'd hoped, but this would protect her from being violated here and now. A guard stripped her, and the sudden burst of cold was white hot, then painful to the touch as she crossed her arms to cover herself. Léger let out a guttural sound at the whip marks on her back, and averted his eyes from her, looking toward the ground.

"Hey! Monsieur Carrier! This one's got leg braces," the guard yelled.

Ani said, "I can't walk without them."

Another guard laughed mockingly and said, "Heh, but I bet you can't swim *with* 'em. Leave 'em on."

The first guard left them on, though he looked conflicted at tying her wrists together with Léger's. "Sorry," he said quietly, his brow drawn. Over his arm he'd draped her removed cloak, and he lifted it and looked at it with fondness, a strange familiarity. "Hopefully your husband can walk you both."

The second guard shoved them forward onto a plank.

"Swim?" Ani repeated, and Léger and she looked wild-eyed over their shoulders at each other and shuffled awkwardly across the plank with the rest of the prisoners boarding the galiot. The waters of the Loire slapped against the boat, fierce and white-capped, reaching to the painted name, *Vrede*. She trembled and shivered at more than the falling white skies. What was happening?

"I'm so sorry to be touching you like this," Léger said.

Ani didn't respond. She was sorry, likewise, but figured it didn't need to be voiced. No one here was unsorry for anything. Léger kept them balanced as they boarded the boat, thrust into a corner on the wide, flat deck, then forced down below it. Rats ran at their bare feet, and Ani now shivered so violently that Léger could feel it from the floor.

"Can you…" Her lips quaked. "Can you reach my right brace?"

"I can try." He strained until the thin twine cut into his wrist, but he could touch her brace. It was sharp and nicked his hand, though he didn't feel it for the lack of circulation. "Ah, I see."

They twisted their hands together and moved back and forth across the sharp edge of the brace with their joined wrists, but it was a surprisingly difficult endeavor. Ani's contorted torso squeezed her lungs, and she felt as if the cold air had frozen them in place. She coughed and cut her hand and pushed hard through her shallow breaths until her chest calmed. Her teeth chattered uncontrollably, and she fixated on it to keep her mind from everything else. The hundreds of naked royalists around them. The stuffy smell of belowdecks. She couldn't help but wonder if this is what happened to Aubrey, if he'd been set adrift in the wilds of the Loire and had never made it any farther. And Breauchard—he'd wonder forever what happened to her. He'd never forgive himself. If he lived. If he was alive. She twisted and pressed harder with the twine against the brace. The boat lurched, its moorings pulled, and a stronger rocking made the cutting harder as they drifted toward Trentemoult, a neighboring fishing village.

"Where do you think they're taking us?" she said.

"They're not taking us anywhere."

She stopped cutting the twine and looked at him.

"Can you swim?" he asked.

From the far side of the hold came commotion, gasps and shouts and pleas for help. "M'aider!" and curses, and the floor filled slowly with freezing water. Ani worked harder at the binds, and they suddenly snapped, propelling her forward, her hands landing in water up to her forearms. The noise of the frantic women in the cramped space grew and amplified as they tried to hold their children up, their hands bound, their desperation deafening, and Ani watched the rats scurry toward higher ground.

"The rats!" she said, hauling herself up, her fingers so cold they could hardly grip. "Follow the rats!"

Ani and Léger fought through the swarm, the water up to their calves, Ani pulling herself along on the cargo ropes attached to the walls. They climbed up and into a wooden loading duct, Léger leading. He reached the top, poked his head out cautiously, and cursed.

"There are fishing boats everywhere. Men with paddles and poles to strike us down."

Ani climbed up his legs as he held on tight, and as she neared the top, it felt as if the bottom of the river suctioned to her. She screamed, and he caught her, but the floor of the boat dropped out, and the water rushed fast. The screams of the prisoners, the prayers of the nuns, the sounds so loud Ani couldn't think. She clawed forward, but the water reached her torso, though she could hardly feel it, the cold spikes shooting through her. Léger pulled her onto a deck overhang, but the boat was sinking, the deck already underwater. Ani crawled onward. Boats and barges packed in the river like the mouth of it were choking. Nearby ships brought up their anchors loaded heavy with dead bodies. Guards shoved poles into the bound prisoners who surfaced, holding the flailing bodies down. One by one, the screams fell silent, the night becoming too quiet but for the creaking of the sinking ship, the shouting and laughing of possessed guards, and the deck suddenly shifted, tilting, the planks disappearing from underneath Ani. *She was in water.*

She kicked, but her braces pulled her down, down. She grabbed the leeboard and hoisted herself on it, catching one breath, but her lungs wouldn't hold it. She coughed into the water and took in the cold waves, and she choked against the side of the boat, then her braces took her down. Dark water filled her nose and mouth. She coughed under the surface, and it filled her with blades of ice. A pounding that belted her brain. Nerves spidering closed, one by one. She couldn't reach the latch, couldn't release… Her fingers were… Her arms too cold, the hands… Her hands curled into themselves. The black encapsulated her, but Léger found her arm and yanked her upward. She shot awake, coughing into the black void, honeyed thick around her, and she found the latch. Her right brace unhooked, and she kicked out of it clumsily, and it fell away. Then the left, easier, and it fell, and they both fell slowly, suspended, drifting as if they weighed nothing. Her braces to the bottom of *la Baignoire Nationale*, as it had been christened by the rabid executioners. The National Bathtub.

Above her head, flashes of lanterns amid pitch black, and Léger and she held on to each other, pushing and pulling against the weight, until they reached the surface and gasped for air, spitting the foul black death from their mouths. Léger vomited into the water. Ani could feel nothing, her lips blue and quaking, but her mind came back to her in flickers. *The snow stopped.* And *the smell of meat grease.* And *I've never seen the ocean.* But when she knocked against the side of a fishing boat, she inhaled sharply and looked up into the silhouette of a guard hovering over her with a raised paddle.

"We're not royalists!" Léger said, but then his eyes closed at the effort, and he sank back limp into the water, letting go of the boat.

The guard grabbed hold of him before Léger drowned and hauled him in over the side, and then another guard lifted Ani into the boat. She shivered and curled into a ball, coughing out the filthy water, then felt the warmth of her cloak wrapped around her, the heat of its familiar wool. She looked into the face of the guard who'd apologized to her on the plank, who had hesitated with her braces and clothing.

"La Capot," he said quietly and took off his red cap and put it on her head. "You're fine," he said, then went to his place at the oars.

The other guard wrapped his coat around Léger, who crawled to the edge of the boat and looked out at the galiot, mostly gone, a swell of disquieted water, the yelling revolutionaries holding down the priests who tried to rise, the women begging for their children to be spared.

"Lot of good their god did them," Léger said, then slumped back to the floor.

The second guard, no more than a boy, built a fire in an enclosed iron pot suspended on bricks, and Ani and Léger circled it, sliding on their sides around its heat. Ani studied the guard who'd called her by her disastrous nickname, but he rowed steadfastly away from the *Vrede*, away from Nantes, pushing hard against the upstream current without explanation. He only looked at her when she coughed. Was he turning her in to the Committee? She coughed violently, dragged herself to the side of the boat, and vomited over the edge, rocking the boat that the oarsman worked hard to steady. There was a reward for her capture in Paris. If he turned her in, there was nothing she could do. Her braces were at the bottom of the Loire. Her weapons were gone. Her insides vacillated between being frozen stiff and igniting. She rolled back and huddled against Léger for warmth, the iron fire only starting to penetrate her topmost layer.

"Léger," she said, by way of comfort and thanks and apology all in one, with nothing to continue.

"My name is not Léger," he said. "That's what that penial-swell senator called me when he put remittance in my hand to translate the farts of his bleating goat."

Ani laughed unexpectedly, the sound of it distant and otherworldly.

"He thought he was so clever."

"I don't want to know your name," Ani whispered with difficulty. "Everyone I know dies."

"All right," he said, closing his eyes and settling into the guard's coat. "It's Rémy Rocher."

Ani let loose a quiet sob into his coat fabric.

"It's all right," Rémy said soothingly. "It seems I'm not dying tonight."

When dawn came, Ani coughed herself awake, a black liquid coming from her mouth. She was burning up. A half-eaten block of cheese sat beside her head, and she vaguely remembered eating the other half. And she'd seen sun, so this wasn't the first dawn, several suns, so it wasn't the second, but they were countless to her. The boat still pushed upstream along the Loire, the apologetic guard on one end of it, and two new men on the other end, taking turns at the oars, trading off at ports. Uncountable birds of prey circled overhead, screeching, feasting on floating bits of flesh. Rémy was gone. She coughed and stirred and felt her forehead, slid her hand down her body. She wore the guard's clothes.

"Eat something," he said, rowing ceaselessly.

"Where is Rémy?" she managed between coughs.

"Got off at Beaugency. Had friends there."

Another man said, "Think the fish is all right to eat yet?"

The rowing guard shook his head. "Still contaminated."

"Without goodbye?" Ani asked.

"I imagine for a man who's already lost everything, goodbyes are rather difficult."

The third man said, "Orléans, Citizen," and pointed.

The guard nodded and steered toward the port. "Not that you would have heard it, anyhow. You been racked for days." The men lowered poles into the water and led inward to the port, shoving off the river bottom, and the guard stood and unhooked the hawser, wearing nothing but his underhose and a thin shirt. He pointed toward one of the men. "Get up there, and buy a space on a cart going to the city." He threw him a coin pouch, then turned to Ani. "Can you walk?"

"I will try."

She lifted herself with great effort, but she coughed and spit up dark water as she crawled to the edge of the boat. He raised her by the arms over the lip and let her lean across his shoulder like a crutch as she dragged her leg, and they moved slowly to the end of the dock and up onto the quay.

"My sister had the misfortune of marrying a rich city lawyer," he finally said, leaning Ani upright against the bulwark, so she could balance herself along the quay. He looked down, then up at her pointedly. "Thank you for saving her."

Her breath caught. "Wh—? Who—"

He put up a hand and shook his head, and the man with the coin pouch came running back down the quay. "Got a horsecart! Going to the city. Man said he'd take her wherever she want to go."

The guard acknowledged the approaching man, then turned to Ani. "Do you know a doctor?"

"Yes!" A tear streamed down her cheek. "My god, yes."

Chapter Twenty-Two

White flag

How have I loved liberty?
With the enthusiasm of religion,
with the rapture of love,
with the conviction of geometry:
that is how I have always loved liberty.

—Marquis de Lafayette

Ani knew they'd reached central Paris by the smell of it. Pig fat and bodystink and moldy wood and dyeing sulfur. She was fevered, exhausted. The streets prepared loudly for sans-culottides celebrations. Women whirled topless on the cobbles, shouting a frenzied carmagnole. Prop guillotines were erected along the rues, their blades draped in swishy red velvet. Each violent bump of the cart had expelled dry heaves and coughs from Ani until she had nothing left, hardly sensing the tiny flakes that lit on her cheeks as the horses came onto rue Honoré, then slowed in front of Boutique de l'aquatinte. Before the cart halted, she had rolled over the edge of it, landing hard on the stones. The driver hadn't even dismounted before Ani was on her hands and knees, pushing forward with her stronger leg and dragging the unresponsive one to meet it.

"I was going to help you," the driver called after her, watching her, but she'd already crossed the road and pulled herself up on a lamppost, though she nearly fell again.

The land swayed. People stared, a wave of red caps and sashes of red, white, and blue. The door to the printshop was open, and a young man walked hurriedly in and out of it to a carriage across the way, in front of whence departed the cart that had brought her. She coughed, spit up bile, and the doorway to the shop confused her. The sound. Crying, sniveling, mewing like a hungry kitten, then moaning. A sudden and unadulterated screaming. Nothing. Quiet. Was it quiet? Her brain throbbed. Her speech slurred with the sound. She thought she formed words, but she was swirling. The young man came back.

"Jacques," she said to him, and he pointed inside, then yelled for Breauchard. Ani balanced from the post to the wall to the doorway and slid against it. Consciousness came back to her; how long had it been? The printshop in flashes, and she was still immersed in water, seeing the lanterns above her. Was there sound underwater? She didn't hear it, blinked, and it was the printshop, the room she knew. Arms she knew.

"Oh, my god, Allyriane," Breauchard whispered into her hair, kissing her cheeks, her lips, her head, holding her against him. "I want to choke you I'm so angry at you."

He shook her, then held her to him and calmed her breathing with his palm in even circles on her back. He motioned for his apprentice to bring one of the tricolored sashes to tie around Ani's waist, so she'd look less suspect wearing the revolution's colors. Her throat was blistered with sunburn, so the apprentice procured a cotton fichu from a trunk—Ani figured it was a trunk of articles left behind by the dead—and buttoned the covering around her neck.

Her body wouldn't move with her mind; her neck stiffened when she tilted it. But laid out on a cot, she saw Grietje, head fevered wet, skin sallow. The girl's clothes stuck to the sweat that soaked into the cot beneath her unconscious body. Where once Grietje's left forearm had been, she now had a space, her infected gunshot wound having spread gangrenously. A stain of brown blood marked what was severed just above the elbow. A ceramic jar of rum sat next to the young girl's head. Wooden sticks that had slid from her mouth rested on the cot beside her neck, and a leather tourniquet squeezed tightly around what remained of her arm.

"Sit here." Breauchard sat Ani where he pointed. He squatted in front of her, touched her face, lifted her eyelids with his thumbs, looked deep into her eyes by the light from the window. "Stick out your tongue."

The young man said behind him, "Doctor."

"I'm coming." He inspected Ani's wrists, the rope burns and cuts, the base of her skull. He felt the nodes of her neck. "You are sick." He put his ear to her chest, pressed into her back. "God, what has happened?"

"Doctor," the young man tried again.

"I said I'm coming, Luc."

He stood and turned and leaned over Grietje, and Ani watched Dr. Breauchard replace arteries that had been fettered aside then tacked with crooked needles into layers of curtailed tissue. He sutured them with stitches and held his stomach and looked away, slowly lipping a count to ten.

"Thank you," he said to Luc, the sandy-haired, twenty-something medical apprentice who'd been holding Grietje's body down from the other side of the cot. "With God's grace, she'll stabilize soon." He ran a hand over her sweaty forehead, then faced Ani when he heard her moaning. "What the hell were you doing in Nantes during a civil war?"

She tried to move, but her body stayed behind. Her tongue felt fat as a bee sting. "I had documents for," she breathed hard, "for Americans to get…Lafayette." The words came out muffled, and she coughed until it hurt.

Breauchard loomed over her and glared. "Jesus Christ. That man. Look at yourself. Even if you could free him, what would happen? Have you asked yourself that? He'd be beheaded. He's safer in a Prussian prison, wherever the hell he is." He hissed through his teeth as he rushed to prepare a medication for her from vials and powders. "What Americans?"

"Diplomats." She coughed and laid her head back against the window and told him about the scuttled boats of prisoners. About Rémy Rocher. Her braces at the bottom of the river. Her stolen inhaler.

"Mercy," Breauchard said beneath his breath.

"There were hundreds of us, Jacques. These boats. They just…" She closed her eyes. "They just *sank them.*" She breathed in, and her chest had a new pain in it, a deep lungful of nettled air. "Why'm I so sick?"

"All the contamination in the Loire. You were insufflating dead bodies and animal waste." He pulled out his pocketwatch and looked solemnly at it. His mouth twisted. "Did they get their papers?"

She grinned.

He grunted and smacked her jaw lightly, and she opened her mouth for a spoonful of whatever he had mixed for her. She laid her head back. They'd get to him. They'd get to Lafayette. And they'd take the tale of what was happening here back to America. Surely then more Americans would come to help. Surely then they'd stop pretending they didn't know what bloodshed ran in France's gutters. Surely then.

"Our names are known," he said. "We're leaving now. You were fifteen minutes ahead of being too late."

"Am I not always?" she said and coughed.

He smirked. "Keep that medicine down." He turned toward Grietje, unconscious and soaked, and instructed Luc in wrapping the girl in dry blankets in preparation for shifting her.

"Are there papers?" Ani said.

"No. Less than half have papers." He wiped Ani's face with a dry cloth. It was instantly saturated in sweat. He looked particularly worried, then rummaged through some documents. "It's going to be a carriage to the brim, and another woman gave me this for you." He slid the sealed parchment marked *Capot* into Ani's hand. "She might have been followed. They might know we're here."

Ani opened the letter with the names and location of the three children of the now-beheaded Girondin leader, Jacques Brissot de Warville, whose wife had encountered Ani in the marketplace months ago and had begged her to take the children.

Breauchard watched Ani's facial expression change with the information the letter contained. "The borders are now secure, so what we're doing is impossible," he said. "I waited too long to get you girls out."

"I never had intentions of getting out."

"Well, I've always had those intentions for you. But we're at the mercy of roadblocks. They know about the doctor carriages. Border patrols are allowing no one to cross without a passport, even the émigrés they once welcomed. They can't bloody tell which is which. They figure we're all to blame, that we can just rot in it, and quite frankly, they're right. This Republic has not an innocent among us. Near everyone I've ever known is dead or deserves to be."

"You know about Évard," she whispered, "and Pere. And—"

"I don't want to think about it." He shook his head. "They were carted to the catacombs. It was the first I'd prayed in years. Never thought I'd be thankful you'd disappeared to somewhere else." He turned and placed a wool cap over Grietje's bandaged stump and buckled it in place with a cord of leather. "That could have been you."

"Jacques." She coughed.

"Keep that medicine down."

"I thought I'd never see you again." She breathed heavily. "I'm... sorry..."

"Save your strength."

"I'm afraid."

"Me, too. Those who aren't afraid are the ones to fear." He slid a blanket down to Grietje's feet and wrapped the edges around her.

"You've had your fight. You've fought it valiantly. Now it's time to forget marquises and save yourself."

She tapped the edge of the chair and frowned. "Have you heard from him?"

He stilled, tinkered with the blanket. "Not since Lyon," he said quietly and didn't look at her. "Ani."

"I know," she said.

"They were outnumbered. Soldiers are being urged by the government to massacre their own officers. They're all dead or dying."

"I know." She rolled her head away so he wouldn't see the tear that slid down her cheek.

"The carriage is ready," Luc said, stepping back from the door. "I'll get the valises in." He laid Ani's white satchel in her lap.

She stared at it, petted it like a curiosity. She fished around inside and pulled out Aubrey's insignia stamper ring, slid it on her thumb, and cupped it to her heart. The room swirled.

When Luc had returned, Breauchard asked, "Can you carry Gret?" and nodded back to the unconscious girl who would have the misfortune of coming-to in a bouncing carriage in France's dark countryside. With any luck, a passenger's stowed whisky may be at hand. Breauchard packed the rum, just in case. As Luc lifted Grietje, Breauchard supported Ani, and the two men helped the young women toward the packed carriage that had picked up most of its passengers prior to this stop. Even the carriage looked antsy, rocking in place.

Ani pressed against Breauchard's shoulder, stared up at his blue eyes, his angular jaw. "Was my father a good man?"

He misstepped but didn't hesitate. "He tried to be."

"I'm not a child. I don't need lies."

"He did what he thought he had to do."

"He was a highwayman."

Breauchard stopped briskly and looked at her. "Did the marquis tell you that?"

"I'm nothing like him."

"You're like your mother."

She half-smiled. "I'm like you."

He grunted, but his heart hammered. "No one's lucky all the time." The carriage door opened, and he slid her upright onto the seat, pulling himself in after her, then situating her across his lap for lack of space. "Don't speak ill of the dead." His arms held tight around her, and he watched out the carriage window as onlookers across the street stopped activity to stare at the coach, memorizing, filing away every detail.

Luc held Grietje in his arms next to the doctor, and they made room for everyone on benchseats intolerably cramped. They rode. Silence shrouded the passengers, heads against the velvet lining of the coach, fingers fidgeting in laps, shoulder to shoulder. At a noise, each jerked in unison, then resettled. Ani rested against the doctor's chest and murmured the contents of Madame de Warville's letter over and over. The children. There wasn't room. They had no papers. Each street passed, each landmark, each faubourg, each department, each arrondissement, and she knew she neared the address of the Brissot children. Her pulse quickened.

"Turn left ahead," she blurted, pulling herself upright on the window ledge.

"No," the doctor said. "What are you doing?"

"Turn left here." She waved her hand out the carriage window at the drivers and pounded on the side panel.

The closest driver nodded, and the carriage took the turn.

Ani ducked back inside and faced Breauchard's angered gaze. "There are children," she said. "They've lost their father. They'll be orphaned."

"There are thousands orphaned by this. We can't help them all. They have no papers. They'll be turned back at the border."

She set her jaw. "I said I would do what I could. Some people still keep their word, Jacques." She closed her eyes and pictured Aubrey signing the confession, those words, then blinked it away.

It was well after dark when the carriage rolled in front of the townhouse, and Luc retrieved the Brissot children. Under the cover of darkness, the children exited the house quickly, and Ani saw shadows of sullen caretakers, perhaps Madame de Warville, slumped in stupor in the flicker of the houselamp's glow, spreading a beacon of needed illumination out the fanlight. If the passengers begrudged the addition of the children in the overstuffed space, they didn't voice it. The carriage rolled through the countryside, silent except for the occasional bubbling of a child's laugh to remind the riders what a future might still sound like. A light snow fell now and again, and the passengers huddled together for warmth, nodding in and out of restive sleep.

Breauchard chose a lightly trodden path through the country, skirting an aggressive Prussia, toward the Dutch Republic to get the passengers to neutral ground with ports where the majority of them could travel to

England or on to America. If he could even get just the papered passengers to Lillo, Kruisschans, or Liefkenshoek in the five-day journey,
he would consider it a victory. The French countryside they'd traverse
prior to this freedom, however, was pocked with battles and armed men
and roadblocks, and each day longer into the realm of the war increased
their risk of capture.

Unknown was that foreign troops entered the countryside north
and east of Saint-Quentin, joined with retreating troops from eastern
France and the Vendée. Unknown was that, thirteen hours and four
horse exchanges into their travels, troops littered the roads and fortresses through Cambrai, Denain, Valenciennes, and well past the border.
Nearing the sleeping outskirts of Saint-Quentin, a glow of lamps to the
northeast put an uneasy feeling deep in the doctor's gut. Ani slept, and
he held her tighter against his shoulder, laying his cheek against her wet
forehead and whispering a prayer into her damp hair. The lamps moved
closer.

Breauchard ordered the carriage lanterns extinguished, but within
minutes, the moving lamplights turned into soldiers riding up to the
carriage on horseback, dressed in whites and reds. Royalist men in arms.
Some French, some Prussian. Others Swiss, Austrian, and German.
Pickets sent to clear the road of insurgents.

"Detach all your tricolors and throw them out the window,"
Breauchard said. He removed the cloth from Ani's head and waved it
high as a white flag of surrender, and two shots rang out. He thought
they were warning shots, but as the carriage rolled to a stop on its own,
he realized the shots had pierced the two pilots, leaving them dying at
the reins while the troops converged on the defenseless coach.

"Godalmighty," Breauchard rasped.

"Get out of the carriage!" one of the soldiers yelled in an Austrian
accent. He stepped down from his horse and approached. "Get out of
the carriage now. Put your hands and papers high."

"You killed my drivers, sir," Breauchard said, "under a white flag?"
The doctor restrained a waking, fevered Ani from groping for the window ledge.

Another soldier waved his bayonet at the passengers. "Step out of
the carriage! Show us your papers."

"I have sick and injured children here," Breauchard protested. "We
are doctors with patients, making our way to hospital. Please grant us
safe passage."

"Is that why you bypassed the city facilities in the opposite direction?" the second soldier said, laughing coldly. "Step out of the carriage."

"They are royalists?" Ani whispered.

Breauchard nodded.

"Please, sir." Ani dragged herself from beneath her wrapped blankets and up to the window of the carriage. Flakes of snow fell on her arm. "I'm the wife of a royalist general. You may know him." She cast a silencing glance at Breauchard. "He will vouch for our safe passage."

The soldier squinted. "What's his name?"

"Beaumercy," she said. "Marquis de Collioure. He is a lieutenant general from the former King's Guard, fighting for royalist troops in the Vendée."

"The only men left in the Vendée is dead men," the man said, opening the carriage door to usher them out. "You're not very informed for a *wife*. He's a major general. He's not in the Vendée; he's right at Port Gayant at the river. And he's not married; every woman north of Reims knows that."

Ani pleaded harder. He was alive. He was so close. "Please. What is your name, sir?"

"Moubray."

"Let him tell you for himself, Private Moubray. I beg you. Tell him it is Joan of Arc."

"What proof have you that you be his wife to persuade me even bothering ask him?" He hauled her out of the carriage and saw for the first time that she was injured. He softened his tone. "Have you a passport?"

"No, sir, I've no proof. You know it is too dangerous to carry that kind of identification through France. The wife of a royalist." She studied Moubray's expression; he was considering it. She tapped a thumb on her thigh, then remembered. "I have his insignia." She looked down at Aubrey's pewter wax-seal stamping ring that she'd kept around her thumb. The oversized ring slid off effortlessly, and she handed it to the soldier.

The first soldier leaned over Private Moubray's shoulder. "No papers, no proof," he said, taking the ring from Moubray's hand. "Any common thief coulda stole this from the major. You want us to believe a girl looks like you be the Marquise de Collioure?" The soldier laughed and tossed the ring to the departing soldiers leading three papered passengers by horse to Port Gayant.

"Where's their cockades?" another soldier said. "They don't have cockades."

Then, a familiar voice came from behind both soldiers. "Do not believe nothing that girl says. She's an insurrectionist."

"General de Béquignol," Ani said brusquely to the officer sitting atop a horse behind the two men. The game had shifted.

The corners of his mouth curled into a snarl. "Shoot her." He waved over the passengers. "Shoot them all."

"Don't do this," she cried. "You know me, General." She turned to Private Moubray. "He knows me. Please. There are children."

"Yes, I know you," de Béquignol said and sidled his horse to face her. "You betrayed him. I'm doing him the favor. Now line up, and don't call me general. Your…*husband*," he smirked, "demoted me to field marshal. I'm not feeling too charitable this fine evening." He yanked on his reins and drew his horse back to take in the full picture. "Get the rest out of the cart. Take their wares. Execute them."

"Some do have papers, sir," Moubray said, waving a document next to one of the standing passengers.

As Breauchard stepped out of the carriage, propping Ani against the side, he reached into his pocket and retrieved his passport. Discreetly, he handed it to the passenger on the other side of him. "Take this," the doctor whispered. The passenger dismissed the action, but Breauchard shoved the document into the man's hand. "Take it, goddamnit. It does me no good if Ani doesn't have one. One of us might as well get across the border with it."

"Who here still has papers?" de Béquignol said. "Step forward. Lafonne, Boucher: Take them to Saint-Quentin. Search the rest. Search everyone. Take the bags. Check for supplies." He alighted and handed the reins to a soldier.

Ani counted the agonizing minutes, watching the disorganized men shuffling about, their rough handling of passengers and luggage, their intricate investigation of passports. "Please, Édouard," she pleaded, "don't hurt the children."

Moubray turned and locked eyes with her when she addressed the field marshal by first name. He looked back to de Béquignol and lowered the musket.

"Line up the children, as well," de Béquignol said, looking directly at Ani.

"But, sir," Moubray protested, "we can't just execute children."

"Do as I say."

"Sir, with all due respect, no one will do it."

"You will do it," de Béquignol snapped.

"No, I won't." Moubray stood erect, dug the stock of his musket into the mud, and crossed his arms on it. "Not kids. You should go to the major on this, and you know it."

"We have orders from higher than the major that insurrectionists is to be shot on sight. We's at war." He walked up to Moubray and stared the shorter man down. "But if you're so soft, Moubray, take the kids to camp, and *you* can be responsible for sending them on a carriage back to Paris to lose their heads for being emigrants."

"You don't know if they be insurrectionists. Some really are injured." Moubray motioned for the kids to be pulled out of the lineup at the point of a bayonet. Another officer rifled through their pockets while Moubray watched, unnerved. The children were shivering.

∾

Back at Port Gayant, the first passengers with passports arrived with soldiers corralling them toward the encampment set up on the river. The soldiers gathered the émigrés into the custody of the barons and officers waiting at the generals' main station. Soldiers lined the walkway to pilfer through stolen possessions of the detained, to hear the tale of the carriage, the firing squad ordered on insurgents, dead carriage pilots. The relating of a young woman dressed like a man who said she was the major general's wife, a fanciful tale, was received with laughter.

But one officer found the description too familiar: Baron Pierrick-Anne Bellon, the Breton who'd watched Aubrey's and Ani's interactions for months. When the pewter ring came around with the looted treasure, Bellon clasped it in his hand and backed away from the gathered men and émigrés with a knot in his stomach.

∾

At the carriage, de Béquignol ordered the men to pop the trundle and remove the trunk, to break the lock if they had to. Men went at the lock with the stocks of their muskets. A soldier going through Ani's satchel lifted the crumpled octavo pamphlet of Hébert's *Le Père Duchesne* and held it up. She'd long forgotten about that.

"Marshal, sir," he said, taking the pamphlet up to de Béquignol, "I found this on one of the women."

The field marshal looked at the extremist sacrilegious pamphlet and muttered, "Proof enough for you now?" He wadded the booklet into a ball and smacked it against Moubray's chest.

Breauchard scowled at Ani. "What are you doing with that?"

"I don't know," she said, her chest deflating, tickling for breath. "It was handed to me. I think. I…I don't know if I even glanced at it. I… can't remember." She went into a coughing fit that bought them time, if nothing else, and Breauchard held her in place, close to him.

The passengers were thrown against the side of the cart, every bag and belonging searched. Some of them were sectioned off in the darkness. She focused on those papered passengers and children already at, or headed toward, Saint-Quentin and Gauchy. Some would get away. She wanted to pray for it. Aubrey would've prayed, but she couldn't muster it. To whom would she pray?

De Béquignol yelled, "Line everyone up! Tell them girls to stand up."

A soldier approached Ani to take her from Breauchard's support, but the doctor pushed the soldier away. "She can't stand on her own. Show some fucking mercy."

"Please, wait," Ani said. "Listen, please. These men are doctors." She indicated Breauchard and his apprentice, Luc. "I know you need doctors. They will serve you and help your injured. They're men too good to waste like this."

"Don't plead for me," Breauchard said. "I'm not leaving you."

Moubray looked once more toward the injured young woman struggling to stand, her face firm as she leaned against the carriage and held hands with the doctor on one side and a trembling woman on the other, comforting her. "Shouldn't we take them back to camp, sir?" he tried again. The thought of sending bullets through trembling, unarmed women—he shook it away. "They rose a white flag."

"It's dark; I didn't see no white flag," de Béquignol said and walked up to the line of passengers. "Any of you among the faithful, start praying now." No one moved. "That's what I thought. Go down the line and say your last words."

"Sir, goddamnit," Moubray said, "there are injured girls. One of them has been amputated within the day. She's not even conscious."

"One more word out of you, Moubray, and I'll have you dismissed. Does the unconscious girl have a paper?"

"No, sir."

"Then put a bullet in her. I haven't got all night."

A voice called out at the back of the carriage, and de Béquignol became engrossed with what the soldier pointed out in the trunks, belongings, and supplies of the passengers. Ani hung her head and counted the minutes again. Had she endured the Loire for this, a fate no better than the priests who survived the shipwrecks only to be drowned by poles? She was thankful Rémy had left at Beaugency—that if he died, she'd never know, never have to see it happen before her. One less death was a tiny mercy.

ℰ

At Port Gayant, Baron Bellon pounded on the door at the marquis' meeting quarters and opened it without any invitation to do so. "General, sir," he shouted.

Aubrey spoke with two other men, hunched over a map. He looked above the rim of bifocal lenses at the baron's sudden entrance.

"I don't mean to intrude. Under any other circumstance, I would not. But, sir."

Aubrey straightened and removed the bifocals, folding them neatly in his hands. "Spit it out, Baron."

"The men from the western front brought back émigrés with papers. There was talk of a white flag. And...and a girl who said she was your wife."

"My wife?" Aubrey chuckled, then his face went waxen and blanked. "My wife."

"Yes, sir. A young woman dressed as a man who had this." He held out the pewter ring. "She said she was Joan of Arc."

He laughed. "Where is she? Where is Allyriane?"

"At the southwest road, west of the city." Bellon pointed, then hesitated. "Facing a firing squad."

Aubrey swore and threw his bifocals onto the map, patted the guns at his hips, and overtook the baron in a single bound. "Who ordered a firing squad on a white flag?"

"You'll never guess."

"I will drag that son of a bitch beneath my horse." He exited at a run.

"Sir, you won't make it."

"Have you heard the guns?" he yelled over his shoulder.

"Not yet," Bellon called back.

Aubrey commanded the nearest mounted soldier, "Chaillon, your horse!" The officer slid wordlessly from his stallion off one side as the marquis simultaneously bestrode the other.

From the port to the southwestern roads outside the city, a fast horse might take nine minutes through the dark, but Aubrey was determined to cut that down to seven. To five. He felt the horse beneath him as if the four legs were his own, let the beast have his head. He whispered for him to go. *Go.* He squeezed his thighs and let his gut guide him through the dark at breakneck speed and thanked God he'd chosen a fast one, despite the jarring gait. His chest pulled and tightened like the wind repeatedly going out of him, and when he tried to breathe, he succeeded only in holding longer breaths. Time refused to bend and bow to suit him. Anchors heaved his heels, honeyed around his horse's knees, moving up a current. Time didn't discriminate, just held so. Even as the sleek, fast horse flew across the countryside toward the faint lamps of the mounted soldiers, the stallion couldn't move fast enough. A half-mile from the scene, Aubrey could make out the lamplights as lamplights, not merely fireflies. Then, too late he rode. The firing squad released its musketfire at once, and the reports echoed again and again across the field, mocking him. The suddenness of the shots induced the marquis to pull up on his reins so abruptly that he nearly took his horse to the ground with the dropping of his insides.

"No," he whispered to himself, then screamed it out long and loud, "No! Hold your fire!"

Another round would go off after reloading or bringing in a second line of squad. Aubrey jerked a pistol from his side and fired it into the air, commanding his spooked stallion forward with all his strength, yelling to hoarseness for the soldiers to hold their fire. They heard him, saw their major general charging toward them, but the damage had been done. The line of prisoners lay straggled on the ground in the dark.

Breauchard was among the lucky ones, grazed in the outer right hip. Two of the three remaining men were dead, and the third had been shot through the lower groin and upper thigh, bleeding out through his femoral artery, screaming. Grietje had been shot point blank through the chest, never regaining consciousness from the shock of her amputation to know what was coming. Breauchard clenched his teeth against the pain as he dragged himself to Ani, and his hands fluttered uselessly over her body where she lay still on the ground, punctured twice through one side. The woman who'd held Ani's hand lay motionless beside her, their fingers linked and now stilled that way.

"Do not fire!" the marquis called, leaping from his horse in mid-stride, recovering his footing, and running, adrenaline-flushed, toward the line of slain passengers. "Oh, Allyriane." He dropped to his knees at her side, lifted her head into his arms. "God have mercy. Please. Have mercy." With one hand, he absently crossed himself again and again, the first time he'd done it in a long time. The movement caused her to inhale sharply and open her eyes, and the marquis moaned softly.

"Aubr—" was all she could muster.

"I'm here. Shhh." His fingers trembled against her. "Don't try to talk."

She reached for the doctor.

"I'm here," Breauchard whispered. He put his hand in hers but gave her over to the marquis. The doctor removed his shirt and held it to her wounds, and the two men wrapped her.

"Tend to that bleeding man!" Aubrey yelled at his soldiers.

"But, sir," a soldier said, "he's—"

"Then put him out of his goddamn misery, for Christ's sake." He didn't cross himself this time.

"Gret?" Ani asked.

Aubrey turned his glance to the dead girl's body lying motionless at the end of the line. "Fuck," he muttered, and his throat hardened. He looked back to Ani. "She'll be fine. Don't fret now." He pulled her into him, and they both jerked when the shot went off next to them.

"Your family," she cried against his neck. "Josephine. I...saw..."

"I know. Shhh now. It's done and over."

She melted into the crook of his arm without resistance. "I'm so tired."

"Stay with me." He pressed his hand to her face, but her responses were imperceptible. He shifted her as the doctor wrapped her wounds.

"I'm so tired."

Her hand dropped, and Breauchard winced through his own pain and lifted her from the marquis' arms to rub salve on her and wrap her with one more bandage. The soldiers, dumbstruck at the depth of their mistake, came to Ani's aid, but Aubrey raised his palm.

"Do not touch her. Get back," he said, his voice cracking as he stood and reloaded his pistol, blood coating his uniform. "Who ordered a firing squad without permission? My God, are we so uncivilized? Are we no better than the animals we fight against? No army of mine advances upon a white flag! What kind of soldiers fire on a woman who says she

is my wife without further investigation?" The men stepped back, and
Aubrey didn't look down at his gun as he finished loading it rotely and
lifted it. "Who?" he yelled, and the men parted and backed away from
de Béquignol, leaving the scowling field marshal open and obvious. De
Béquignol blubbered something ineffectual, but Aubrey breathed quickly, pulled the trigger, and sent the bullet into the marshal's chest. Pink
sprayed the night, and the men gasped, looked down at the body, then
up at their major general, stunned. He dropped the gun and lifted the
bandaged Ani into his arms and headed toward his horse. He propped
her on the saddle with considerable effort and hauled himself up behind. "Moubray, get the injured bodies to Gauchy. Be careful with that
doctor." He pointed at Breauchard. "Any man who fired a shot will give
proper burial to the dead at first light. If any of you ever goes above
my command again, mark me, I will not bother with a court-martial."
He secured the reins and aimed his horse back toward Port Gayant,
and from behind him, he heard curses and moans of agony; in front of
him, he heard her breaths shallowing. He wrenched his stallion toward
the encampment. With the weight of another person, and fragile as Ani
now was, the return was slower, but he still took the horse as fast as he
could command it, speaking against her cheek, "I know you are tired,
but stay with me. Do not close your eyes. Focus on me."

The rocking motion of the horse, arrhythmic, jolting, put her into a
daze. Her face bounced against his chest, in and out of consciousness.
His body was warm, and hers was getting colder. The horse beneath
her, so futile, and Aubrey—unwashed, salty. His uniform tasted of dirt,
and it filtered in and out of her open mouth, and she let it, tasted him.
The moonlight silhouetted his tight jaw. He looked so angry, looked
older. Warred, battletorn and broken, determined but lost. While he
held her, his hand with constant pressure against her bandage, she let go
of him, unable to grip as she bounced into his chest, into the home that
he was. Her eyes lost focus. He squeezed his thighs against the horse
until they cramped, and he gritted his teeth and groaned and squeezed
harder. It seemed too long before he approached the camp's sick-bay
quarters and slowed the stallion, slicked with sweat, and unloaded Ani's
unconscious body with assistance of the surrounding soldiers.

Dismounted, he took her again and pushed through the crowd.
"Doctor!" he called out. "Lemieux. Beaudin. Anyone!" He elbowed the
door open, and a doctor rushed toward him, directed him to a cot, and
helped him lay her on it gently.

"What happened?" Dr. Lemieux asked, feeling the head of the woman and rubbing her cheeks and arms to revive her consciousness. "This girl is deathly fevered."

"She's shot."

"She's more than shot."

"Lemieux," Aubrey panted, his breath still out of him, "keep my wife alive."

"Your wife? What is she doing out here?"

"Surviving." The marquis looked at her closely one more time. "There will be more injured coming, but her care is first and last, understand? If she dies—"

"General, I am a doctor, not a miracle worker. This woman looks like she's been through hell."

"She has." Aubrey glanced back as he reluctantly walked to the door. "It's called France."

Chapter Twenty-Three

Bokhoven; or, the epilogue

*One forgives
to the degree
that one loves.*

—François de La Rochefoucauld

Aubrey took a swig, paced the floor, and lifted the flap over the make-shift window. No riders yet. He could smell the stink on himself, and he involuntarily murmured little nothings as he paced. Then he'd stop and stare as if he weren't quite sure what he saw, his vision blurry. The quietude unnerved him.

Ani lay sleeping on the cot, her face soaked with sweat. Aubrey stared at her through a drunken haze, a leather-encased glass flask in his hand. He hadn't been quite so drunk in a long time, but it kept him from thought. Too much thought. He was transfixed on her bare right foot that edged from the bottom of the blanket. He'd break his stare, then pace the floor beside her, then come back to her small foot. Beneath the blanket, she wore nothing but his clean shirt, long enough to reach her kneecaps. Her pants lay folded at her bedside.

"You said you were always sober on duty," Ani spoke, startling him out of his trance.

He met her gaze swiftly and took a drink. "I've been drinking for four days straight waiting to hear your reprimand." He raised his flask and nodded at her. "You know what I always say about idle hands." He looked at the flask. "My only duty now is watching you recover. I've," he cleared his throat, "*retired* from everything else."

"You're still the only general I would follow into battle."

"God knows I've lost more battles than I've won, so I wouldn't follow too close."

"If I follow too close, I'll like to die from your fumes." She coughed and winced. "Bathe yourself, sir."

"There's been no women to mind." He chuckled, handing her the flask of whisky as he sat on the edge of her cot and tucked the blanket in around her.

She took his flask and held it shakily to her lips, the whisky tasting too expensive for the time and place. They passed it back and forth. A year and a half floated between them, all it entailed, feeling both longer and shorter than that.

"Jacques tells me you saved hundreds of people. Even swam out of the infamous Baignoire Nationale and lived to tell it."

"Jacques," she echoed, listlessly. A worried look washed over her. In it: the doomed journey, Luc, Grietje, Pere, Rémy, all the things that went wrong. "How is he?"

"He's piqued by a sore hip, but it's healing to minor inconvenience, at most. He never even rested it. He's been in Gauchy around the clock these past days designing you new braces."

Her eyes lit at the mention of it. "And Grietje?"

He lowered his eyes. "She was already at rest. I couldn't say it."

"Oh. Oh."

He stood and stepped toward her with purpose. "But Émil Gagnon's wife and children joined him safely in Switzerland. There are some things that turned out all right. Brissot's children are en route to a safe haven in England, where we can get them to America. Henri Sault's at Liefkenshoek. And I negotiated the release of your friend, Béatrice Meschinot, with an American senator who's now in Prussia. I believe you may know him." He smiled.

"Then we lost five to your firing squad."

"Not *mine*. I have never ordered a firing squad in my life." He tinkered with the folds of her blanket. "You lost eight. Two carriage drivers, and the one bleeding out couldn't be saved." He sighed. "And I can't get you out of here. They aren't giving papers to get you and Jacques across the border. Most of the roadblocks and patrols are unfriendly, and no one crosses without a passport. My own passport could get us both arrested and sent back to Paris, and it wouldn't be a leisure trip. The royalists aren't winning."

"Jacques has a passport."

"No," Aubrey said, handing her the flask of whisky. "He gave his to another passenger so he could stay with you."

She moaned, "What a foolish thing."

"You think so? I can't blame him. I'd've done the same." He took hold of her hand and leaned in. "I told Jacques, when this was over, I'd come back for you, to Paris. I'd risk it. I hoped after every livre and deed and title was stripped from me and I was leveled to a commoner, that one day I could return to my city, and you might find no more reason to refuse me."

"You could not be a commoner. Have you any idea how much money you have?"

"Yes." He cocked his brow. "Although, I'll wager, a lot less than I once had. Yet, you're still wearing men's clothing on the income of a marquise. Imagine that." The humor in his face fell. "Ani, I know I'm not your first choice. But I figure since Lafayette's already spoken for…" His smile returned, and he shrugged. "Given where we are, what's become of us…if I asked you now—"

Dr. Breauchard opened the door, carrying new copper leg braces, and his face lit to see her awake. His whole chest fell with his thankful sigh. "I know I'm a few weeks too early for your nineteenth birthday, but I'd be awful cruel to make you wait." He pulled back her blanket to reveal her bare legs.

Aubrey glanced away, then back, flushing.

"This is the best material that the marquis' money can buy." Breauchard paused long enough for that to sink into a grin on Aubrey's face. "It's thinner copper, but more structurally sound, so, lighter weight but better support. The springs are tighter, and pull and release with a wider range of motion, so you get a springing step that works with your kneecap. And here—" He pointed as he slid the brace onto her leg. "No more clicking steps. I've padded the heel sole with felt." He laced the braces in place, then instructed both Aubrey and Ani in the new buckle system. "The latch is different, so there is no chance of it coming off or loosening unless that is what you choose for it, with this mechanism right here." He guided Aubrey's hand to the buckle just above her kneecap, showing him how to lift the clasp up and out, then back in. Breauchard then did the same for Ani, propping her up with one arm, locking and unlocking her brace, then setting her back to the pillow carefully.

When Breauchard returned to his spot across the cot from Aubrey, the doctor noticed the young man's hand grazing slowly across the buckle, along the seam of her kneecap, his fingers caressing a patch of skin between the knee buckles. The doctor bunched his lips and raised his eyes to the marquis' face, to see Aubrey staring at Ani, and Ani staring right back. Breauchard looked away from the silent exchange as if he'd been an unwelcome voyeur. His throat tightened until he had to focus on swallowing the lump in it. He took a step back.

The marquis shifted his gaze to the doctor. "Perhaps now is a good time to tell her."

"Keep still, sir," Breauchard said.

Ani asked, "Tell me what?"

"Jacques has something he'd like you to know," Aubrey said.

"No," the doctor answered curtly, "I don't."

Aubrey shook his head at the doctor's cowardice, about to say more when a knock arose at the door. "Come in," he said, lifting the blanket over Ani's legs to cover her.

A thin man came into the room in an air of vainglorious self-admiration. He had the appearance of a dandied squire, a white sash across high shoulders. The arbiter for the Austrian branch of Aubrey's noble family—he made sure everyone knew it, no matter how out of place he looked. He entered and stopped with a start, unsure how to proceed with the addition of Dr. Breauchard to the room.

"Go ahead, Monsieur Joncheray," Aubrey said. "We're all family." He glanced at Breauchard.

Joncheray pulled from his breast pocket a batch of folded papers and leafed through them, handing the first to the marquis, who approached. "It's not what you had in mind," Joncheray said, "but it's all we could achieve at this time. Half the documents are forgeries, but quite undetectable. The good news is your cousins and uncle in Austria have granted you a townhouse in the neutral northeast of the Dutch Republic. It's large and roomy with space for lots of children." He looked at Ani. "Or dogs or whatsoever. The countryside is beautiful there, and your land is—"

"And the bad news?" Aubrey said, looking over the papers that the arbiter laid out.

"They can't give you anything else. It gets complicated, and the war is expensive. You understand. You won't have any personal wealth if you can't access it here, and your property in France has been confiscated by the First Republic. They'll take the rest once they learn you've emigrated. We can give you the shelter, but—"

"Baron? It says here I'm a baron," Aubrey said. "I'm being stripped of my hereditary title?"

"No insult meant, sir. The demotion must be done for your safety. We pray it shall all be reinstated upon your prospective return to France. Sooner rather than later, let us hope."

"Aan de Kerk? You're turning me Dutch?" Aubrey laughed shortly, but in looking over the two papers on deed and passport, there was no mention of Ani. "And what of my wife?"

"Sir, she's not your wife," Joncheray said.

Aubrey looked up from the papers. "That's not what we agreed on."

The arbiter reached into his pocket without breaking eye contact with Aubrey. "Sign it." He held out a piece of paper. "This does not please your family."

"Nothing new there." Aubrey opened the document.

It was a Dutch Republic marriage license, notarized and filled out with his faux Dutch surname and a false date putting them at one month of wedded bliss, linking her name to his. All he had to do was sign it with the pen Monsieur Joncheray extended between bony fingers. Aubrey took the pen and dipped it into the ink, pausing when he noticed the document contained but one line for signature.

"There's no place for her consent," he said, placing the pen to rest in the jar of ink and stepping away from the paper as if it had sprouted thorns.

"Sir," Joncheray said, scoffing in Ani's direction, "she is an orphan with no inheritance, hereditary lineage, title, dowry, or father to give a blessing; and you are a high-ranking nobleman and general who has inherited your father's entire estate." He unfolded another paper of deed and title to the late Duke de Collioure's entire duchy, lands, estate, and accounts, and handed the deed to Aubrey. "With all implied respect, *Duke*, her permission is not required."

Aubrey took another step away from the paper.

Ani wondered what this arbiter would do if he learned the reason the duke was dead, how the entire palace must have been silenced in one way or another. She shuddered to think of the way most of them had been silenced.

"If you don't sign it," Joncheray said to the marquis, "she's not your wife. If she's not your wife, she doesn't go. And if she doesn't go, you're still leaving without her. These are orders from your family, and I intend to carry them out as instructed. Some things are still sacred here. Your cousins are sore enough about this, but there are no other Beaumercys left in France. They are willing to overlook her improper lineage for the prospect of male heirs to carry the name."

All three men turned to look at Ani, and she laughed at their serious expressions. "Why're you looking at me?" she said. "I'm sure I look no more a duchess than I look Dutch. Just sign it, you fool."

He snatched up the pen, then paused, turned to Breauchard, who stood at Ani's side with the expression of a dam on the brink of bursting. "Dr. Jacques Breauchard, sir." The duke removed his hat and erected himself. "I would like to ask for your blessing in taking the hand of your...of...Allyriane." He looked down to the floor to complete the sentence, then up to the doctor with that understood exchange between them. "Please, sir, with your permission."

"It is not mine to give," the doctor spoke quietly, stonefaced. "But for what it's worth, you have every blessing I'm allotted the grace to grant."

"Thank you, sir." Aubrey grinned. He reached for the pen before the doctor could retract the blessing or Ani could change her mind. He signed the certificate, the deeds for both the townhouse and his father's estate, and his own passport, sliding the certificate along the desk to Monsieur Joncheray.

"I will witness, yes," the arbiter said as he signed. "Marriage certificate, yes." He passed it back. "Deeds, yes." Joncheray gave each of the papers to the duke and retrieved the last one from his own pocket, opening it and looking it over. "All right, sir, consider yourself married. Here is a consul paper for the Baroness aan de Kerk to sign." He placed a wetted pen into Ani's fingers and the passport just beneath it. "Give him a male heir, Baroness. And soon. We're counting on you." To Aubrey, he said, "Make your wife happy, sir, and I'm quite certain you will have been the first Beaumercy ever to do so."

"That name is gone."

Joncheray snapped up. "It will be restored."

"We'll see," the duke said indifferently.

The arbiter gave him a stern glare but followed it with a forced smile. "Now is a good time for both of you to start learning Dutch."

Aubrey laughed. "Laat dat nou toevallig een de vele diensten zijn die ik aanbied."

"Why am I not surprised?" Breauchard said.

"You leave immediately and ride through the night on a papered

escort," Joncheray said. "Do not enter France's borders, hold corre-
spondence with French noblemen or entities, or mention the name
Beaumercy until it is safe to return." He turned toward the door, but
Ani's voice stopped him.

"What about Jacques?"

The arbiter flinched. "We can only secure papers for the two of
you."

Ani said, "I won't go without him."

Aubrey's grin faded. "Let Jacques go in my stead. I will join them at
the townhouse when I can."

"Apologies, sir," Joncheray said, "but it is your cousins who have secured the papers, with the emphatic order that one of the passports be
used to get you, yourself, out of France. You are the eldest remaining, of
age to take over the family deeds, the sole male, and heir to the rest of
your father's estate upon your twenty-fifth birthday. Until you and your
wife conceive a son, you are the last bearer of your family name. Your
cousins want you safely out of France without delay until the monarchy
is restored and you can regain your wealth and stature, as well."

"Then I will wait and go with Jacques," Ani said, taking the doctor's
hand.

"That's for your husband to decide," Joncheray said. "He speaks for
you now."

"You'll never silence her that way," Aubrey said. "I won't——"

"Ani, I'm not going," Jacques said unexpectedly. "I'm traveling back
to Paris."

"What?" Ani frowned.

"I'm going to continue what your bravery started. There are thousands who need rescue. And once you are better, we could use your help
from the Netherlands, to provide haven or to secure outside documentation from neutral ground."

"You can't."

"I can." The doctor laid a hand on Aubrey's shoulder and placed
the nobleman's palm over the top of Ani's clenched fist. "You are out
of my hands now, my girl." His eyes watered, and he rubbed them
and softly whispered, "Live a real life, Allyriane." The doctor placed his
hands over the top of both Aubrey's and Ani's and smiled. "Don't let
those legs slow you down."

A tear trickled toward her temple. "But you'll come when you can,
won't you?"

"When I can, girl, sure," he said. "You'll never leave my heart. For all time. I swear it." A pain visibly needled the side of his hip, and he drew a sharp breath. He'd been standing too long. He kissed her on the forehead and pulled his hand from the pile to smooth her hair back along her damp hairline. "Get some rest. You are your husband's problem now. I'll take no more responsibility for the trouble you're sure to cause him." Breauchard smiled, but Ani didn't return it. Before he could lose his composure, he exited with Monsieur Joncheray, leaving Aubrey and Ani alone.

"Jacques is right; you should get some rest." He patted her arm. "It will be a long ride. I'll come for you at first nightfall." He turned away, then back, his fingers fidgeting with his buttons. "The name you despise is gone, Ani. I'll bury it and leave it dead. But it is only a piece of paper to free us. Should it not be your desire," he paused, cleared his throat, "paper burns as portraits and martyrs do. I'll even light the fire."

"I know you would," Ani whispered, and she held out her hand to him. "But the words will long outlive the fire."

Aubrey's eyes glassed, and after a soft silence, she drifted, the hooting of an owl beyond the tent, the rustling of nighttime guards, and he whispered, "Sleep," left hesitantly, and she pressed her head back into the pillow, letting her exhaustion take her into rest.

Hours later, under the quiet of darkness, the coach pulled up outside the hospital quarters of the port. Aubrey's closest officials and the major general relieving him helped load belongings into the carriage trundle. Two carrier bags and one portrait. Everything to which the nobleman had been reduced, save a townhouse in Bokhoven. He was adorned in plain, yet respectable, clothing—his military uniform now worn by his replacement. Two state-of-the-art revolvers lined Aubrey's waist sash. Should revolutionaries find the émigrés before royalists or neutral borders, he'd be ready.

Ani lay sleeping in the hospital quarters. Dr. Lemieux had bathed and dressed her in a simple shift, letting her rest the last few hours before her fever would be challenged again by a journey of another ten hours, at best. Aubrey came for her in the twilight, her face lit in the casting glow of an oil lamp from the far desk. Careful not to wake her, he slid one hand beneath her shoulders and one under her knees and lifted her, propping her head in the crook of his neck. He held her there for a moment, wanting to pray. Wanting to pray that when she woke, she would be safe in Bokhoven, their townhouse, with a view of the English Channel. But the hope wouldn't come to him so easily. Something had been lost in all his unanswered prayers, and now he was afraid to utter more. He stood there until Dr. Breauchard ushered them to the carriage and helped Aubrey slide Ani into a restful position on the bench.

Before Aubrey stepped in, he went around to the rear of the carriage. When he reemerged, he held the rolled portrait of Ani and extended it to Breauchard. "It's only right that we both ought see her every day."

"I can't take this," the doctor said, holding the portrait between them.

"I have the source. I won't need the replica." Aubrey climbed into the carriage and situated himself on the bench, lifting Ani's head into his lap and taking a blanket from the doctor to lay over her as she slept. He turned to Breauchard. "I assume you're going back to Paris to decorate some exiled nobleman's abandoned palace."

"Something glamorous like that, I'm sure." He tried to smile, but it faltered on his lips. "Here, you will need this, too." Breauchard slid Ani's carrier bag along the floor at Aubrey's feet, then closed the door beside the two passengers. Through the open window, he added, "Take the best care of her. Anything she needs—"

"She will have it, sir…" Aubrey paused and extended his hand. "Father."

The doctor smiled gradually and nodded, taking Aubrey's hand. "Son." He swallowed. "Tell her now and again that you've heard from me. That I'm alive and well."

Aubrey's eyes misted, and he blinked rapidly. There was something in the words, so final, so resigned. It wasn't until the coach moved that the two men let go of hands and let the darkness finish what had come to pass between them, what would never pass again. Breauchard watched the coach disappear with his daughter. He could still hear its haunting rattle long after it had gone from sight.

A little over two hours out from Port Gayant, after a tranquil and black landscape surrounded them, a faint light arose at the road ahead of the coach. Aubrey espied it through the window. He figured he must be just outside of northwestern Mons, and he bounced his nervous legs against Ani's sleeping head. The carriage approached the lantern of a roadblock—whether hostile was undetermined—and the light illuminated a circle of guards and a wooden bar across the path. Aubrey realized he was breathing erratically and calmed himself, eying the horizon for landmarks to identify his location. When the carriage rolled to a stop, an armed officer in what appeared to be a Dutch police guard uniform approached the window, though it was too hard for Aubrey to distinguish the insignias in the dark. The man rested his hand on a gun. Aubrey slowly placed a hand on his own and placed his other hand across Ani's shoulder, trying not to wake her, but ready to roll her to the floorboards should bullets fly.

The officer kept his gun at his side and slid his other arm into the carriage window with his palm up, his fingers flicking in a come-on motion. He spoke in different languages, "Pas, paspoort, papier, passeport, reisepass, papers, passports."

Aubrey thought he detected a Dutch accent underneath it all. He took the chance. "Goedenavond, meneer." He pulled Ani's and his passport papers out of his breast pocket and handed them to the officer. The man looked curiously at him, and Aubrey smiled, telling himself to keep calm, keep constant eye contact. He broke it only long enough to spot another guard with a bayoneted musket standing at the head of the carriage.

The first officer looked at the papers meticulously, holding them to his lamp and near to his face, then peered nosily into the carriage at the sleeping Ani in Aubrey's lap. The man lifted the lamp to the window of the carriage and looked about it for other passengers, for anything out of place, then beneath the cart, then at the back amongst the carrier bags, walking all the way around to ask the driver for papers, as well. He conferred with the other officer, but Aubrey couldn't make out their words. A couple minutes later, the man returned to the window.

"Waar ga je heen?"

"Bokhoven."

The officer broke into a smile and handed the papers back to Aubrey, waving the travelers through the roadblock with a relaxed hand. "Goedenavond, Baron aan de Kerk. Welkom terug."

"Dank u, meneer."

Aubrey held the papers in his sweaty palm, unable to sit at ease until he felt the carriage move far enough past the roadblock that he could look back and see no lamplight. Only at that point did he let out a relieved sigh. His heart raced. His fingers shook. He looked down at Ani, the curve of her mouth creased into a thin crescent. Beneath his fingers, he felt her skin cooling, her temperature lessening. Her face stirred against his leg, and where her mouth pressed into his thigh, he could feel the warmth of her breath through his culottes.

He reached down and unbuttoned Dr. Breauchard's carrier bag to insert the passports and gasped when he pulled back the leather flaps. There at his feet was the majority of his spendable fortune: livres, gold marks and Louis d'or coins, English pounds, banknotes, property deeds and accounts, family jewels, priceless heirlooms he'd thought long lost—everything from his deserted palace that Ani could possibly have squeezed into one bag, brimming with what remained of the fortunes he'd once amassed. He closed the bag and leaned his head back against the wood paneling with a bout of quiet, happy laughter leaving him. He trailed his fingers through Ani's hair. It was more than enough for a new start. The air was cool and fresh and calm as it filled the carriage. The earth was quiet; the night pleasantly, not bleakly, dark; and the coming dawn seemed not unfriendly. He looked out over the dim horizon, pinching tiny spots of glowing cities between his thumb and forefinger like tally marks and smiling into the night.

Ani opened her eyes at his quiet laughter and looked up at him. She smiled and whispered, "*Candide.*"

*The French people have
too well known their rights
to have forgotten them.*

—Marquis de Lafayette

GLOSSARY OF DUTCH TRANSLATIONS

Vrede: [Ship name] Peace.

Aan de Kerk: [Capitalized as aan de Kerk] A Dutch surname meaning "of the Church."

Laat dat nou toevallig een de vele diensten zijn die ik aanbied: Let that, by coincidence, be one of the many services that I offer.

Pas, paspoort: Pass, passport. [The languages that follow the Dutch are **papier, passeport** = paper, passport in French; and **reisepass** = passport in German/Austrian.]

Goedenavond, meneer: Good evening, sir.

Waar ga je heen?: Where are you going?

Bokhoven: A city in the then-Dutch Republic [United Netherlands].

Goedenavond, Baron aan de Kerk. Welkom terug: Good evening, Baron aan de Kerk. Welcome back.

Dank u, meneer: Thank you, sir.

ACKNOWLEDGMENTS

Special thank you to my faction: Michael Litos, Hannah Keeton, Paige M. Ferro, Jamie Vincent, Eric Shonkwiler, Dawn Raffel, Constance Sayers, Nina Shope, Stephanie Dray, and Ashley Shelby for the edits, beta reads, and endless inspiration. Selma Oeke Algra for accuracy in my Dutch translations and Fanny Dufour Sood for accuracy in my French translations. Elizabeth Copps of the Copps Literary Agency and Jaynie Royal at Regal House Publishing, whose dedication to this book shaped it into its own kind of revolution. Love to those I only want to guillotine on rare occasion: Mom, Dad, Karen, Marta, Denny, Ethan, Cammie, Doug, Lacy, Nick, Melody, Mama Bear Sarah, Ted, Grandma Bev, the nieces, nephews, cousins, and all the extended. Dr. C. H. Uties: *Je t'aime plus que la vie.* And my German Shepherd, Torgo, *mon bon chien*, who receives every sentiment I skip in my books.

I could not have written this book without the inspiration of the Marquis de Lafayette in my life since childhood. Some letters, journals, and firsthand accounts that shaped this book include *Introduction to the French Revolution* by Antoine Barnave; *History of the Guillotine* by John Wilson Croker; *Jacques Pierre Brissot in America and France, 1788-1793: In Search of Better Worlds* by Bette W. Oliver; *Memoirs, Correspondence, and Manuscripts of General Lafayette* by the Marquis de Lafayette; *Declaration of the Rights of Man and of the Citizen*, compiled by the Marquis de Lafayette; *Rights of Man* and *The Age of Reason* by Thomas Paine; *The French Revolution: A History* by Thomas Carlyle; *Reflections on the Revolution in France* by Edmund Burke; "Making History: How Art Museums in the French Revolution Crafted a National Identity, 1789-1799" by Anna E. Sido; *Mémoires sur la Révolution de France* by Vincent-Marie Viénot, Comte de Vaublanc; *Mémoires de Bertrand-Molleville* by Comte Antoine François Bertrand de Molleville; *Mémoires de Louvet de Couvrai*, edited and prefaced by historian François Victor Alphonse Aulard from the memoirs of Jean-Baptiste Louvet de Couvrai; *The Parisian Order of Barristers and the French Revolution* by Michael P. Fitzsimmons; "Notes on Conversions between Eighteenth-Century Currencies" from Appendix 2 of *The Washington-Rochambeau Revolutionary Route in the State of Delaware*; and numerous contemporary accounts, including material from the French Revolution Digital Archive collaboration between Stanford University Libraries and the Bibliothèque nationale de France.